The Rehearsal

THE MEN . . .

ANDREW—The handsome, wealthy bachelor almost convinced Valentina to believe in love once again. Until tragedy struck . . .

ALAN—A tough, rich entrepreneur with a tender soul, he gave Val the kind of close, comfortable love that kept her heart safe. But was it enough?

GLEN—The Texas high-roller took Valentina to new heights of ecstasy, but he played for keeps, and he played to win . . . whatever the cost.

THE WOMEN . . .

TEDDIE—The daughter whose birth shaped Valentina's life is the one thing standing in the way of her happiness . . .

JESS—Valentina fought desperately to adopt the orphaned daughter of her best friend, never knowing the heartbreaking aftershocks that would result . . .

DIANA—A child born of passion and forced to become a pawn in her own father's game, she learned early on that love can be war . . .

Invitation to a Wedding

Angelica Moon

FAWCETT GOLD MEDAL • NEW YORK

A Fawcett Gold Medal Book
Published by Ballantine Books
 Published in the United States by Ballantine Books, a division of Random House, Inc., New York, and simultaneously in Canada by Random House of Canada Limited, Toronto.

http://www.randomhouse.com

Library of Congress Catalog Card Number: 97-90053

ISBN 0-449-14852-1

Manufactured in the United States of America

First Edition: July 1997

10 9 8 7 6 5 4 3 2 1

For “Jewels”—
Forever sparkling in memory

I

Invitations

Miss Valentina Cummings

requests the pleasure of your company

at her marriage to

the Man of Her Dreams

to be held on

The First Day of the Rest of Her Life

Three o'clock in the afternoon

in Paradise

Regrets Only

One

Malibu, California
Easter, 10 A.M.

Just before the invitation was delivered to her, Teddie Darian was coming to the end of her preparations for yet another wedding—one of the most spectacular Hollywood had seen in years. The director of four of the biggest-grossing movies of all time was marrying the young actress whose last two pictures had both been number one at the box office. This wasn't just Hollywood's wedding of the year, but its wedding of the decade.

As usual, Teddie had done an impeccable job, living up to her reputation as the movie capital's most inspired and sought-after wedding planner. Two thousand extra plants—bougainvillea, jasmine, orchids, dozens of unusual varieties—had been shipped in to turn the garden of the groom's Malibu estate into a tropical paradise. Discreetly placed behind foliage were laser-light installations that would produce a towering web of beams after nightfall—a chapel of light over the whole four acres. The luncheon after the morning ceremony and the evening's ten-course wedding dinner were being prepared under the supervision of four of France's three-star chefs—at a fee of twenty-five thousand dollars each.

It all added up to a cost of over a million dollars—and a fee for Teddie herself of seventy-five thousand, though that was only a fraction of her income. Some years earlier Teddie Darian had foreseen that as much as she might earn from producing these wedding extravaganzas, the richer market would be selling the same once-in-a-lifetime romantic dream to the masses. So she had sunk her earnings into building Darian Villa, a ballroom complex in the San Fernando Valley, where weddings with spectacle and pomp could be produced at assembly-line cost. The current national average for a formal ceremony and reception exceeded twenty thousand dollars—though at Darian Villa the usual wedding for two hundred fifty guests went for fifty thousand dollars and there were enough customers longing for that never-to-be-forgotten perfect day that the ballrooms and party rooms were booked solid year-round.

So Teddie didn't need to be as nervous as she was today—except she still had a hunger to be the best, to be the one that the biggest stars counted on when they wanted a wedding for their third marriage that topped the ones they'd had for their first two. Today she felt confident she'd lived up to that expectation. Pridefully she surveyed all the little extra touches—like the dozens of doves floating on the swimming pool in buoyant cages, cages that would spring open, releasing a cloud of the lovebirds at the moment the I-do's were said. Teddie gave herself extra credit, too, for complying with her client's demand for a morning ceremony. An unusual request, but the groom was an insomniac who said he didn't want to spend half the day shuffling around, waiting to get married, so a morning wedding it would be, even though Teddie and her crew had to work through the night to arrange it.

"Listen up, everyone!" Teddie announced abruptly to her assistants, who were scattered around the garden doing last-minute tasks. "The guests will start arriving in fifteen minutes. Everyone ready?"

One by one they replied that they would be done in the next minute or two, knowing that their employer would tolerate no other answer at this stage.

Even when she wasn't demanding attention, Teddie Darian cut an imposing figure. Tall, blond, she had chiseled features and ice blue eyes. Once she changed out of her work clothes into the designer original she had bought for the day's event, it would be hard to distinguish her from any of the more mature movie queens who would be guests.

After a final satisfied glance over the scene, Teddie started toward the house to inform her client all was ready. She was intercepted by a young man wearing a plain dark suit, his face masked by sunglasses. "Miss Darian . . . ?"

"It's Mrs., actually," Teddie said. Though not presently married to Mr. Darian—the most recent of her husbands—she thought it best for business to fudge the fact that weddings settled nothing forever.

The man held out an envelope. "I'm to deliver this to you."

As soon as Teddie accepted it, the man turned and left. She almost stopped him to ask who had sent him, but she was more curious about the envelope itself. From her extensive knowledge of such matters, Teddie had no trouble recognizing the stationery as Cartier's best ivory card-vellum; "T. Darian" was inked on the outside in graceful calligraphic writing. A wedding invitation, probably. Highly unorthodox for anyone to arrange the delivery of such an invitation to take place at someone else's wedding, but Hollywood people had their own strange ideas of proper etiquette.

Teddie opened the envelope and extracted the card within. For a few seconds she stared at the engraved writing. It was an invitation, all right. But what was this mysterious bullshit code—no groom's name, no real time or place given.

Even so, Teddie had no doubt it was serious. And this wasn't just an invitation, she knew at once, it was also a message . . . even a kind of challenge, a flinging of the gauntlet.

A surge of fury boiled up within Teddie, and she gripped the edges of the card to the point of tearing it in half. Damned if she'd even consider going to—

She stopped herself and smothered her anger. Imagine, after all these years it was happening. In spite of herself, Teddie couldn't help the onset of a grudging admiration. Never mind, she thought, whether she went after the answers to the riddles or actually accepted the invitation. All that mattered was that Valentina Cummings was getting married. In that very fact

Teddie suddenly saw an opportunity beckoning, a chance for herself as bright and promising as any wedding could ever be.

Washington, D.C.
Noon

At the Georgetown home of Jess Calder, the doorbell rang on the dot of twelve as she was rushing into good clothes to keep a lunch date with a White House staffer who had indicated he had a few juicy tidbits to give her "off the record." As always on weekdays, Jess had spent the morning at her word processor preparing her newspaper column for the next day. Hearing the doorbell, she rushed down from her bedroom on the second floor, brush in hand as she gave the last few strokes to her pale blond hair, her sky-blue silk blouse not yet tucked into her black skirt.

"Wait there," she said, grabbing the envelope from the young man on her doorstep and scanning for her purse to dig out a tip.

Realizing her intention, the courier said, "That's not necessary, ma'am. I've been very well paid."

That was certainly unusual, Jess thought as she closed the door, someone actually declining extra money—in Washington, no less. Rushing to keep her appointment, she put the envelope aside on a hall table and went to finish dressing. She could guess what it was anyway—an invitation to another last-minute embassy reception for a visiting dignitary, or a supper party given by one of Washington's rich behind-the-scenes kingmakers. Jess's popular column of political gossip, *Calder's Call*, made her a sought-after guest in Washington's inner circles.

Yet the messenger's saying he'd been "well paid" for the delivery stuck in her mind, and it occurred to Jess he might have brought something extraordinary. She went back to the table and picked up the envelope.

As soon as she read the card inside, any concern with being on time for her appointment fled her mind. She hurried to her study off the foyer and grabbed the phone.

There was no answer at the private number, so the call switched automatically to someone who would answer.

"Is Miss Cummings available?" Jess asked.

"I'm sorry, she's out for the next few hours," said a secretary.

"This is Jess Calder. . . ."

"Oh, Miss Calder, I know she'll want to speak with you. I wish I could tell you where she is—she usually leaves a number—but today—"

"Never mind, we can talk later." If this wedding invitation was for real, Jess reflected, the prospective bride's phone was probably going to be ringing all too much.

"Do you want me to give her a message?"

A moment's thought. "Just say . . . I called to tell her whatever she does is fine with me, and I'm very happy for her. Got that?" Jess added, not really doubting the secretary's ability, but wondering if the question might prod the woman into revealing how much she understood of what was behind the message. Just how much, Jess wondered, was Val keeping secret?

"Oh, yes," the secretary replied, "I've jotted it down exactly as you said it."

Jess hung up. Gazing down at the engraved card still in her hand, she had to smile at Val's curious intrigue. What was she up to? Surely it was a breach of etiquette to send out such a wedding invitation. There must be chapter and verse written about the proper form, and no doubt it would be frowned upon to subvert it so frivolously. Indeed, Jess happened to know that Tiffany's and Cartier's absolutely refused to print any invitation that departed from proper, traditional form.

Yet it didn't surprise her that they hadn't refused to print *this* one. Maybe it did break the rules, but if anyone had a right to break them, it was Valentina Cummings.

Rome
8 P.M.

In the great ancient arena of the Eternal City, the audience waited to see whether the combatants could win their favor and earn the crucial thumbs-up at the moment of truth.

But on this night, two thousand years after those life-and-death contests between lions and gladiators had been waged here, a different sort of fight for survival was being staged. Giacomo Angeloni, current favorite among the Italian designers of fashion apparel, had persuaded the mayor of Rome to allow him to use the unique and historic Coliseum to stage the show of his latest designs. Though half in ruins, the world-famous building still made a magnificently dramatic backdrop for his spring show. As they made their entrances through various arches on the circumference, the world's most stunning models were backlit by the lavender evening sky, their march along the runway dividing the spectators punctuated by a sound track of lions roaring, and crowds screaming, as if for blood—Angeloni's comment on the ethics of the whole fashion business.

Near the old dungeons where the Christians had been kept before they were sent out to die, the "backstage" tumult of the show was at its peak. Half-nude models dashed through the area in a frenzy, stripping off one dress, slipping into another, being pinned into it for maximum effect by the designer's assistants.

But at the fringes of this maelstrom of activity, one young woman stood calmly as she was prepared for the show. To those in the fashion business and its followers, she was known only as Diana. She had a second name, but it was no more used than for that namesake of all Dianas, the Greek goddess of the moon. Indeed, this Diana had the sort of classic beauty associated with goddesses, and coloring that suggested a luminous moon shining through a dark night—pale skin, jet-black hair, and silver-gray eyes.

In almost every showing of a designer's spring collection the traditional finale is the presentation of a wedding gown. In the quest for originality or attention-grabbing sensation, designers try every variation on the theme. There are full-skirted white lace creations with fifty-foot trains—and bodices that leave the bust totally exposed. White silks with elaborate veils, tops, bare midriff, and bikini bottom. Wedding gowns of black rubber and snakeskin.

Giacomo Angeloni knew that the combination of the gown he had designed for his own finale and the woman who wore it was sure to make a sensation. Diana, he thought, was the most uniquely lovely of all the women in this business where beauties were so commonplace. He was glad he'd been able to persuade her to do just one more show for him. Weeks earlier she had announced that after tonight she was giving up modeling forever, eager to launch the other career she had always really wanted.

Angeloni smiled as he remembered their first encounter, the day ten years before, when she'd walked into the House of Angeloni seeking work only as an apprentice, a chance to learn firsthand the art of cutting and draping material. Already she'd been to Paris and been turned away by every couture house: There were already waiting lists for such jobs—what Parisian girl didn't wish to learn design? So she had moved on to Rome.

The day she had entered his establishment on the Via Veneto, it happened that the designer himself was in the main showroom. On his knees before one of his secretaries, swathed in the strips of raw muslin many designers use to experimentally drape designs on the female body, mouth full of pins, there was nothing to reveal he was anything more than one of the craftsmen who simply executed the designer's conceptions. He continued to kneel and pin as the American girl addressed herself to the secretary, asking in English if an apprentice position was open.

"Dispiace," the secretary replied, "nothing at all."

"I'll work for very little. Can't I talk to Signor Angeloni, ask him if he'd be willing to try me out?"

Since the girl obviously had no idea of what Angeloni looked like, and the designer made no move to identify himself, the secretary went on answering for him. "No use, *ragazza.* He has offers by the dozens from students—many who'd happily pay him to be able to work here."

The designer glanced over his shoulder as the American girl walked away. He was struck at once by the way she moved—a languid walk, long legs sheathed in the ever-present blue jeans, kicking out in loping strides. Masculine somehow, the designer thought. The walk reminded him of . . . Clint Eastwood in those spaghetti westerns he'd made in Italy before he'd gotten big in Hollywood. That was it: a cowboy's walk.

Intrigued, Angeloni shot glances at the many mirrors that lined his showroom, trying to see the girl's face though she was heading away from him. *There.* A quick look, but enough.

"Aspetta!" She turned. "I am Angeloni," he said. "And I will give you a job."

What he had proposed after crying out for her to wait was that she accept employment as a mannequin, someone he could use to drape clothes over, see how they fit and flowed; and if she could learn how to do the runway walk, she might wear a dress or two in his next show.

Her first reaction was to laugh. Be a living doll who created nothing? No, *signor*, not for her. Anyway, she couldn't fit in with the young women who did that kind of work. Diana used not a dot of makeup, confined her wardrobe to what could fit into a small backpack—two pairs of jeans, a sweater, a few Ts—and wore her black hair in a ragged mop, not as a style, but as a result of the haphazard shearings she gave herself, letting her hair stay pretty much as it was when she got out of her sleeping bag each morning. Ragged, unkempt, taken as graceless because of that odd, loping stride, she wasn't regarded as particularly attractive.

But Giacomo Angeloni had seen so many conventionally pretty girls that he valued the spark of unconventionality. He let the American's laughter subside and continued his pitch. "You want to learn *sartoria*—dressmaking—so why care if you learn it standing around and wearing the result, or working on your knees with pins in your mouth?"

"I care if somebody's going to want to get me on my knees with a prick in my mouth," she shot back. "Isn't that what you all want your models to do?"

Was this girl going to be worth the trouble? One more try, he decided. "You seem able to protect yourself from being misused. I offer you a chance to be where creation happens. Not the way you planned, but you will learn, I promise you. So what do you say, *bovaro*?"

"I don't speak Italian," she said.

"*Bovaro* means cowboy. I call you this because you walk like Clint Eastwood."

She laughed—a warm sound, it told him she wasn't vain. "*Bovaro*, eh? I like that. Though I used to be told I walk more like John Wayne." She paused another moment. "Okay, what the hell. I'll give it a try."

Once she'd agreed to put herself in the designer's hands, the girl not only wore whatever was assigned to her, but did everything else he demanded. Hair, maquillage, exercise to tone her body. Her attitude didn't change—there still wasn't an ounce of vanity in her character—but the veil over her beauty formed of her indifference was dissolved almost overnight by the designer's attentive ministrations.

Angeloni had used her for the first time to show the very collection she inspired, adaptations of themes and colors and patterns associated with the cowboys and the Old West. Bold black and white silk prints like the hides of pinto ponies, skirts and blouses woven with Navajo and Zuni designs. Diana was featured, loping along the runway in a succession of chamois miniskirts and leather pants burned, like the hides of cattle, with oversized branding marks. They proved so popular, they were the basis for the whole "Bovaro" line that had been franchised and sold worldwide. The American girl had more than justified Angeloni's belief in her. Soon her name was on the lips of all the people in the business. Diana.

He allowed her to take other offers that poured in, expecting loyalty only to the extent she would come whenever he needed her. She made her home in Rome, flew all over the world and spent weeks at a time in other cities, but always came back to the rooftop apartment she found in a narrow back street of the Trastevere. Usually there was also a man to come back to—though a different one each time, she met so many in the merry-go-round of Roman nightlife. For a while it was an aging but still charismatic Italian movie actor, then the son of an Italian industrialist. The succession continued over the years, some famous, some poor and unknown.

Now, after ten years of that life, while still young, she

wanted to get back to her first ambition. Success at that would allow her to stay in one place, settle down—and perhaps let her heart settle, too, on one man with whom she'd share her life. If she could stop being indifferent about herself and her work, she believed, it would end her indifference to love. Succeeding on her own terms would also make it easier to go home, back to America.

So tonight her entrance at the climax of Angeloni's show was to be her last time ever on the runway. The wedding dress she would wear was made of a fine mesh of tiny round solid gold bands, small wedding rings, draped and layered in such a way over her nude body that it looked as if she had been caught in the net of a gladiator. To emphasize the point, as Diana made her way in a spotlight from one of the topmost arches, through the benches that circled the great arena, she would be followed by a muscular young man, half nude, carrying a triton. Another of Angeloni's ironic comments, this on what marriage in the modern age had become—a kind of gladiatorial contest entered into by a strong, independent woman only when subdued by a man in primal battle.

To get the proper drape and the effect of her being "netted," the gown had to be assembled around the model, sections of links connected and closed with pliers, so it took the duration of the show to put Diana into it. The elaborate process was approaching completion, when a loud disturbance broke out at the roped-off entryway leading into the dressing area.

Angeloni hurried over to investigate. A young man in a motorcycle helmet and goggles was shouting angrily in Italian at the two guards who had been hired to see that unauthorized personnel were kept away from the models.

"What's all this?" Angeloni demanded in Italian.

The young man rattled back that he was a messenger and he had instructions to deliver a special document to one of the models. He produced an international express mail pouch, and showed it to Angeloni.

The designer looked at the name on it. "All right. I'll give it to her."

"No. My instructions are—"

"Screw your instructions. Leave it with me, or else piss off."

The messenger hesitated, shrugged, gave that Italian twist of an upthrust hand that simultaneously conveys surrender and a curse upon the beholder, and stalked away.

Angeloni regarded the pouch in his hand, addressed to Diana. Some sort of legal document? Or a love letter . . . ? If she read it now, would it upset her too much to do her job well? On an impulse, he tore open the courier's pouch.

Inside was an envelope addressed with her full name—including her rarely used family name—in calligraphic writing. Angeloni couldn't stop himself from tearing open the envelope too. If he was even going to consider showing her this thing now, he ought to know what it was.

The moment he saw it, he realized that right then was the perfect moment to make the delivery. He hurried over to Diana, her preparation nearly complete. "This just came for you," he said, holding out the card removed from the envelope.

Diana took the card and read it. Instantly her hand began to tremble. A liquid sheen came to her pale gray eyes, giving them the cast of molten silver. Angeloni was worried. He'd thought a wedding invitation—surely from a friend, someone she cared about—would be just the thing to show her right before she went out to portray a bride; its arrival had seemed a lucky omen. Now he realized it had seriously upset her.

"What's wrong, *cara*? This is an invitation to a wedding, a happy occasion, *sì*?"

"Maybe it will be," the model said cryptically.

The assistants clustered around her did their final touches on her hair and makeup. She moved toward the stairway she had to climb to make her entrance at a high point in the arched perimeter of the ancient arena. Angeloni moved alongside her. Was there something else he could say to soothe her? Tears were spilling from her eyes, her makeup could be ruined. . . .

No, he realized then, he could ask for nothing better. The bride, the tears . . . *perfètto!* Evidently this "bride's" tears didn't spring from joy, but some darker emotion. The audience wouldn't perceive that though.

An elaborate trumpet fanfare began to play on the sound

track. Diana started up the stairs, moving as quickly as she could in the heavy gold mesh. A minute later she appeared in the spotlight. Even at a distance the crowd could see the tears glistening on her cheeks.

Watching from a shadowy place on the sidelines, Angeloni wondered why the invitation had upset her so much, though he didn't regret giving it to her. Diana's appearance as the trapped, tearful bride touched the audience as few performances in a fashion show ever did. They rose to their feet and cheered.

New York
3 P.M.

Today Valentina Cummings sat alone at her customary corner table. It was rare for her to come to the popular restaurant alone. Since it was only a block away from the building where her business was located, she used it somewhat as an extension of the office, meeting two or three times a week over lunch with advertisers or travel agents, hotel owners or book publishers, home decorators or dress designers. But today she had felt a need to be alone, to have a chance to reflect on the past while, in distant places, her plans for the future were being made known.

The headwaiter, used to seeing her surrounded in lively purposeful conversation, had come over several times to ask if everything was all right, obviously concerned at her solitude. Now as she ended her meal with coffee, he returned once more.

"Anything else I can bring you, Señora Cummings?" He was a gracious Spanish gentleman.

She pondered a moment. "What time is it, Manuel?"

He checked his wristwatch. "Five minutes after three o'clock."

Which made it six hours later in Rome. So by now all three invitations had been delivered. "Yes," Val decided abruptly. "I think I will have something else. Champagne—a split, so you can join me. Would you mind, Manuel? I feel like making a toast, and I couldn't do that alone."

"I would be honored to join you, Señora Cummings." He told her the brands of champagne available in splits, and she chose the best. In a minute he returned with the chilled bottle and two crystal flutes. The lunch crowd had gone, and they were alone in this corner of the restaurant. The headwaiter deftly popped the cork and poured two glasses.

"Bueno . . . la salud. What is it to be?"

Valentina Cummings lifted her glass. "To the bride, Manuel," she said. "To *all* brides!"

"Ah, *sí*! To all brides." He drank his champagne, and then he laughed. "I should have guessed, Miss Cummings. What else would you drink to?"

He gave a slight courtly bow, and left her again with her thoughts.

What else, indeed. Brides, weddings—for a lifetime they had been her preoccupying concern. All the ceremony and symbolism, the singular beauty of a bride in her gown, the intensity of hopeful and joyous emotion that flowed on a wedding day as on no other, they were always in her thoughts, at the heart of her dreams.

And yet until now, as much as she had wished to be part of the pageant, to be a bride, all of life seemed to have conspired against that wish—fate, ambition, history, not to mention the peculiarities of the human heart that sometimes refused to cooperate. Though if her wish had been fulfilled right at the beginning, wouldn't her life have been poorer, duller . . . ?

Her mind drifted back to the very first days of longing. She filled her champagne glass again and raised it in another salute, joined this time by her ghosts.

"To the bride," she said solemnly, remembering. . . .

Two

Buffalo
December 1946

She would always remember waking that morning to a faint frosty touch on her cheek. She had a vision of a prince from a land of crystal castles bending over her, the touch of his lips, cool and refreshing as dew, breaking a spell.

As soon as she opened her eyes, Valeskja Kumeniczi saw the fresh mantle of white clinging to the tree branches outside the bedroom window. The window was slightly open and the winter wind blew an occasional swirl of snowflakes into the room. She brought a hand to her cheek and felt the wetness of the snow that had kissed her awake.

Raven-haired, with eyes the color of summer sky at evening, porcelain skin, an oval face marked by high cheekbones, and a narrow straight nose, if there had truly been a prince anywhere in the vicinity, he could not be blamed for taking this girl of eighteen to be the fabled Sleeping Beauty.

Abruptly Valeskja tossed back the covers and ran to the window. Overnight, an enormous amount of snow had fallen, blanketing everything, softening all the lines into undulating curves that glistened in the rising sun. Normally the view outside was far less magical: the scrubby backyard of her uncle's house, beyond that the property of a neighbor who did carpentry so that his yard was used for storing spare lumber, old window frames, and other eyesores. But what was usually so ordinary and ugly sparkled today as though nature itself had put on a gown in anticipation of the great day to come.

As she had been doing every morning during the past few weeks after she woke, Val went to the closet to look in at the wedding gown hanging in its protective cellophane wrapping. It was not a dream. She and Ted were going to be married! Exactly one month from today.

She could hardly stop thinking about it—how magical it would be, especially if it was a day like this one. She hardly had to worry here in Buffalo if there would still be snow in January.

How wrong they all were! Her uncle, her cousins, the girls at the factory, even Ted and his family. They'd called her spoiled for insisting on a church wedding, a bridal gown specially made and costing nearly a hundred dollars, all those fresh flowers placed around the church, and then having everyone fed at Molvina's Tavern, each and every free feast with wine costing no less than three dollars! Squandering money on dress-up church weddings with lavish parties was only for rich society girls, they scolded her. Her money should be used to start out life with her husband, make a decent home. Sure, this was America, a woman didn't have to bring a dowry to secure a husband, but that didn't mean a girl like Valeskja should be tossing away all her savings on empty vanities.

Such arguments! Even when Val insisted that the money was hers to spend any way she pleased, that wasn't the end of it. If she had to put on airs, they said, at least do it *all* as the rich girls do—marry in June, when you can take pictures in the sunshine on the church steps, and flowers won't have to be shipped across the country, doubling the cost.

To quell objections, Valeskja had gone so far as to visit the local library to research wedding traditions, to find out if there was any particular reason for spring to be favored over winter, and indeed, she'd learned that by some traditions January was the most favored time. The ancient Greeks had called January *Gamelion*, which meant "wedding month," and it was considered sacred to Hera, the goddess of marriage. Val proceeded as she wished. At Christmas Ted would finally return home for good; they could enjoy the holidays together, then be married in the New Year.

She simply couldn't, *wouldn't* wait until spring. These past years when he'd been thousands of miles away there were times she had been so desperate to belong to him, she felt the futile longing eating her up, almost making her ill. Her impatient hunger for him had become even more consuming, perhaps, because he hadn't taken his discharge like so many others when the war ended. The child of German immigrants, raised in a household where German was spoken, Ted's fluency in the language made him particularly valuable to the army. After the Nazi surrender, he'd been transferred to a special section that took statements from the highest-ranking Nazi leaders who were slated to be tried for war crimes at Nuremberg. The extended service was voluntary. He had seen firsthand, he had written Val, that the evil of the Nazis was unparalleled, and he was proud to contribute to bringing them to justice. His idealism made her love him all the more, but made it no easier for her to go on waiting.

Even as she gazed at the glistening world outside her window, Val couldn't help thinking of summer, that evening in August when he'd been home on his last leave. As the memories came rushing back, both wonderful and cruel, she closed her eyes against the sparkling whiteness.

"Can I look yet?"

"Just another minute. Careful. Take it slow. . . ."

She kept her eyes squeezed shut and gingerly put one foot forward, then the other, feeling for the ground in front of her. Ted had one arm around her shoulder to guide her gently along; in his other hand he held a kerosene lantern so he could see the way and provide light when they arrived at their destination. He had a surprise for her, he'd said when he picked her up after work that evening—and from the way he made the announcement, she could tell it was something very important to him, so she made up her mind it would be important to her too. Whatever his dream, she wanted to share it.

He had owned her heart and soul right from that day he'd seen her being teased outside school by her classmates and he'd moved in to stop it. She had been new to this country then, one of the lucky ones evacuated from war-ravaged Europe because there were relatives willing to take her in, and he had been the first stranger to make her feel welcome. This tall, handsome boy with blue eyes and golden hair, a student leader, a star athlete, all of five years older . . . God, she'd felt her heart would burst with excitement the moment he spoke his first words to her.

"We're almost there," his voice coaxed gently.

This August evening they were on the old dirt towpath that ran beside a stretch of the Erie Canal, where once workhorses had plodded along, pulling the craft through the water by long ropes. As Val walked, eyes closed, she was more than usually aware of the smells around her, stronger as the sun went down and the air cooled, not only the fragrance of greenery, but the oily water of the canal, and the rot of old timbers that had drifted up along the banks.

Ted pulled her to a stop. "All right . . . we're here."

She opened her eyes. They were at a place on the canal bank where an old barge was tied by ropes running to metal stakes pounded deep into the ground. The barge was about fifty feet long with a large flat cargo area in front, and a square, hutlike cabin at the stern. In the fading twilight Val could see through the cabin windows that the forward part was a wheelhouse. The barge had evidently stood unused for a long time. The hull's dingy green paint was flaking, the metal fittings were pitted with rust, and bird droppings covered the dull varnish of the railings. She turned questioningly to Ted.

"It's mine," he said, smiling. "Mine and Willy's."

Willy—Wilhelm—was his older brother. Not a golden boy like Ted, not as bright, nor as popular in school, nor a soldier who had risen despite his youth to become an officer during the last days of the war. Willy had been able to avoid military service because after Ted's enlistment he could plead he was the sole support of their widowed mother.

Val stood trying to form words that would conceal her dismay. If Ted was going into a business with his brother, then Willy would always be part of their lives. But Val had assumed they would be freer to carve out a path for themselves, even to leave Buffalo. Before she could say anything, however, Ted stepped to a gap in the railing and held out a hand.

"C'mon aboard," he said, "I'll show you around." He raised the lantern so she could see to step safely onto the deck.

He led her past coils of oily rope and old barrels filled with fetid rainwater to a door at the side of the rear cabin. Pulling a key from his pocket, he unfastened a brass padlock and opened the door.

It led not into the wheelhouse, but revealed a larger cabin area behind it. Portholes framed in polished brass shone in the lamplight, walls paneled with dark oiled wood gleamed warmly. At the edges of the cabin were bunks covered with red and blue plaid wool, used for sitting in the day, sleeping at night. Through an open passageway Val saw a trim galley. Opposite one bunk a table had been set up on brass poles inserted into floor fittings. She gave Ted an appreciative smile as she saw a vase of fresh roses on the table along with wineglasses and champagne in a "silver cooler"—a paint can, label removed. She was touched to realize he must have spent odd hours all during his two-week furlough to secretly refurbish this part of the barge for this night.

"Well?" he asked hopefully.

"It's so . . . cozy."

"Then you like it?"

"Certainly I like it."

He poured their champagne and made the toast: "To us, and our new life."

They sat down at the table and he explained his plans in an excited rush. With the war over, a boom in business was already developing, factories were switching from war production to making cars and refrigerators and lawn mowers. Buffalo—always one of the great manufacturing hubs—needed transport to get the goods to market. Barges left to molder during the war by owners occupied totally with the transoceanic shipping would start to flow again along the Erie Canal. Ted boasted that he and Willy had been able to get this one cheap. Not only would it be the foundation of a business, it would provide a home. Living aboard while making cargo runs, he and Val would be able to save . . . to buy a second barge. In a few years he and Willy could build a fleet, take advantage of circumstances to become "kings of the canal."

She loved his optimism and ambition. She didn't care what Ted's dream was as long as she could be part of it. So she drank down the champagne happily with each toast to their future. And when she lay down with him on one of the bunks, she concentrated on how idyllic it could be to share this cozy cabin someday as they plied the canal together.

Warmed by the vision, relaxed by the wine, she was emboldened to show the urgency of desire that had been building all the time he was far away and she had been growing to womanhood. Feeling him grow hard below, she slipped her hand down to caress him, then undid his belt and put her hand inside his pants.

For all the petting they had done, this was the first time she had ever touched him there. A thrill went through her as she grasped his hardness, and she pressed her lips to his more hungrily to let him know that she could wait no longer.

But he eased himself away. "Val . . . sweetheart . . ."

"What's the matter? Am I doing it wrong?"

"No . . . not at all. But . . ." He trailed off, embarrassed.

"Teddy . . . darling . . . I can't wait any longer. All this time you've been away . . . all the nights, when I'm alone, and I think of you, I want you so much. . . ." She looked into his eyes, put a hand to his face. "You want me too, don't you?"

His embrace tightened. "My God, of course I do, more than I can say." He smiled. "You know, I've had plenty of my own nights alone, thinking of you, imagining what it would be like."

From listening to the talk of girls at the factory, Val guessed that he had slept with women who were so readily available in the devastated countries of Europe. It only made her more eager to fill that need for him; maybe then he wouldn't ever want anyone else again.

"Haven't we both dreamed enough?" she said. "Let's make it real for each other. . . ."

He looked at her searchingly, still uncertain.

Until now, especially because of her age, it had long been an unspoken vow that she would bring herself to him as a virgin on their wedding night. She had first noticed him when she was only twelve, after all, and he was in his last year of high school; and it was only on one of his army leaves two years before—she had just turned sixteen—that he had taken notice of the way she had grown. Even then he hadn't actually asked her on a date, but had met her after school, walked her to the part-time job at the factory. Then a couple of times he'd been outside the factory gates when she emerged in the evening and he'd taken her home, stopping to buy her an ice cream soda on the way. In two weeks, after just one kiss good-bye when he caught the bus, he was gone again. But they had begun to exchange letters, and on the next leave they were together constantly. There had been many more kisses and embraces, and she encouraged him to touch her everywhere.

When her stern guardian, Uncle Jovan, had noticed how much time she was spending with Ted, he wasn't pleased. "In the old country," he'd said, "a girl doesn't spend so much time with a boy unless they're engaged. Has he asked you to marry him?"

Of course he hadn't, she told her uncle, the days they'd spent together barely added up to a few weeks. Yet she also said that she knew Ted truly loved her and she would be his wife someday.

"Someday," her uncle had repeated dubiously. "If he lives through the fighting, if he asks you to marry him—if he doesn't find some slut of a Fräulein over there who suits his nature better . . ." A dig at Ted's background, she understood; because of the way the Nazis had raped their own homeland, Jovan couldn't shake off his prejudice. "So, until all those ifs are out of the way," her uncle had concluded, "you'd better stay away from Ted Gruening . . . and make damn sure he doesn't get in your pants. The way soldiers behave, he'll give you a disease. . . ."

After that their letters and most of their meetings when he was home on leave were clandestine. The situation would be better, they both felt, as soon as Ted could go to Jovan, abide by the custom of asking his permission to wed Val. But that had to be timed carefully too. Val should turn eighteen first. And Ted should have come home for good, with the anti-German bitterness of the war as far behind as possible.

She had turned eighteen in May, and his discharge was already set for Christmas, so that was when he planned to ask for her hand. But that was still months off. . . .

And now, here in the lamplight, she could see that the longing in his eyes matched her own. Yet he was still hesitating, perhaps doubting what the effect might be, wondering whether or not to abandon his own ideal of their wedding night.

The time for persuading him with words was over, Val resolved. Raising herself up, she began to unbutton the simple shirtwaist dress she was wearing.

He watched her as she slipped her arms free, then unhooked her bra and let it fall away. Seeing the firm round whiteness of her breasts, an eager gasp of approval escaped his lips, and the doubt fled his eyes. Suddenly he could restrain himself no longer. He reached up and pulled her against him, breathing warm against her bosom, his mouth finding her nipple, giving her an electric jolt of pleasure as he kissed and sucked at her avidly.

They were swept away now in a wave of urgency, fumbling at buttons, helping each other undress as they kissed and whispered endearments and impatient confessions of need. Tumbling around on the narrow bunk, elbows and feet thumped against the wooden paneling and the sides of the cabin.

A bumping sound alarmed Val for a moment. It sounded, felt, almost as if someone outside had jumped aboard the boat. She sat up. "Did you hear that?"

He listened for a second. Silence. He chuckled. "Am I making too much noise?" he said.

"No, I thought . . ." She didn't want to lose their momentum. "Never mind." She had only her pants left to remove, and now she slipped them off.

"Valeskja," he murmured, grasping her arms, his gaze

sweeping up and down over her body, "you're the most beautiful thing I've ever seen—ever will. . . ."

"I'm yours forever, darling."

He hurried to remove his underpants too, and as she saw him naked for the first time, she had an urge to kiss him in places that were only for the most intimate lovers. Her mouth went to his chest, his hard, muscled stomach, moved down—

A creaking noise froze her again.

He understood. "Just the movement of the boat on the water," he assured her. His hands cupped her breasts, then he reached lower, fingers gently touching her at the very core of her pleasure, and the urge rose again to serve him too. She went on kissing him, tasting him, and then he pulled her up and rolled her over, and knelt between her legs. She opened herself for him to enter, opened wide, feeling like a flower blossoming as his warm, hard shaft glided down into—

The door burst inward, flying back into a wall and shaking the cabin with an explosive bang.

The reflexes of war made Ted jump as if a grenade had detonated, while the terrifying shock completely paralyzed Val. Still on her back, naked, Val turned her head toward the source of the noise.

Framed in the open doorway stood the hefty figure of her uncle. For an instant he paused there, glowering fiercely, his black eyes taking in the sight of the two bodies, naked and gleaming in the lamplight with the sweat of passion and an August night. His black mustache quivered like the stingers of a huge poisonous insect as the rest of his body shook with rage. Then he flew across the cabin. Grabbing a mass of Val's long, raven hair in one of his hands, he dragged her off the bunk onto the floor, making her scream with pain. Then he lifted her and flung her against the table, causing the wineglasses to fly onto the floor and shatter.

"Slut!" he roared, glaring at her. "Filthy whore! I took you in, and you dishonor my name this way!" Val cowered and he moved toward her, raising a hand to strike.

But Ted sprang off the bunk, ignoring the shards of glass

that cut into his bare feet, and grabbed Jovan in a fierce grip from behind, immobilizing him.

"Let go of me!" Jovan shouted. "I'll kill you next!"

"Reason enough to keep a tight hold," Ted said. "Until you swear not to touch her again."

"Who are you to ask me for promises!" Jovan bellowed. "The man who raped my niece."

"He didn't!" Val cried out. "It was me! I wanted him!"

"Quiet," Jovan commanded. "Whatever you think you wanted, where I was born a man who'd do this to a young virgin would be castrated like a sheep, and his balls stuffed down—"

"Where you were born," Ted shouted over him, "many more terrible things have been done lately. But we're not savages here. Whatever you think you can do to me, I want your promise that you won't hurt Val anymore."

Jovan was silent. Clamped into immobility by the younger, stronger man, his irrational rage seemed to ebb away. He glanced at Val, then modestly averted his eyes. "For God's sake," he snapped at her, "cover yourself!"

She scuttled meekly back to the bunk and went about putting her clothes on.

"Well . . . ?" Ted asked.

"I won't hurt her," Jovan muttered at last. "She's done damage enough to herself."

Ted released his hold. But he stood ready to defend himself as the other man started to turn. Seeing Ted still naked, Jovan looked away again and growled, "You too, dammit, get dressed. I don't want to see your goddamn bare ass anymore."

Ted edged backward, pulled his clothes together, and began to slip them on, never taking his eyes from Jovan.

Hunched over, depleted by his explosion of rage, the older man kept facing away toward a corner and said nothing for a few minutes. In the silence, unobserved, the lovers cast wondering glances at each other as they dressed.

"There is only one honorable thing you can do now," Jovan said grimly at last. "And if you don't do it, soldier, then I *will* kill you, I swear."

Ted understood what he meant. "I *want* to marry her. I love Valeskja. I'd have married her anyway, was going to ask you properly when—"

Jovan seethed. "Don't even speak of what's proper. You've done nothing but dishonor her and yourself."

Val had to speak. "I wanted him, Uncle. I'm not ashamed. We love each other."

He turned, his eyes burning at her through the dim lantern light. "If he loved you, he would not have stolen your virtue."

Before Ted could say anything, Val shot back, "He stole nothing. My only regret, Uncle, is that you found us too soon, and I didn't have the chance to give myself completely."

Jovan studied her a second, then his eyes switched to Ted, examining him. Whatever he saw seemed to satisfy him. "Well then," he said, "it seems I was sent just in time."

Sent. Both lovers caught the word, and they glanced at each other, curious as to how they had been betrayed. Some neighborhood busybody, probably, seeing them stroll off along the old towpath, popular as a lover's lane.

"Come now, Valeskja," her uncle said gruffly. "I'm taking you home. You'll bathe in the hottest water you can stand, and say your prayers, and hope that God forgives you for acting like a whore."

Ted lurched toward him furiously, his fists clenched. "Goddammit, you treat her with respect! There's nothing wrong with what we did."

Jovan stared back at him unapologetically. "With respect, you say. Very well. But then you will respect her too—by not seeing her again. . . ."

"Not—" Ted was stunned. "But we're to be married. You said—"

"Yes, eventually. But if you want to respect *my* wishes as Valeskja's guardian, then you will not see her again during your leave. You will wait until you return from abroad for good."

"Christmas," he said quickly. "I'll be discharged at Christmas."

Jovan went to the door of the cabin, still open, half broken off its hinges. "Christmas," he said. "You may see her again then. And you shall be married." He motioned brusquely for Val to join him at the door.

With a glance, Ted told her to obey.

She paused, longing to kiss him good-bye. But neither wanted to risk reigniting Jovan's furious temper. Anyway, his leave did not end for several days; they could probably find a way to meet secretly.

"Good-bye, my love," she said brokenly.

"Good-bye, Val," he said. "I love you."

She ran out the door, crying.

Her uncle started after her, then turned to glare once more at Ted. "Don't forget, Gruening. From tonight, you are officially engaged."

So that was how their engagement had happened. No sweet proposal on bended knee, no thrilling presentation of a ring, no chance to give him an exultant embrace—or tease him a moment by pretending she needed to think about it. That part of the romantic dream was forever lost to her; she grieved for it a little at times.

Yet that had only made the romance and tradition of a beautiful wedding all the more essential to her. Especially because they had been kept apart, forbidden to each other until their marriage, all her dreams were built upon the time when they would take their vows, and then at last they would have the right to love completely. In her reading on wedding customs she had also learned that women of ancient Greece did not count their age from the day of their birth, but from the day of marriage. That was the real beginning of life for a woman. And Val felt it too. She was waiting for her life to begin.

On this snowy morning, the jangle of the telephone ringing downstairs brought her out of daydreaming in front of the wedding gown, and she closed the closet door. Glancing at the clock on her dresser, she saw it wasn't yet eight o'clock, which explained why her uncle hadn't wakened her. Very rare for a phone call to come so early. Perhaps with the snowfall already so deep outside, she might not have to go to work. One of her girlfriends at the factory might be calling to consult about whether to go in on the shift. She hurried out of her room just as she heard her uncle pick up the receiver downstairs. His voice, low and indistinct, floated up from below. A few exchanges, then he hung up.

"Who was it?" she called down.

There was an odd silence.

"Uncle . . . ?"

Now she heard his footsteps on the stairs, a slow, heavy tread, ominous in its cadence. She went to the landing and looked down. When he saw her waiting above, he stopped halfway up the flight.

"Who was calling?" she asked again.

The expression on his normally somber face was not quite like any she had ever seen before. A chill ran through her even before he spoke. "Mr. Gruening," he said.

"Ted?"

"His father. They've just been informed, and he thought you should know right away. . . ."

She took a step down. "Know what?"

"Your fiancé—" Jovan paused heavily. "He has been killed."

"No, it can't be," she said automatically. There had been so many times in the past years when she'd imagined it happening, feared it, hearing this news. But now the war was over. The shooting was done.

"They received the telegram this morning. From the army."

"The army?" The war was over. The danger was past. This made no sense.

"I'm sorry, Valeskja. . . ." But there was no comfort in his sympathy. No comfort anywhere.

Except in believing that it couldn't be true. In a month they would be married. Yes! Then her life would begin. With him.

She turned and walked slowly up the stairs, back into her room, and across to the closet. The wedding gown hung there, waiting.

Of course it couldn't be true, she told herself again and again as she stared at the gown. The war was over.

Three

The body came home on an army plane. Only then—with proof it was no nightmare—was Val able to bring herself to sit with Ted's mother and hear exactly what had happened.

As part of his duties in preparing for the Nuremberg trials, he had been in a group of investigators led by a suspected Nazi war criminal to a rural field where a mass grave of concentration camp victims was located. An army demolition team had cleared the field of the dozens of land mines laid by the German Army, but it wasn't unusual for one or two to escape detection. Ted had stepped directly onto a stray mine.

During all her grieving, the one memory of their love that taunted Val more than any other was that night on the barge. If only they hadn't been discovered—if once, just *once* she could have known all of him, belonged to him in that way. Perhaps then losing him forever might have been the tiniest bit more bearable.

The pain never left her. Weeks turned into months, and still she felt an agony that made her want to die too. It was always worst at the start of a day, or the end, when she went to her closet to dress or undress . . . and she saw the wedding gown hanging there at the back. She thought of giving it away, but she was unable to let it go because there was so much meaning attached to it. Not only as the vestige of his desire to have her as his wife, but as the reminder of the last promise she had made to her mother.

Her mother had been a dressmaker, well known as the finest in Budva, their town in the small seaside kingdom of Montenegro that had become part of Yugoslavia. Hired frequently to make bridal gowns for the daughters of the affluent Montenegran families, it was her custom when delivering a gown always to include a bouquet of wildflowers taken from the hills above the town. Once Val had asked why, and her mother had replied that to be a bride was the most special of all times in a woman's life, and every single moment leading up to it should be made as beautiful as possible.

One spring evening in the last summer months before the onset of war, after returning from a walk with Val to gather such a gift of flowers, her mother had taken her up to the attic of their house and had brought out a gown from its packing in an old trunk. It was the most beautiful article of clothing Val had ever seen, yards of ivory lace, and silk with swirling designs sewn on in tiny pearls. "This is for you, Valeskja," her mother said.

"For me?" Val had laughed. "But why make a gown for me?" She was only eleven at the time.

"This one, my darling, I made for myself. I wore it at my own wedding. I know it's many years before you will marry. But I saved this for you: It's yours. I want you to know that—in case . . . in case you ever want to take it away with you."

"But why should I want to take it away, Mama?"

"The world is changing, Valeskja," her mother said. "And I'm afraid no one can tell what may happen in years to come. So promise me now you'll take care of this, and wear it at your wedding."

"Oh, I do, Mama," Val crowed with delight. "I promise!"

But like millions of other such promises, the war had made that one impossible to keep. The family's house and every last thing in it had been taken over by Fascist sympathizers when it was left abandoned. Valeskja's father, a rough-and-ready man who made a good living as a carpenter, had gone into the hills to fight with the partisans, and soon afterward Val's mother and her relatives had been picked up by the Gestapo and questioned about her husband's partisan activities. The answers were judged "unsatisfactory," and they were sent to a concentration camp in Poland, where all had been gassed. This in turn fueled her father's hatred of the enemy, and he had fought more recklessly until he was killed in a skirmish.

The family's one piece of good luck was that in the last days before war was declared, they had decided to use all their savings to send their daughter out of the country. Val had gone first to England, where after a few months she had been put aboard a "liberty ship" to join her father's brother, Jovan, who had gone to America years earlier. In Buffalo, where he had settled and bought himself a house in a neighborhood of other Slavic people, Jovan, who had never married, lived alone. It was thus assumed he would appreciate having Valeskja—as a "woman" to look after him. After all, when she came across in 1940 she was eleven, more than old enough, by old-country standards, to cook and do all the other housework.

Val didn't begrudge the arrangement. Her uncle turned out to be a gruff, humorless man, but he provided her with a warm room, she ate well, and she was able to continue her education free at an American school. As her uncle never stopped reminding her, she was just "goddamn lucky to be alive." She felt even luckier after she met Ted Gruening.

As soon as she could be used even part-time, Valeskja went to work in one of Buffalo's many factories and began saving her money. By then she knew that as soon as the war ended she and Ted would marry. If she couldn't wear the very gown her mother had shown her that spring night, she was still determined to come as close as possible to fulfilling the promise.

She paid to have her wedding gown specially made, describing from memory the one she had been shown by her mother. Skirt of ivory silk, bodice of lace; she couldn't afford real seed pearls to limn the outline of little flowers and the hem as on her mother's, merely tiny pearlescent plastic beads, but the effect was lovely.

Would have been lovely.

Each time she saw the gown now, it tortured her with the reminder of all the vows that would never be made.

Finally, it became unbearable. One evening, the autumn after his death, she took the gown from the closet and laid it out on her bed for a last look. Then she bundled it into an empty burlap potato bag and walked down to the towpath where they had walked that fateful night. She filled the bag with stones, heaved it into the canal, and watched it sink.

She was tempted, then, to walk farther along the towpath and revisit the barge. But she stopped herself. It would only make her wish more desperately for the impossible.

Month after month Val remained numb to the world. She went to her job, she kept house for her uncle, that was all. There was no shortage of men who wished to know her better, entertain her. But she refused all their invitations, never gave them the least encouragement.

Another winter came. This time she saw nothing pure or magical in the blanket of snow that covered everything. This snow was no gown of white, but a funeral shroud.

Her uncle observed her brooding night after night, but he never urged her to end her mourning. In his eyes, Val knew, she was permanently dishonored, the only man who might have erased the stain was dead, and he would take no part in foisting her on any other.

Yet there was one man who was never turned away from the house when he came—Ted's brother, Willy. He alone could share some of what she felt, Val thought. He, too, had needed Ted, was nothing without him. One or two nights a week for the first year of her mourning, he came to sit with Val—in the parlor when the weather was cold, on the porch when it was warm. He talked only when she wished to talk—about Ted, or her feelings, or just the small daily events of their lives. Willy worked in a factory that had produced tank treads during the war and had now switched to auto parts. Without his brother to energize the plan, he could do nothing with the old barge. It sat rotting in the canal, an old plank propped on deck, painted with the words For Sale. But no one wanted it. As Val had foreseen, even in the postwar boom canal transport wasn't reviving.

On the second Labor Day after Ted's death, there was a picnic at one of the local churches, and Willy persuaded Val to go with him. It was a hot, windless day and the evening brought little relief from the heat. Seeing that Val wasn't enjoying the boisterous atmosphere of the picnic, Willy proposed taking a walk to the canal. It would be cooler, he said. They might go to the barge, bring out chairs from the cabin, and sit on the deck.

She was reluctant at first, but Willy persisted. Whenever he went there, he said, he remembered the plans he and Ted had made and felt closer to his brother's spirit. It truly helped.

Perhaps then it could be a balm for her too—to be in the place where they had come so close to possessing each other.

Arriving at the old barge, she thought it looked more forlorn than ever. What a dreamer Ted had been to think of turning this old hulk into the foundation of a fortune! Yet any negative thoughts evaporated as Willy opened the brass padlock on the door of the cabin. It all came rushing back then, the candlelight, all the preparations he had made to convince her that their life together would be wonderful. And their touches . . . a memory of desire so keen, it went beyond pictures in the mind to a glow within, a sense it was Ted at her shoulder in the doorway, his warm breath wafting faintly onto her neck.

"Willy," she said, "would you mind terribly . . . if I were alone in there for a little while? Sit on the deck and I'll join you. Soon . . ."

He smiled understandingly. He took two deck chairs stowed in the cabin and went out.

The sound of the door latch clicking shut was a trigger to unleash the full torrent of passionate longing Val had bottled up since Ted's death. Arms wrapped around herself, she pretended she was in *his* embrace. "Oh, Ted . . . my love," she moaned softly, "come to me. . . ."

Dissolving into wordless sobs, she moved to one of the bunks and stretched out on it. Her thoughts went back to the only other time she had lain there—with him, naked, hearing his words of love. She seemed then to enter a kind of trance, where she believed she could feel his body against hers. Giving herself over to the fantasy, she put her hand under her dress, slid her fingers inside her panties, imagined the way it would have been that night if they had not been interrupted—

The click of the latch jolted her back to reality as if the whole terrible episode were repeating itself. They were being invaded again by Jovan! She rolled over quickly toward the paneling along the bunk, facing away from the door as she heard footsteps on the cabin floor. She was trembling, still in the momentum of self-induced passion.

"Valeskja . . . are you all right?"

She couldn't bring herself to answer. Could Willy have *seen*? She lay motionless in a pretense of dozing.

"Val," Willy said softly, his voice nearer, "don't be so sad . . . please. . . ."

He must have seen her body shaking, have believed it was from sobbing. She felt him sit down behind her, then his hand on her shoulder. "He wouldn't want you to suffer so much."

"I can't help it, Willy," she murmured at last. "It doesn't help to be here after all. Not for me. I . . . think of him bringing me here once . . . to show me where we'd live after we were married."

His hand stroked lightly down along her arm. "I know. He worked so hard to make it nice before he brought you, and he told me later how it had ended."

"He did?" she asked, staring more rigidly at the paneling. She had always assumed the episode would never be revealed.

"You shouldn't be angry," Willy said. "We told each other things that were on our mind—plans, worries, disappointments."

She rolled over to look at him. "I'm not angry, Willy. Just surprised."

He shrugged. "We were brothers. We didn't keep many secrets." He was quiet a moment. "There was one big secret I kept from him though. Something I could never tell him."

She realized he wanted to be asked. "What was it?"

"About you."

"You knew a secret about me?"

"Just . . . the way I felt about you." His eyes came back to meet hers. "Still feel . . ."

It was another second before she could take it in. Then she

felt a rush of tender sympathy. "Oh, Willy." She brought her hand over his where it rested on her arm.

"Never could say, not then," he stammered. "I understood . . . he was better—the right one for you. But now . . ."

She smiled, touched. "Willy, you're so dear. All through this you've been—"

His hands went suddenly to her shoulders, gripping them hard. "He's gone forever, Valeskja. But *I'm* here. Let me be the one." He pressed himself over her, his face close.

Now Val noticed the pungent smell of whiskey strong on his breath. He must have had some already stashed on the barge. She saw his eyes, bright with frightening determination, roaming down her neck to her breasts. When they lifted again to her mouth, she was impelled to respond. "Willy, you're very important to me . . . but this can't—"

His grip didn't loosen. "I want you so much, Valeskja. And you *need* me." Abruptly, he brought his mouth down onto hers, and she could feel the swelling rod of muscle inside his pants grinding against her.

Jerking her head sideways, she tore her lips free from his, began arching and twisting her body to wrestle him off. "Willy, stop!"

His voice came back in a growl. "You didn't want him to stop, so why me?" He had moved one arm across her chest to hold her down, while his other swung down to his side, and his hand worked to free himself.

Wild now with fear and desperation, she thrashed about. Yet she could hardly budge him. Even within all the other sensations, she was aware of the hot, sinewy flesh rubbing against her thigh, his hands tearing at her panties, then his penis starting to push inside her. A scream of protest ripped from her throat, but as she felt him penetrate, it died to a whimper. "Not you . . . not you . . . I want *him*."

Panting, his mouth beside her ear, he murmured in short bursts as he pumped in and out. "Close your eyes . . . let it be him . . . if you want . . ."

Because at last there was nothing else to do, she

surrendered to the fantasy. Closing her eyes, she began a kind of chant in her mind, telling herself to forget the violation, imagine it *was* Ted, it was that night, it was all she had dreamed it would be.

No! In love it would have been tender, beautiful. This was horrible—the cloud of whiskey breath, his raucous gasping as he drove himself savagely into her. Her fists started violently pummeling his back, but he seemed not to notice at all. He kept heaving himself up, pounding down, harder and faster, until suddenly he went rigid and let out a long, rasping groan. At last he tumbled off to one side of the bunk.

The only sound for a while was her sobbing.

"I'll marry you, Valeskja," he said finally. "I've always wanted you. I'm not sorry Jovan stopped you when he heard you two were alone here. . . ."

The sobbing died in her throat. *Heard . . . ? "Sent" was the word she remembered Jovan saying after he burst in.*

It came to her now that Willy must have been the one who'd told Jovan and robbed Ted—robbed them both—of that night of love. But she was too emotionally drained by the rape to condemn him for that earlier crime.

Slowly, she pulled herself up to sit on the edge of the bunk. She examined herself bleakly and saw that her underwear was too ripped even to put back on. Tearing it away, she tossed it off to one side, then stood and straightened her dress. She stumbled to the cabin door, her mouth, arms, legs, her very core, feeling tender and bruised.

Quickly, he was beside her. "I'll see you home, Valeskja." He put his arm around her. "Are you all right?"

How could he even ask? He seemed absolutely unaware that he had done anything wrong.

"Forgive me, Valeskja. It was only because I want to give you everything he would have. I didn't mean to hurt you. . . ."

There were so many different curses she wanted to scream at him, so many prayers she wanted to offer, but her mind could only form a kind of static, like the sound of all those voices she had heard during the war when she tried to tune in the shortwave to get news from the other side of the ocean. She felt indeed as though one part of herself were that far away from the other part.

He stayed beside her as she drifted numbly along the canal, heading home like a wounded animal seeking its nest so it could curl up and sleep forever.

Neither spoke until they approached the porch of Jovan's house, and a fresh plea burst from him. "You must forgive me. It came from love."

It couldn't have been love, she answered as she mounted the porch steps, but she answered only in her mind, unable to speak.

As she reached her door, he caught her hand from behind, holding her back, needing absolution. She left her hand limply in his and did not speak. "Will you tell your uncle?" he asked. "If you do, he might kill me. That's what they'd do in the old country."

Without looking at him, she shook her bowed head. However frightened Willy might be that Jovan would harm him, Val was sure her uncle would only demand that Willy marry her. So it would be all the worse for telling. Better that no one ever know.

"Thank you," Willy said quietly. Still holding on to her hand, he walked around in front of her, then leaned over and kissed her on the cheek.

She stood like a statue, feeling almost as though she had been turned to cold marble by an evil curse.

"I'll call you tomorrow," he said. After a moment he turned and went down the steps, and she went inside.

Across the threshold she was seized again by confusion. What had been done to her was a crime, wasn't it? If she reported it to the police, wouldn't he be arrested? Then what would people say about her for putting the brother of the man she'd intended to marry in jail?

Limbs heavy as lead, she climbed the stairs, went into the bathroom, ran a tub of water as hot as she could stand, then got in and scrubbed herself down until her skin was raw.

In bed she lay staring at the ceiling, so filled with the

memory of the rape that it almost seemed to be happening over and over and over again.

Val's dull factory job was not at all what she'd dreamed of doing when she was younger. All through high school she'd been encouraged by art teachers to believe she had extraordinary creative ability that might be used to earn a living. She had put those aspirations aside at first because the war was on, then because she couldn't give up the steady paycheck while she was saving for the wedding.

Since Ted's death she had no ambition. The daily drudgery of operating a die-cutting machine was anesthetic . . . and an accepted part of her life, as much as meals she ate without appetite, nights of restless sleep, bad dreams.

When she returned to work after the rape, she felt even more numb and apathetic. Accepting what Willy had done to her without protest deadened all her feelings, led her to believe that everything else must be accepted in the same way.

She did not even shun her attacker. On a few recent evenings Willy had stopped by the house, bringing flowers or candy. She couldn't rouse herself to react to him with fury or contempt or hatred. She knew if she did, there were bound to be questions from Jovan, then the whole thing might be blown into the open. Her uncle would insist that she marry—or else throw her out of his house.

So she accepted the gifts and sat in the front parlor, staring at her hands as Willy talked at her or with her uncle. When Jovan left them, Willy might ask in a whisper, "Are you still angry with me?" to which she would answer always that she didn't feel anything about him, and she wished he would stop coming.

He didn't though. Because, he told her, he wanted her to know he would always be sorry, and he felt certain she'd have to trust him again sooner or later. And then they could be married.

She found herself at work one day in October, standing in front of her machine in the midst of a crying jag, as surprised by her own tears as if she had been caught by a rainstorm breaking from a cloudless sky.

An older woman who operated an adjacent machine came over. "What's the matter, honey?"

"I don't know. Everything, I guess. . . ."

The other woman put a sympathetic arm around her. Everyone at the factory knew she'd been engaged to a man who'd been killed. "Go home, kid," she said. "I'll tell the foreman you felt sick."

"But I don't really—"

"Sweetie, you've got the blues, and who can blame you? Take a break, cry it out."

At home Val made tea for herself and got into bed, but she couldn't stop crying. The overflow of emotion puzzled her. Not that there wasn't a lot to be miserable about, but nothing she couldn't have cried about yesterday, or all the days of the past year, for that matter. Perhaps she was just at that time of the month when her emotional balance became most delicate.

That time—? It struck her suddenly that she was already *weeks* beyond her usual time. Her tears stopped abruptly as a bolt of panic went through her. How long had it been since that awful night with Willy? She'd worked so hard to erase it from her mind that she'd lost track of time. Now September was already past. More than half of October.

Dear God! She wasn't being hysterical, she knew; now that her mind was no longer blotting out the full impact of what had been done to her that night, she was possessed by a strange clarity of vision. She had a sense of knowing her body as she had not known it before; without being able to define exactly how or why she could be so certain, she felt another life growing within her.

Oddly, the panic subsided. For a while as she lay in bed it was sorrow that filled her instead. She had dreamed once of the children she'd have with the man she loved. Instead, she was going to have a child by a man she ought to despise.

But then even her sorrow gave way to more positive feelings. No matter how different his brother was from Ted, they'd come from the same blood. For that alone, couldn't she cherish this baby?

She could not abide the idea, however, that the man who had raped her should ever be able to claim it as his own, or use it as a lever to possess her.

To keep the child. To make it hers alone. With those two vows to guide her, a long list of other necessary choices followed.

Four

New York City
1948

Pausing outside the loft building in lower Manhattan's Flatiron district—named for the tall, triangular structure built at the turn of the century on the nearby corner of Twenty-third Street and Fifth Avenue—Val looked at the slip of paper on which she'd noted the details for the job interview. Mr. Geller from the employment agency had made it sound somewhat more interesting than the usual run-of-the mill office work.

"It's in a print shop," he'd told her. "Pays forty-eight bucks a week. This place does posters, and you've got down on your application that you won a prize for art in high school, so that may help."

She'd been in New York a month looking for work. Not that jobs were so hard to find; there was no lack of openings for women to work as waitresses, sewing machine operators, or salesclerks for twenty dollars a week. But if it made sense at all to have run from her old life, Val felt she had to try for something more than the low-salaried drudgery she'd left behind.

Then, too, she needed a salary sufficient to put money aside so she could take time off when the baby came. And it had to be work that kept her off her feet so she would be able to keep earning right up to the time of birth. In a perfect world it would also be a job where she could prove herself so useful, she would be taken back again once the baby could be left in the daily care of someone else.

Hard demands to fill, especially when her education hadn't

gone beyond high school. And, too, she'd learned, her obviously foreign name deterred many agencies from giving her first preference. It seemed odd, since Americans had been so ready to fight and die to protect Europeans, that she should find them reluctant to give opportunities to anyone whose name was foreign. Yet needing every break she could get, Val gave the agencies an Americanized name. Unfortunately, Valentina Cummings hadn't been any luckier than Valeskja Kumeniczi.

The money she had brought with her to New York was dwindling away even though she kept expenses to a minimum. Thirty dollars a week for her room and board in Brooklyn, some new clothes to make her more presentable for the interviews, a dollar here and there for a movie to soothe her loneliness. The city was so expensive and unfriendly, she was doubting her decision to come. At least Willy wanted her . . . the baby could have a father . . . they would be sheltered and fed.

In fact, if she didn't land a good job in the next day or two, Val was resigned to going back to being . . . Valeskja Kumeniczi. She looked again at the slip from the employment agency. Forty-eight dollars a week. Today it seemed like a fortune.

"What about experience?" the stocky man in the ink-smeared smock shouted at her over the noise of the half dozen printing presses in the huge, open loft. "The stuff we do here, drawing don't matter a damn. You gotta know how to set type, do layout."

Val glanced around as her mind worked to find some way of persuading the man not to send her away. Her gaze fell on a poster on the wall, a remnant of a past job, she guessed. Printed across the top of the card was the date September 18th beneath a photograph of the great heavyweight boxer Joe Louis, and details of the championship bout that had been fought on that date. Val recalled her uncle reading a newspaper report the next morning.

"Are those posters the kind of thing you do?" she asked.

The man nodded.

"I know about boxing. Louis won that fight by a knockout in the first round."

The man smiled wanly. "Yeah, kid, who *doesn't* know he decked Mauriello in under two minutes. Look, you seem like a nice girl, but this isn't the place for you." He hurried back to work.

Val went to the elevator that serviced the loft and pushed the button. Waiting, she wondered if she should even bother trying further. Thanksgiving was only a couple of weeks away. No time to be alone.

The elevator opened and she got on. On the way down, she noticed that the young man beside her was holding two large boxes with engraved cards taped to the sides, samples of stationery in the boxes. The Flatiron district was an area where many printers and engravers had their shops. As the elevator descended, Val idly read the words engraved on the sample card: "Mr. and Mrs. Archibald P. Winston III request the pleasure of your attendance at the wedding of their daughter Justine Carter Winston to Mr. Hugh Spence Dwyer at . . ."

She got no further before her vision blurred over at the reminder of what fate had stolen from her. The invitation to a true society wedding reminded her, too, of all the well-meaning warnings she'd had that such grand events were for the rich and privileged, not for ordinary people like herself.

Bowing her head to conceal the tears spilling down her cheeks, Val didn't notice that the elevator had arrived at the ground floor. The other passengers exited around her, and as new people came aboard, Val realized her lapse and dashed off the elevator. Head down, blinded by tears, she was only faintly aware as she ran out of the building that during the time she'd been inside, it had started to rain. Turning, she collided abruptly with a man walking ahead of her. The impact sent him sprawling, but Val reeled only slightly before managing to catch her balance. Looking down, she saw her victim was the young man with the boxes of wedding invitations who'd been in the elevator. He'd dropped the boxes, and all the pristine engraved cards and envelopes had spilled out across the wet, grimy sidewalk. "Oh, no!" she cried.

The young man, somewhat stunned, rolled over and propped himself up on his elbows to survey his losses.

"I'm so sorry, really so terribly . . ." Val said brokenly.

"Why the hell can't you watch where you're going?" he barked as he got to his feet. Val saw now that he had torn his pants at one knee.

"I should have, yes . . . you're right, the whole thing's all my fault." Her abject guilt resonated with everything else plaguing her, and her crying intensified.

"Okay, okay, settle down," the young man said impatiently. "I'm the one who came out of this with all the problems."

"No, no," she sobbed. "I have problems too. I mean . . . I just feel so awful about what I've done." She regarded the hundreds of cards scattered on the sidewalk, all ruined.

Looking at her, his expression softened. With the initial shock of the collision behind them, they became aware of the chill November rain pelting down. Val realized, too, what a good-looking man he was, tall, with long brown hair, and hazel eyes that gazed back earnestly at her.

"Hey, come out of the rain," he said, grasping her arm to pull her toward the nearest shelter, the entrance of the building they had just left.

"What about those?" She looked back at the invitations lying under the downpour.

"Those are useless now. They'll have to be redone."

Which would cost . . . goodness, how much were invitations like that? From the way the young man was dressed, windbreaker, dusty corduroys, Val realized he must be the printer's delivery man; paying for the replacement would be a hardship. And already he would be in trouble, the new invitations would not meet the schedule. Val felt she had no choice but to make the offer. "I'll pay to replace them. . . ."

He looked at her with surprise. "It's very expensive."

In the doorway she had gained control of herself and stopped sobbing. "It's only fair," she said firmly. "It was my fault."

"But it was an accident," he said.

"Maybe," she sighed. "Or maybe when it's anything to do

with weddings, I'm bad luck. You shouldn't suffer because of my jinx."

He regarded her curiously, but seemed to decide against asking her to explain. "The engraver's in this building. Come back upstairs with me, and we'll see what can be worked out."

They rode the elevator up to a loft two floors above the place where Val had been rejected for a job. A sign in a small waiting room said: R. DURER, ENGRAVING & FINE PRINTING. The young man led Val through the door into the loft. At a long counter running down one side of the room, men sat on high stools, peering closely under bright lights at work they were doing with tools in their hands. Some wore a band around their head with a magnifying lens attached so that it could swivel down over their eyes. In the farther recesses of the loft were printing presses.

As soon as they entered, a man on the stool nearest the door rose and came over. He was elderly, with snow-white hair, smooth, pinkish skin, and a wide, friendly face. He wore a linen printers' smock, but it was unstained by ink.

"Back so soon?" he said to the delivery man.

"It's my fault," Val interjected quickly. "I knocked him down, and all the invitations fell and got ruined."

The printer buried a hand in his full white hair. *"Gott in Himmel,"* he said.

Realizing he was a German immigrant somehow made him seem less a stranger to Val because of Ted's family.

"They'll have to be redone, Mr. Durer," the delivery man said.

The printer's white eyebrows flared. "All of them? *Ein unglück!*"

"But not a total disaster," Val said. "I'll pay for new ones."

Her ability to understand his German drew a curious glance from the printer. Then he looked to his delivery man and raised his eyebrows, seeking assurance her offer was genuine.

"She's insisted on paying," the delivery man affirmed.

"One problem solved, then," the printer said, his German accent more noticeable as he had more to say. "But the poor bride will have to wait another week now."

"But this was a rush order to start," said the delivery man.

The printer grew agitated. "And didn't I do my best to oblige? Eight hundred invitations, ready as ordered. What am I to do when people throw my fine work into the gutter?"

"No one threw it away," Val protested. "Mr. Durer, I know how upsetting it is if . . . if things don't go exactly as planned for a wedding. Tell me what can be done so the new invitations will be ready as soon as possible."

The old printer pursed his lips. "Well, we still have the engraved plate—and I suppose we could work late tonight, and tomorrow. But of course that makes the job more expensive, and there are also setup charges. . . ."

"I'll cover the extras," the delivery man said.

Val shook her head. "I can't let you. . . ."

"Miss, please—"

"No! I'm responsible." If it were anything but wedding invitations, Val might have acted differently. But she felt the cloud of the jinx hanging over her, and was seized by a superstitious notion that settling this account could change her luck.

"Gut," said the printer. "I'll have them by Monday afternoon."

"How much deposit will you need?" Val asked nervously.

"Pay in full on Monday. I'm not sure yet how much overtime will be required."

Monday. With her money all but depleted, she'd been considering going back to Buffalo within the next few days. Now she wondered if she'd even have bus fare left once she met her obligation for this catastrophe. "Can you give me an approximate idea of the amount—so I can bring it with me?" She held her breath.

Durer calculated. "Eight hundred . . . best quality . . ." He glanced at the young man. "Envelopes again?"

"They were ruined too," the delivery man said.

Durer did some more mental arithmetic. "Sixty dollars—"

Val started to exhale with relief.

"—per hundred," Durer finished. "Invitation and envelope."

The breath caught in her throat. She could only stare at the printer. Sixty times *eight*! Four hundred eighty, more than three times what was left of her savings.

Impossible. She ought to admit it right now.

But then who would pay? It would be no easier for this young man. The rich society bride—let her deal with it, plenty of money there. But it wasn't her fault. And Val felt a curious kinship with this unknown bride at imagining her suffering over a mishap that threatened her plans.

"Monday," she said quietly. It was settled.

The printer went back to his work, and Val headed for the elevator. "I'll go out with you," the young man said to her. "That mess on the street needs to be cleaned up."

He tried to make pleasant conversation, but Val could only give perfunctory replies, her mind bedeviled by what she needed to accomplish. Outside, the rain had completely soaked the stationery, which still littered the street. She helped the young man put it into garbage cans in an alley between buildings.

"Where are you going now?" he asked when they'd finished. "I was going to have lunch. . . ."

"I'm sorry, I can't join you," she said with a consoling smile. "I . . . I have shopping to do."

He was clearly disappointed. He hesitated, as if considering another proposition, then he shrugged and said, "Maybe I'll see you on Monday. . . ."

"Yes. Maybe."

They said their good-byes and walked in opposite directions.

Mr. Durer was in the midst of giving instructions to a group of three other men in printers' smocks when Val walked back in. Noticing her, the white-haired printer broke off his conference and came over. He could see the distress plainly written on her features. "*Noch etwas?* You have lost something here?"

"Only my senses," she said. "Mr. Durer, those invitations—I'm sorry, but I don't have the money to pay you."

"But then why did you say you would?"

"Because it was my fault."

"*Verstehen.* But that young gentleman was willing to pay, and you refused."

"It didn't seem fair. What you pay him to make deliveries can't be very much."

"To make deliveries," the old printer repeated, his brow furrowed as though he was trying to recall some English words he'd forgotten.

"I'll be honest, Mr. Durer. I came to this building today looking for a job, but I didn't get it. I might even be leaving the city . . . but I feel I have to make this right. If you'll do those invitations, I'll pay you back. Not Monday, not all at once. But I'll save . . . wherever I am . . . and give you something every month. I'll repay you . . . even if it takes years."

He gazed at her steadily, and she saw a gentle concern in his faded blue eyes. "Ozzie!" he called out. "Set up the run on that Winston job. I'll be in my office awhile." To Val he said, "Come, Fräulein. I think you need to sit down and have some tea, maybe even with a little schnapps, yah?"

She pulled back slightly to look at him, and he nodded and smiled with a warmth and assurance that made her feel better already. "*Danke schön,*" she said as Ted had taught her.

His office at a rear corner of the shop floor was enclosed by glass partitions with a window that looked out on an air shaft. Still, it had a cheerful quality. It was clean and uncluttered, with a comfortable chair facing the desk. A painted cuckoo clock and posters of the Alps decorated the two corner walls, and a hot plate with a flowered crockery teapot and cups stood on a cabinet. He gave her the tea as promised, and offered to add a few drops of schnapps from a bottle in his bottom desk drawer, which she declined.

As he brewed the tea he gently and patiently asked Val about herself. She gave her name as the one she'd adopted to seem less of a refugee, and talked a little about how and why she had come to America.

After the tea was poured, the printer sat down opposite her. He had been moved by hearing how the war had destroyed her family and forced her to emigrate to relatives in America.

"Young lady, you have endured much bad luck. You are past due, I think, for some good luck to even the account."

"It would be nice if there were such an account book in life," Val said. "But the way things are going, Mr. Durer, I'm afraid I see only the bad luck side of the ledger getting longer."

He eyed her thoughtfully over the rim of his teacup. "You speak a little German," he remarked then. "How does that come about?"

"The parents of the man I was going to marry came here from Germany."

"Yet you had no trouble loving him?"

"We're all Americans here, Mr. Durer. My fiancé fought for this country during the war."

"When are you to be married?"

She looked down and shook her head. "It . . . it ended" was all she could bring herself to say.

"I see—more bad luck." He set his teacup aside. "So let us see what can be done to balance accounts. If you will come to work for me, Miss Cummings, I will pay you a salary of thirty-eight dollars per week. It's not a great amount, I know, but I will increase it quickly as you learn."

She gulped her tea. "You're offering me a job?"

He shrugged. "It's one way to be sure your debt to me is repaid. Actually, I shall be starting you at forty-two dollars per week, but with four dollars deducted for the invitations."

Val was so excited, she nearly leapt up though the cup and saucer were balanced in her lap. She stopped herself in time, but was still bubbling over with gratitude. "Mr. Durer, I don't know how I can ever thank you. I'll have time to work things out, see if there's some way I can possibly stay here and still have my—" She clapped her mouth shut: She had said nothing about the baby, and if she did she felt he would surely withdraw the job offer.

Almost as if he hadn't heard the half-finished sentence, he said, "*Nun gut*. You will start Monday, then." He rose from the desk. "Now I must get back to work."

He told her she could relax and finish her tea, but Val took the cue to leave.

"Forgive me if this is prying, Miss Cummings," he said as they were walking to the elevator, "but are you . . . longing for the fiancé you lost. Or . . . might you consider receiving the attentions of a new suitor?"

Was this what lay behind offering her the job? An old man's desire? Val answered carefully. "I don't know if I'll ever forget Ted. And I doubt I'm ready for courtship. But I can always do with a new friend."

"Ah, well, unless my eyes deceived me, the man in question was attracted in a way that suggests a desire for more than mere *Freundschaft*."

"What man is that, Mr. Durer?"

"The fellow you knocked over in the street."

"Your delivery boy?"

"Delivery boy!" The old printer erupted into a boisterous guffaw. "Sweet girl, you don't appreciate how much good luck entered your 'ledger' today."

"But I do. I couldn't hope for more than a job."

"Yes you could. That 'delivery boy' who obviously can't wait to see you again on Monday—he is the brother of the very lady for whose wedding those invitations are intended. Young Andrew Winston is one of the most desirable *jungeselle* in New York!"

"Jungeselle?" Val repeated questioningly.

"Excuse me, Miss Cummings, perhaps your fiancé didn't teach you that word: bachelor. And not only is Mr. Winston one of the most eligible in New York, but one of the richest."

Eligible as he might be, Val thought as she left, it was no good to her. Romance with a socialite was surely out of reach for a woman of her background who was pregnant by another man.

She wasted no time feeling sorry for herself, however. The job was good luck enough for one day.

Five

She arrived for work Monday morning promptly at eight o'clock, and was instructed in her duties, a combination of secretarial work and assisting in the print shop—answering the telephone, making out invoices, packing up finished stationery, paying bills, showing sample books to the walk-in customers. During lunch hours and other quiet periods, Mr. Durer said, she would be instructed in the engraver's craft.

Val made an effort to approach each chore with a display of enthusiastic cooperation, determined to make herself no less than indispensable in the next few months so that even after her pregnancy became apparent, she would be able to hold on to the job. Another incentive to keep her working, of course, would be her debt for the Winston wedding invitations: At just four dollars a week, it would take two years to repay.

The invitations were ready as promised on Monday afternoon. Andrew Winston had phoned to say he would collect them personally at four o'clock.

As the hour neared, Val begged her employer to let her avoid Winston by staying out of sight in a rear office. It would be too embarrassing, she explained, to have him know she'd been forced to take the job to fulfill her obligation.

"You don't have to hide from him," Durer said. "I won't tell him about the job. You can pretend you're here just to pay me."

"No, please. I think it's better if I don't see him again."

Her reticence baffled the printer. "Dear girl, why behave like a *schüchtern Kaninchen*? Do you think it's every day you'll have the chance to meet such a man?"

He meant well by chiding her for running from the opportunity like a timid little bunny, Val knew, but she also realized that given Andrew Winston's social station and her circumstances, pursuing a romance was impossible. To squelch the old man's benevolent meddling, she fibbed. "Mr. Winston may seem wonderful to you, but . . . I've already had hints that he's much too fast for a respectable girl. Another word for some bachelors, Mr. Durer, could be *ein ordinërer Kerl*, the German for cad."

"Ah, yes," Durer allowed, then, "perhaps the whole family's no good. You know why they came to me for their wedding invitations? Top society folk like that normally go to Cartier or Tiffany—but neither of those would deliver quickly enough, and the girl was in such a big rush to get them. So perhaps there's something more than meets the eye about that marriage, eh? You know what I mean?" He winked, and patted his stomach lightly.

Later Durer reported to Val that when Andrew Winston had come to pick up his order he had again inquired about her, wanted to know when she might be coming to pay the bill, evidently prepared to wait. Obliging Val's wishes, Durer replied that the bill was already settled. She had been and gone.

Val had no regrets. At this point it was surely best not to become involved with *any* man.

There were times it was hard being alone. The pangs of isolation were especially acute at Thanksgiving.

She had left Buffalo abruptly without explanation to anyone but Jovan. To him there had been only a letter taped to the door of her room, thanking him for taking her in, and saying that remaining in the place where all her dreams had died only kept stoking her grief. She needed a fresh start far away.

By now she had written her uncle from the city to tell him she was "doing well," but she had provided no return address: That might be passed to Willy, and he might even come after her. She wanted to forget him, *everything* to do with him. Indeed, as the weeks passed, Val kept buried any thoughts about her pregnancy.

Then one evening, walking from the subway to her rooming house, she passed two pregnant women chatting outside a store, overheard them comparing notes on their doctors' advice. Mortified by the prospect of admitting to any doctor she was unmarried, Val had delayed going for medical advice. It dawned on her now that she was long overdue to start.

The next Saturday morning she went to the free clinic at nearby Brooklyn Samaritan Hospital. After telling the nurse at a receiving desk that she thought she *might* be pregnant, she was given a form to fill out and pointed to a hallway lined on both sides with chairs occupied by waiting men, women, and children.

Periodically, young interns appeared and called out a name. As Val waited, her attention was drawn to one young woman in particular. Seated along the opposite wall, she had yellow-blond hair that trailed over her shoulders, pale, almost translucent skin and a very slight build, thin arms and legs that gave her a fragile, vulnerable look. Her face was very pretty—large green eyes, high cheekbones, and a thin, straight nose—yet the sad set of her mouth and dark circles under her eyes gave her a haggard aspect. She sat with one arm across her body, clutching at the other arm, which bore ugly purple bruises by the elbow.

She must have arrived only a little before Val, because as names were called, she remained there. A moment came when Val found the stranger looking back at her and they exchanged a smile.

Val opened the bridge of conversation: "Long wait . . ."

"You have to come very early on Saturdays," said the fragile blond woman.

Shifting along her row to an empty seat directly opposite her, Val said, "Sounds like you've been here before."

"A few times. I live in the neighborhood." Her voice was soft with a pleasing lilt.

"What happened to your arm?" Val asked.

"Fell off a bicycle."

There was a silence. Val felt she was racing the clock, that any moment a doctor would call the other woman's name and they'd never see each other again. Yet she had a powerful intuition they could be friends. Having someone like herself to talk to, someone who seemed hurt and vulnerable, was so rare and valuable, she didn't want to let the contact wither. "I'm here because I'm going to have a baby," Val said. "Do you have children?"

Affected by the intimacy of Val's confession, the blond woman's expression lost its guarded tightness. "Yes. I have a little girl, six years old. And she's the light of my life," she added, evidently sensing Val's anxiety, and wanting to reassure her.

"I hope I can say the same thing someday," Val said. "Right now I'm pretty scared."

The other woman moved across to an empty seat beside Val. "I'm Josie MacMoran. Who are you?"

After using her new name so much at work, it came naturally: "Val Cummings."

"Don't be scared, Val," Josie said. "It's great to be a mother; it's the best part of my life. As for having a baby, long as you're healthy, and do the right things, it can be easy as—"

"As falling off a bicycle?" Val put in mischievously.

Josie paused before giving a little laugh. "Yeah—and it hurts at least as much. But if you learn certain exercises, that helps a lot, how to breathe and stuff." After a second, Josie asked, "Is your husband excited about it?"

The truth was too much to admit. "Yes," Val said. "Very."

A white-coated resident appeared through the door to the examining section. "MacMoran!" he called out.

Guilty about her lie, Val was relieved to be off the hook but also disappointed the encounter had to end.

The other woman rose. "Nice meeting you, Val. Good luck with the baby."

"Thanks. Nice meeting you too."

Val wanted to add something—an opening to greater friendship. But the resident called impatiently, "Coming, Mrs. MacMoran . . . ?"

Josie moved ahead. As she disappeared through the door to

the examining section, Val could faintly hear the intern say to her, "So. I see we've had another bicycle accident. . . ."

It had an odd ring to it, Val thought, as though the doctor were teasing, more snide than sympathetic.

Soon Val was called in for her examination. A resident introduced himself as Dr. Kendall and motioned her to get on the table of a white-curtained cubicle. He began asking questions to complete her written form.

She found Kendall very likable, short and chubby with a round, smiling face topped by a mop of light brown curls, and gentle hands. Still, the examination was an ordeal for Val, not only the probing of the most sensitive parts of her body, but the questions.

"How's your husband's health history?" the doctor asked while completing the form.

"It's fine," Val said.

"No abnormal births in any of his close relatives?"

She shook her head.

But that wasn't the end of the embarrassing questions. "You wrote down that this is your first examination," Kendall observed after stethoscopically sounding her abdomen. "I'm already getting a heartbeat from the fetus. Have you felt any movement?"

"No."

"You will soon, I think. I'd guess your baby is already at the end of the first trimester, Mrs. Cummings. Maybe even starting the second. Why did you wait so long to come here?"

"I . . . I just felt fine . . . so . . ." She looked away guiltily.

"Were you aware of your condition?"

Head bowed, Val murmured, "Yes."

Softly, the doctor asked, "You aren't happy about the baby?"

Her head came up. "Yes, I am!" she said with a force that took her as much by surprise as it did the doctor. It hadn't been crystallized until then, but she realized the baby was everything to her, her hope of belonging with someone, existing *for* someone.

"And your husband?" the doctor said. "You wouldn't be trying to keep this a secret from him . . . ?"

Val's eyes met the doctor's, which were a soft brown, and conveyed a kindness suited to the rest of his teddy-bear look. Lying again was suddenly impossible. "I don't have a husband," she admitted.

"I see. But the father, how does he—"

"He doesn't know," Val broke in. "He doesn't *deserve* to know." Val's hurt and anger at Willy spilled out.

The young doctor studied her for a long while. "Mrs."—he caught himself—"Miss Cummings, from all appearances, both you and your baby are doing fine. We'll want to get results on the blood samples, of course, but I expect there'll be no special cause for concern. Except one. It sounds like this child has no one to depend on except yourself, which means you can't be as casual as you've been about your condition. You have to eat the right things, take care of yourself . . . and plan how you're going to manage when the baby comes."

"I know," Val said in a shamed whisper, tears forming.

The doctor put a hand on her shoulder. "I'm sure it'll be all right . . . as long as you begin today." He moved to a cabinet and took out a few pamphlets. "Here are some things to remember about your prenatal care and diet."

She took the pamphlets and thanked him.

"If you'd like, I can continue to be your physician, and you can make appointments for when I'm on duty. Otherwise, just come to the clinic whenever—"

"I'd like to have you," she said quickly. She didn't want to have to make the confession to a different doctor every time, and had a good feeling about Kendall.

"Fine," he said. "Get dressed. That's all for today." He started out. "Unless there's anything else you'd like to tell me . . ."

"No," she said. "Not today." But sooner or later, perhaps.

When she went out into the hallway, the chairs were all empty, the clinic done for the day. Spotting the resident who'd called Josie for treatment, Val asked if she was still around.

"No, she's gone. Are you a friend of hers?"

"Sort of. Why?"

The doctor gave a twisted little smile. "I was thinking someone ought to talk to her about . . . the bicycle that keeps making her black and blue." He walked away.

There it was again, his strange tone when referring to Josie's mishaps. Val considered going after him to ask just what he meant. But after all, she wasn't really a friend of Josie MacMoran's, so it was no business of hers.

At Christmas, Val received a holiday bonus from Mr. Durer of an extra week's pay, and on his card fronted by a picture of the Nativity he added a note saying he was glad she had come to work for him and, as an extra gift, he was forgiving the rest of the debt for the Winston invitations.

Andrew Winston, still unaware Val had gone to work for Durer, had called the printer—luckily for Val at a moment when she was out making a delivery—to ask if he had any idea how she might be located. "Forgive me for bothering you, sir. But I can't get that girl out of my mind."

"Yes, she was very pretty," Durer said, plumbing the sincerity of the young man's interest.

"It's not just that, sir. I feel bad about letting her pay your bill. It was an accident, and the more I think about it, the more I suspect it might've been a stretch for her, while for me . . . well, anyway, I was just hoping that if she paid you by check, you might remember the bank, and I could call them to—"

"She didn't pay by check. I'm sorry, but I'm afraid I'm unable to tell you anything." In fact, Durer had given Val a pledge that if Winston called, he'd get no help or encouragement.

When Val returned to the print shop, Durer reported the call and suggested she might reconsider meeting Andrew Winston. "He certainly sounded honorable enough, whatever his sister's peccadilloes. Why not try him once more, see what he's like?"

"There's no point in it," Val answered so emphatically that the printer resolved not to meddle in her personal business again.

* * *

Early in the New Year, Reinhart Durer finally took the trip he had put off since leaving Germany fourteen years earlier as the Nazis had begun gathering power. He had a brother and sister in Munich, and he wanted to visit and try to persuade them to leave their war-ravaged country and come to America. Though Val had worked for him only a couple of months, the printer had noted her competence, and felt confident she could run the office during his three weeks away. The production and engraving would be overseen by his principal assistant, Oskar Samstein—"Ozzie"—a hefty refugee from Belgium with a bushy gray beard.

All went smoothly for Val most of the first week. Then on Friday, a man appeared in front of her desk with a large black morocco portfolio in one hand. Though a stranger to Val, she realized he must have been there before. As he made his way from the elevator, she heard him call greetings to the printers.

"Hi, there, beautiful," he said, giving Val an approving once-over that was too much of a leer for her taste. "I'm Bradley Smythe." He was about forty years old, dressed in a well-fitted dark brown suit that looked to be made from the expensive new miracle fabric, rayon. His brilliantined dark hair was perfectly cut, and he had a trim mustache.

"What can I do for you, Mr. Smythe?"

"Not a thing, really. I like looking at you, but it's your boss I really *need* to see." He glanced around, already looking for Durer so he could simply bypass a secretary.

"Mr. Durer's not here."

"Listen, gorgeous, I need an okay on something pretty big. Maybe I shouldn't have left this to the last minute, but Durer's always here, so I never expected there'd be all this trouble."

Val's back stiffened. "There isn't any trouble," she said starchily. "If you'll explain what this is about, I'm sure I can help you. Mr. Durer's gone abroad; he's left me in charge."

"Abroad, eh?" Smythe said with another leer. Then he walked to the side of the desk, ran the zipper around the edge of the portfolio, and plopped it open in front of Val. "These are the printer's pages for this year's annual. I figure Durer wants to take the same space again. If he wants to leave the decision to you, fine—but I need the word right now. We print next week."

Val looked down at the pages in front of her. They were blocked out in sections that quartered the space or broke it into eights. Each box was blank except for a name handwritten in ink—"Durer" was in one corner box, and Val recognized others as belonging to other printers and engravers. A heading across the top of both pages read: For Your Invitations. Flipping forward, Val saw similar sections for other bridal needs—gowns, veils, coiffure, floral arrangements. Turning back to the cover of the book, she found a pleasing full-color illustration of a bridal bouquet on thick, glossy paper, with *Bride's Annual* printed in gold across the top. She understood now that "the *Annual*" offered advertising to those who provided goods or services specifically to brides, geared to come out a few months before June.

Smythe pulled the portfolio away. "In or out, that's all I need to know. I can use the last year's copy, or tell me if there's something new. Costs have gone up though, so your space'll cost twice as much as last year. Of course, with the boom in big weddings since war's end, we're also printing a lot more copies."

She looked up at him. "Then, for our ad you're asking . . . ?"

He gave her an oily smile. "Two thousand dollars."

This was a big investment to take on her own authority, Val thought. A car cost less! "Sit down a moment, Mr. Smythe." She gestured to a chair and hurried over to consult Ozzie at his engraver's bench.

"Smythe is a snake," Ozzie said. "But he's put himself in a position where it's hard to say no. Reinhart doesn't like him, but I think he'd take the same space as last year. It brings in more than enough business to pay for itself."

Val went back to Smythe and said Durer would take the ad.

"A thousand now," Smythe said, "the rest when the book is delivered. Check made out to me." He stood, preparing to leave as soon as the payment was in hand.

When Val looked at the check ledger she wavered again. With payrolls to meet while collections often remained outstanding for months, the firm never ran a large balance. After paying Smythe and weekly wages, Val saw only four hundred dollars would be left.

"How many copies are you printing?" she asked.

"Ten thousand. Sent all over the country."

Twenty cents per copy for Durer to advertise. Fair enough, Val supposed. She started to make out the check.

"How long you been here, gorgeous?" Smythe asked as he stood over the desk, watching her write.

"A couple of months."

"I should try to get here more than once a year," he said, "keep . . . abreast. You really are quite a looker, Miss—"

Val tore the check from the ledger and pointedly held it out without speaking.

"I could arrange a discount just for you—a very *substantial* discount, if you're willing to . . . discuss it."

The proposition suddenly tripped a circuit in Val's mind. Did this oily character have any more right to treat her as if she were available for the right price than Ted's brother had been entitled to take her without consent? Her outstretched hand went rigid as she stared at him coldly. When he reached to take the check, her fingers were clamped so tightly together, his quick pull tore the paper in half.

He smiled slowly. "So—you *are* interested in . . . renegotiating?"

His misinterpretation only infuriated her more. "Not one bit, Mr. Smythe," she snapped. "I've just changed my mind: This firm will not be taking an ad in your publication."

His smile changed to an ugly smirk. "Not smart, sweetheart. Just three or four jobs for fancy invitations you've covered your cost, the rest is gravy. So I'll give you a chance to write that check again—for the full amount."

She couldn't yield to anything that gave him a reward. "This firm will survive very well without you, Mr. Smythe. Good day." She slammed the check ledger shut and started clearing her desk.

"Yeah, you're beautiful," he said, picking up the portfolio

and starting for the elevator as he called loudly over his shoulder, "Beautiful . . . but dumb!"

The panic struck as soon as he'd gone. How much business had Mr. Durer lost because of her willful indignation? He'd been so good to her! And this was how she repaid him. . . .

Hearing Smythe's parting shot, Ozzie came over. "What was that about?"

"I lost my temper." Val's voice sank. "And . . . I didn't take the ad."

The engraver pulled over the deskside chair and sat down. "Never mind, Val, you must have had good reason. Nobody likes Smythe. They'd all tell him to fly a kite if they could; but there's nothing else like his catalogue."

She shook her head. "A man like that could give the whole wedding business a bad name. How did he get to be so important?"

Ozzie told her about Bradley Smythe. Until sixteen years ago, he had been an ordinary salesman in the silver department at Tiffany's. Observing the prospective brides who came not only to buy engagement and wedding rings, but to register for expensive china settings and silverware, he had realized what a ripe market they were. In the midst of the Depression only the rich had been able to afford lavish weddings. Those young women and their friends were the cream of society, with endless amounts of money for their trousseaus, and for friends to spend on gifts. Tapping into that specialized market, Smythe realized, would earn him far more than being a silver salesman.

Until then, wedding gowns and other bridal finery were advertised sparingly along with all other fine apparel and luxury goods in the pages of *Vogue*, *Ladies Home Journal*, or other glossy magazines aimed at women. Smythe began spending time stolen from his job to approach those who made or sold any product that would appeal to prospective brides with the idea of paying for space in an annual catalogue to be distributed free each June, giving prospective brides a full year to plan. The recipients would be purely from the most affluent group of bridal prospects, he told clients, their names culled from engagement announcements on the society pages of the newspapers. A second mailing could be done six months later, targeting names that appeared on bridal registries of the better stores.

The idea was successful immediately, especially since Smythe began by asking only nominal advertising charges. As soon as he enlisted a fairly representative group of suppliers of bridal finery, the rest fell quickly in line rather than give their competitors any edge.

"Smythe did well right from the start," Ozzie said. "But in the past couple of years I think he's actually begun to grow rich. During the war, almost no one took time out for a big wedding. Now people can again put time and money into it, even middle-class. So Smythe's catalogue gets quite a response. The advertisers know it and they're willing to pay."

"From the sound of it," Val said glumly, "I've cost our firm a lot of business."

Ozzie stood to return to his bench. "We don't depend on wedding business, Val." He was obviously trying to spare her feelings, though he couldn't disagree that her dignity had been purchased at a high price.

For the rest of the day, and after she got back to her room that night, Val thought about what Ozzie had told her: how clever Smythe had been to find a way of making money for himself out of brides and weddings.

Thinking of weddings, Val was overcome with memories of planning her own. God, how she wished— No use making any of those wishes though. She wasn't going to be planning a wedding for herself again. Who'd marry her when she had a bastard child by a man she'd refuse to name?

Yet her nostalgia for the pleasant part of that experience—when she'd been looking forward to that wonderful day—made her think it might be nice to help other brides make their plans, as Smythe did in his way. But what Smythe had done couldn't be repeated, Val thought. Anyway, how could she hope to start any business of her own? Having the baby and finding a way to survive—together—would be miracle enough.

Six

In the first week of March, a blizzard descended on the city. On the Saturday when Val had her regular checkup at the clinic, the streets were piled with drifts, the sidewalks treacherous with ice. Val wasn't sure it was wise to venture out, but in return for Walter Kendall's dedicated care—he had told her his first name at the last exam—she was keen to show him she wasn't neglecting her condition.

As the weeks went on, she had felt the doctor developing a personal interest—nothing improper, simply the degree of extra attention one might receive from a friend or even a brother. But his warmth and guarded affection inspired Val to trust him fully and be more open with him about her circumstances. Over several visits, she had talked about Ted's death and confessed that in the aftermath she had "allowed things to happen" she would have avoided if she hadn't been in such a despondent state. She remained ashamed to confess her pregnancy was the result of rape, but admitted to Kendall she'd left Buffalo rather than be forced to marry her baby's father.

The clinic wasn't crowded this snowy morning, and she was taken as soon as she arrived. Walter Kendall went carefully through his exam. "Everything's excellent," he said at last. "Come again in three weeks." As he was about to leave the cubicle, he paused. "Val, last time you explained to me why you'd left home. I understand your reasons, but for the baby's sake, perhaps you should give some thought to going back."

"I can't," she said flatly.

"You'll need help caring for this child," he persisted. "You mustn't try to deal with this all alone if there's any way—"

"Whatever I have to deal with by staying here," she said, "it could never be as bad as going back."

But as she dressed, she wondered if the answer she'd given was still true. When the baby came, how would she manage? Where would the money come from? What would happen with her job?

As soon as she emerged into the waiting area, Val recognized instantly that the lone figure occupying a chair was Josie MacMoran. Josie didn't see her though. She was slumped down, blond hair curtaining her face, possibly even dozing.

Val lowered herself into the empty seat beside her. Bending down, she saw that Josie's eyes were open, staring at the floor.

"Hello again," Val said softly. Josie turned. As her face became fully visible, Val gasped. The lower lip was split, crusted with dried blood, and there was a terrible bruise around her right eye and cheekbone, the eye reddened by a hideous blood spot. "My God, what happened?"

Josie's lip curled in what might have been a smile, though her injury made it grotesque rather than winning. "Damn bicycle again," she said.

But something in her tone told Val a bicycle had nothing to do with it—and never had. Val didn't ask more though. What mattered now was to comfort Josie. "I was so hoping I'd run into you. Well, not like this—but . . . you were so sweet, reassuring me about having a baby, I would've liked to talk more."

Josie gazed back as though understanding that Val was proposing not merely a conversation but a friendship. "Me too. You here for your checkup?"

"Just finished. I'll wait for you though. . . ."

"I could be here a while—might need X rays." Josie put a hand to her chin. "My jaw feels broken . . ." Val gave a sympathetic shake of her head, but Josie went on without milking any sympathy. "I would like to talk, if you're sure you don't mind waiting."

"I'm sure. But maybe you ought to go straight home. Doesn't look like you should be up and around."

"I got myself here, didn't I? I'll be okay."

A white-coated resident appeared at the door to the examining section. "Mrs. MacMoran!"

Watching Josie go, Val was filled with curiosity. What had caused those injuries? And if Josie was married, and so badly hurt, why did she have to bring herself here?

When they sat down to talk at a coffee shop near the hospital, it was soon apparent to both women that they were involved in a rapid, intense bonding unlike any either had experienced before. Perhaps it was because they had met at the clinic—where each had come with a problem she'd been forced to keep secret too long—that they found in each other an immediate and essential support, but each woman knew at once she had found an irreplaceable friend.

Coffee led to hot turkey sandwiches, then glasses of milk with cherry pie. And all the time they talked, exposing secrets and sharing deep feelings almost as easily as if they were tossing a ball back and forth. Despite her injuries, Josie was in an upbeat mood, encouraged because the X rays had shown her jaw was not broken.

Sitting in the booth of the diner, Val told Josie everything about herself—how she had come to live in Buffalo during the war, her love for Ted, his death, and even the way the baby had been conceived. Josie in turn revealed the whole history behind her persistent "bicycle" accidents.

She had been born in the Red Hook section of Brooklyn—along the East River under the Brooklyn Bridge—where many residents were families of dockworkers. Josie's father, Tom Duffy, was a longshoreman; so was one of her two younger brothers until both of them had enlisted in the navy two days after the Japanese attacked Pearl Harbor.

During sailors' boot camp, the Duffy brothers had befriended a man in their barracks who also came from an Irish background, and on their first leave they brought him home. He had no home of his own to go to, they explained, since both his parents had died in a fire when he was small, and he had been raised in a Catholic orphanage. His name was Sean MacMoran, and it was clear at once that the brothers Duffy had selected him as a good match for their sister.

"I was the oldest," Josie told Val, "twenty-four and still unmarried, so they were worried I'd be an old maid."

She had found nothing to object to in her brothers' choice. Sean MacMoran was trim and tall, with blue eyes and black hair and a sweet smile that dimpled his cheeks. Nor did Josie fail to live up to the advance praise her brothers had heaped upon her. She was a year older than Sean, but it didn't matter to either of them. Sean returned to duty thinking of Josie as "his girl."

He was ordered to serve on a troop ship traveling between England and the States, so for a while she saw him every two months. The Duffy brothers, having both distinguished themselves in gunnery courses, went to serve in the Pacific aboard the aircraft carrier *Yorktown.*

Eleven months later, the *Yorktown* was sunk at the Battle of Midway, and both Duffys had perished along with hundreds of others. Josie's father had taken their deaths so hard that ever since he had anesthetized his pain with heavy drinking. Josie believed, too, that inconsolable grief had been the seed of the heart condition that had killed her mother years after the war ended. For Josie herself, the loss confirmed that she ought to marry the man her brothers had chosen for her: It would be a kind of memorial.

"We got married two months after my brothers were killed," Josie related, "at the start of one of Sean's four-day leaves. Then we took a bus to a little place a couple of hours from the city, where a lot of sailors took their new wives for quick honeymoons. I'd never been with a man—I mean, *that* way; I'd been brought up thinking that joining the flesh out of wedlock was a guaranteed one-way ticket to hell. Now, there I was. For the next three days—right up to the time he had to leave and report back to his ship—Sean kept me in bed."

Some wives might have recalled a husband's boundless desire on their honeymoon with glowing nostalgia, but it was obvious to Val that for Josie it had been anything but that.

Tears sprang to her emerald-green eyes as she told how her new husband expected to be satisfied sexually by her any way he wanted, anytime. If she resisted, he grew so angry, it terrified her into compliance.

"By the third day of our honeymoon," Josie said, staring down into her cold coffee, "I was so tired and sore. Then he wanted something that . . . didn't even seem natural. I told him I wouldn't, no matter what. He got crazy mad then, and grabbed me and tried to turn me over and force me. I ran in the bathroom and locked it. But Sean broke the door in easy. . . ."

Right then was the first time he had hit her, Josie said, a closed fist driven into her stomach as she cowered by the bathtub. When she was doubled over in pain, he had turned her around and forced himself into her.

Listening, Val was aghast, not just that such brutality could be inflicted by a man upon a woman he had supposedly wed for love, but that Josie was still married to that man.

Yet Val knew well enough from the silence she'd kept after being raped that making such choices was a complex process. Whatever Josie chose to reveal had obviously been wrenched out of herself with as much pain as she could bear. Understanding would come, Val felt, as she got to know her better.

It was well past two o'clock, and they had sat in the diner for three hours when Josie realized the time and said she had to go. "Sean will be wondering what's happened to me. He gets so worried when I'm gone too long."

"Worried?" Val repeated the word with amazement. Not so worried that he had come with Josie to the hospital—not so concerned that he hadn't caused the injuries that sent her there.

Josie raised her eyes a moment, as if seeking wisdom from the heavens. "I know, it doesn't make a bit of sense." Her eyes met Val's again. "But you see, that's the hell of it, Val. He loves me. When he goes wild and does something like this, he cries for hours afterward, cries like a baby." She reached across the table and clutched Val's hand as if only the intensity of her grip could affirm her words. "He swears he'll kill himself if I ever leave him, and I don't think there's any doubt he means it."

"So that's why you stay?"

"Each time he hurts me, he's so sorry, I think it can't happen again. But then it does." Josie pulled some money from her purse for the lunch. "Oh, God, I don't know the reasons anymore," she added wearily. "Maybe, after all, I really like what he does to me." She stood up and headed out of the coffee shop.

Catching up to her, the only thing it occurred to Val to say was that Josie shouldn't tolerate her situation for another day. But that seemed such a foolish platitude. Josie had obviously told herself the same thing a thousand times already—and continued to ignore it.

Outside, it was snowing again, a biting wind swirling around. "It helped me a lot to talk to you," Val said, "and I hope it helped you to talk to me."

"Oh, Lord, so it did, Val," Josie said. "There's been no one I can tell this stuff. I want to see you again soon."

"Again and again," Val said. She dug in her purse and found a pencil and paper to write down the phone numbers at Durer's and her rooming house. She held the slip of paper out to Josie. "And how do I reach you?" she asked.

Josie took the paper. "I'll call you," she said. "Promise."

Val guessed that she might be afraid to have her husband know about her new friend. They hugged each other tightly and went in different directions to catch separate buses.

As an afterthought, Val turned to call: "Be careful, Jos."

But the wind was blowing hard, the veil of snow was thick, and the way Josie kept melting away into the whiteness, it seemed she hadn't heard.

It became a regular thing on Saturday mornings. Not at the hospital again—Josie had not returned—but on a bench in Prospect Park when it was sunny, or while they did their wash at the new coin-operated laundry near Josie's walk-up. A stolen hour or two when Josie could leave Sean at home with their daughter, telling him she had shopping to do, or was visiting her father—who would watch the little girl—for a longer time than she would actually spend with him.

As Josie revealed more of the history of her marriage, Val began to see how it had endured. Those first years, the war was on so she saw Sean only rarely; when she did she told herself that his rampant sexual needs resulted from long periods without gratification, heightened by battle stress.

After their honeymoon he'd taken up duty on a cruiser involved in the invasions of the Japanese-held islands. By the time he was rotated back to San Diego on leave, he had seen some of the worst fighting. Josie took a train to the West Coast to meet him. They had not seen each other for a year, and during that time his letters from the battlefront had been frequent and loving.

To make the most of their reunion, Sean suggested a trip down to Mexico. They passed first through the border town, Tijuana. Josie knew it was a wide-open town where sailors went to drink and whore, and when Sean suggested stopping over, she was afraid to protest. They checked into one of the nicer hotels, then left their room to get a meal. Sean had led the way into one of the dives lining the main street, and made Josie watch a show where pairs of naked men and women had sex in different combinations. Shocked and disgusted, she had run back to the hotel and crawled into bed while Sean stayed and drank tequila.

He returned to the room in the small hours, drunk and bringing along one of the female Mexican "performers" from the club. Waking Josie, he insisted she join in replaying some of the sexual acrobatics they had seen earlier. When she resisted, he had grabbed her and punched her until she submitted.

The mild day in mid-April when Josie told this story to Val, they were sitting on a bench in Prospect Park, and Val began to cry. She would have asked Josie to stop, except she knew her friend had waited all these years to tell anyone, and sharing it was like lancing an infection, maybe even a step toward changing her life for the better. So Val sat crying through the rest of it:

The morning after the threesome, while Sean slept, Josie had left the hotel and traveled alone back to New York. Her parents never questioned the story she told to explain her rapid return—the reunion had gone just fine, but Sean had received emergency orders to return to his ship—and they never heard otherwise from him; he did not call before sailing again.

Then his letters started to come, pleading for understanding that the war did strange things to a man, declaring that he knew he didn't deserve her, but he still adored her and if only she would give him one more chance. She had decided to grant that chance even before she realized she was pregnant.

Josie told of her husband's solemn oaths to love and respect her and never again harm her in any way, but Val could not forget that every oath had been broken, every hope violated.

Of course, once the child was born, Josie had been bound to the marriage even more firmly, for Sean adored his daughter, and the little girl loved him.

"He's so perfectly lovely with her," Josie said. "When I watch them together, I see such goodness in him, Val, that I have to believe what Father Kerrigan says must be true—that whatever battles with the devil Sean's fighting, he's bound to win if I keep praying for him. Then everything'll be the way I've hoped."

Val struggled to find the proper response. "While you're waiting for the prayers to work," she suggested, "there are some practical steps you could take. Sean's a veteran—the battle stress might still be affecting him. He should talk to the doctors at the Veterans' Hospital. . . ."

"I've asked him," Josie said. "But he doesn't think there's anything wrong with him. Just a bad temper, he says—runs in his family; he had to put up with it himself from his father."

Val could only add her own prayers that Josie's husband would undergo a miraculous transformation.

At work Val had continued to hide her condition. Through the winter it hadn't been too difficult; whatever bulge she showed as her second trimester progressed was easy to camouflage beneath the loose woolen skirts and bulky sweaters worn during the cold weather. She laughed off the occasional teasing remark by Ozzie or one of other printers that she might be having a few too many doughnuts at the coffee break. But now warmer weather had arrived, and people in the shop began to remark that she was overdressed.

It had become impossible, Val realized, to go on keeping the secret. Either she must tell Mr. Durer about the baby or leave his employ without giving any explanation. What made it all the harder was that he had been so understanding when he returned from Germany and learned what had happened with Bradley Smythe.

"If you fired me, Mr. Durer," she had said, "I wouldn't blame you."

"*Unsinn, susskind,*" he answered—he often called her "sweet child," as now, when he declared her thought of being fired was nonsense—"I've put far too much effort into training you to ever let you go now."

After a weekend of brooding about how to tell him, she arrived one Monday morning and took Durer aside at once to say she would like to talk to him privately, she had a serious confession to make.

"*Ein ernst Bekenntnis*, eh? Well, let us go to the confessional." He led her back to his office and told her to sit.

"So . . . what is it now? You've chased away more customers? Never mind, they must have deserved it."

There was a lightness to his tone, and a twinkle in his eye that disconcerted Val even more.

"No, this is nothing to do with business, Mr. Durer. This is . . . well, it's something I should have told you before you hired me. It was wrong of me not to, but . . . well, I . . . I . . ." She started to cry.

He came over and put a hand on her shoulder. "Never mind, *Liebchen*," he said gently, "if this is about your baby, I know."

She looked up. "You *know*?" She was astounded.

"The story you told when you first came here, combined with my powers of observation, gave me enough of an idea."

"And you don't mind?"

He waved a hand toward the area outside the office. "None of us do. We are all delighted."

"All?" Not a single person in the print shop had ever given the faintest indication they knew. "But you never said. Not Ozzie or anyone—"

"Sweet girl, it was plain you preferred not to speak about it, so they were under my strict orders never to say a thing unless you did first."

All this time she had thought she was being clever, she was the one who'd been fooled. A rush of embarrassment gave way quickly to appreciation for the protective affection surrounding her.

"If you want," Durer told her now, "this child of yours can have a dozen godfathers."

While relieved to know she had the affectionate acceptance of all her coworkers, Val knew it was something quite different to expect them to provide for her.

"You know," she said hesitantly. "I won't be able to continue working . . . at least for a while."

Durer said nothing for a moment. "Let's cross that bridge when the time comes" was all he said before sending her back to her desk.

On the first Saturday in May, Josie met Val outside her rooming house for a walk to the park. Josie was bursting with excitement, happier than Val had ever seen her. Some miracle must indeed have happened.

"Sean's bought a house! We're moving next week," Josie announced. It was in a place miles outside the city, she went on, with grass in front and a big yard in back where their daughter could play. "The house is on a street called Greenapple Lane—doesn't that sound peaceful? Sean says it's what we've needed all along, a place away from all the noise and dirt, the roughness of the docks. He swears it'll make the difference."

"But how . . . ?" Val asked. "I mean, isn't it expensive?" She knew Josie's husband had been trying to get dock work, but the union kept the jobs limited, and in the meantime he'd worked only part-time as an auto mechanic.

"That's the most amazing part," Josie said. "For any veteran these new houses are only a hundred dollars down—and just five thousand to pay off. Sean's got a friend from the navy with a house-painting business who lives out there on Long Island and he's going to take Sean in with him. Isn't it wonderful, Val? Our own backyard! Mandy can have a swing, and I'll grow things."

As sincerely happy as Val was for Josie, there was also a shadow of regret. "I'm going to miss seeing you so much, Jos." She stopped herself, not wanting to spoil Josie's excitement.

"Val, this won't stop us from being friends. It's only a short train ride to Long Island. You'll come to visit as soon as we're moved in."

Val wasn't sure how to respond. Visiting Josie's new home would mean meeting her husband, and by now he had become such a villain in Val's mind that she was afraid to face him, not out of concern for her own safety so much as because she feared she couldn't keep from denouncing him.

Josie understood Val's reservation. "Don't worry about Sean, Val. He'll like you. And I bet you'll like him."

"I couldn't, Jos. Not unless I know he'll never hurt you again."

"Oh, Val," Josie said dreamily, "it's the start of a new life in every way. I'm sure of it. So you will come, won't you?"

Val nodded and smiled. She wanted nothing more than for Josie's belief to be fulfilled—though she wondered how she could survive the challenges she was facing herself without even this one friend to lean upon.

A week later Josie called Val at work with an invitation to visit her new home the following Sunday. Val was eager to see her friend again, and a day out of the city would be welcome on these warm spring days.

Sunday morning she went to Pennsylvania Station and took a train on the Long Island Rail Road. She brought along an electric coffee percolator for a housewarming gift, and a stuffed animal for Josie's little girl. In less than an hour the conductor called out the stop at Hicksville, where Josie had told her to get off. From the train window Val could see trees, and neat white houses with yards, and an endless expanse of blue sky, but nothing like real rural countryside.

Josie was waiting on the platform of the small station with her young daughter at her side. The little girl had an angelic face accented by big round blue eyes, framed by hair like spun sunlight. Having already been to church with her mother, she was turned out in her Sunday best—a powder-blue topcoat with a collar trimmed in blue velvet, the trim of a frilly white dress peeking out from beneath, black patent leather Mary Janes over snow-white socks on her feet. Seeing the child gave a lift to Val's maternal feelings. Whatever hardships she would confront as an unwed mother, she wanted her baby.

Josie greeted Val with a hug. "Mandy," Josie said then, "this is Mommy's friend I've been telling you about."

Mandy nodded at Val but said nothing.

Val bent down to her. "I've brought you a new friend too," she said, removing the stuffed panda from a big paper bag.

"Black and white," Mandy said, seizing the furry toy. "Are there black and white bears?"

"It's a kind of bear that comes from jungles very far away from here," Val said. "It's called a panda."

"Panda," the little girl echoed. "Sounds like my name."

Val smiled. "Mandy," she said, "meet Pandy."

"Pandy." The child's face lit up, and she clutched the animal tighter.

"Say thank you, Mandy," Josie said.

"Thank you, Auntie Val." With the animal's leg still gripped in one hand, the child threw her arms around Val.

"Gently," Josie cautioned. With two months to go, and dressed today in a tan cotton shift with a short jacket over it, Val was showing a noticeable bulge. Val grinned and cast her eyes happily at Josie as she returned the little girl's hug.

Josie led the way to the parking lot and stopped at a dark blue prewar Hudson sedan.

"You have a car!" Val said, impressed.

"Sean bought it for almost nothing and fixed it up," Josie said with pride.

The mention of Sean sparked Val's curiosity to know if the

move was proving to be as good for the marriage as Josie had hoped, but she couldn't probe too deeply with Mandy listening. Josie did look better than in the past though, the dark circles around her eyes gone—and all her injuries healed.

"You look well, Jos," Val said. "Things working out okay?"

"Fine," Josie answered. "This was all we needed."

They had driven a few miles from the station, just coming over the crest of a hill, when Val noticed the most remarkable view: On a plain below were hundreds of houses, every one absolutely identical to every other. It was as if the houses had sprouted there like rows of corn. All the same size and design, all with the same length of concrete walkway running straight across the same size lawn to the same color door flanked by a window on each side. Seeing so many, made tiny by the perspective of distance, they looked unreal, like toys laid out by children at play.

Soon Josie turned off the main road into a side street lined with the cookie-cutter houses. To live where everyone's home was exactly the same little white box seemed strange, Val thought, even scary, as though it took away a piece of each person, took away what made them special and unique.

"Well, this is Levittown," Josie said brightly. As if she had read Val's thoughts, she went on. "I know, it looks sorta weird at first. But this is why the houses are affordable for people like us. Mr. Levitt, the man who built them, figured he could build cheaper by making only a couple of basic designs. They're what's called prefabricated—windows, doors, sides, everything made in a factory, then brought here on trucks and put together."

They were driving within a maze of streets now. As the houses passed at closer range, Val noted small efforts being made to personalize them, window boxes on some but not on others, various plantings of flowers or shrubs. Still, it made only a small dent in the overwhelming uniformity.

"If I lived here," Val said, "I'd probably walk into the wrong house half the time."

Josie laughed. "It happens now and then. Tired men come home at night and walk into the wrong one. I've heard one man kissed the wrong wife before he realized he wasn't home. But the houses are really well built and you can do whatever you want inside. Sean and I could never have afforded a place of our own if they weren't selling these so cheap."

Val was sorry if anything she'd said had made Josie feel defensive about her home. "You're lucky, Jos—and you, too, Mandy." She turned to the child, who was cuddling her new toy in the backseat. "There's nothing like having a home of your own, a place where you feel safe, and things are just the way you like them." She looked back to Josie. "I hope I can find a place like that for me and the baby."

Josie showed a smile combining forgiveness and reassurance. But she said nothing, as if she thought encouraging words might sound hollow.

They turned at last into one of the concrete parking pads separating one lot from the next. The front door of the house opened at once and Josie's husband stepped out. Mandy ran straight to him.

He swept her up in his arms. "Hi, poppet! Hey, what've you got there?"

"Pandy," she said. "Auntie Val gave him to me."

"Nice of her." His eyes shifted to Val as she walked across the band of grass leading to the door. "Hello, Val. I'm glad to meet you at last." He gave Mandy a quick nuzzle before setting her down to extend his hand in greeting.

From Josie's stories, Val had built up the image of a man she couldn't possibly like. What she had not anticipated was that Sean MacMoran would strike her as overwhelmingly friendly and attractive, his smile so broad and genuinely warm, his manner with his little girl so disarming. What she had not thought conceivable was that in an instant she would set aside all that she knew about him, willingly put her hand in his, and return his smile.

"Hello, Sean," she said. "It's very nice to be here."

Josie looked on, pleased that her best friend and her husband were ready to give each other the benefit of the doubt.

While Sean went with Mandy to the backyard to continue setting up for a barbecue, Josie proudly took Val on a tour of the house. Keeping expenses to a minimum, Josie had nevertheless turned every room into a sweet, comfortable haven. The walls of Mandy's room were decorated with balloons and little carousels and clown faces that Josie had painted herself. The other furnished bedroom upstairs had been painted a shade of rose, then stenciled by Josie with tiny flowers. Downstairs, the living room was filled with cast-off furniture received from her parents, but all had been brightened with fresh coats of varnish and home-sewn slipcovers. The kitchen had all brand-new appliances supplied by the builder.

"You have a lovely home," Val said sincerely when they ended the tour in the kitchen, where a screen door opened to the small, neat backyard. "You're very lucky."

Josie put her arm around Val. "That's how I feel, Val. Sean likes his job, and we all love the house. We have nice neighbors too. A lot of young newlyweds. Seems everyone's getting married now that the war's over, and there are these homes where they can afford to start out. One couple was given the house by their parents as a wedding present! Can you imagine?"

From the yard, Sean called that he was ready to put on the hamburgers. Josie and Val went out. The yard was mostly a level square of grass, but Josie had planted a few flowering shrubs along the rear fence that marked the boundary with an identical property to the rear. In a corner a slide and a swing had been erected for Mandy. Nearer the house was a pine picnic table, where they sat down to a lunch of hamburgers and corn and salad.

While Mandy was with them, Val included her in the small talk: how did she like her new home? had she started school? She welcomed the child's presence, for she felt uneasy about being alone with Josie and her husband. Finding Sean MacMoran actually likable made it somehow as difficult for her to be with him as if he had proven to be a monster.

Finally Mandy asked if she could play on her swing, and Josie let her leave the table. Silence descended, the heavy silence of people who know each other's secrets and pretend they don't.

Josie broke it. "You're really looking well, Val. Blooming. Isn't she, Sean?"

"Gorgeous. There's something about a woman when she's having a baby." Josie was on the bench beside him, and he put an arm around her. "You looked so grand when you were expecting. I can't wait for the next time."

A wistful expression came over Josie's face. Val guessed they might be trying to conceive again.

"How much longer?" Josie asked Val.

"Dr. Kendall says early next month."

Josie looked at Sean. She seemed to be asking permission to go on. He nodded, and she asked Val, "Have you thought about how you'll manage when the baby comes?"

Val had wanted to talk out her problems with her friend, but it seemed odd to discuss these things in front of Josie's husband. "I'll figure something out when the time comes. Now, can we talk about other things?"

"Not yet." It was Sean. "Josie's explained everything to me, Val—about why you can't go back to your home. We thought—knowing you had nowhere else—we'd ask you to come here, you and the baby. . . ."

Val turned to look at him, hardly able to absorb the meaning of the words, especially coming from him.

"You'll need some taking care of, at least for a while. Knowing your situation . . . well, it's no more than the right thing to do, the Christian thing."

That made her feel like she was a charity case. She frowned, opened her mouth to refuse, but Josie headed her off. "It's friendship, Val, that's all. You need help, we want to give it."

Val stared back. Knowing what she did about the marriage of these two people, it was hard to imagine sharing their house.

"Josie's told me that you know everything about our troubles," Sean said. "But you don't have to be afraid of me, Val. I've . . . well, I'm better. Everything's better."

Val's eyes went to Josie, needing confirmation from her.

"When I asked Sean about it," Josie said, "he agreed right away. Let us do this, Val. Please." She asked so fervently that it seemed there was something she needed from the arrangement too. Perhaps it would be the final proof for her that she could trust her husband, and he deserved her complete love.

"It's kind of you to ask," Val said finally. "Both of you. Let me think about it."

"Sure," Sean said. "Just so you know, we're here for you."

"Well . . . I've got strawberry ice cream," Josie said, determinedly lightening the mood. She started gathering the used plates. Val moved to help. "No, you take it easy," Josie insisted. "Sean will help."

He rose too. Val was relieved not to be left alone with him. Even if she had discovered he was not a monster, she wouldn't have known how to relate to him left on their own. So what would it be like, she wondered, if she were living in the same house with him?

It worried her. But though she'd asked for time to consider his and Josie's offer, Val realized already that she would accept it. There was simply no better choice.

Seven

Walter Kendall was not the scheduled resident on duty on the second Sunday in June, but the staff had been advised to call him if Val was admitted. He lived in a rented room close to the hospital, so he arrived in plenty of time to perform the delivery.

At the instant the baby girl was first placed into her arms, Val felt all the worries and regrets of her situation cleansed away by an overwhelming gratitude for the beauty and perfection of the child, for the miracle of creating life. She could feel no bitterness toward fate, no anger toward Willy. Her little girl, she told the nurse who asked how to fill out the birth certificate, would have only one given name: Theodora.

Late in the day, after Val had rested in a ward shared with other new mothers, Walter Kendall came to visit. He didn't examine her, but immediately pulled a chair up to the bed.

"I'm concerned, Val. Are you still determined to deal with this on your own?"

"I won't go home," she said. "But I'll be staying with a friend, Josie MacMoran—we met right here at this hospital's clinic, your clinic."

"So you'll be nearby. . . ."

"No. Josie lives on Long Island now."

The doctor's round, pleasant face took on a look of disappointment. Val had a momentary image of a teddy bear neglected in a corner. "And after that? Can you support yourself?"

"I'll be going back to work as soon as I'm able."

"Then who'll care for the child during the day?"

"Josie. She already has a daughter of her own."

Kendall nodded thoughtfully, then stood and reached down to take Val's hand in his. She had always found the way he touched her exceptionally comforting.

"You're a brave young woman, Val," he said. "Raising a child alone these days is very hard, practically and . . . socially. I admire you for it. If there's any way I can help, I'll always be happy to do whatever I can." He hesitated, as though there was something else he wanted to say, but then simply smiled and laid her hand down on the sheet.

Val detected an intensity in his words that went beyond his kindness as a professional caregiver. For a moment she was lost in a daydream of Kendall as a companion, guardian for her fatherless child—but she dismissed the notion. Why would he burden himself with the responsibility for another man's bastard?

"Thank you, Walter," she said. "I'll never forget your kindness."

He paused another second, gazing down at her. "Well, I have patients waiting. Congratulations, Val, you have a most beautiful daughter."

Several times after his visit she found her thoughts drifting back to her fantasy of the doctor as her savior. Yet even if he might accept caring for another man's baby, why choose for himself a woman who had been used as she had—raped, and accepting it without complaint. Damaged goods, as the people in business said. She had not ever told him that part of the story; but she would have to if they became more intimate, and she was sure it would keep him from holding her in the same high regard.

The third bedroom upstairs in the MacMoran house had been furnished with a bed and a crib, and Josie had done more of her fanciful paintings on the wall next to the crib so that at least part of the room looked like a nursery.

The first two weeks, while getting accustomed to the routine of caring for Teddie—as Theodora was immediately called—Val spent sitting in the backyard recovering her strength. During this time Josie was at Val's side, guiding her through the steps of motherhood.

"How does anybody do this when they're on their own?" Val often asked. She couldn't have possibly managed without Josie's help.

"If I weren't here, you'd figure it all out," Josie said. "Being a mother is pure instinct for a woman, Val. You'll realize it even more when your kid learns to *talk*. You'll need all your instincts then to come up with the right answers to all the crazy questions she asks."

Well, Val thought, in some women the instinct must be more highly developed than in others. Josie seemed to be an unusually good mother, a ready source of comfort whenever Mandy had some mishap, always generous with the nuzzling hugs and kisses that left no doubt in the little girl's mind that she was—as Josie had said from the first—the light of her life. Some children, feeling their position challenged by a new baby being welcomed into their home, reacted in ways that further upset the family balance. But Mandy showed nothing but pleasure and warmth toward Teddie.

One hot August day, while Val was letting Teddie lie in the yard on a blanket, Mandy came out and lay down next to the baby. "Can Teddie be my sister, Auntie Val?" she asked.

"You can certainly love her as much as if she were. But if you really want a sister, Mandy, I think you'll have a real one of your own one of these days."

"I don't know if another one would be as nice as Teddie."

Val laughed. "All babies are nice."

"Anyway, Mommy isn't sure she wants more children."

Val was in a folding lawn chair, doing a needle-and-thread repair on an old baby dress of Mandy's that Josie had passed along for Teddie. She glanced in surprise at the blanket where Mandy lay gazing at the baby. Val had frequently heard Sean express his eagerness to have more children; she recalled Josie echoing it—though only when Sean was present. Was Josie only parroting what she knew her husband wanted without truly feeling it? Then what did that say about the true state of her marriage? Mandy's remark had betrayed the sort of knowledge children came by accidentally, and without recognizing its importance.

In the days following, Val watched for clues to a concealed tension between Josie and Sean, but saw nothing. At night sometimes she could overhear sounds through the walls from their bedroom—the low hum of quick conversations, sometimes low moans or sharp cries from Josie that, as long as Val believed all was well with Sean, she assumed were the result of their lovemaking. But were they cries of pain? Close as she felt to Josie, Val couldn't bring herself to pry. Outwardly, Josie appeared content. If it was a lie, it was one maintained with determined effort. Would it be right to strip that away?

On the Tuesday of Val's fifth week as a guest, the two women sat down to breakfast together. Having poured coffee, Josie discovered there was no milk in the refrigerator.

"I should have asked Sean to drive me to the store over the weekend," she said, "but he had that extra job. . . ."

"Let me do the shopping. I can't stay any longer without paying my way."

"When you go back to work, Val, then you can pay."

"I'm going to call Mr. Durer and say I'll come back next week."

"Don't you want to spend at least a couple of months just being with the baby?"

"I'd like to spend a couple of *years*—there's nothing more wonderful than being with Teddie. But it's not the same for me as for you, Jos. You have someone to support you. I can't ask your husband to take over responsibility for me too. I have to get back on my own two feet—and make a home of our own for Teddie and me."

Josie gazed at her wide-eyed. In all the hundreds of identical houses that surrounded them, just as in the tens of thousands of houses in every little town across the country, only the tiniest percentage was occupied by unmarried women with children earning a good living for themselves. Divorced women or those widowed young by the war or other misfortune were on their own, but they had alimony, insurance, other benefits. Or they lived on charity. What Val was talking about, being as independent as if she were a man, seemed as thrilling as . . . discovering a new continent, as daring as setting out on that voyage.

"But how can you do it?" Josie asked. "To have a house—that costs money. And with a child there are clothes, toys, the extra food. Then, later—"

"I know," Val said, "there's a mountain to climb. But that's why I mustn't wait to get started."

"Val, lucky as you are to have a job waiting, you've told me it hardly pays enough for you to take care of yourself."

"It's just a stopgap while I set some other plans in motion."

"What sort of plans?"

Val hesitated. She had been considering the idea for weeks—a chance to provide a good life for her new daughter. But that was daydreaming. How would the idea sound if she spoke it aloud? She needed to know.

So she told Josie now about the incident with Bradley Smythe, and what she'd learned about the lucrative business of publishing a catalogue of wedding services and supplies. "I've been thinking about trying to publish a catalogue of my own," she concluded.

Josie gazed back blankly. The absence of encouragement for which Val hungered was no less chilling than a plunge into freezing water. "Well . . . say *something*," Val begged at last. "The idea can't be that bad, it's already working."

"That's why I don't understand. This man Smythe is already doing it. Why would anybody need the same thing from you?"

"Smythe is a snake," Val snapped.

"He sounds awful, Val," Josie agreed. "I understand why you got mad at him—but other *men* wouldn't. And men run all the businesses that pay to advertise in his catalogue."

"True. But what you just said, Jos, is the heart of why I feel I can compete. Smythe is a man . . . but his business, every business he advertises, is built around serving *women.* Brides! That's where I've got an advantage. I can put together something that appeals to more brides than Smythe can. That'll be my pitch to advertisers anyway. I've got to know better than a man what it means to dream about—" Val broke off, filled suddenly with the memory of having come so close to fulfilling that paramount dream of a woman's life . . . then having it shattered.

Suspecting what had come over Val, Josie spoke quickly to divert her. "Okay, I get it. Maybe you're right, being a woman gives you an advantage. But what do you know about how to publish something like that?"

"Not a damn thing. But I didn't know anything about being a mother either—until I was forced to start learning."

"That's different. You knew that by instinct."

Val smiled. "You know, Jos, I think I may have an instinct for this too."

It was only her second day back at work when Val told Reinhart Durer she needed his help and advice with a business matter. They went into his office, and while Val outlined her moneymaking idea, the printer sat at his desk doodling an elaborate calligraphic T on a sheet of scrap paper.

"Well, there it is," she said at last. "I was hoping you'd be my partner. I think I owe it to you—to make up for what I cost you when I lost my temper with Bradley Smythe."

Durer added a curlicue to the tail of the T and held up the paper to display the design. "What do you think? I'll engrave it on a little silver baby cup I've bought for your Theodora."

"Lovely," Val said, plainly deflated by Durer's eagerness to avoid discussing her proposal.

He put down the paper and leaned forward. "*Liebchen*, I respect the way you behaved with Herr Smythe. There's no need to go whistling up this notion of a rival catalogue for the sake of recovering what was lost."

"But that's *not* why I want to do it! I've just got to do something to earn more money."

"You know, if you stay with me, someday you'll—"

" 'Someday' won't take care of my baby now—or buy us a home."

"A home. I see. So you think you can earn the price of this home, and everything else you need, with your idea?"

"Smythe makes a good living."

"What makes you think even one of his advertisers will feel a need for a second wedding catalogue the same as the first?"

"It *won't* be the same. Mine will be much better."

Durer's thick white eyebrows rose like two tiny clouds. "Oh? How better?"

She was going to repeat what she'd told Josie: that she could improve the catalogue by applying her instinct about what would make it more appealing to a bride. But she realized a general answer wouldn't suffice. As Durer argued to protect his own interests—his desire to keep her working for him—his Germanic hardheadedness took over. He wanted details, wanted to hear some new element before he could believe Val's youth and inexperience wouldn't doom her to failure.

Under pressure, it popped out of her. "I won't just print up a list of things brides need, or a bunch of pictures of gowns. I'll supply . . . advice!"

"Ah," Durer said, "advice. Based on your experience . . ."

Val couldn't tell if he was intrigued by the notion or mocking it. "There's so much a bride needs to know, so many decisions to make . . . a wedding is a time when we're all so nervous about doing it right. We want it to be perfect. I'm sure brides would like a few pages on the rules of etiquette, ideas for gifts, how to put together a wedding bouquet. There are hundreds of things I could advise brides about."

Durer leaned forward, his expression of concern deepening. "Then what you're talking about, *Susskind*, is not publishing a catalogue . . . but a *magazine*."

"I guess so," Val said slowly.

Durer tossed up his hands. "*Ach!* Bad enough to start a business you know only a *little* about. Turns out you want to start up something even more complicated . . . that you know *nothing* about." He rose and came around the desk to Val. "Dear girl, I care for you too much to encourage this *wahnsinnige Torheit*."

Crazy foolishness. Val had heard the words when Ted's family gossiped about an aunt from Milwaukee who lived with twenty stray cats. Her confidence plunged.

Seeing the effect of his words, the printer's manner softened. "Sweet girl, I tell you for your own good. If you want to rise up in the world, it can't be done by exchanging a secure position for a pipe dream." He patted her shoulder consolingly. "But—so you have no doubt where your best interest lies—here and now I promote you to my executive assistant, and lift your *besoldung* to eighty dollars per week."

She looked at him, startled. The title he'd given her meant nothing . . . but in one leap he had nearly doubled her salary.

"*Jah.* Good," he said, seeing her stunned approval. "You see? I will take care of you, and your little Theodora. So back to your desk now, eh?"

She started from the office, so off balance that only at the last moment did she turn and say, "Thank you, Mr. Durer," at which he smiled paternally.

For the rest of the day, and as she lay in bed that night after supper with the MacMorans at which she had reported the raise and they had all celebrated, Val kept going over and over the arithmetic. Eighty dollars per week added up to more than four thousand per year. Josie had told her Sean was earning ninety-five a week, including veterans' benefits, and that had been enough for them to buy a home, a car, provide for Mandy.

Oddly, rather than feeling a gain at having security within reach, she was filled with a sense of loss. No matter how much she was paid, she couldn't get excited about going to work every day in the print shop. But she *was* excited by the prospect of helping brides plan their weddings. Her own had been stolen from her by fate, but the catalogue—no, a magazine, Durer had rightly called it—would give her a way of sharing the happiness of that special occasion. The time was surely right to launch such a venture. There were so many recently married couples in Levittown, hordes of others must be having weddings all across the country, part of the postwar boom of national optimism, belief in the future.

Dear God, how she yearned to be part of all those sweet moments of love's essential celebration . . . even in a vicarious way.

But the baby's needs were more important than her own. She didn't dare gamble away security, she realized, for the sake of fulfilling that hunger.

Eight

As soon as she'd gone back to work, Val had started contributing twelve dollars each week to the MacMorans' food budget, and insisted on paying Josie twenty dollars for the five days she looked after the baby. Even with these expenses, by the end of October she had $520 saved. Though she feared that landlords of any decent building might refuse to rent to an unwed mother, Val felt it was time to start looking for an apartment of her own.

Heading home on Friday evening of the last October weekend, she stopped at the newsstand in Pennsylvania Station and bought all of the city's four evening papers to study the classified ads on the ride to Levittown. From previous browsing of the ten dailies, she knew there were walk-ups available at rents she could afford. Tomorrow she planned to start trekking around Manhattan.

Settling into a window seat on the train, she had just begun scanning the small print of the ads, when a voice close to her ear said quietly, "Is that really you? I'd given up on ever finding you again. . . ."

Dumbfounded, Val looked over her shoulder. A young man in a dark business suit who'd stood up from a seat in the next row back across the aisle was leaning over her. He was quite attractive . . . but a total stranger.

"It *is* you," he said as she stared at him nonplussed. Realizing she didn't recognize him, he prompted, "Andrew Winston . . . the wedding invitations . . ."

Without the rough, baggy clothes, and with his light brown hair recently cut, he looked totally different from the way he had standing soggily in the pouring rain almost a year before. "Oh! Mr. Winston, yes. Sorry I'm in such a fog. . . ." Her head was full of rent figures and apartment details.

"I'm so glad to see you. I tried every which way to find you after we bumped into each other."

"I did all the bumping, as I recall."

He smiled. "You know what I mean. . . ."

Other commuters streamed along the aisle, having to push past him. He gestured to the vacant seat next to Val. "Mind . . . ?" She shook her head, and he sat down. "You have no idea how much I wanted to find you again." He looked suddenly embarrassed by his admission. "I mean, to thank you for being so decent about the invitations, paying to replace them."

He was more than just nice. For the first time since Ted's death, she'd met a man who attracted her. He was someone who she might even have—

But getting swept up in romantic dreams was a futile exercise. Val felt miserable as she thought of the possibilities that might have existed . . . if only there had been no Willy, no baby. As it was, there could be no serious future with Andrew Winston. In the end he would have to know she had a bastard child; even without a scandal in her past, the interest of a man from a family like his would never survive knowing her background.

Deflated, she had little appetite for conversation. She looked to the papers in her lap, hinting that she wanted to get back to them.

But as the train pulled out of the station, he took up the slack. "I feel so lucky to have run into you again. It's been a while since I took this train. I'm going out to Oyster Bay for the weekend—my uncle has a home out there. Where are you going?"

"To stay with friends," she said, "but not on the shore." That was putting a thick layer of gloss on the truth, but Val was helplessly intimidated by the awareness of his wealth and position. Oyster Bay, out at the end of the line, had long been a fashionable beach retreat for New York's most established society members. From high school American history, Val remembered that Teddy Roosevelt's family had a summer home in Oyster Bay.

"Where do you live?" he asked.

"Actually, I'm just about to change addresses. I'm looking for a new apartment in the city."

"I might be able to help. My older brother's got very good connections in real estate."

Top end of the market, no doubt. "Thank you," Val said. "But I've already got a few leads on the kind of apartments I like."

He leaned away slightly, studying her. "I wasn't expecting any favors in exchange, if that's what you're thinking. I'm just happy to help out if I can."

She realized now how coldly offputting she'd acted with him, and it filled her with regret. It wasn't his fault she'd gotten her life in a mess and couldn't be receptive to his offer. "Mr. Winston," she said contritely, "I'm sorry if I haven't been polite. It has nothing to do with you. You've never been anything but extremely nice."

"I did bark at you a little after you knocked me down."

She smiled. "I couldn't blame you for being upset after all those invitations got ruined."

"But the way you made good right away was very decent. A lot of people wouldn't have done that." He gazed appreciatively at her. Self-conscious, she averted her eyes. "So," he went on, "if you're turning a new leaf, is it too soon to tell me your name?"

"Oh—excuse me. Val Cummings." She put out her hand to make the introduction proper.

He shook it. "Val," he mused. "Is that for Valerie . . . or are you, like the girl Maurice Chevalier sings about, Valentina?"

"Valentina," she said, and smiled.

"I had a feeling it might be something close to a valentine." He still held her hand.

Now Val withdrew it, but he kept gazing at her. Embarrassed, she broke the silence. "By the way, how was your sister's wedding? Everything go all right?"

"Perfectly—if you like that kind of thing."

"Who wouldn't? There's nothing more wonderful than a wedding."

"Depends on the wedding, doesn't it?"

"What could be wrong with *any* wedding? It's a magic time when reality becomes most like a fairy tale. Every girl gets to believe she's a princess who's won her prince."

Winston shrugged. "I've been to quite a few, and usually it seems to me everyone is working too hard at pretending to be in the fairy tale. The only ingredient you really need is love, true love, but if it's there at all, it gets practically buried under the *show*. So many people, flowers, so much champagne, food, cake, so much . . . spectacle. At least that's what my sister's was like." He paused a moment, reflecting. "Well, it was what Justine wanted. But when I get married I won't want a crowd watching—all those fourth cousins you can't remember ever meeting before, celebrities to dress things up, politicians who did you favors . . ."

Val remembered the order was for eight hundred wedding invitations. Andrew Winston's list of the sort of people in that crowd underlined how different the wedding for a daughter of the Winston family would have been from her own. It wasn't unreasonable to feel it became a kind of performance that lost a measure of its true meaning for the sake of solidifying social position. She examined Andrew Winston with fresh interest. Apparently he had a romantic spirit.

"What kind of wedding would you like for yourself?" she asked.

"The most important thing, I guess, is what my bride wants. Naturally I hope she'll feel as I do—that all the fancy trappings aren't the things that are really meaningful."

"What things are?"

He thought. "A ceremony—in surroundings of beauty . . . and being with the people you truly care about. That's all that matters."

"Suppose your bride wants all those things you think are unnecessary?"

"Everybody and his uncle . . . and feeding the whole lot

bushels of caviar," he said, summing it up. "I doubt that's the kind of girl I'll choose to marry."

"But most girls love a big, traditional wedding. Don't you think a man sometimes has to go along with a wedding that doesn't exactly suit him to make his bride happy?"

He sat back, eyeing her. "How did we get into all this talk about weddings? It's too soon for *us* to be making plans."

Val flushed. Eager to let him know she hadn't meant to be provocative, she said, "I'm interested in the subject for a project I have in mind."

"What sort of project?"

"A magazine. All about brides and weddings—for women planning to be married."

"So you're in the publishing business?"

Publishing . . . printing. Close enough, Val persuaded herself. "I have connections to it."

"A magazine for brides," he said, weighing the notion. "Not a bad idea. Tell me more."

Should she confess it had been empty boasting? Well, it was *true* she'd had the idea. "It's just in the earliest stages."

"You have a publisher lined up? Or are you going to publish it yourself?"

"I, uh, haven't made those decisions yet."

"Got a name for the magazine?"

In fact, she had been playing with names, though only as part of the idle imagining she indulged in when she got bored at work, fancying herself overseeing a wildly successful venture, running meetings with writers, editors, advertisers. But freeing the daydreams from her mind would make them a little more real. "I've narrowed it down to two," she said. "Since it's a growing trend for more young women, not just society girls, to want bigger weddings, and since I want them to know the advice they'll get is up-to-date, I thought *Today's Bride* might be good."

"Today's Bride." He waggled his head in a mime of deliberation. "Not bad. And the other?"

"Well, I want every girl getting married to read it—and to

think it's about every girl who gets married . . . so I thought *Every Bride's* might be good—*Every Bride's* magazine."

"That's it!" he said emphatically. "You've even put the possessive in a much better place—not on *Today's* but *Bride's*, so it's like the magazine belongs to her, was made for her, as much as a gown. *Every Bride's* magazine. Perfect!"

His approval was gratifying—though it struck Val he might be playing a game as much as she was. "The way you gave your opinion," she remarked, "it sounds as if you're familiar with the magazine business."

"Not very. But my family has friends in publishing."

"What business are you in?"

"Nothing so interesting—though you and I do have one thing in common: I'm also just trying to get started."

"In what?"

"Delivering freight."

It did sound dull. But as she realized that right at the start she had mistaken him for being a delivery man—and, after all, he was—she had to laugh.

He asked why she was laughing, and she told him.

With the soothing rhythmic click of the wheels as background music, their talk flowed on easily. She asked what sort of amusements he would pursue over the weekend, and he answered that the main reason he was going to Oyster Bay was to participate in a polo match.

His involvement in a game reserved for the rich was one more reminder to Val that her world and his were too far apart, but while on the train she let herself pretend there were no barriers. She told him nothing to compromise any of her previous fibs, but obliged his curiosity by filling in personal history—coming from Montenegro to live with relatives in Buffalo because of the war, the loss of her parents. In sympathy, he mentioned that one of his older brothers had been killed in the D-day landings, which led to talk about his other siblings, a second older brother, two older sisters, a younger brother.

Before she knew it, the conductor was calling out the stop for Levittown. As the train slowed, Val felt a tremendous letdown. She'd enjoyed being with Andrew Winston—liked pretending that all the possibilities still existed for her.

"When can I see you again?" he asked eagerly as soon as she said they had reached her destination.

The more appealing she found him, the more she feared the eventual mortification of being unmasked as an impostor with a buried scandal. "I'm sorry, Andrew—"

"No, Valentina! You're not going to tell me we can't meet, you just can't do that. I don't want to lose you again."

The train was slowing. She rose, and he stood to let her pass into the aisle. "I wish things were different," she said. "But—"

He snatched up her left hand and glanced at it, obviously looking at the bare ring finger. "You're not married. Are you engaged?"

"No."

"Then please—meet me next week. I'll be anywhere you say. . . ."

The train was in the station. She edged away. "It's too hard to explain, but I'm sure it would be a mistake."

He moved along the aisle with her. "That magazine of yours—I can help, introduce you to people who could get behind it. Would that be a mistake?"

They reached the vestibule by the exit door. She turned to say the magazine was no more than a dream, but when she looked into his handsome face, her tongue froze.

"Next weekend," he urged. "We can meet at Penn Station . . . then have supper, go dancing. . . ."

Supper? Dancing? To keep any relationship from ending in disaster she would have to go on concealing too much. "I don't think so. . . ."

He heard her uncertainty and took it for progress. "Where we met tonight," he repeated. "I'll be waiting at the information booth at the station next Friday."

Val hadn't the will to refuse again, nor was there a need. She went down the steps, and the conductor closed the door.

As she went along the platform, she could see him moving back through the car, tapping at windows of vacated seats to attract her attention, and mouthing his pledge again: Six. *Friday . . .*

When Val rose the next morning, the baby was still asleep. She went down alone to have breakfast and found Josie already at the kitchen table, in her bathrobe, sobbing quietly. One side of her face bore a large red welt.

"Oh, no," Val moaned. Pulling a chair close, she asked in a whisper what had happened.

"You don't have to whisper," Josie said. "There's no one else here. Sean's taken Mandy shopping for winter clothes. . . ."

In fact, as Val drew out the story she learned the new clothes had caused the fight. Josie had been putting aside all the money Val gave her for tending Teddie to use for Christmas gifts, but that morning Sean had demanded it for Mandy's clothes. Josie resisted giving up her small nest egg. Sean earned more, he should pay for their child's clothes. Her answer enraged him, and he had hit her, promising worse if she didn't hand over her savings. Only then, remorseful as always after hitting her, he admitted he'd been fired from his job two weeks earlier, after losing his temper with his boss. All these recent days when he left the house, it was to hunt for new work.

Val sat comforting Josie, but she held back from discussing the heart of the problem. She guessed now that Josie had hidden other episodes of Sean's mistreatment. If Josie was going to be helped, Val thought, she needed to get her away from the house—if only for a day; it might give her some perspective.

"I was going to take Teddie into the city today," Val said. "Come along, Jos. We'll go to the park . . . maybe the zoo, have some fun."

Josie's eyes lit up. "Gosh, I haven't been there in years." The spark died. "But I should be here when Sean gets home."

"Leave a note, say we'll be back for supper. C'mon, Jos, it'll do you good."

"He could be out all day with Mandy, I suppose." Josie jumped up. "I will! I'll go with you, Val. Why shouldn't I?"

Just for Josie to ask that question, Val thought, was the first step in making a change for the better.

It was a glorious Indian summer Saturday, the fields and paths crowded with families and couples appreciating an island of nature in the midst of the towers of concrete. At the zoo, Josie took as much delight as Teddie in watching the antics of the monkeys in their indoor cages, the seals swooping through the water of the large outdoor pool. Teddie couldn't talk yet, but her laughs and squeals as she saw the animals perform conveyed her delight.

After visiting the animal houses, they went to the cafeteria and sat at a table on the outdoor terrace to eat hot dogs and ice cream. Val had brought along baby food in jars for Teddie.

"I'm so glad I came," Josie said, spooning down chocolate ice cream. She glanced around at the children, their helium-filled balloons floating above strings tied to their wrists. "I wish Mandy could be here too."

"Next time." Val tucked a baby blanket around Teddie, who had fallen asleep in her stroller.

Josie looked down pensively. "It should be so easy to have a day like this. But sometimes, Val, I don't feel so different from those monkeys we saw, locked in a cage."

Val had been waiting, hoping Josie would bring up Sean's mistreatment. "You have to change that, Jos," she said. "You shouldn't be living in fear."

Raising her eyes to meet Val's, Josie said weakly, "He doesn't mean to hurt me. He's always so sorry."

Val had some insight now into how difficult it was for Josie to condemn her husband no matter how much he hurt her. She had seen for herself a side of Sean MacMoran that was basically decent. There had been times she was busy with some task and Teddie would start to cry, and Sean would scoop her up before Val could get there and have the baby gently pacified in no time.

Yet hearing Josie defend him, Val couldn't keep her anger from flaring. "For God's sake, you've got to stop *apologizing* for him! You talk as if you're to blame for making him mad.

But you're the victim. It's wrong to hit you. And if you can't speak to Sean about it, then I will."

"No," Josie cried in alarm. "You can't do that!"

"Can't? Jos, what I can't do is say nothing—watch you get hurt and pretend it isn't happening." Val leaned across the table. "Please . . . let me help."

"You are helping! Just having someone else in the house reminds him he has to control himself."

Val grabbed her friend's hand. "You can't go on living this way. It's no solution to keep me around as a witness. We've got to get this situation fixed—for Mandy's sake too. I'm getting my own place soon. Maybe you should tell Sean that you and Mandy will be staying with me until he—"

"No!" Josie erupted, so loud that people at neighboring tables on the terrace looked over sharply. "It will make him so angry, Val. He'd hurt you too!"

"I'll take that chance."

"It's *my* life, Val. I don't want to leave him. So promise me, please. Promise me you won't stir things up, won't say a word to Sean about this."

Val's heart ached as she looked at her friend, her frail body trembling. She reached out again to touch Josie, not knowing what to say, wanting only to comfort her.

But Josie shied away, as if being threatened. "You've got to promise . . ." she begged.

Val could do nothing but enter the conspiracy of silence. "All right. I promise," she said.

Reassured, Josie finally picked up her spoon and finished her ice cream.

As soon as they entered the house, Sean stormed to the door to meet them. "Where the hell have you been?" he screamed at Josie.

She could scarcely find words to counter his rage. "I . . . I went with Val. . . ."

Sean turned on Val. "Where?"

"To the city," Val said. "The park, the zoo—Josie needed to have a day out."

"You're going to tell me what she needs?" he demanded fiercely. "She's *my* wife."

From the stroller beside Val, Teddie whined a complaint, upset by the angry shouting. "Sean, let's talk about this later," Val urged. "Where's Mandy?"

Sean ignored the question. "I want to know *now*: What else do you think my wife needs?"

Josie tried to intervene. "Sean, where's Mandy? Let Val put Teddie—"

"Shut up! Mandy's playing across the street." He glared at Val. "Tell me. What other good advice did you give my wife all day?"

More concerned with saving Josie than with violating any pledge, Val replied, "I told her she has a right to feel safe in her own home."

He spun to Josie. "You don't feel safe with me? You don't know I'd do anything to protect you?"

It would have been laughable if the sad lack of logic didn't have such a destructive core. "It's *you* she's afraid of!" Val erupted. "She doesn't want the pain anymore, doesn't want to be knocked around, and . . . practically raped!"

"What the hell right have you got to talk for her?" he roared, his face turning red. "What goes on between us is our business and nobody else's."

Teddie began to bawl. The baby's upset only heightened Val's anger. "No, it's not. I can see what goes on, I know it's not right, and something has to be done about it."

His eyes blazed hotter. "Right! You don't like what you see so something has to be done!" Abruptly he snatched her arm into such a strong, tight grip that her fingers started to go numb. He yanked her roughly over to the stairs and started pulling her upward, half dragging her as she struggled to keep her footing. "We'll do something right now so you'll never again have to see what goes on around here."

"Let her go!" Josie screamed, climbing the stairs after them.

"She says something has to be done!" he seethed. The menace in his tone and his loss of control terrified Val.

Below, the baby had begun to shriek, reacting to the sounds

of fear and fury. Val tried to free herself, but Sean's grip was an iron shackle. With Josie pleading at their heels, he dragged Val up and into her bedroom. With his free hand he opened the closet and started pulling clothes off the hangers, flinging them to the floor. "All right, something's being done. You won't see what goes on here anymore because you're going to get the hell out. Now!" He threw her down roughly on the pile of clothes.

Stunned, Val sat in a daze as he moved to the dresser and turned all the drawers over into another heap. The baby's shrieking seemed to come to her from a great distance.

Josie protested. "Sean, you can't just throw them out. Think of the baby. . . ."

He turned very slowly to her and lifted a fist. "Go to our room before you get hurt."

The gesture alone terrified Val. "Go, Josie," she said very quietly. "I'll be all right."

With a last apologetic glance at Val, Josie retreated.

"You just should've kept your fucking mouth shut," Sean shouted at Val as he finished emptying the drawers.

She pulled herself to her feet. "Like Josie? Not all women are like that, Sean."

"Too damn bad," he said. "I'm phoning for a taxi now. I want you and your bastard out of here in ten minutes. We'll send the rest of your stuff later."

When she was packed, going down the stairs, Sean came out of his bedroom and stood like a sentry barring the entrance. Val could only call good-bye to Josie.

"Good-bye, Val." The answer came back in a weak, shaky voice.

Now wasn't the time, but Val knew she had to do something to rescue her friend.

Clutching Teddie, she caught the last train into the city and checked into a cheap hotel downtown. Teddie slept at last while Val paced the floor, plotting out the future. Except that it had happened so brutally, Val wasn't sorry to be on her own; she'd planned to leave anyway. She had money saved for an apartment, and taking the baby to work with her might be manageable—for a while anyway. But now, on her own, she realized the enormity of the task facing her.

Tomorrow was Sunday. As she lay down at last, Val resolved to find a decent place to live for herself and Teddie. But after that . . . ? To fulfill the dream of giving her child a real home, perhaps the only chance she had was to keep that date next Friday.

Nine

Approaching the information booth at Penn Station on Friday evening, she saw him waiting as promised, scanning the crowds criss-crossing the vast terminal floor. In a sleek black overcoat, his hair neatly combed, he looked even more handsome than the last time. A fresh flutter of nerves swept through Val, a reprise of the dire certainty that any involvement with this man was doomed. She had an impulse to turn and run before he noticed her. Adding to her other reservations was a mother's guilt—this was the first night she hadn't been with Teddie since the baby's birth. Not that she doubted Mrs. Falconi's ability to look after a child; the Italian widow had raised seven of her own. In fact, the large supply of neighbors who loved children was a wonderful fringe benefit of the four-room railroad flat Val had found in the downtown section of Manhattan called Little Italy. The apartment was on the top floor of a run-down walk-up tenement. It had floors covered in ancient cracked linoleum, poor light, a bathtub in the kitchen, and leaky plumbing. Yet when Val had moved in with Teddie the previous Sunday, there had been children playing around the stoops on the block, and babies being rocked in carriages by their grandmothers. Even before entering the tenement for the first time, Val was stopped by women with compliments about Teddie and friendly questions about the baby's age. Val realized that this neighborhood was a kind of gigantic family where it would be easy to find someone to look after Teddie when needed.

Now, on the brink of leaving, Andrew spotted her and rushed over, beaming. "Bless my stars, you came!" Then his face darkened with disappointment. "You didn't dress up though. Don't you want to go dancing?"

"Frankly, Mr. Winston, I thought it would be less confusing if we didn't mix business with pleasure." Not to mention that she had no money to spend on a dress for a date she hadn't even been sure she'd keep until the last moment. She'd worn the best thing she owned, though she knew it was rather severe—a dark blue wool suit with white piping, purchased at the time she was job hunting.

"So . . . this is only business?" He didn't hide his disappointment.

"You offered to help with my project."

"Your—? Ah, yes, the magazine . . ." He gave a resigned shrug. "All right, business it is. But would it be out of the question to discuss it in nicer surroundings? Or do you want to just take a bench over there in the waiting room?"

She reminded herself again not to be so deliberately off-putting. "I'd be glad to go somewhere more pleasant."

He took her straight across the avenue from the terminal to the Pennsylvania Hotel. Val thought of it as a glamorous place, since the song "Pennsylvania 6-5000" derived its title from the phone number of the hotel where Glenn Miller's band had appeared regularly before the war. Winston continued through the lobby to the nightclub where Tommy Dorsey's orchestra now played. The headwaiter at the door greeted him by name and seated them at a table beside the dance floor. A small lamp glowed on the table, as on scores of other tables around the room, and colored lights shone down on the floor. Beyond shadows of dancing couples, Dorsey stood onstage performing a trombone solo as his band played "I'll Be Seeing You." The song, popular during the war, had been a favorite of Val's and Ted's.

A waiter came to ask if they wanted drinks, and Val asked for an old-fashioned. She'd never had anything alcoholic but wine, and chose the cocktail only because she'd heard it ordered by sophisticated women in movies. Winston asked for a whiskey.

"You look sad," Winston said when the waiter had gone.

"This song brings back memories."

"You told me about your parents dying in the war. Was there someone else?"

"No," she said cryptically, "not in the war."

He regarded her pensively another moment. "I've got a terrible nerve to pry, I suppose, but I haven't hidden that I'm very attracted to you, Valentina, and it might clear the air if you'd explain why I shouldn't think of tonight as anything but business. Is that fair?"

"All right. Explaining some things might also help you understand why I've thought so much about this idea of mine, even though"—she took a breath—"well, to be perfectly honest, I don't know the first thing about publishing a magazine." He didn't look surprised, but just sat waiting for her to continue. "You see, I was almost a bride myself once. . . ."

Now she told him about Ted, their plans to marry, the way it had ended. During her account the cocktails came, and the alcohol relaxed her, made it easier to speak about her loss. She was careful, though, not to hint at what had happened with Willy, saying only that she had come to New York to escape unhappy memories and make a new beginning.

"Maybe it's because I got so close to actually taking the vows that I've felt haunted by a longing to . . . finish the ceremony." She gave him a melancholy smile. "I suppose that's why I've kept such an interest in weddings, spent time in libraries reading about them, thought so much about what it's like to be a bride."

He nodded. "I can understand your sympathy for my sister when the invitations were ruined. Though I've always regretted letting you pick up the bill to replace them."

"Never mind, it all worked out." Because there were other secrets she had to keep, she decided to balance them with honesty wherever possible. "To tell the truth, I didn't have the money to pay for those invitations when I said I would. So I went back to Mr. Durer and offered to work off my debt. He gave me the job I still have. In his print shop . . ."

"Your 'connection to publishing,' " he said, laughing. He paused to gaze at her with fresh admiration. "You're quite a girl, Valentina. I think the least I can do to make up for taking your hard-earned money is to help with your plans."

"You don't owe me anything. I'll accept help, Andrew, only if it's given because you truly believe my idea can succeed."

"I think you've got more than a chance. You'll make this work because . . . it's your way of finishing the ceremony." He smiled. "Though maybe someday you'll find out there are other ways. Now, let's order dinner. Then you'll tell me more about what'll be in this magazine, and I'll tell you what I can do for you."

Over a delicious steak—meat still seemed a luxury after the years of rationing—Val kept up a steady, informative patter about the things she was sure prospective brides wanted to know. A monthly column on etiquette would be a must; there were always questions about what was proper in different situations, and while books on the subject existed, they were expensive. There could be suggestions for different kinds of honeymoons, with photographs of beautiful places for them. Articles might be included about the history of wedding customs: where did the tradition and symbolism of the ring originate, for example? There could be a fashion element, as well, detailing the latest designs in gowns for brides and their bridesmaids. Advice, too, to help women meet the demands that came with being a newlywed, tasks they'd never faced before—furnishing a first home, cooking for a husband.

Andrew listened intently, interjecting an occasional question to satisfy his curiosity about details Val touched on and test the depth of her knowledge. For instance, what exactly was the origin of the wedding ring?

"It goes back as far as the wedding ceremony itself," she told him, "which was being performed in the most ancient civilizations. There was a belief that a vein ran from the fourth finger of the left hand directly to the heart, so by placing the ring around this finger, the source of a woman's love was captured by the man, made his property as much as if he'd put a round metal fence around a piece of land. Gold was always used because it was the purest, most valuable metal. In ancient times the ring might bear a symbol—a common Persian one was clasped hands, and the Elizabethans inscribed very short love poems inside that they called posies—but now the plain band is preferred."

"I can tell you've done your research," he said.

"As much as I've had time for. But there's a lot more to know that I'm sure would interest readers." Val paused. There was one more element she believed essential for young women approaching marriage. "It's occurred to me, too, that most women getting married might also need advice about . . . the wedding night."

"You mean sex," he said offhandedly. "That's pretty daring. Advice to the lovelorn is common, but anything too explicit would be attacked, perhaps even enough to kill the magazine."

"There's a limit to what we can write," she said. "But I'd like to find a way to make it easier for women who haven't had much experience, and feel . . . a kind of terror about a time that ought to be part of the magic."

"Home furnishing, cooking, travel, I see where all that makes a nice complement to the basic wedding stuff. But sex? Are you thinking of trying to put too much in the magazine?"

"They're just ideas," she said, reluctant to make an issue of anything that might chase away Andrew Winston's support.

He deliberated for a few moments. "Val, I'm going to introduce you to some friends who can help get you started."

"You don't want to be involved yourself?" Was he passing her along because he didn't really believe in her ideas?

"I will be. But you also need the help of people who know a lot more about publishing than I do. I couldn't give your business much time either. As I mentioned, I'm trying to start a company of my own."

"Some sort of delivery service."

He smiled. "More or less."

She wondered how that could be more interesting to him than what she'd proposed, but she said nothing.

"It would be a good idea," he continued, "if you put your ideas in writing. I'll call you during the week after I've set up the weekend with my friends."

"Weekend? What do you mean?"

"I thought you'd come out to Oyster Bay. It's an ideal setting to present your project."

"Andrew, I can't! It isn't possible for me to—" She stopped. She'd almost blurted out that she couldn't travel away from her baby. How would his rich friends like investing in a bridal magazine run by a woman with an illegitimate child? Good for laughs, maybe, not for business. She finished lamely, "I just don't think I'm ready to talk about it."

"Look, Val," he persisted, "hiding your lack of experience in publishing would be hard. But people who spend time with you are bound to see you're a smart, determined young woman . . . and a relaxed weekend is an ideal opportunity for them to get to know you. If you want this to go through, you'll be there."

Even if the problem of Teddie's care were solved, could she fit into such a rarified social atmosphere? She owned none of the right clothes. She went on hesitating, wondering if she could possibly sell total strangers on her idea.

He noted how grimly anxious she looked. "C'mon, it'll be fine," he said encouragingly. "Now, how about we take a spin around the dance floor? Even if I won't be full partner in your magazine, I'll make a swell partner for a fox trot."

She thought of being in his arms, moving slowly to the music—and suddenly she could only look ahead to the point where he would expect more of her. She wasn't sure if it was the way Willy had betrayed her trust, or loyalty to Ted's ghost, or the fear that intimacy would lead to having her shameful secrets exposed, but she was afraid of getting too close to him.

"Hey, it's only a dance," he coaxed.

Only a dance. But already she was much too attracted to him—and, she knew, too much in need of love. It would surely lead to disappointment . . . or worse.

"Remember," she said, forcing a smile, "this was going to be just business. And I think our business is done for tonight."

He looked at her for a second with longing and regret, but then he called for the check.

When they were outside, he offered to escort her home. But

he didn't protest when she said she preferred going alone in a taxi. Learning about the death of her fiancé had evidently convinced Andrew Winston that Val knew her mind and heart, and that her desire to be left on her own was unchangeable.

Ten

The Tuesday following their "business" dinner, Andrew called Val at work. "The weekend is all arranged," he told her. "Meet me at the same train Friday evening."

"I'd prefer to come Saturday—around noon," she replied firmly.

"All right. But you'll stay over, won't you? I've got a polo match in the afternoon, and then there'll be a chance for everyone to talk in the evening. Once you've charmed them all, we can get down to brass tacks on Sunday."

"I'll stay," she said. She was prepared to be away from Teddie for one night, not two.

"Good. I know this is going to pay off for you, Val. You won't be sorry."

Won't I? Part of her was sorry as soon as she hung up. Once she was scrutinized in Andrew's sophisticated milieu, she was sure to be exposed as a fraud. A one-time factory girl who didn't own a single fine dress sitting down to dine formally with people who had closets full of them—and asking them for money to run a business she knew nothing about.

But even if she failed, she told herself, it would be in a good cause. A chance to be something more than a secretary in a print shop. A chance to do more for her daughter.

That evening when she stopped at Mrs. Falconi's door to pick up Teddie, Val asked her to take care of the baby overnight on the weekend. Mrs. Falconi agreed—conditionally: "I don't help-a you," she announced, "if it's-a cause you gonna be in a love nest with-a some no good *mascalzone*."

"I'm not going to be in a love nest," she said, laughing. "I'm going away to meet a few people and try to interest them in a business I'd like to start."

"If it's-a not monkey business," said the Italian woman, "then you can count on me." But, with a conspiratorial nudge, she added, "And maybe I don't even mind if it's-a really to be with a man, as long as you let me first-a make sure he's not a bum. I gotta keep-a your sweet little *bambina* away from bad men."

"Mrs. Falconi, I am going to be with some men . . . but they'll be gentlemen, the kind who play polo and get dressed in tuxedoes to eat dinner. If anything, they may be *too* good for me."

"Valentina, what-a you mean? You're the most-a beautiful woman on the street. No man's too good for you."

"Thanks. Maybe I'll feel that way too . . . if I can figure out a way to look the part. I can't afford to buy any new clothes, and nothing I have is right for being in this kind of company."

The old woman gave a smile that looked all the more crafty because of her crooked teeth. "It's important you look-a good for business, eh? I fix."

Val asked how, but the widow would say no more on the subject for tonight. Val would find out tomorrow night, Mrs. Falconi said, when she came to collect the baby.

When Val arrived the following evening, Lelia Falconi was waiting with a friend of hers, another elderly Italian woman named Giuletta Randazzo. "Gigi," never married, had worked until her recent retirement sewing costumes at the Metropolitan Opera House and had a collection of old costumes in her apartment down the block.

Val had visions of being fitted into something that made her look like Carmen, or Madame Butterfly. But Gigi Randazzo turned out to have a well-developed sense of style. After taking Val's measurements, she appeared the following night with a stunning midnight-blue velvet gown recut from an old costume from *La Bohème*. To complete her outfit for her high-society weekend, Val felt the only purchases she had to make were a blouse and a pair of white flannel slacks to wear with the navy jacket from her suit—to pass as a blazer—the right sort of clothes, she imagined, for watching a polo match.

Saturday morning Andrew met her at the Oyster Bay station and they drove to the Winston estate in his two-seat vintage Jaguar convertible. Val was awed by the property, an immense redbrick mansion that sat on the shore of Long Island Sound. A butler met her at the door to take her one small valise, and she was ushered inside. The entrance hall of the house was as big as the lobby of a hotel, and there was as much art all around as in a museum.

She was put at ease, however, when Andrew led her to a solarium at the back of the house to meet his aunt and uncle, Charles and Beatrice Winston. They rose from the wicker love seat where they were sitting as soon as Andrew entered with Val. Both were trim and gray-haired, dressed casually, and had smiling, friendly faces.

"Aunt Bunny . . . Uncle Charlie, this is the girl I told you about," Andrew said, introducing Val.

She put out her hand, and Bunny Winston pressed it warmly between both of hers. "Welcome, Valentina. I can see now why you made such an impression on our Andy."

Eyeing Val, Charlie Winston said gruffly, "If you ask me, from the description I heard . . . I think it's time the young buck started wearing glasses." Val shied, and the others looked at him in shock. Then his face split in a wide grin. "The way you described this young woman, Andy, doesn't half do her justice."

"You'll get used to Uncle Charlie," Andrew said to Val, seeing that his humor had given her a bad moment.

"I'll look forward to it," Charlie said.

With the charm and skill of practiced hosts, the Winstons launched a conversation designed to learn more about Val, but in such a way that it made her feel it was because she was an interesting person, not because her social credentials were being investigated. As they chatted, Val discovered that the couple looked upon Andrew as a son. They had two grown daughters, but their own son had died young in a summer polio epidemic.

For all their obvious wealth, the Winstons struck Val as very down-to-earth. Both in their early seventies, they had been married for more than fifty years, and still seemed to be in love—fond of teasing each other, and touching, in a way that seemed unusual in elderly people.

Finally, Bunny suggested that Val might like to change clothes before they left for the polo match. Lunch would be a picnic, Andrew explained, served while they watched him compete. The other people he wanted Val to meet were joining them for lunch.

The match was played on a private polo pitch at an estate adjoining the Winstons'. The spectators sat in lawn chairs along the side of the field, and were served picnic food. Before the match began, Andrew came to the sidelines and introduced Val to three men, contemporaries of his—Philip Longworth, who had been his roommate at Yale and now worked in his family's investment firm on Wall Street; Franklin Storrow, who also worked in the family business, a chain of newspapers; and Nathan Palmer, who was Andrew's partner in the business he had started himself. Val understood now how a couple of these men, with their experience in publishing and finance, could be especially helpful.

Never having seen polo before, Val was both thrilled and alarmed by the spectacle of horses galloping headlong from one end of the pitch to the other while men in the saddles tried to hit a ball through a goal with long-handled mallets. Nate Palmer came to take a seat beside Val and explained to her what a chukka was and other details of the game. Talking with him, Val learned that his friendship with Andrew Winston dated from the army air force, when both had piloted paratroop planes. It was Nate, too, who revealed that the new venture in which he and Andrew were partners was actually an airline called Atlas Air, which hinged on the idea of flying nothing but cargo, no passengers. So this was the business Andrew had modestly played down as "freight delivery." At the moment it consisted of four war-surplus DC-3s, which Nate and Andrew piloted themselves in shifts with several other war buddies.

Watching him score the decisive goals in this dashing sport played on a brilliant autumn afternoon, and hearing from Nate about some of Andrew's exploits as a wartime pilot, Val felt her interest in him deepening. But she warned herself that she was bound to be rejected if it were ever discovered that she was "not respectable"—as a single woman with a child was bound to be perceived. She had heard the rumor that Andrew's own sister had become pregnant before her wedding, causing embarrassment for the family. That situation involved "one of their own," however, and had been resolved by a marriage. As nice as Charlie and Bunny seemed, Val doubted they'd welcome her so warmly if she linked the Winston family to more scandal.

The evening's formal dinner was served by the butler and a maid in a long dining room with a wall of French doors that looked out to the water. Crystal, silver, and fine china glittered by candlelight. On the sprawling lawn outside, a dozen torchères were lit to add to the ambience. The meal was lobster bisque followed by quail cooked with brandied cherries, tender white asparagus, and strawberries soaked in frosty kirsch and topped with whipped cream for dessert—all new tastes to Val. If not for Charlie and Bunny, who continued to display a knack for putting all their guests at ease, Val would have felt seriously out of place.

Tonight, Philip Longworth and Franklin Storrow were accompanied by polished young women, prewar debutantes, and Nate Palmer was with a young radio actress who had arrived late from the city—with whom he was staying at a nearby inn. Val realized then that Longworth and Storrow must have family homes of their own nearby, so that she was the only overnight houseguest.

With the conversation ranging over books and politics and travel to foreign places, coffee had already been served before there was any mention of Val's purpose in being there. And then it came down only to Andrew saying to the men, as they rose from the table, "Don't forget, we'll meet for breakfast tomorrow at ten to discuss the proposition." That was all.

Had the dinner really been meant for her to make an impression on these potential investors? Could she have done it with the few things she'd said? Or could Andrew be playing on her ambitions simply to achieve a conquest of his own? After all, she was the only unattached woman staying overnight under the same roof with a man known as one of New York's most eligible bachelors.

Rather than tempt fate, Val didn't join the others when they adjourned to a drawing room after dinner, but took Andrew aside to plead fatigue.

"Let me see you up to your room," he said.

Enough rooms lined the upstairs hallway that she wasn't sure of finding her way to the right one. "Thank you."

He stopped outside the door. "It hasn't been so bad, has it?" he asked.

"No. I've had a lovely time."

"Were you bored by the polo?"

"Not at all. It looks like a sport you have to be very brave to play."

He chuckled. "Not as brave as you have to be to start a new business, Valentina. Are you sure you want to go ahead?"

"Yes. Do I seem afraid?"

He paused, choosing his words. "You do seem nervous about . . . something. At least when you're around me."

Again he'd perceived her defensiveness. She felt bad about it—yet equally wary of letting her guard down while they stood at her bedroom door. Struggling to be honest about some of her feelings, she said, "You've been wonderful, Andrew. If I seem a little unsteady, it's because I'm in uncharted territory. I'm not used to being in high society. You're all educated, rich, you've already seen the world. I'm—" She shook her head. "I worked in a factory up to a few months ago. I can't stop worrying that I really have no right to be here—I mean, asking other people to pay for my own little dream. I could easily end up losing all their money."

He smiled. "Your dream isn't little, Valentina. And don't think my friends will give you money as a gift either. They're hardheaded businessmen. If they write checks tomorrow, it'll be because what you say persuades them you have a chance to make even more money for them. But they know it's a risk too. There aren't any absolutely sure things in life." His voice grew gentler. "You of all people should have learned that.

Because if there were, you'd be somewhere else, happily married—and you and I would never have met. Good night, Valentina. Sleep well."

He gave her another smile of assurance, then walked away down the long hall.

His words, and his gentle manner, left her feeling more confident, and ashamed of her doubts and suspicions. Yet the horrible experience with Willy—the utter betrayal of trust in mere friendship—had left its mark on the way she judged all men.

In bed, she lay thinking about Andrew, all his kindnesses. How long would it be, she wondered, before she could trust again . . . and let herself believe in love?

Breakfast was all business. Even Bunny Winston didn't come to the table, so that Val was the only woman present. Acting as an informal chairman, Andrew gave a short preface to the presentation Val was to make:

"From the moment I met this young lady, I can say without exaggeration I was completely bowled over . . . by her energy and determination. We met through a matter that involved publishing—I won't bore you with the details except to say she was kind enough on that occasion to finance the project in full. . . ." When he gave her a mock-serious glance, the shared conspiracy in knowing the truth of their first meeting somehow gave her a necessary lift, chased her nervousness.

"Now she's got something bigger in mind," he went on, "and I thought it only fair to return the favor. Much as I believe she'll make a success of it, it's too big for me to handle alone—so that's why I'm giving you all the opportunity to join in. Val . . . ?" With that, he turned the meeting over to her.

She had armed herself today not only with written notes, but also a pasteup of what an issue of *Every Bride's* would look like, with pictured gowns cut from Smythe's catalogue, an imagined question and answer column on etiquette, and an article on the Grand Canyon from an old *National Geographic* to serve as an example of honeymooning advice. Drawing on what Ozzie had told her about the success of the catalogue and the reasons wedding customs were changing, Val had also written up some notes on why she believed there would be a wide audience for a popular magazine directed at brides. During the war years there had been no time or money or incentive for an average couple to get married in any way but the quickest and simplest. Honeymoons, too, were not much more than two-day affairs, usually in the handiest hotel, before a soldier or sailor reported back to duty. Niagara Falls might be the butt of jokes, but for decades it had also been the true Honeymoon Capital of the World as proclaimed by its chamber of commerce. But all that was changing now, Val suggested. Romance would be able to bloom again, and the essence of its expression would be in the moment that love was sanctified by marriage. Women would want to prepare themselves as well as possible, spending a lot of time before the event dreaming about and planning every phase of it. This magazine, Val concluded, would not only fulfill her dream . . . but also the dreams of tens of thousands of women who married every year. She would start, she said, by publishing an issue every three months, four the first year; if she started now, she thought she would be able to put out the inaugural issue in March or April—early enough to get the attention of June brides.

The group listened politely, then asked a number of questions. Frank Storrow, trained in his family's newspaper business, wanted to know if Val had already arranged "distribution through a wholesaler."

Val drew a blank immediately, and Andrew spoke up to cover her ignorance.

"Isn't that something you can help with, Frank? Val should have her time free to concentrate on the editorial stuff. . . ."

Storrow's glance switched shrewdly between Andrew and Val. He seemed to realize then that she had given no thought to distribution, might not even know how magazines arrived on newsstands. But he could also read Andrew's expectant, hopeful expression. "Sure," Storrow said, "I can help there."

It was the same with Phil Longworth when he asked about how Val's company would be "structured financially," whether she was setting up a corporation or partnership, and what sort of return on investment she envisioned.

"I'm sure Val would appreciate having a financial adviser," Andrew said before Val could even think of admitting that she had no answer. "You might even look after the checkbook, Phil. The important thing here is whether or not we think Val can create a magazine that young women planning to be married will read. All the rest is just . . . minor detail."

Charlie Winston took Andrew's cue. "Well, I've heard enough to know it's worth a flyer. I'll put in six thousand dollars—if the rest of you will each do the same. That will make a total of thirty thousand. Is that enough for you to meet all your expenses, Val?"

It sounded like such a tremendous amount of money. "I'm sure it is."

"Out of that amount," Storrow said, "you'll be expected to open offices, pay yourself and your employees a sensible salary, and budget to publish the first two or three issues, at least. You can't assume you'll make a profit right away."

"I know that," Val said.

"We'll set it up as a limited partnership," Longworth said. "Your investors will own fifty percent of the company—you'll own the other half."

Oddly, she hadn't given a thought to owning any part of it; she would have been willing to have no share, only to be employed as the editor, if it would be the magazine she had in mind. "That sounds fine," she said.

With the commitments made, the breakfast ended. Val was dazed by the ease with which this first crucial step had been accomplished. Of course, it was Andrew who had made it possible.

"Well, now that that's done," he said after the others had dispersed, "how would you like to spend the rest of the day?"

She looked into his eyes, and was so filled by a wave of gratitude that her first thought was only to be with him, do whatever *he* wanted.

But the same cold fear stifled the impulse. The closer he got, the more he would have to know; and there was nothing more to know, she believed, that would not disappoint him—and make the other men reconsider their investments. "I think I ought to go home," she said. "Now that this is a reality, I can't wait to get down to work."

"Not even a Sunday off?"

"Please . . ." she said, begging him, as much as anything, not to make her explain more.

He drove her to meet the next train. Waiting for it to arrive, she thanked him effusively, and told him she owed him more than she could ever repay.

"Don't give me too much credit, Val. Nothing would have happened if your idea wasn't a good one and you weren't burning to achieve it. Remember, it was one of the first things you told me—about your need to finish the ceremony? If I hadn't helped you, I know sooner or later you'd have told someone else who would have."

"Funny," she said, "I think you believe in me more than I believe in myself."

"Maybe I do."

The train was coming into the station. She watched it, avoiding his eyes—steeling herself against her own impulse to kiss him.

Abruptly, he said, "You're still in love with that man you were going to marry, aren't you?"

No, she had accepted Ted's death. But it was an easier way out than admitting the truth that she was sure would make him judge her as promiscuous and immoral. "I . . . I guess I am," she said.

The train stopped and he helped her up the steps. "You shouldn't ever forget him, Val," he said, handing the valise up to her. "But maybe it's time to make some room in your heart for somebody else."

All the way back to the city she cried. She had the room . . . she wanted to let Andrew Winston in. But she had already known the devastation of losing the love of one man. If she lost another—lost his respect along with his love—she might not survive so easily.

Better to keep the door to that empty room in her heart closed and locked. With the work of fulfilling a dream to keep her busy, perhaps it wouldn't be too hard.

Eleven

"That's one of the most beautiful paintings I've ever seen," Val said, and the women flanking her laughed and applauded. The four of them were standing together in the dingy corridor watching as the black letters were stenciled onto the frosted glass of the office door: EVERY BRIDE'S MAGAZINE.

These first few months, she'd settled for a penciled sign taped to the door of the three-room office suite. Soon, in early March, the April issue—the first one—would go to press. Three weeks later the magazine, with its glossy cover of a veiled woman swirled into a long-trained white silk bridal gown, would be distributed to newsstands. Time to believe she might be here long enough to make it worth painting the sign on the door.

Since she'd deposited the thirty thousand dollars in the bank, Val's life had been consumed by the magazine, all plans subordinated to the need to get research done, articles written, advertisers signed up.

Mr. Durer had been disappointed when she told him she was quitting the print shop to pursue her dream, yet he had been very understanding, had even given her a severance bonus. She tried to refuse the extra money, but he insisted. "You're smart and lovely, *Liebchen*, but you're young—and a woman. You'll be up against men who have no pity when it comes to business. Remember, you can always come to me, and I'll give you back your old job."

Discouraging as it was, she knew he meant well. She thanked him . . . and used the money to start a savings account for Teddie.

After locating cheap office space in a building right across the street from the print shop, Val hired two employees through publishing agencies. One, a woman in her forties named Madge Truesdale, had spent nine years in the advertising department of *The Saturday Evening Post*, then had left to get married. She was looking for work after her childless twelve-year marriage had ended in divorce. Madge was tall and buxom, with red hair a shade too vivid to be genuine. When she showed up for an interview, she had already tried for months to get hired at the more established magazines. Divorced women were still rare in the workplace, more likely to live off alimony than to go back to a job—and when they did show up on the hiring lines, they didn't have an easy time.

"We're about as welcome in an office as lepers," Madge explained to Val. "The guys who run things would much rather hire young women for peanuts than pay more to someone like me for my experience. They think divorcées are gonna be hard to work with, too, bitter toward all men, or sex-starved—apt to stir things up in a way that throws business off track."

But Madge struck Val as energetic and eager to reassert her independence. "I can't offer a big salary," Val told her, "but if you're with me at the beginning, I promise you'll do well if the magazine succeeds." Selling advertising, of course, would be central to any success, so Madge's ability could be crucial.

Madge surprised Val by being hesitant about taking the job. "Honey, I didn't realize until I got here that this thing of yours is aimed at brides . . . and I'd hate to cripple your chances from the start. A divorced woman isn't the best person to tell advertisers there's a long future for a sheet about the golden dream of married love and happily-ever-after."

Not a bad point. The best sort of person to sign up advertisers would be a dewy-eyed newlywed who could gush about how she wished something like *Every Bride's* had been available when she planned her own wedding. But by the same standard, Val herself didn't qualify to publish and edit a magazine for brides. She insisted Madge take the job.

Before long, Madge had signed up a full complement of ad pages from jewelry manufacturers who made wedding and engagement rings, dress companies that had begun to produce ready-to-wear wedding gowns, makers of cedar-lined hope chests in which young women kept the items they were collecting for their trousseaus, and producers of china, furniture, appliances, kitchenware, and other items for new homes. The same no-nonsense honesty and directness that caused Madge Truesdale to underline her own shortcoming for the job made her a terrific saleswoman.

Val's other paid employee was Connie Marcantonio, a thin girl of twenty-three from Brooklyn with long black hair who had graduated City College, then taken some accounting courses, hoping to earn money as a bookkeeper while trying to fulfill her cherished ambition to be a writer. When her first bookkeeping position proved hatefully boring, and all the short stories she wrote were rejected without a single word of encouragement, she decided to find a job in which her writing would be utilized. For fifty dollars a week she was Val's editorial assistant, who also did accounts, answered the phone, and happily produced articles and a Question-and-Answer column for the first issue under half a dozen different names.

Connie also provided an authentic window into the heart and mind of the audience *Every Bride's* was intended to reach. For the past two years she had been engaged to a boy from another Italian family who had grown up on the same block in Brooklyn where she lived. He worked in his father's seafood restaurant in Sheepshead Bay, and they were waiting to be married until they had saved enough money to, as Connie said, "start out life on the right foot." Tapping into Connie's dreams for her own wedding gave Val a vision of subjects that might be covered in future issues.

Finally, there was one unpaid employee. Katharine Storrow was the lanky blond debutante sister of one of the investors, Frank Storrow. Val had taken her on at Frank's request—to help break her idle routine of lunch with girlfriends and shopping for clothes to put in already bulging closets. Val couldn't refuse, particularly when told Katharine would work without salary.

Though Val expected she'd be getting a spoiled young

woman who would arrive late for work and leave early, Katharine Storrow proved to be a bright, eager volunteer with contacts from the highest social level who were a distinct boon. A magazine based on a vision that more and more girls from every social level were going to aspire to imitate practices once reserved to the weddings of the rich was helped by having the viewpoint of a genuine society girl as a guide to the last word in wedding customs. It was Kath who had observed that with so many boats that had served as troop ships during the war being restored to cruise ships, cruises would make an excellent topic for the honeymoon section.

Small as her staff was, Val felt it was diverse and well balanced.

As the painter completed stenciling the name on the door and gathered up his materials, it was near the end of the day and the three other women lingered with Val, admiring the words on the door as if standing before a treasured painting in a museum.

"Looks great," Connie said.

"Tasteful," Kath remarked.

"But he left something out," Madge observed, pointing to a lower corner of the frosted glass pane. "Right there it should say Valentina Cummings, Editor in Chief."

Val shook her head. "This is a team operation. My name will go up when we have the kind of office—with enough doors—so you can all get the same treatment."

"You mustn't be so modest, Val," Connie said. "You're the one who started this."

"It's not modesty," said Kath, always free with a tart comment. "Until we know we're profitable, Val doesn't want the bill collectors knowing only *her* name."

They filed back into the small suite consisting of an outer reception area leading to two side-by-side small rooms, each with a grimy window facing an air shaft. At first they had made an effort to organize it, with one office for Val, one for Madge, the outer space with two desks for Connie and Kath. Over the months, the free trade of responsibilities, and the unending flow of paper being stacked everywhere, had blurred the boundaries. The women often plopped down to do their work at any desk that happened to be unoccupied. The office designated for Val, commonly the scene of group meetings, had evolved into a conference room, where chairs were left in a permanent semicircle around the desk, and a hot plate and coffee percolator were installed.

A phone rang. Kath answered, told Madge the call was for her, and Madge went into Val's office to take it.

"It's early," Connie said to Val, "but would it be okay if I leave for the day?"

"Sure," Val said. Connie rarely balked at working overtime, but Val knew that some evenings she went straight from this job to help wait tables at her fiancé's father's restaurant.

Kath had been neatening clutter atop a file cabinet. "You can also go, Kath," Val said. "It's winding down for today."

"Are you staying?" Kath asked.

"I'll lock up after Madge."

"Then I'll stay too."

"That's not necessary."

"You always lock up alone," Kath said. "I'm invited to a party later, Val; I thought you might like to come along. My friends are fun, you'd like them."

"I'd love to meet your friends. But some other time."

Kath gave a resigned nod. That evening's invitation was hardly the first any of the staff had extended to Val for dinner out, a movie, or a party. They were always fended off with excuses—work to do, a previous engagement, a sniffle coming on. By then it was clear Val was anxious to keep part of her life strictly private.

It was Teddie, of course, whom Val wanted no one in the office to know about. Keeping the secret required an effort, but having concealed it from Andrew and his friends at the time she'd accepted their money, she knew it would be all the worse if they were to learn now. And if she was to keep them in the dark, then the women in the office couldn't know either, since the story was bound to filter back through Kath to her brother. For all Katharine Storrow's good qualities, Val had heard her express a snobbish disdain for women who got themselves "in trouble." In an office gossip session she had told the story of the younger of Andrew's sisters being forced into a hasty marriage because she was "knocked up." Hearing Kath describe the way the news made the rounds in society, and the other women in the office clucking over how sad it was for a girl, Val was reaffirmed in her belief that if Andrew knew her situation, he and his friends would have never become involved with her.

Madge finished her call and came out of Val's office. "A new account—electric blankets. Just the thing to heat up the marriage bed."

"You're doing an incredible job, Madge. I'm lucky to have you."

"Lucky my husband didn't want me," the divorcée said wryly, unhooking her coat and purse from a rack. "Funniest damn thing that I'm here every day, selling the great American wedding dream, and I couldn't buy it for myself."

"You may yet."

"Looking over our first issue does make me wish I could be a bride all over again. It was the happiest day of my life—if only a day." Madge sighed and said good night, then stopped at the door. "By the way, is there anything in the budget for travel? I got a call earlier from a guy who owns an inn in the hills of Pennsylvania. In the war years he had a lot of servicemen running down there for quickie honeymoons. Now he and some other local businessmen think the area could be developed, made more popular. They heard about us, and want us to come look it over, then do a feature on the region."

"What's it called?"

"The Pocono Mountains."

"We can certainly afford train fare to Pennsylvania."

"Why don't you go, Val? A day or two in the country—wouldn't you like that? They'll give us a hotel room gratis in exchange for the publicity."

She could bring Teddie, Val thought at first, nice for both of them to have a couple of days in the countryside. Then she realized it risked having the baby's existence exposed—if, say, the innkeepers later mentioned it to Madge. "No," she said, "you take the trip."

"All right," Madge said happily.

After Madge left, Val signed letters Connie had typed to go out to new advertisers. She had just unhitched her jacket from the rack when there was a knock at the outer door, a shadow looming against the frosted glass. It was late for an office caller, and she'd made no appointments. "It's open," Val called.

Andrew walked in. He was wearing khaki pants and a leather flying jacket, his eyes were masked by sunglasses, and his brown hair was tousled by the stiff breeze of early March blowing outside. It was the first time she had seen him since the weekend in Oyster Bay. Phil Longworth and Frank Storrow had both been to the office often, Phil in his capacity as the company treasurer, checking the books, advising Val on how to conserve her money; Frank Storrow helping her negotiate with the printers, and the wholesalers who would put her magazine on the newsstands. Andrew, however, had stayed away. Val supposed the feigned coolness she had exhibited had convinced him he might as well not bother, and she had heard from Kath Storrow that over the past few months Andrew had continued reinforcing his reputation as most eligible bachelor, dating one young woman designated Debutante of the Year by *Life* magazine, and another who played the beautiful Eurasian ingenue in *South Pacific*. The report assured Val that she could never have been more than another in Andrew's string of conquests.

Even so, when she saw him now, her heart skipped a beat. At the same time, the unannounced visit made her curiously anxious, fed into an intuition that something bad was about to happen.

She gave him only a very reserved hello.

Catching her tone, he said, "Is this a bad time . . . ?"

"No, I'm through with work for today. I'm just . . . so surprised to see you."

"A last-minute idea. I'm having the airline's new business stationery printed at Durer's, and I was just there picking the typeface. Since it's right across the street . . ."

"Well, if you're checking up on your investment, there's not all that much to see, but I can give you a quick tour."

"I can see it all from here. What I really want to check up on, Val, is you."

"Why do you think it's necessary to check up on me?" she asked.

"Not necessary, Val, friendly." He hesitated, glanced at the jacket she was holding. "If you're done for the day, maybe you and I could go and—"

"Andrew, I'm truly sorry, but I can't." The baby was waiting.

He stood looking at her. "Okay. Then I'll talk now—just for a minute. Val, you've made it clear in a number of ways that you'd be happier if I kept my distance, and I've been respecting that wish. But then I started hearing that it wasn't only me you keep at arm's length. Frank's heard about it from his sister—how you cut yourself off from everyone except during the hours when you're here in the office. I've been listening to them gab about it for weeks, and it started to worry me."

"I'm . . . a private person, Andrew. It's nothing to concern yourself about."

"I told you I want to respect that. But for a girl like you, Val—beautiful, with such bright prospects—well, it just doesn't seem quite . . . well, not quite . . ." He kept searching for the word.

"Quite what?" she prompted.

"I was going to say . . . not normal. People need friends. They don't usually chase everyone away. Unless, maybe, you're in some kind of trouble, then it would make sense. So when I did find myself right nearby, I came to say, if there is a problem, and there's any way in which I can help . . ." He trailed off.

Of course she was touched—and still she couldn't let down her guard. "That's sweet, Andrew. But let me assure you I'm not wanted by the law, afraid of a vendetta, hiding out from bill collectors or anyone else. In short, I don't think of myself as being in trouble."

"Living alone with memories can be a kind of trouble," he said quietly.

"I'm not alone," she said almost as a reflex—anything to stop him being so damned . . . *nice*. He was wearing her down, bringing her to the point where she might break down, lean on him, and tell him everything . . . and she couldn't imagine it would be good for either of them.

He gave her a dubious glance, but then he shrugged. "Okay. I tried. I'll butt out. Since I'm here, though, the least I can do is give you a ride home."

Home was where she kept her secret. But his impulse was so good, and she'd run out of evasions. "Okay. Thanks." It would work if she had him drop her on a corner a block from where she lived. She put on her jacket and was moving to turn off the lights when the phone rang.

"Let it go," Andrew said. "They'll call back tomorrow."

She almost did. But as long as she was in the office, she had to tend to business. She picked up the phone on Connie's desk.

A high-pitched whining was the first thing she heard, then a pounding behind it, followed by an incoherent babble, words run together so fast, it sounded like a foreign language. "Who is this?" Val said.

"Zozie!" came the answer in a desperate wail. "Izzozie, 'Al!"

She knew the voice. "Josie? What's wrong?"

Crying hysterically, Josie forced out some garbled words. "Zo' 'fraid, 'Al. Try to cho' me . . ."

Val didn't have to ask anything else. An image shot through her mind of Josie at the clinic the time she'd thought her jaw might be broken. If she was having trouble speaking, it must be because Sean had again beaten her terribly. Along with the pounding in the background, Val could make out his furious shouting, though muffled by a closed door.

"Get out of there, Jos. Get out now!"

"Can' doot 'Al. He's ri' ou'si'."

There was a phone in their bedroom, Val remembered. Josie must have locked herself in, and Sean was trying to break down the door. "Call the police, Jos. Right now, hang up and call them."

"No. Poliz'll hur'im."

Hurt him? It was the same crazy logic Val had run into every other time she'd tried reasoning with her friend. Even now the sick bond of devotion wouldn't allow Josie to summon the police because of what they might do to the man threatening her.

Val could hear Sean's muffled shouts grow louder. "You've got to call the police, Jos. Or I will."

"Nee' you, 'Al, 'atsall," she wailed. "You come!"

Her desperation matching Josie's, Val also began to shout. "I can't get there fast enough. Call a neighbor, call out the window. What about Mandy—is she all right?"

"Wouldn' hur', Man'. Oh, 'Al . . ." Josie was overtaken by her hysterical howling.

"I'll be there quick as I can!" Val bellowed. "Just keep away from him. Do anything you have to, but stay safe."

Only when she banged down the phone did she again become aware of Andrew nearby, listening. "My friend's in terrible trouble," she said, grabbing up the phone again to dial for an operator.

"I'll help any way I can," he said.

"There's nothing you can do," Val said as an operator came on the line and she asked for the police in Levittown. It was a precious minute before the connection was made. Hurriedly, Val told the policeman who answered that there was a woman in danger, and gave him the MacMorans' address.

"In danger, ma'am? You mean a burglar's inside the house?"

"No. Her husband's trying to break into their bedroom."

"She's locked him out of their bedroom? I can understand he might—"

"You *don't* understand. He's crazy, he might kill her."

Another pause. "Who are you, ma'am?"

"I'm her best friend."

"I see. Well, if this is a domestic dispute, we can't—"

"For God's sake," Val pleaded, "get over to that address. You'll be saving her life."

"All right, I'll check into it, ma'am. Thank you for calling."

Check into it? Look in a rule book and see if it was allowed? She might have stayed on the phone, pleading, but from the policeman's bland reaction, Val doubted he'd do anything beyond what was customary. And the custom was for the police not to interfere in matters between husbands and wives. Exasperated, she banged down the phone. Rather than argue, she could be on the move.

"I've got to get to the train right away," she said, heading out of the office. "Would you take me?"

"Of course, but you don't have to take a train," Andrew said, punching the elevator button as Val locked up. "I'll drive you out there."

"That's not necessary."

"Sounds like an emergency, and it'll be faster. . . ."

Riding down in the elevator, she debated. If Andrew brought her to Josie, it could be hard to keep him from learning the rest of her secrets. It was because of Teddie that the two women had become friends. And what would be gained? She didn't think going by train would take that much longer than driving. Anyway, if the police hadn't responded at once to her call, a difference of twenty minutes one way or the other wasn't going to save Josie.

In the street Val said, "Just take me to Penn Station, Andrew. I've already called the police, they'll do whatever has to be done for my friend long before I can get there."

He bit back a response and pointed her toward his car.

Only once on the way to Penn Station did he break the silence. "It's not too late to change your mind. I can turn here, and—"

"I don't want you mixed up in this. That's final!"

"For God's sake," he said hotly, "I can tell this *is* trouble. Why in hell do you have to keep me locked out? I want to help."

"You have helped, Andrew. But you've done all you can do for tonight, believe me."

"And what about tomorrow night . . . or the night after? Don't you think you might need help then?"

She still hadn't answered the question when he stopped in front of the railroad station and she ran from the car.

The train ride seemed endless. Val wasn't given to praying, but she did pray now that the police would have intervened and Josie would be all right by the time she arrived.

On the long ride, Val castigated herself for not maintaining closer ties to Josie in the past few months, even though she had made the effort. After Sean had thrown her out of the house, he had also forbidden Josie to take Val's telephone calls. Still, Val had gotten through several times when Josie was home alone. On those occasions Josie would always swear up and down that things were fine, Sean was treating her well.

Finally, in their most recent call, Josie had asked Val not to call anymore—no, not merely asked, Val recalled, she had pleaded, urging Val to believe that it only made things worse. When Val resisted giving a pledge to cut off contact, Josie had shouted at her angrily, accused her of interfering where she wasn't wanted.

So Val had listened, had given up. And now she knew it had been the wrong thing to do.

A police car was standing in the driveway of the MacMoran house when the taxi from the station pulled up. Was it a good or bad sign that the police were still there more than an hour after Val's request for help? Had they arrived in time . . . ?

The door of the house was open, and Val dashed straight inside.

Two policemen stood in the living room, one young, the other a veteran. Sean and Josie sat on the sofa facing them. Josie stared glumly ahead, holding a dishrag wadded around a bunch of ice cubes against the side of her face.

Val went straight to Josie and knelt in front of her. "I'm sorry I couldn't get here sooner. . . ."

"You didn't have to come at all," Sean snarled.

"Are you the woman who called?" the older policeman asked.

Val nodded, her eyes still on Josie. "Is Mandy all right?"

"Mandy's fine," Sean snapped. "We don't need you here, Val."

Josie pulled the ice pack down. There was a huge bruise on her cheek, her lip at the corner of her mouth was puffed up and bloody. "She wo' up," Josie said. "But I pu' her ba' to slee'."

Val looked over her shoulder at the police. "What are you going to do now?"

"We're about done here, miss," said the young one. "Mr. MacMoran has apologized to his wife, and she's told us she definitely doesn't want to press any charges, so—"

Val turned back to Josie, wide-eyed. "Nothing? Is that what happens now? An hour ago you thought he was going to kill you!"

Sean looked to the young policeman. "I got mad, but I'd never—"

Val cut him off, her focus still on Josie. "I can take you with me, you and Mandy. You'd like that, Jos, I know you would."

Josie avoided a reply by putting the ice pack back on her lip.

"She doesn't want to go anywhere with you," Sean said.

"Then let *her* say it!" Val snapped. Lowering her voice again, she said, "Josie, now's your chance . . . while the police are here. You can come with me. Even for just a day or two. You could take Mandy to the zoo, and the Empire State Building."

Josie went on staring silently back with frightened eyes from behind her ice pack.

Val turned to Sean. "Please . . . give her a chance. Tell her it's okay . . . let her go."

"She belongs here," Sean said implacably.

The older policeman spoke up. "What do you want, missus?" he asked Josie. "Speak for yourself."

Slowly, Josie lowered the ice pack. "Li' to ta' Mand' to the zoo."

Val breathed a sigh of relief. "Go and pack," she said quickly.

Josie looked questioningly from Val to the policemen,

who nodded reassuringly. "Fi' minu's," she said, rising from the sofa.

Sean was back on his feet. "You can't walk out on me!" he raged at her.

The younger policeman, after observing all the interplay, had changed sides. "She's invited to the city for the weekend, she wants to take the kid to the zoo, I think you should let her."

Sean glared at him furiously. But then suddenly all the fight went out of him and he slumped back down.

He didn't move or say another word until Josie came down with two suitcases, Mandy at her side. Still groggy from being wakened and dressed, the child seemed only vaguely aware of what was happening. She greeted Val with a smile, then went and hugged her father. "Bye, Daddy," she said. "See you soon."

Sean hugged her back. There were tears in his eyes as he turned to Josie. "You know I'm sorry. Don't stay long."

"I won't," she managed to say.

Val took a deep breath. She would do everything in her power to give Josie a chance to break out of the cage.

She made the weekend a kind of holiday, as promised. Josie and Mandy stayed in an unused bedroom of Mrs. Falconi's apartment, but they all ate together at Val's. She had fixed her place up by now, tearing up the linoleum, scraping and polishing the old wood floors, hanging curtains, buying a lustrous old cherrywood tabletop to put over the kitchen tub so it could be used for dining when not for bathing. During the days Val and Josie and the children toured the city, not only fulfilling Mandy's desires to go to the zoo and see the top of the Empire State Building, but enjoying a meal in Chinatown, and a show at Radio City Music Hall. All the corny things every tourist did, and Val enjoyed them no less, for she had never made time to be a tourist herself.

Late Sunday afternoon, after a ride on the Staten Island ferry, they went to the Automat in Times Square for supper. Mandy was enchanted by the little windowed boxes that opened to provide a sandwich or cupcake when a few nickels were dropped into a slot. At the end of the meal Josie allowed her to go off by herself to buy cake and milk.

"I've had the best time in years, Val," Josie said. "I wish we could stay a little longer."

"Why can't you, Jos? The weekend was to give you a chance to think about whether you *should* go home. If you want to stay, I'll give you a job, and we can find a larger apartment, big enough—"

"Val, I'm not brave or strong enough to make a life for myself the way you have. I need someone to take care of me."

"Sean doesn't take *good* care of you though."

"He wants to."

"Oh, Jos, whatever he wants to do, he's still—"

Josie broke in again, more assertively. "I'm going back, Val. Try to understand: I don't have a choice. Not every woman does. I wish I did, but I don't. So I'm going back, and I'm going to make the best of it. And you've got to understand that. Look, I love you, but I don't expect to see you again."

"No!" Val said. "I was wrong last time not to—"

"Listen, listen!" Josie pleaded. She was speaking very rapidly, eager to say certain things before Mandy came back to the table. "My best hope is that Sean can learn to be . . . gentler. But you saw those cops, you know which side the law is really on. If I'm the one who walks out—who brings things to a head—I know I'll end up paying for it one way or another. He might even be able to take Mandy away from me."

"I wouldn't let him!"

"You? Val, dear Val, I know you mean well, but please, just listen, I have something important to ask." Josie glanced anxiously to where Mandy was watching an animal-headed spout dispense a glass of milk in return for a nickel. "If anything does happen," she continued, "I mean, if Mandy ever needs help and I can't give it to her, I want you to be there, to stand in for me. Will you do that?"

"Of course. You know I would."

"With Sean in and out of work, and . . . our other troubles, it's the one thing that has me worried out of my mind—that

Mandy could be the one to suffer. I just want you to swear to me you'll do everything you can to take care of her if she ever needs it, the way I took care of Teddie for you."

"Count on it," Val said solemnly as her mind teemed with the implications of Josie's plea.

Despite her assurance, Josie kept eyeing her worriedly. "You understand, Val, I'm depending on you. This is a sacred vow."

Val reached for her hand. "Josie, if you're this worried—"

"All I need is your promise!"

After another moment Val said steadily, "You have it."

Josie sat back and breathed deeply. "Good. That makes me feel so much better." The sudden way she pasted a broad smile on her face indicated that she had noticed Mandy approaching the table.

Val accepted that it was too late to change Josie's mind. It had been too late, surely, before they had ever met.

Twelve

"Seen enough?" Andrew said as they walked out of the Astor Hotel into the heart of Times Square. The hotel was one of the biggest in the city, and Val had wanted to be sure the large newsstand in the lobby was stocking issues of *Every Bride's*. The ballroom was popular for debutante cotillions and other big social events; dozens of society girls planning wedding receptions were bound to pass through that lobby.

"Not yet," Val answered. "It's a thrill every time I see the cover looking back at me—something that wouldn't exist if I hadn't created it. Sure, it's not Beethoven's Ninth . . . or *Hamlet*, but . . . to have created something of my own . . ."

He laughed. "Okay. On we go! There's a newsstand in front of Child's." He took her arm to guide her across Broadway.

On this April day, the first of the magazine's distribution, Val had spent the afternoon walking all over the city, checking corner kiosks, good hotels, stores where all the other popular weeklies and monthlies were on view. Her magazine wasn't in every location, but she was content to find it in most of the better hotels like the Astor, and the Pennsylvania, propped up on stands alongside *Life* and *Look* and *The Saturday Evening Post*. There were dozens of copies of each of the others, only two or three of hers . . . but it was a beginning.

It felt right to have no one but Andrew at her side for this "victory walk." No matter how often he might say that one way or another she would have fulfilled her ambition, Val doubted it would have happened without him. Except for Josie and Mr. Durer, neither of whom had been encouraging, Andrew was the first to whom she had told her idea. That had been just six months ago—and now here they were, enjoying the achievement together.

The turning point in their relationship had been that night when Josie's call had led to the argument about her evasiveness. After the couple of days she devoted to Josie, Val had called Andrew to apologize for chasing him away. Not that she wouldn't have done it again in the same situation—she still didn't want to let him into the private corners of her life—but she did want him to know she appreciated his friendship and didn't want to lose it.

Since then, Andrew had begun passing by the magazine office occasionally just to say hello, or to take Val out for lunch, or a cup of coffee at the end of the day before she went home. He seemed eager for her company whenever he wasn't flying, though these days that was rare. With the need for faster transport of goods growing as peacetime industrial expansion picked up, his all-freight airline was developing rapidly. He and Nate had added six more war surplus planes, the larger DC-4s. When Val reflected that Ted's plans had been based on going back to one of the most old-fashioned forms of transport, the barge, she wondered if perhaps he had been too much of an impractical dreamer to have made a good life for them even if he'd lived.

As she grew closer to Andrew, Val felt a time coming when she ought to trust him with the knowledge of her child's existence. A friend would surely understand, she told herself. Though would a *lover*? And it was as a lover, she knew, that she wanted Andrew. . . . Whenever she thought about being completely honest with him, she went back and forth on when and how and if. Fortunately, though, she felt no pressure to decide. In all their time together since the night they'd argued, Andrew had never again criticized her secretiveness or asked prying questions. They talked about work, about events in the news, shared anecdotes and gossip—they simply enjoyed being together. Merely by his manner he let her know he was ready now to take no more than she was prepared to give. He had not, after all, given up his nights on the town with debutantes.

"You've been very patient putting up with my nonsense," she said to him after she'd looked at the news kiosk outside Child's, content to see four copies of *Every Bride's* in a rack. "Let me buy you a cup of coffee to show my appreciation." She nodded at the entrance to Child's.

"Coffee! Madam, this appreciation of yours knows no bounds."

She laughed. "All right, coffee and a doughnut. It's too early for champagne."

"I'm sorry, Val," he said then. "But I should be getting out to the airport. I'm flying to Chicago."

"Do you still have to do it yourself? I thought you had ten pilots working for you now."

"Matter of fact, twelve as of last week."

"So why do you still have to do the flying? You're the owner."

Andrew smiled. "I don't *have* to fly, Val. I work as a pilot because I like it. No matter how big Atlas Air gets, I don't ever see myself being tied to a desk. Nate's doing most of the corporate stuff, he doesn't seem to mind, but I'll always need more adventure in my life."

He kissed her on the cheek as they said good-bye, and said he'd call when he got back—it might be a couple of days, since the company was developing a new terminal in Chicago.

"I'll be back on the weekend though. Let's get together then."

"I can't, I'll be away."

He was obviously disappointed. "Where?"

"The Pocono Mountains."

"Where's that?"

"Pennsylvania. It's getting popular with honeymooners."

"Going alone?" Andrew asked quickly, showing a hint of alarm.

"I'm not going on a honeymoon, if that's what you're thinking. The magazine may do an article." After making the first trip, Madge Truesdale had told Val that unusual things were being done in the area that might make it especially appealing to honeymooners. Madge had cagily withheld specifics, however, advising Val she had to see and judge for herself.

Andrew's relief was palpable. "Well, if you're going to be on your own . . . what would you say to my going along? I'll drive you down. And I'd get my own room, of course. But it could be fun, don't you think?"

"I'd like it, Andrew," she said. "I'd like it very much. But . . . well, it wouldn't be . . . convenient."

"Oh, I see. There *is* someone else."

Yes—she'd been thinking of taking Teddie along to the country. But she didn't want to lose this chance with Andrew, to be alone in circumstances where all the barriers might finally come down. "There's no one else. I meant it wouldn't be the best time because it's for work, and I wouldn't be free . . . just to play."

He shrugged. "I'll take whatever I can get."

She stood at the crossroads for another second. "I'll arrange for the extra room," she said. "Pick me up on Friday at the office around three o'clock."

Mrs. Falconi agreed to take care of Teddie for the whole weekend, moving up to Val's apartment so the baby could remain in familiar surroundings. By now the Italian woman was a full-fledged surrogate grandmother who took care of Teddie each weekday while Val was at work, or any other time Val was unable to be home. Yet as comfortable as Val felt leaving the baby with Mrs. Falconi, she kept having second thoughts about going away for this longer stretch of time. It seemed wrong not to give her child more of herself. Equally difficult, however, was to think of putting off any longer a chance to explore a deeper intimacy with Andrew—to be loved again.

On Friday morning, when Mrs. Falconi arrived, Val wrote down the name and phone number of the inn in the Poconos where she would be staying in case any emergency arose with the baby.

"So this-a for your job?" Mrs. Falconi said. "You go away to a place called The Rainbow Inn for-a work?"

"I'm doing research for my magazine, looking at places that honeymooners might like to stay."

"How you gonna know what's-a good for a honeymoon just by looking? You gotta try it out you-self."

Val laughed. "This will have to do for now."

"You goin' alone?" When Val hesitated, Mrs. Falconi added, "You could-a take the baby if you go alone. . . ."

Val sighed. "No, I'm not going alone."

Mrs. Falconi gave her shrewd crooked-toothed smile. "A nice-a man?"

"Very nice. But we're just friends, Mrs. Falconi. He's got a car, so he offered to drive me."

"Just friends," Mrs. Falconi said knowingly. "That's-a nice."

They reached the Poconos after a drive of two hours. The region offered pleasant scenery, low mountains, and green valleys painted in sharp relief by the golden late-afternoon sun, though Val's first impression was that there was nothing of such spectacular interest that it deserved to become a particular favorite of honeymooners.

Her opinion was only reinforced when she and Andrew arrived at The Rainbow Inn, where Madge had convinced the proprietor to provide two free rooms. Though set back from the road down a nice winding tree-shaded drive, the establishment appeared to be little more than a large colonial farmhouse with a modern wing of one story constructed to jut out at an odd angle. It sat on several acres of meadow that embraced a pond which might have been charming except that the water looked rather muddy. One touch that had probably been installed specifically for honeymooners was a wishing well that stood near the edge of the pond. From the look of it, little had been done since the war years, when this was exactly the kind of getaway that would do for couples who'd have only a day or two after a quickie marriage.

"You sure we took the right turn?" Andrew asked as he steered his station wagon up to the door fronting the main part of the house.

Val pointed to the sign hanging over the door. "Says Rainbow Inn right there."

"And they think they're gonna make this the honeymoon capital of the world. . . ." Andrew shook his head.

"There must be more than meets the eye. Madge says she thinks this place has possibilities. That's all she'd say though—insisted I had to see and decide for myself."

"Maybe she just wanted to be sure you had a free weekend in the country."

"With you along," Val said, "that's good enough."

He smiled, and it seemed he was about to move toward her, but just then a man emerged from the inn.

"Greetings! Greetings!" he hailed them loudly, striding toward the station wagon. "Welcome to The Rainbow Inn, where all year round love's in bloom, and day or night you'll see stars in your room." The little piece of doggerel was obviously tailored to the honeymoon crowd.

Val got out of the car. "Mr. Wellstrom?" Madge had given her the proprietor's name.

"That's me all right, Rudy Wellstrom." He was a burly man in middle age with a broad, weathered face under a thatch of unkempt graying hair. Wearing overalls and a plaid woolen shirt, he looked more like a plumber interrupted in the middle of a job than a professional host, but he had the hearty welcoming demeanor of someone sincere about wanting strangers to feel at home. "You folks sent by a friend of yours—or mine? Either way, we'll make your time with us a dream of romance, a ride on moonbeams, when two hearts dance."

"Mr. Wellstrom, we're not honeymooners. I'm Valentina Cummings—from *Every Bride's* magazine."

"Ah, Mrs. Cummings, yes! We've been looking forward to your visit." He turned to Andrew, who was out of the car by now. "And Mr. Cummings, I'm glad you could come along. Never too late, or even too soon, for lovers to take a *second* honeymoon."

Andrew cast a glance at Val, not certain how she wanted to handle his being mistaken for her husband.

Val was momentarily at a loss for words. Would it be better

to say they were *not* married, just friends? Or was the innkeeper just being polite? What sort of marriage could he think they had if they had booked two rooms?

Suddenly Val regretted allowing Andrew to accompany her to this place. Though he'd suggested coming along, he hadn't bargained for being dragooned into playing the part of her husband in a tawdry honeymooners' hideaway.

Yet he didn't seem to mind letting the mistake stand. Before she could decide how to respond to Wellstrom, Andrew said, "Can we see our rooms now?"

"Sure enough. Sort of the whole point of your being here is to see the rooms. That's what you're going to want to tell the world about. C'mon inside and register, then I'll show you the way to . . . well, I like to think of it as paradise."

They followed Wellstrom into the colonial house. Inside, sitting rooms with fireplaces flanked a central hall where Wellstrom had set up his counter. Behind it was a board hung with a dozen room keys affixed to large red numbered cardboard tags cut in the shape of a heart. The keys were all in place, Val noted, indicating no other guests at the moment. Glancing into the public rooms, she saw they were decorated nicely in the Pennsylvania Dutch style, with furniture that appeared to be genuine antiques.

When the innkeeper slid a registry and pen over in front of Andrew, Val peeked over his shoulder and saw him sign "Mr. and Mrs. V. Cummings." Even as a lighthearted joke it troubled Val. If she had begun to hope for intimacy with Andrew, it wasn't because she was scheming for marriage, but because she simply yearned to have a man she truly desired make love to her, longed for his touch as a cure for the trauma she had suffered being so cruelly handled by Willy.

"Very well, Mr. and Mrs. Cummings," Wellstrom said after a glance at the register, "now that you've signed your name on the line, allow me to show you to your den divine."

As he led them out of the old portion of the inn to the new wing, he began what sounded like a tour guide's lecture on a natural wonder of some sort. "What you are about to see is unlike anything you have seen before. It is unique to this establishment . . . and a few others in this area owned by friends, because I have shared my creation with them . . . an innovation that will do no less than revolutionize the tradition of the honeymoon, that special time when lovers all through history have consummated marriage with the ultimate gift they can make to each other."

By now they were at the new wing, in front of one of a row of doors all painted the red of valentine candy boxes. Inserting the heart-tagged key into the lock, Wellstrom opened the door with a flourish.

As soon as they stepped inside, Val and Andrew both froze in amazement. The room was a sea of red in the same shade as the door—walls, silk curtains, plush carpet, and most eye filling, an enormous heart-shaped bed covered with a quilted satin spread and tented over with a satin canopy. Vases of red silk roses stood on a dresser and night table, and lamps glowing at the bedsides had red heart-shaped shades that bathed the whole room in a glow, making the red of everything else even more intense.

Val and Andrew glanced at each other, making a silent pact to do everything possible not to collapse into laughter. The innkeeper, who'd boasted of being the creator of this "paradise," was waiting for a word of praise.

"You were right, Mr. Wellstrom," Val said. "This certainly is unlike anything I've ever seen before."

"Or me," Andrew said.

"You haven't even seen the best part yet," Wellstrom crowed, "*my* invention." He went across the room to a pair of extra-large doors set into a wide portal. With a sweeping movement he sent them sliding back into wall pockets . . . revealing the bathroom, and virtually making it a part of the sleeping chamber. Again red was the dominant color: red tile, red bathroom fixtures, red towels. Dominating all else, however, was the red tub, set into an immense stagelike platform and reflected in mirrors above and on all sides. Looking at the mirror on the ceiling, Val could see that the enormous tub was heart-shaped.

The bathroom only confirmed Val's feeling that perhaps this

was all a practical joke of Madge's, and she had actually wandered into a bordello.

"Well, there it is," Mr. Wellstrom declared proudly, "my own contribution to furthering the evolution of the human race."

What could he be talking about—the all-red bathroom? She glanced at Andrew, who gave a barely perceptible shake of his head, confessing his own confusion.

Wellstrom noticed their uncertainty. "The *tub*, Mrs. Cummings—you won't find anything like it anyplace except where I've installed it myself—I'm not just an inventor, I'm also a plumber. How much more a honeymoon can mean, when people can make love . . . while getting clean. What do you think?"

He took their momentary speechlessness for a lack of observation. "Well, don't you see? It's heart-shaped. Nobody ever thought of that before, the heart-shaped tub, not a living soul. I've even got a patent pending."

"A patent, really . . . ?" Val said. Wellstrom's enthusiasm for his own creation was curiously infectious. Perhaps there was something more unusual here than she'd recognized at first.

"Oh, yes," the innkeeper went on, "the government recognizes how special this achievement is, even if the rest of the world is slow to appreciate it." He paused thoughtfully. "Could be I'm just a little ahead of my time. Took the Wright brothers a while before people shared their vision, didn't it?" He gave Val a modest smile. "Or could be I just need to spread the word a little farther and wider. That's why I got so excited when I heard about your new magazine, Mrs. Cummings. I knew it was just the thing to bring the business flooding in. Write this up in your magazine and young lovers will beat a path to my door, see that this is their honeymoon dream come true."

Val pondered. She couldn't promise space in her pages to this bizarre notion, yet Wellstrom was so endearingly devoted to the cause of love that she felt it would be like Scrooge calling Christmas humbug if she did anything to discourage him.

"I'm surprised you need publicity, Mr. Wellstrom," Andrew

put in. "I'd imagine all the happy honeymooners who've stayed here would pass the word along."

"We get recommended, sure. But I just finished these new honeymoon suites a couple of months ago, and winter's always a slow time, so there's only a handful of guests who've tried it so far. Tell you the truth, I'm not sure all those young folks really understood it. My idea was to help put them in the mood, y'know. Honeymoon's a time when a guy and gal are feeling shy with each other, and I figured a thing like this . . . getting them to step into a kind of fantasy, would be a help to shaking off their whatchamacallits—habitations?"

"Inhibitions," Andrew offered.

"Yup. It's natural to be slowed down by those inhibitions on a wedding night, and they need something to get over that hurdle, right? I thought this'd kick 'em right over."

Val regarded Wellstrom with growing appreciation. There was, after all, a basic down-home wisdom behind his observations and impulses. She was no longer quite so inclined to dismiss his vision as simply ridiculous.

"Problem is," he continued, "I may have gone just a bit too far. I guess some people could look at this the wrong way, see it as"—his voice fell nearly to a whisper—"too much like a place of . . . ill repute, if you know what I mean. But enough of my sales talk. You folks must want to get settled, relax a bit. Maybe take a bath, eh? Got no other guests right now, so we'll have dinner anytime you're ready—Mrs. Wellstrom's home cooking!"

He gave Andrew a second key for the adjacent room, and left.

The moment he was gone, Val was seized by the sort of tension she expected she'd be feeling if this were her honeymoon. Here she was with Andrew, their relationship delicately poised to move to another plateau, and they were virtually imprisoned in a place that insisted they set aside gentle courtship and jump with lightning speed straight into a fever of carnal passion.

"We don't have to stay," she said.

"I'll leave if that's what you want," he said. "But you know, I doubt I'd ever have another chance in my life to see a place like this . . . and something about this guy Wellstrom tells me he's sincere: He really thinks this is the way to play Cupid."

"I felt that too," Val said.

"Then don't you think a story on that would be right up your alley?"

"I suppose it's worth doing a little more research." She realized how suggestive that sounded only after it was out, but Andrew didn't seem to mind.

Moving close to her, he said, "Why don't we do it together?" He tossed a glance toward the tub. "Start right there . . ." He waited a second, then walked into the bathroom and turned on the taps over the tub.

For only a moment she weighed the question of what he might think of her if she gave in too easily.

As soon as she joined him, sliding the doors shut behind her, he took her into an embrace. The instant she was in his arms, her lips meeting his, she felt unbound from all the restraints and conventions that had shackled her choices for as long as she could remember. All she knew at that moment was that she was glad to be desired again, and to feel desire. Only now she understood that since the rape she had condemned herself and punished herself by believing no man, at least no one as decent as Ted, would want her again.

But Andrew was every bit as good . . . and he did want her.

Matching her passion to his, swept up in a fever of hungry kisses, an urgent need to feel his touch everywhere, they undressed each other and lowered themselves into the water-filled heart. Instantly they were entwined again. She could feel the length of him against her, feel his hardness, yet the enfolding warmth of the water, by itself like a caress, calmed the urgency for a while, and it was enough to hold each other, to go on exploring with lips and hands.

At last the nexus of shared need had become too much to deny any longer. Val opened herself to him so easily, the buoyancy of the water making it seem that she was floating up into him as they were joined. They called to each other in a quickening chorus of whispers as the sensations overtook them, coming faster, bringing them together in a tight, thrashing knot that churned the water around them into waves that splashed everywhere. And as if they were part of the same natural force that whips up an ocean, not merely in a heart-shaped bath, when they came together it was as if a huge wave had crashed down onto a shore, all its inexorable power spent, quiet pools running slowly back to become part of the source.

They lay back in one curve of the heart, Val nestled in his arms. "I'm definitely persuaded that Mr. Wellstrom deserves praise and publicity for his invention," she said.

He stayed quiet a bit, stroking her slowly. "As quick as this happened, Val, I want you to know it doesn't mean any less to me. I've wanted you all along, that's why I stayed near. But just as you kept your friends at a distance before, it seemed you weren't ready. . . ."

"No," she said, "not until today."

"And the way I feel myself, I don't think of this as . . . a passing fancy. In case you haven't guessed it by now, I'm in love with you."

Hearing it thrilled her . . . and frightened her. All this had happened the wrong way around, she realized too late. She should have told him about Teddie before they'd ever made love. How much worse she would feel now if exposing her secret caused him to lose respect for her, turn away.

She must tell him everything. This wasn't the time or place, but she must find the moment soon, before the weekend was over. She turned to look at him, then embraced him tightly, clinging as the possibility of losing his love—just when they had found each other—loomed in her mind.

"What's wrong?" he asked, seeing the distress in her eyes, feeling it in the intensity of her touch.

"What you said just now . . . it made me realize how much you mean to me too. I don't want to lose you, Andrew," she added earnestly.

"Why should you? I just said I love you." He touched her cheek, gently turned her face to his. "Maybe it's crazy to do it now—I mean usually the honeymoon comes after the wedding—but if you really want to make sure I'm yours, perhaps you'd agree to be my—"

"No," she murmured quickly, and laid her fingertips over his lips. She knew it was going to be a proposal, and she couldn't bear even to think about it until she had been completely honest with him. "Not now. Not yet."

He looked puzzled, even a little hurt.

"I do want you though," she said to soothe him. "Make love to me, Andrew. Make love to me all night."

She kissed him then, passionately, and his strong hands slid down along her body while she reached to grasp him below. The feel of their wet skin sliding over each other in warm, soapy water aroused them quickly. She climbed up over him, opening herself, ready to take him in—

Then they became aware of the knocking at the door, not soft, but insistent enough so that the noise penetrated all the way to the bathroom.

Wellstrom's voice called. "Mrs. Cummings . . . are you there . . . ?"

They remained motionless a moment, hoping he'd go away.

But he didn't. "I'm terribly sorry," he called. "They insisted. . . ."

They? Val scrambled out of the tub, wrapped herself in a large towel, and went out into the bedroom. "Yes, I'm here," she called back through the door. "What is it?"

Andrew followed, muttering, "If he crashes in like this on real honeymooners, he'll never have too many customers."

Wellstrom obviously understood what a serious violation he had committed. "Forgive me for busting in on you, Mrs. Cummings," he called from the other side of the door, "I'd never do this ordinarily . . . told 'em you couldn't be bothered, but they ordered me to get you at once." He sounded very upset.

Val pulled the towel closer around her and opened the door a crack. "Who, Mr. Wellstrom, who needs to talk to me?" Whoever it was must have called her home, got this number from Mrs. Falconi.

The innkeeper's eyes shifted from Val to Andrew, standing just behind her, as if he weren't quite sure he should answer her, even in front of the man he believed to be her husband. Then he said, "It's the police—from up in New York. With this kind of thing they waste no time doing whatever they have to do."

"With what kind of thing, Mr. Wellstrom?" Val asked with rising panic.

"Someone's been murdered," he said. "And somehow you're wanted in connection with it."

Thirteen

Standing at the phone in the lobby of The Rainbow Inn, Val shivered violently from the chill of lingering wetness under the clothes she'd thrown on—and the shock of listening to the police detective's report. She might have collapsed at the phone if Andrew hadn't been standing with her. Seeing her slump, he threw a steadying arm around her.

It wasn't simply a murder, Val was told, but murder-suicide: After stabbing his wife to death late last night in the kitchen of their home, Sean MacMoran had gotten behind the wheel of his car, a vacuum cleaner hose attached to the exhaust pipe and fed back through a window. A neighbor had noticed the car sitting in the driveway, the lifeless body in the driver's seat, when he went out early this morning for his newspaper.

Val remembered Josie telling her that Sean had threatened to kill himself if she ever tried to leave him. He'd only left out that he planned to kill her too.

Painful as it all was to hear, there was one mercy: Mandy had apparently slept through the fatal argument, was still asleep in her bed, unharmed, when the police arrived. In sifting through Josie's belongings, they had come upon a sealed envelope marked To Whom It May Concern. Inside was a letter Josie had penned herself, dated several weeks earlier. It was the letter that had made the police call Val. The man on the phone, a detective named Connelly, read the letter aloud to her:

"It also starts off To Whom It May Concern, then Mrs. MacMoran writes: 'I hereby express my wish that if my husband is responsible for anything happening to me that makes it impossible for me to care for my child, Amanda, then Valentina

Cummings has my permission to take care of Amanda for so long as I am unable to do so.' That's all, Miss Cummings. Did you know about this?"

"She'd asked me to take care of Mandy if . . . she wasn't able to, but I didn't know she'd written it down."

"Seems like she was expecting something bad to happen. . . ."

How much had Josie known? Val wondered. Whatever dark fears motivated her to extract her promise surely didn't include the possibility that her daughter would be left without either parent. Yet that was the case. "Where is the little girl now?" Val asked. "I should be with her."

"That isn't necessary," the detective said.

"But isn't that why you're calling?" Val said. "That poor child must be terribly bewildered and frightened. . . ."

"The Department of Social Services has responsibility for the girl, Miss Cummings. They'll decide the most appropriate way to deal with her."

Social Services? Val had a vision of anonymous matrons in uniforms leaving Mandy to sit in drab, lonely rooms. "This is a *child*, Detective, she needs more than 'dealing with' at a time like this. For heaven's sake, you've got the letter. It's her mother's wish—her dying wish, as it turns out, that I'm to—"

The policeman cut her off. "It's not that simple, Miss Cummings. There are blood relatives too, but in a situation like this, even they may not be allowed to take the child."

"I thought you called me because of the letter."

"That's right. It indicates you're her closest friend. We figured you could tell us why Mrs. MacMoran was killed."

Val sighed deeply. If she had to guess, Josie had finally told Sean she was leaving him, taking Mandy, and he wouldn't stand for it. "I doubt anyone could explain it," Val told the detective. "But I suppose I can give you some information."

He must have heard the strain in her voice, the shivering effort not to fall apart. "No need to say more now. But come in as soon as possible, and tell us whatever you know."

"I'll come now," she said.

It wasn't to help them understand that Val felt she was

racing the clock; she had made a promise to Josie. Every second that passed until it was kept would be measured in the suffering of an innocent child.

Andrew drove her back to the city. Along the way, he made gentle inquiries about Josie and her history with Val—not prying, Val understood, only thinking that talking might ease her distress more than bottling up her feelings. Yet the trauma of having to deal with the horrible death of her friend left Val unable to cope with any additional upset that might be caused by revealing too much of her own past. She did explain to Andrew why the police had called her, and then talked about Josie, but without revealing the genesis of their friendship, or making any reference to Teddie.

"I got to know her when I first came to New York," Val said. "We were both living in Brooklyn then. Later, when I was trying to save money, she let me live with her for a while. That's when I got to know her husband too. I saw the marriage was bad, and tried to get Josie to face it, do something about it. But he threw me out. I moved back to the city and tried to stay in touch with her, but it didn't work. She was too afraid . . . not just of him, but of trying to make a life alone, without him."

"It's terrible that she couldn't save herself," Andrew said. "It does seem that she knew what the end would be when she wrote that letter. Do you think you'll be able to manage taking care of her child? It'll mean a tremendous change in your life."

He was talking, of course, as if she'd had no experience caring for a child. And she might have said it right there: *not so big a change, I already have one, I can manage one more.*

But she let the moment go by. In a few days, she promised herself, after the emotional hurricane of Josie's death had subsided, she would be able to choose the right words, tell the whole truth, and have the emotional resilience to absorb the consequences. But there was no way she could do it just now.

It was past eight o'clock in the evening when they approached New York. Val told Andrew to bring her to the train station, she would go the rest of the way to Long Island alone.

"I'm not going to leave you alone now, Val."

"Listen, I could be with the police in Levittown for an hour or two. Then I've got to try and see Josie's little girl."

"All the more reason for me to stay with you."

She couldn't tell half-truths to the police. Letting him come ran the risk of having him find out everything. But he insisted on driving her to Long Island, at least.

When they got to the police station, she asked him to let her go inside alone. Though puzzled by the request, Andrew agreed rather than do anything to upset Val's obviously precarious equilibrium.

For more than an hour she answered questions about the MacMorans. When the men interviewing her said they were finished, Val declared that she wanted to see Mandy. The ranking officer on duty was brought in to repeat what Val had been told earlier: Josie's daughter was in the custody of the authorities and being well cared for. Val wouldn't be allowed to see her until certain formalities had been observed.

"How the hell can you put formalities ahead of this child's heart and soul?" Val appealed. "Right now she should be with someone she knows and loves. I'm the person her mother *wanted* her to be with. I gave my word I'd be there when I was needed!"

"I understand how you feel, Miss Cummings. But there's a grandfather who has a priority, no matter what you or Mrs. MacMoran wanted. For that matter, we don't even know if Mrs. MacMoran was in her right mind when she wrote down her wishes. All of that has to be investigated."

"And while it's 'investigated,' " Val said bitterly, "that child's heart is breaking."

"She's with good people," the police officer assured Val. "Go home now, Miss Cummings. Get some rest, and I'm sure you'll be allowed to visit the child soon."

Val was too drained to protest further.

Andrew was waiting outside with the car. Exhausted, on the ride home Val put her head back and tried to sleep. But all the way to the city, she debated with herself whether to confess all that she had been concealing from him. Right before the awful news about Josie had arrived, he'd been on the brink of proposing marriage. In the glow of making love, she had also been sure she loved him. But her mind was in such a muddle, she wasn't sure when it would ever be right to accept such a proposal. Josie had been sure, once, that she loved Sean MacMoran. She had to know Andrew Winston better before they could enter a lifetime partnership—one that could involve his being father to not one, but *two* children who weren't his own. He had to know her better too. What were the chances he'd even finish his proposal once he knew all that marriage to her would mean?

Before taking even a small step toward confession, she decided to test the solidity of the ground. They had crossed the Brooklyn Bridge into Lower Manhattan, when she said, "Can I ask you something very personal, Andrew?"

"Anything."

"It's about your sister—the one whose invitations I knocked out of your hands."

He chuckled lightly. "Lucky, wasn't it?"

She went on soberly. "There was talk around the print shop that those invitations had to be done faster than usual . . . so the wedding could be held that much sooner, because—"

He erupted. "Because it was a shotgun wedding. Is that what you want to know? If it was true? Well, if it makes a difference to you, yes, Justine was—what's the popular term?—knocked up. Four months pregnant when she married. What about it?"

The passing shadows of the bridge cables flickered over his face, accentuating his angry expression, making it seem even more demonic. But Val continued to probe methodically.

"I imagine it was very hard on your family. . . ."

"Hell, yes. Do you think it wouldn't be? In a family like ours, those things aren't supposed to happen, are they? Remember once when you and I talked about that wedding, how I said it was too much of a show? It was partly to cover up my parents' shame—putting on the dog, acting as if everything was all right. That was one of the main reasons I hated it—though I didn't tell you *that* at the time. . . ."

She nodded, thinking now that the debate was over, her course was clear. She could never tell him about Teddie and still expect to marry him. His family had bent the rules for a daughter of their own—as long as they were marrying her off. But they would never bend them far enough to accept an outsider and her bastard child. And now there would be Mandy, too, orphaned by a murder-suicide.

Andrew glanced from the road to give her a hard look. "So that makes a difference to you, does it? You don't want to be mixed up in a family that might be the target of a little nasty gossip."

His misunderstanding was so topsy-turvy that all she could do was stare at him with her mouth open. And when a sound finally emerged, it was half laugh and half gasp. "It doesn't matter to me. All I wanted to know was how it affected you."

"Me? I was just glad when it all died down and was forgotten. It was so hard on my mother and father. Frankly, I think they actually lost friends because of it—people who cut them, and whose gossip was too cruel to forgive."

"I see," Val said. "That must've been very difficult for them."

"Terrible. But it's over now, thank God."

Over. Val knew she never would be the one to put them or Andrew through it again.

It was nearing midnight, but on a mild Saturday night in Little Italy there were still people strolling, cafés and small grocery stores open late. Val asked him to stop on Mulberry Street, at the corner of the block where she lived. "You can leave me here, Andrew. I want to buy a few things before I go home." Baby food, but she wouldn't tell him that.

He came around the car to open the door for her. "You're sure you don't want me to stay with you?"

"I'll be fine now."

For a second they stood on the curb, facing each other. It should have been so easy to kiss, except that the tragedy smothered all passion. Josie's tragedy—and the end of a love just begun.

"We were going to have such a beautiful time together," he said. "It's such a shame this had to happen. But don't let it completely erase what was good, Val. I mean, when we were together, it was wonderful. And I meant everything I said. . . ."

"I won't forget, Andrew."

"Right now I know you have other things to deal with, but I'd like to help any way I can. And in a while we can pick up where we left off. Next week maybe you could come and meet my parents. I know they'll love you too."

As long as they don't think I might drag in more scandal, lose them some more friends. "I can't make those plans now," she told him.

"I understand."

He bent to kiss her, and she turned slightly to offer her cheek. She wanted his kiss—but knew it would be better to start right away getting used to never feeling his lips again.

"I'll talk to you in the morning," he said as she turned to walk away. He had said earlier that he would escort her to Josie's funeral if she wanted.

"I may be out," she called back. "Trying to see Josie's little girl."

"I'll just keep calling until I connect with you. . . ."

At the foot of the stairs to her apartment, she spent a minute in tears, mourning for the love she'd surrendered. Then she thought of Teddie's darling face waiting to greet her when she got home. And she thought of Mandy, waiting to have her own grief mended.

The tears stopped coming. There were much more important things to attend to now than her own broken heart.

Two mornings later, Val stood at a grave site in a Brooklyn cemetery along with a handful of other mourners. As the priest intoned the burial rites of the Catholic service, Val whispered her own solemn message to Josie's spirit.

"I'm sorry, Jos . . . I don't want to let you down, and I'll keep trying . . . but see if you can give me a little help from up there."

During the past two days, Val's persistent efforts to see Mandy had been rebuffed. The little girl was in the care of experienced foster parents, Val was told by the child welfare agency, and would stay until the best course for her was determined. When Val asked where to reach Mandy—even for a phone call—she was refused the information. She had screamed furiously then at the caseworker, and was passed to an agency psychiatric worker.

"I understand this is hard for you, Miss Cummings," he'd said, "and I'm sure you have the best interest of the child at heart. But from our point of view, it's not as easy as simply turning the child over to you. There are legal procedures that must be followed. . . ."

Having been kept away from Mandy, Val half hoped that she might see her at the cemetery, yet she understood when the child did not appear. Apparently the authorities had deemed it too traumatic.

The one other mourner, an elderly white-haired man with a ruddy face, Val assumed to be Josie's only immediate family survivor aside from Mandy, her father.

As the burial service ended and the few mourners dispersed, Val went over to Tom Duffy to offer her condolences.

"Mr. Duffy," she began. "I'm—

Before she could say her name, he bellowed at her, "I know who y'are, miss, and you best know right now, I ain't ever gonna let you take that kid away from me. I've lost everyone else; she's all that's left of my blood, and I'm not going to give her up, 'specially not to no scarlet woman. Understand? Never!"

"Mr. Duffy," Val said sympathetically, "I don't want to take her away from you. I just want to keep a promise I made to Josie that I'd give Mandy the same care and love her mother gave her. But it doesn't mean you won't still be her grandfather, spend all the time with her you want. I'd never do anything to cut Mandy off from what's left of her family."

"She's not your blood," he said gruffly, "so there's no damn reason she should be with you. No damn reason at all." He turned on his heel and walked away.

But there *was* a reason, Val thought as she watched him go, one that had been instantly apparent when the poor man bellowed and she could smell the liquor coming from him. Josie's father had every right to be upset today, but his heavy drinking in midmorning was obviously more than a rare attempt to dull the pain. Val remembered Josie mentioning that her father's turn from a controlled social drinker to an alcoholic stemmed from the wartime deaths of both her brothers.

Unfortunately, the implacable figure of justice not only wore a blindfold, it had no sense of smell. Two days after the funeral, Mandy was delivered into the hands of her grandfather. Like the welfare agency, Mr. Duffy seemed determined to keep Val from his granddaughter. Val called his house in Red Hook a few times, but he answered the first calls by roughly declaring that Mandy had no desire to speak to her, before he banged down the phone. Later on he simply hung up as soon as he heard her voice.

Finally, Val stopped calling. Surely Mr. Duffy loved the child, would do the best he could for her. With all that Mandy had suffered already, would it be right to put her in the middle of another battle? And for now she already had one child of her own to worry about.

She was the last one left in the office the following Tuesday evening when Andrew walked in briskly and confronted her. It had been more than a week since she'd seen him last. She had made curt excuses to get off the phone quickly whenever he called, which wasn't very often since he had evidently been busy piloting a full schedule of cargo flights.

"What's going on, Val?" he asked with more than a hint of anger. "A week ago we were—well, maybe it was a dream, but I thought we'd . . . found each other. Suddenly you won't talk to me. I know it's been a rough time for you, but all I wanted to do was help. Why are you avoiding me?"

She took her time, sorting through all the possible tactics for defusing the situation. At last she said, "I care for you, Andrew. You've done more for me than anyone else ever has. So the least I can do for you . . . is keep your life free of unwanted complications."

"What are you talking about? Is this something to do with your friend's murder?"

"Not only that."

"What, then?"

She paused, then made the decision. "I was just leaving," she said. "Come home with me tonight." She had never asked him home before, never allowed him. But simply letting him see her baby would be the quickest, easiest way to make her explanation—and discover if there was the least chance he'd still want her.

"I can't tonight," he said. "I was on my way to the airport. In fact, I've got to fly cargo to St. Louis—but this was eating at me so much, I had to get it off my chest before I climbed into another cockpit. I've been thinking about you so much, I'm not even sure it doesn't affect my judgment, make it dangerous for me to be up there in the clouds. . . ."

"All the more reason we should clear it up now." For herself, she knew if it didn't happen tonight, she'd resume avoiding him.

"All right," he said. He moved to a desk and grabbed the phone there. "I'll see if I can get someone to take over my flight."

Atlas Air had an office in New York and a depot at LaGuardia Airport. The office was closed, but the desks at the airport were still manned. It was Nate Palmer who picked up the phone. He had arrived not long before, having completed a round trip to Pittsburgh. Andrew told him that he was looking for a pilot to substitute for him.

Listening to Andrew's end of the conversation, Val could tell that Nate himself had volunteered.

"I don't know, pal," Andrew said. "You're just coming off duty. I hate to make you turn right around. Isn't one of the other guys available?"

Evidently there was no one else, and Nate was insisting.

Andrew hesitated, looking thoughtfully at Val. "Okay, buddy, thanks," he said at last. "I owe you one. See you tomorrow."

They hardly spoke as Andrew drove her home. She felt he was angry for making him change his plans—or perhaps he thought of it as deserting his duty—and for keeping secrets in the first place. But she wasn't apologetic. Not yet anyway. Only when he saw Teddie would she know if she'd been right or wrong in the decisions she'd made.

He had never actually been to her building before, and as they climbed the stairs in the dingy hallway, she could tell that the first shock for him was to see she lived in conditions so different from his accustomed luxury.

She opened the door of her apartment with the key and entered, Andrew following close behind. Immediately through the door was the small living room that also contained the dining table. Mrs. Falconi was at the table, feeding the baby her evening meal. Pleased at seeing Val with an attractive man, she smiled at them.

"*Buona sera,*" she said.

"Hi, Mrs. Falconi. This is Mr. Winston."

Andrew nodded at her, but his eyes were on the baby. Val went to lift Teddie out of the high chair into her arms, then came back to him.

"She's mine, Andrew." She paused to read the shock on his face. "How much more do you want to know?"

He groped for words. ". . . The man you were going to marry, the one who—"

"No," she said. "I wish it were his."

"But, then . . ."

"Does it really matter who? You told me how hard your own sister's 'trouble' was for your family. Would you have wanted to be involved with me at all if you'd known about this from the start? Can you still want to 'bring me home to mother'?" She gave the last question a bitter twist.

He ran his fingers through his hair, turned one way and the other, clearly in torment.

Realizing she was in the middle of a wrangle, Mrs. Falconi had risen from the table, picked up some dishes, and moved quietly into the kitchen.

Andrew faced Val again. "Listen, I won't lie to you, this knocks me for a loop. But I . . . I do love you, Val. And I don't feel myself falling out of love right this minute because this isn't turning out to be a perfect fairy tale. Fairy tales and Prince

Charmings may be the stuff that sells your magazine, but hardly real life. So just give me a chance to get used to this. Then maybe we can iron things out."

"Maybe," she repeated. "But you're not sure, are you?"

He looked at her bleakly, unable to answer.

"I don't know if that's the kind of love I want," Val said, moving closer to him. "Or that's best for my daughter. A love that has to have wrinkles ironed out, that has to be trimmed around the edges to make it fit, a love you'll always have to defend against the attacks and snide remarks of other people who are closest to you. And," she added, "if I love you too, I don't think I can ask you to make the sacrifices."

"Dammit, Val," he answered now. "We don't have to draw the line here and now. Give me time."

"Time is something you can take for yourself. When you have, if you want me, you know you can always find me. Then we'll see if I still want you."

He stood for another few seconds, searching for words that might shine a new light on their dark prospects. But then he went to the door and opened it. Before going out, he turned and looked back at Val, the baby in her arms. Val saw the shine of tears in his eyes. Then he was gone.

At the sound of the door closing, Mrs. Falconi emerged from the kitchen. "I think-a he come back," she said quietly, moving up behind Val. "He look like a good man, sound like he really love you. That-a one, he come back soon."

Tomorrow, Val thought, might be soon enough.

The next day went by without a call from him, then the day after. Her thoughts kept going back to the plea he had made: *Give me time . . . a chance. . . .* With the passage of a few days, she began to see her own actions in a harsher light. She had kept a secret, then sprung it on him—as abruptly as springing a trap. It was her fear as much as his that had caused the rupture.

And she didn't want to lose him.

On the third day she called the office of Atlas Air in New York and asked to speak to Andrew.

"I'm sorry, he's not here," a secretary said.

"When is he expected?"

"I don't know. He hasn't been in the last few days."

That touched her. She imagined him lost, hurt, trying to come to terms with their situation. "Is Mr. Palmer available?" she asked. Nate was his closest friend, perhaps he would be able to advise her.

The secretary's somber voice broke through her thoughts. "Obviously you haven't heard. Mr. Palmer died Tuesday night."

"Died—?"

"His plane crashed." There was a pause. "He was taking over a flight for Mr. Winston at the last minute. They said the crash was due to pilot error, that Mr. Palmer was tired. That's why Mr. Winston hasn't been in. He feels—"

Val lowered the phone into the cradle without listening to the rest. She didn't need to be told what he felt. Because she had kept her secrets, because she had demanded he learn them when and how she wanted, his friend had died. Did he blame her? Even if he didn't, he must blame himself. Either way, it put one more burden on his heart, and made their reconciliation too hard.

This chance for love was gone forever too, she knew—this one, ironically, not because the man she loved had died, but because he had lived.

Fourteen

New York
Autumn 1955

A hired accordionist played the wedding march, and the five-tiered frosted wedding cake was wheeled into the reception area for Val to make the first cut. No marriage was being celebrated, however. The ceremony was merely a way of recognizing the source of *Every Bride's* healthy success on its fifth birthday.

To mark the occasion, Val had moved the magazine into new offices, a full floor in a building on Madison Avenue. Nearby buildings housed many of the other magazines—*Life*, *Look*, *Collier's*—that were currently the third most popular form of entertainment for Americans after movies and radio. Being at the center of the nation's advertising and magazine businesses, Val could feel that *E.B.*—as all the insiders called it—had truly *arrived.*

For the past several weeks the staff, numbering seventy-four, had been shifting operations from smaller offices farther downtown. Now the move was complete; time to celebrate. Val stood by the imposing desk; she was dressed in a long-skirted beige Dior suit, one of the luxuries on which she had only recently begun to spend her sizable salary. As she cut the cake, the staff cheered, then lined up quickly to get a slice with a glass of champagne to take back to their desks. Valentina Cummings was revered as a generous and inspiring boss, but it was well known she had little patience for idle partying, and rewarded only the hardest workers.

Passing the knife over to one of the secretaries to continue doling out the cake, Val started back to her own office. Madge Truesdale fell in beside her as they went down a long corridor.

"How soon before we have to move again?" Madge asked wryly.

Val laughed. "This time I think I've been brave enough."

"Well, I'm hoping for at least a couple of years," Madge said just before she peeled off through the door to the separate suite she now occupied as director of advertising. "I'm getting back strain from packing up my desk so often."

It was the fourth move to new headquarters in the past five years. Unable to foresee how quickly the business would grow, the past three times Val had leased only enough space for modest expansion, and within months everyone was crowded again. The wedding ceremony might be as ancient as history itself, the desire of man and woman to form a permanent bond as much a part of the human biological imperative as the urge to perpetuate the species, yet the new era of optimism that came with the restoration of freedom in Europe had brought a surge of appreciation for the old traditions beyond what anyone could have predicted. With it had come a boom in the commercialization of everything to do with brides. More dress companies were producing ready-made gowns, more diamond engagement rings were being sold, more fathers of middle-class daughters were saving for more expensive weddings—and more people wanted advice about all of it. The modest printing of 35,000 copies of that first April issue five years earlier had sold out. At the end of the first year, each issue was selling over 90,000 copies at fifty cents each, and ad revenue was climbing rapidly. The next year Val raised circulation more cautiously, but switched to a bimonthly schedule, six issues annually instead of three.

Though a boom in the bridal business could be attributed to a mushrooming of American optimism in general, Val believed that one fairly recent event had, more than any other, imprinted the beauty and romance of the formal wedding on the public mind. In September 1952, a young woman named Jacqueline Bouvier had married the youngest U.S. senator,

Jack Kennedy, in a formal ceremony held at her stepfather's estate in Newport. Because Kennedy was a dashing figure—with a rich father eager to spend his fortune to make his son president someday—the wedding had been arranged to garner wide coverage in the news. From her own sources, Val knew the bride's mother had wanted a small family event, but the Kennedys had won out, and used the wedding as the first phase in a campaign to implant images of the young couple in the national consciousness as a kind of royalty waiting to be crowned. Three thousand spectators had thronged the church in Newport. *Life* had been there to photograph the event, and pictures of the lovely twenty-four-year-old bride in her long lace mantilla had been seen everywhere, igniting the desire of young women across the country to copy the image. Whether or not Jack Kennedy would ever become president, Val was grateful for the boost his marriage to Jacqueline Bouvier had given her own enterprise. Circulation for the issue following the wedding had leapt another 60,000, and had gone on climbing since.

In the new offices, Val had made sure there was ample space in which to keep expanding. She had realized at last that the market for the prime commodities she was selling—romance and dreams—could only grow bigger. As the world became more complex, love would be the most enduring source of comfort. And a bride was the eternal living symbol of ideal romantic love at its purest moment.

But she didn't rely solely on gut instinct to gauge the potential for growth of her business. Even before the Kennedy wedding, Val had detailed one young woman to do research into the trends in marriage by gathering statistics from marriage bureaus in the largest urban centers, and selected rural sites, monitoring sales of gowns at the best stores, checking regularly with major hotels and the developing chains on the size and number of wedding receptions being booked, polling department stores to learn which wedding gifts were most popular. This information added up to a profile of national trends in marriage, and the research could be broken down to tell how much was spent on each and every aspect of the average wedding: The total figure now spent on each of the 60,000-odd formal celebrations annually was up to $3,500 and climbing, more than double the cost of a family automobile.

Originally, Val collected and analyzed these details to use them as a tool in assessing the potential of her own business. But it didn't take long to realize it would all be useful to advertisers. Providing them with reports on the state of the wedding business soon became a separate, lucrative service. *E.B.*'s research department now consisted of eight people. As the magazine's circulation mounted steadily, the tens of thousands of monthly readers became a valuable source of information in themselves, their letters and the questions they asked indicative of the way tastes were developing. Being in a position to provide an overview of the bridal market to both the buyers and sellers was beginning to make *Every Bride's* itself a pivotal influence in the market. Whatever dress was chosen for a model to wear on the cover of an issue—a choice that Val always made personally—was bound to be ordered by hundreds of readers within days of publication. The bridal bouquet the cover bride held would be duplicated exactly by florists in dozens of cities and towns.

As the magazine thrived, some of the original group of backers took an opportunity Val offered to give them a sizable profit, selling their shares for several times their investment. In the third year, Val bought out Phil Longworth and Frank Storrow for $35,000 each—by itself more than the entire original capitalization; in the fourth year Andrew Winston's uncle Charles was happy to sell his share for $60,000. Val borrowed heavily to finance the transactions, using her own shares as equity for the banks, but she had no doubt it would be wise to buy them all out if she could. She also wanted to obtain the shares held by Andrew and Nate Palmer—but that had presented more of a problem. Andrew not only managed his own shares, but as Nate wasn't married at the time he died, Andrew had been named executor of his estate.

They had not talked since the night she had brought him home to see Teddie. The long letter of sympathy and apology she had sent to his office after Nate's death had been answered—but only by a printed form of the kind used to answer the general outpouring of condolences that came to a company when it lost one of its leaders. In its way, it said enough.

Her one other attempt to communicate since had involved the magazine business. She had sent letters offering to buy both Andrew's shares and Nate's—at amounts that increased each year. She also sent annual reports of the magazine's financial results.

There was never a reply.

As she returned to her office that morning, the first order of business was to decide which of six gowns would appear on the cover of the issue currently in preparation—for four months hence. The gowns under consideration were draped on mannequins that stood at one end of the office.

Val found it impossible to concentrate on the decision. All she could think of was that those six forms facing her looked like the front row of a jury, waiting to judge her. She turned from the gowns, went to her desk, and quickly placed a phone call.

"What's the decision?" she said when she got through.

"None yet," said the man on the other end of the line. "The judge has delayed his ruling."

Val's stomach felt instantly as though it had turned to molten lead. This was almost worse than hearing that the ruling had gone against her. "Again?" she said in despair. "I can't believe it."

"The other side sent word at the last minute that they were bringing in new facts relating to the case."

The man on the other end of the line was Gary Felsen, a lawyer who for a good part of the past five years had handled Val's attempt to obtain custody of Amanda MacMoran. Last night he had not only assured Val that the decision would finally be handed down today, but that this time all indications were that it would be in her favor.

"What new facts?" she asked wearily.

"I don't know yet. Whatever they have will be spelled out in legal papers I'll get later this morning. Call me after lunch."

Val hung up. Outside her office, she could hear the voices of her staff, excited as they trickled back from the gathering that marked yet another high point in the magazine's constant upward graph of success. But at that moment she felt lower than she had at any time since the day she'd received the news of Josie's murder. *New facts?* Which way would they swing the decision this time? Even if it came down in her favor, how much longer would it take? A week, a month? Or another year . . . ? After five years, how much damage had already been done to poor Mandy?

In the beginning, certain that Mandy's primary need in the wake of the traumatic loss of both parents was to recover some sense of security, Val had stepped back rather than put the little girl at the center of a battle for custody. She could only pray that Tom Duffy's love for his granddaughter would impel him to remain sober and responsible.

But two months after Duffy had taken charge of Mandy, one of his neighbors reported to social services that the child was being left unattended night after night while Duffy sat in a local bar. A social worker came to check the report, found the old man drunk, and returned Mandy to foster care. Even though Duffy had forbidden her access, Val had continued to check regularly on Mandy's progress, and when she learned of these developments she engaged a lawyer and renewed her efforts to have Josie's express wishes fulfilled.

The initial hearings went against Val on every count. The very promise she was fighting to fulfill made her suspect in the eyes of the authorities. If Josie MacMoran had felt endangered enough to extract a pledge from Val, why had Val done nothing more to help her friend? If she was so ineffective in saving a woman's life, was she qualified to be a child's guardian? Added to that, she was a single parent, and there wasn't enough room in her apartment to take in another child.

Val had no difficulty solving this last problem. With her increased earnings, she was able to move quickly to a spacious four-bedroom apartment in an old elevator building on upper Riverside Drive. This even provided a place for Mrs. Falconi to stay when necessary. Although the widow had been happily taking care of Teddie for years, she still refused to give up her old tenement flat in Little Italy.

To counter the absence of a blood relationship, the best Val could do was present a sworn affidavit of her willingness to legally adopt Mandy.

That left the matter of marital status. Over the past few years, Val had met a number of attractive men through business who had been interested in her and asked her out; she had tried to be open to their advances. But none had come close to engaging her emotions. It seemed possible that the earlier heartbreaks had left a scar, hardened her so she would never love again. Aware that if only she could find a partner it would ease all her battles, she longed to be married. Yet she refused to take wedding vows merely as a strategy in a courtroom battle. To marry for that reason alone might result in a marriage that failed quickly, destabilizing Teddie's life and bringing Mandy into one more home that fell apart.

Mandy went on living in foster care—though she was moved through a few homes because, visiting social workers reported, she continued to have trouble adjusting. What she didn't want to adjust to, of course, was not living with Val.

At last Val obtained the right to make visits, and thereafter, throughout the child's pathetic odyssey, Val managed to remain the one constant, visiting Mandy wherever she lived, assuring her that someday the absurd decision to keep them apart would have to be changed. Miraculously, Mandy retained the sweetness and essential balance that had stamped her personality when Val first knew her. Her strong character simply fought back against being demolished by events that would have left other children in permanent despair. But a linchpin of hope for her was that Val would be able—someday—to keep her word.

It was nearly two years after Josie's death when Val's growing income finally allowed her to hire Felsen, recommended as the top specialist in family law.

"I don't care how much it costs or what it takes," she instructed him, "just keep going back to court, appeal every decision—go all the way to the Supreme Court if you have to—but I have a promise to keep, a sacred vow. I may have let Josie down in the past, but I'm not going to do it again."

That had been three years before. If the ordeal could only have ended now, even with all the trauma and disappointment Mandy had suffered, Val believed she had a good chance to come through as a basically happy person.

But if the ordeal went on . . . if the promise was broken . . .

Val took the leather chair across the desk from Gary Felsen, who sat with a closed file folder in front of him. She could never enter the presence of this rumpled bear of a man who smoked too many cigarettes and drank too much coffee without a moment of amazement that his field of expertise was family law. With his sturdy build and thatch of unruly gray hair, he looked like a brawler who should be defending murderers or negotiating at union tables. In fact, it probably took substantial brawling to carve out and refine a new area of law, as he was trying to do. The idea that children had rights—that Mandy should have a say in where she was allowed to spend her life—was all but revolutionary. Yet this was what he saw at the heart of the case, even beyond Val's desire or Josie's "bequest" of her child. It was the principle that had driven him to fight tirelessly on Val's behalf since she had come to him—taking a fourth of his usual fee once he saw his bill climbing to the tens of thousands.

"Well . . . ?" Val asked nervously. In the call she had made after lunch, he had not told her the details behind the latest delay. Instead, he'd said, "I think it would be best if you came right over here." That had been ten minutes earlier, as long as it took for a cab ride from her office to his.

Felsen's very pale blue eyes bored into Val. "Do you know a man named William Gruening?" he asked.

Staring back into the lawyer's eyes, Val felt suddenly as if she had fallen into a place so cold, she was instantly turned to ice. "William?" she said. "I guess that's what he calls himself now. When I knew him, his name was Wil*helm* Gruening."

"Would you like to tell me how you knew him?"

She was jumping out of her skin. "Don't treat me like I'm in court, Gary. You've got a file there that probably explains how I know him. Just tell me why he's been brought into this."

He tapped his finger on the file folder in front of him. "Val, you've waged a long uphill fight to become the guardian of your murdered friend's child. Because you're unmarried—already raising one child—it's been tough to justify to the authorities. But you've made great strides in the past few years, demonstrated with your remarkable success that you're the one woman in a thousand who can probably be both mother *and father* to two kids. Up to this morning you'd earned the sympathy of our judge." He opened the folder and riffled through a couple of pages. "One thing that helped tremendously was your explanation that the man you planned to marry died in an accident during our occupation of Germany, and after his death you learned you were pregnant with his child. Investigators found the name of your fiancé, *Theodore* Gruening, in the war files, and a record of his death. They didn't look any deeper than that—and neither did I. We were all prepared to take your sworn statement. Until now." The lawyer fixed his eyes on Val. "Because this other Mr. Gruening, who says he's the brother of the man you would have married, claims that he is, in fact, the father of your child. On examination, Teddie's age tallies with his version of events—not yours."

Val took a breath, gathering herself. "Why should that change things? I've admitted from the beginning that my child was born out of wedlock."

"It matters if you lied in sworn statements made to the court."

She looked off through a window at the jagged skyline. Easy to say now that the lie had been rash and foolish—except that she had known it was important to put the most sympathetic slant on her situation, and it would look so much better if it was believed that the child's father had fought in the war, died while doing service for his country. So much better than if she'd become pregnant in one night spent with a shiftless nonentity.

"How did Willy get involved?" she asked. Her use of the familiar name was a signal to her lawyer that the new version of events was the truth, though she wasn't ready to admit perjury.

"I don't know. But the case has been going on a long time. He might have gotten wind of the state investigators looking into your background and come forward to volunteer his information."

If Willy had named himself the father, then surely he'd also had to tell some lies; he couldn't have admitted to being a rapist. "What other information did he provide?" she asked.

"That's the most serious part. He says you took the child away, and kept her away from him without his knowledge or permission. Strictly speaking, it could be called kidnapping."

It burst out of her now. "Gary, he *raped* me. But I was sure no one would believe me then—I was lonely, he was the brother of the man I'd loved, there were no witnesses—"

"I understand, Val. He could have claimed you lured him on."

"Yes! So when I found out I was pregnant, I ran. The child wasn't born when I left. Is that kidnapping—to run away with an unborn baby? Willy couldn't have known about Teddie until lately—learned the same way he found out about this case."

"It's rotten luck that he did, Val. But what it means is that until his claims are cleared up, you won't get Mandy. And if they aren't knocked down, if they're substantiated . . ." He didn't say the obvious: that all hope of winning in the future would be gone.

"What can I do?" she asked in despair.

"Only one thing that I can think of . . ."

"Tell me."

"Get Mr. Gruening to withdraw his claims."

"How?"

"How*ever*! Write to him. Speak to him. Hell, beg him if you have to. Just do whatever you can to—"

"No," she broke in, "I couldn't." A letter or a call wouldn't accomplish the task anyway. If she had the least hope of changing his mind, she would have to go to him, throw herself on his mercy. But she couldn't bear the thought of facing Willy, much less to plead with him for anything.

"Think about it, Val," Felsen urged. "You want the girl, it may be your only hope. For your sake—and hers—think about it."

Val thought of nothing else from that moment. Walking back to her office, sitting at her desk, on the taxi ride home, all through dinner and a game of Chinese checkers with Teddie, lying awake all night.

The next day Felsen informed her that the judge had issued an order that Amanda MacMoran was to stay in her current foster home until the new claim was resolved. Val could visit twice a month—so long as the foster parents did not object.

For the past eight months Mandy had been living with a bus driver and his wife who had successfully taken in six other foster children over the years. A childless couple named Brodie, transplanted from Ireland, the similarity of their background to Mandy's birth parents was another factor in the placement.

Val had already visited Mandy more than a dozen times at their trim redbrick two-family house in Queens. Though they knew she had been fighting for custody, they had never made it difficult for Val to visit, seemed to accept her place in the child's life. Val had even been allowed to take Mandy away for a day in a park, or to see a Broadway musical.

As soon as she heard about the judge's decision, Val called Mrs. Brodie to ask if she could visit Mandy that evening.

"Would you be good enough," the foster mother said, "to wait until tomorrow, Miss Cummings? Mandy's got her lessons to do tonight, and then early to bed. . . ."

Val didn't object. She asked only that nothing be said to Mandy about the latest disappointment so that Val herself could break the news.

After the call, Val wondered if she'd been too hasty in

agreeing to visit the next day. That would be Saturday—a day she always devoted to Teddie. Recently her times for Mandy had been carved out of an evening or late afternoon of a weekday, because as Teddie grew older, she had become increasingly sensitive about the time Val gave to her efforts to obtain custody of Josie's child. Two or three times Teddie had even sullenly expressed such wishes as that Val would "drop the whole thing," or "leave Mandy where she is." Val understood that her commitment to help the other little girl might challenge the security of her own if she wasn't careful, yet she couldn't ignore the pledge she had made to Josie. She hoped that once Mandy was in her home—if ever—a sisterly affection would develop between the two girls.

Late Saturday morning, as soon as Mrs. Falconi arrived to take over from Val, Teddie became upset. "Why is *she* here?" Teddie demanded. "You're supposed to be with me. Where are you going?"

"I'll be home soon, darling," Val tried to placate her.

"You didn't answer me." Val hesitated only a moment before Teddie cried angrily. "You're going to see *her*, aren't you?"

Val knelt and tried to gather Teddie into her arms while she explained, but Teddie ran into her room. Val followed her in and sat beside her crying form on the bed, and talked about the debt of honor to a friend and the need to reassure Mandy—and, most of all, about how much she loved Teddie and nothing she did for Mandy would diminish that love. But Teddie kept her face buried in a pillow and wouldn't speak to her.

"Maybe I shouldn't go," Val said to Mrs. Falconi when she came out of Teddie's room.

The Italian woman spoke with the plain, practical wisdom of having successfully raised seven children. "It's no good lesson to teach-a Teddie that if she cry and-a shout, then you gonna do whatever she wants. You go, come-a back soon as you can, and take-a Teddie to that-a new Walt Disney movie. She be okay."

Val traveled to Queens on the subway, arriving at noon to take Mandy out for lunch. Mrs. Brodie met her at the door and said that her husband had taken the child with him on a short trip to the bakery. Meanwhile, Mrs. Brodie took Val into the small front parlor and offered her a glass of iced tea. Seeing the pitcher and glasses already waiting on a tray, Val suspected that Mandy's absence was planned so that the two women could talk alone. Val steeled herself for what she anticipated Mrs. Brodie would say.

The foster mother was a heavyset woman with thin, frizzy red hair and a round, pleasant face. Val had never been to the house when she wasn't wearing an apron, as though she had no other life but cooking and cleaning.

"I don't have to tell you that our dear little Mandy has experienced the worst thing any child ever can," Mrs. Brodie began. "Now the child needs someone to replace the mother she's lost, but she hasn't known who she could turn to. You have to ask yourself, Mrs. Cummings, if it's fair to keep telling Mandy that you're going to be the one if she's going to go on being disappointed time after time. It would be better if you just let her get used to things as they are."

Before Val could protest, Mrs. Brodie added forcefully, "We do love the child, my husband and I, we'll continue to take good care of her."

"What you're really asking," Val said after a moment, "is for me to give up my efforts to adopt."

"I am," the woman said.

It wasn't an unfair request, Val realized, either for Mandy's sake or her own, even if she could read between the lines that she was also being asked to see much less of Mandy. Yet the thought of surrendering Josie's daughter to these strangers, good-hearted as they might be, tore at Val.

"I know you mean well," she answered the foster mother. "I will think about what you've said."

"Good. That could make it easier on all of us."

There was the faintest hint of a threat in those words, Val felt: To do anything but yield, she was being told, would mean a fight. Val hadn't forgotten that the judge's ruling allowed her to visit Mandy only so long as the foster parents didn't object.

The brief exchange had barely finished when Mandy

returned with Mr. Brodie, as if on schedule. As soon as she saw Val, Mandy ran to her and hurled herself into Val's arms. For a long time they clung to each other.

Which way would the least damage be done? Val asked herself, agonized. How much had been done already?

"Is it today?" Mandy said as soon as she broke from the embrace. "Am I going home with you today?"

Her first words were always a variation of the same question. Looking at Mandy's adorable, eager face, Val regretted having asked the foster parents to wait until Val could break the disappointing news herself.

"We can't do it today," Val said, and watched as the little girl's expression crumbled into disillusionment. Yet Mandy didn't cry—which almost seemed worse. "The judge wants to wait a little longer before a final decision."

Mandy stared back at Val, her blue eyes wide and direct behind the latest pair of plain wire-rimmed spectacles exactly like those Josie had worn. At eleven, she was slim, and beginning to look a little gawky, but already it was clear that when she finished developing, she would be a beauty. "It's not just a little longer, is it?" she said. "You told me it would be only a little while so long ago, right after Mommy . . . after she died. But I'm still not with you. Sometimes I think I never will be, Aunt Val. Is that the truth? Tell me. Will I ever be yours?"

It was Val who could no longer keep herself from breaking down. Sweeping Mandy back into her arms, clinging to her slim frame, Val let the tears course down her cheeks. Over the child's shoulder she saw Mrs. Brodie staring at her, hanging on the answer.

"No, no, darling," Val cried, "that *isn't* the truth. I won't give up until you and I are together, I gave your mother my oath. I've told you that before, haven't I?"

She felt Mandy nodding, even as she saw the foster mother's jaw set.

"Don't give up believing it," Val said. "Please. If you don't give up believing, then I won't. I swear I won't." Val pulled back to look into Mandy's face. "Cross my heart." She made the sign across her breast. "Okay?"

The child nodded again, and then leaked the faintest smile.

In that smile, Val perceived beyond doubt that if Mandy had miraculously survived without being damaged beyond recovery by fear and insecurity, then it was only this fragile hope that had made the difference: that someday she would belong to her mother's best friend. And in telling her not to surrender that hope, Val wasn't cheating her of the truth. It was simply the only answer she could bear to give—the only one, she knew, that either of them could live with.

Fifteen

Val stepped out of the taxi onto the curb and stood in the darkness, composing herself. The legal papers had shown Willy's address remained the same. He still lived in the house bought by his parents when they had emigrated from Germany . . . the same where, so long ago, Ted had kissed her for the first time on a porch swing.

At last she forced herself to look across the street, past the yard, into the yellow square of light cut out of the evening gloom. Her heart lurched as she saw him through the window, sitting next to a lamp while he browsed the evening newspaper. He was in his late thirties now, but looked older. His dirty-blond hair had thinned, his body thickened, the profile she saw through the window looked puffy—the corruption within showing on the surface, she thought. Could she hope to win any kindness?

She had given no advance warning of the visit. She couldn't be sure how he'd react if he knew she was coming. Hide, leave town? Better to gamble, she'd decided, catch him off guard.

Pressing the doorbell, she remembered all the times she had run to this house, evenings after high school—

The door opened. Old dreams of seeing the boy she had loved gave way to the nightmarish confrontation with a man she despised. She caught a faint glimmer of surprise in his eyes, then he let out a little grunt, a sound of self-congratulation, pleased that his tactic had been so successful as to bring her back from obscurity. "Come in, Valeskja," he said. "Or I suppose these days you prefer Valentina. . . ."

When she hung back, he said, "So you're still afraid of me?"

"I have reason to be, don't I? You're still trying to hurt me."

He paused, as though to consider exactly what impulses he was harboring. "You came here to see me, Val. You can come in, or we can stand out here to . . . talk about old times."

At his callous sarcasm, she could feel the rein she had on her self-control already fraying. But losing her temper would destroy her chances. She crossed the threshold. He closed the door and led her into the parlor, where he'd been reading the paper. Evidence of a solitary life lay everywhere—old newspapers scattered on the rug, empty beer glasses and bottles standing on dusty surfaces.

"You live alone?" Val asked.

"My father died two years ago. Mother went to her sister in Florida. Too much snow in Buffalo, she says. May I take your coat?"

By reflex she pulled the coat tighter around her. "No, thanks."

"I wish you wouldn't be so afraid of me, Valeskja."

"Once I wasn't, Willy. You know why that changed."

"Yes," he cried out suddenly. "It was cowardly, criminal! I should have been sent to prison! But I wanted you so much . . . and I knew you would never give yourself to me—I wasn't half the man my brother was."

She stared at him for another moment. Remorse and repentance seemed to charge his words, but could she trust it? "It would be easier to believe you have those regrets," she said, "if you weren't forcing yourself back into my life."

He opened his hands to her, a gesture of helplessness. "Same as before, Valeskja. I couldn't stop myself. Please, won't you sit down? Let me explain. . . ."

A small payment of trust would buy more of his confession, she supposed. She went to the nearest faded easy chair.

He took a place at the far end of the sofa. "When you went away I thought I understood the reason," he began. "I thought it was because after I . . . I dishonored you, you were afraid I would defend myself by making other claims, and they would be believed, and then the only way for you to keep a good reputation would be to marry me. That's true, isn't it? You thought we'd be pushed together, so you left . . . ?"

Val nodded.

"It never occurred to me, though, that I'd guessed only half the reason. All these years, Val, I never imagined that I'd given you a child."

She looked at him stonily, but he guessed the thought in her mind. "I understand. You felt I had no right to know."

She didn't bother confirming it. "How did you learn, Willy?"

"A social worker came here. He told me he needed to verify a claim that Ted had fathered a child of a woman named Valentina Cummings who lived in New York City. I realized at once the child must be mine." He gazed pensively at the floor. "That was more than two years ago. I could have chased you down right then, you know. But, you see, I'm not so bad: I left you alone. I thought, like you, that perhaps I had no right." He shook his head, then looked up at her again, eyes burning. "But all this time, knowing this little girl was there with you, I came to think differently. The child comes from my seed, does it not? This is *my* daughter. I'm the *real* father."

With each assertion of his presumed status, Val's spirit took another blow. "You think I had no other men after you?"

"I know your daughter is six years old now, Val. I'm not so stupid that I can't do some simple arithmetic."

She saw that the old feelings of inferiority still inflamed him. She mustn't let him become too upset or there would be no reasoning with him. "I don't think you're stupid, Willy," she said gently.

His expression softened. "Maybe just unlucky. But since I've learned about you—about the child—I've felt this could be my only chance."

"Chance? For what?"

"Look around, Val. You see how I live. I'm in the house where I was born. I work in the same factory where I got my first job. I haven't found a woman who wants to make her life with me. If I could have changed any of that for the better, maybe you never would have heard from me. It hasn't changed though. While your life . . ." He smiled thinly. "Imagine what you'd be if you hadn't run away from me. But since I found out where you were, *who* you were, I've been able to learn the rest. You're a great success. You started a magazine and it's doing well. I bought a copy, very nice, all about being a bride. And seeing you've done so well, I thought—"

She knew now where this was going, and she was impatient to have it over, to be able to bury this part of her life again. "How much, Willy?" she put in. "Just tell me how much you want to withdraw your claim. I'll give you as much as I can afford."

He looked back at her as if she'd spoken in a foreign language. "Money? You think it's about money?" He shook his large head vigorously. "Oh, no, Valeskja. It's about the *child*—about being the father of a child by a woman like yourself, beautiful and successful. That is what gives me a chance to be something . . . to be more than a nobody. *That* is what I will never give up!"

Hearing his pitiful declaration, Val despaired of winning this battle. If he had intruded himself into the case out of pure meanness or greed, she might have had the weapons to fight. But he was driven by a more basic human need—for a little dignity: If he had created just one good thing in his life, he wanted all the world to know.

Her best hope, she thought, was to use whatever compassion he could feel—not for her but for his own child. "You say you care about being a father, Willy. Does that mean you're capable of showing even more love for your daughter than for yourself?"

"Certainly. I know such feelings are part of the job," he said, unaware of any irony in defining the role as a job.

"Then let me tell you why I've lied about the identity of Teddie's father," Val said. "I thought it was essential for her never to know she was the accidental result of violence and lust. Teddie hasn't had an easy time, having no father; but for all she's suffered, she believes she was created by two people out of true love. I'm sure that has made all the difference, it gives her a core of trust in herself, her importance. She can be moody sometimes, but she's basically strong and—"

"Good," he interrupted. "I'm glad to hear she's okay. But if part of what's wrong is not having a father, why shouldn't that be fixed?"

It was as if he'd heard nothing. "Willy! Even if she learns the truth, understand this: You're never going to become a part of Teddie's life. I'll fight you on that, and don't doubt for a minute I'll win."

"You'd never be able to keep me away altogether," he warned.

Probably not, she thought to herself. But she skipped over it, still trying to reason with him. "Willy, how much do you know about the case the social worker came here to investigate?"

"I was told you were trying to adopt another child, an orphan. Kind of you, Val. But nothing to do with me."

"No," she agreed. "Except if it's proven that I've lied about Teddie's father, the court will never let me adopt the other little girl. It could ruin her life too."

Willy shrugged. "A shame. But it's her life against mine."

"Ted would have put her life first," Val said.

That stopped him cold. He had always wanted to be like his brother. Before the advantage was lost, Val went on, hurrying through all the background to her fight to adopt Mandy MacMoran, the circumstances that had orphaned the child. At the end she said, "I don't know what kind of father you'd make, Willy, if you ever have another child—one conceived in love. But if you want to show you have a heart that's capable of the right kind of caring, you'll do what's best now for both these children. You'll renounce any claim to Teddie."

He gave her a sharp, burning glance, then bounded up from the sofa. For one frightened instant Val thought he might be going to attack her. But he did no more than pace back and forth in extreme agitation. At last he stopped and turned to her. "Even if I agreed, isn't it too late? I've declared my rights. They know your story was false."

"You'll have to say *you* lied, Willy."

"But why would I?"

She'd thought of that too. "I'll tell them it was a scheme to extract money—"

"You want to make me out to be a blackmailer."

She had to take one gamble with his pride. "Not so bad as a rapist," she said. He looked away and started shaking his head. Val plunged ahead quickly. "I'll pay you though. Seventy-five thousand dollars if you'll do what I ask. No one will ever know. With money like that in the bank, you could be someone too."

He stiffened his back indignantly. "I'm not a blackmailer!"

"I know. You're not forcing me to give this to you. I'm offering it, Willy—yours as soon as you provide an affidavit that says you lied about being Teddie's father. The payment will be kept confidential."

He lingered over this, rubbing his face, pacing a few steps then stopping again. She wished she could up the ante to clinch his agreement, but even what she'd offered was going to be hard to deliver. She had thirty thousand saved, and counted on a bank advancing her the rest if she put up her interest in the magazine as collateral. If not, she could sell out. . . .

"Tell me," he said, "is she beautiful?"

"Yes. Very lovely."

"Then I made something good," he murmured to himself.

She held her breath. It seemed he was going to yield.

"Once," he declared, "once at least I want to see her. Sometime . . . somewhere. Will you grant me that?"

"If you'll wait until it won't disrupt anything."

After a moment he lowered his eyes and nodded.

The coiled spring of fear that had been tightening ever since she had seen him through the window unwound all at once. She jumped up. "Thank you, Willy. This means more than anything."

He came nearer to her. "Enough to forgive . . . the past?"

"Yes."

They locked eyes, and for an instant she could remember how it had been before the rape, when she had cared about him because he was Ted's brother, and seemed so kind.

She explained the kind of affidavit her lawyer would need,

left a card printed with Gary Felsen's address and telephone number on an end table, and repeated that the money would be forthcoming as soon as he signed.

He walked her to the front door. "One more thing," he said just before opening it. "A bargain like this should be sealed with a kiss, don't you think?" He looked at her longingly.

So he understood nothing, it seemed, repented nothing. Yet it was a small enough price to pay to complete the purchase of Mandy's happiness. Val prepared herself, muscles flexing already to halt him if he was incited by the kiss to want—

Suddenly her body, her whole being, rebelled, all reason forgotten as the memory of his past sin against her was revived. "No!" she cried shrilly even as she wished she could stay her tongue rather than lose all she'd gained. "No, damn it, I don't *want* to kiss you!"

There was a frozen silence before he said, "I understand." Pulling open the door, he added. "Good-bye, Val. Your lawyer will be hearing from me."

The following week, Gary Felsen informed Val that his office had received an affidavit from William Gruening, though it was not one hundred percent what Val had prescribed. The document attested that Gruening's claim to be the father of Val's child was being withdrawn, and admitted his initial action had been commenced "without good cause." But the wording omitted any outright declaration that he had lied. The result, Felsen warned Val, was to leave some doubt about what the facts were, even an intimation that Willy might indeed be the father but had withdrawn the claim due to outside influence. In the judge's eyes, Val's moral character might not be sufficiently exonerated to grant her custody.

Val called Willy. "It's not what we agreed," she charged angrily.

"I won't admit to being a liar," he replied. "Especially if I'm going to accept money from you." This curious paradox came not from any moral concern, but self-preservation. He was afraid that once Val paid him, she might charge him with extortion and have him sent to jail.

As hard as she tried to convince him she would honor their agreement without any attempt to seek retribution, Willy wouldn't budge. He would provide this affidavit and no other. Val had no choice but to accept, and she made arrangements to honor her part of the bargain.

On a Friday morning, one month later, in Part 19 of the state Supreme Court building in lower Manhattan, Val sat at the plaintiff's table beside Gary Felsen waiting for the judge to enter the courtroom from chambers. At a table across from them were the two lawyers from the child welfare agency who, for five years, had alleged that an unmarried woman, already the mother of one illegitimate child, was unfit to receive a second child into her care, regardless of the wishes of that child's mother. Val tried to read their faces. Did they look confident, pleased?

As she waited, Val's agitation was heightened by the memory of the distress she'd had to cause Teddie just to be in court this morning. In the way that fate had of contriving to make one need collide with another, today's hearing had been scheduled for the same morning that Teddie was appearing as Cinderella in a play being presented by her class at a school assembly. Val had been forced so often by her work to be away from her daughter that she was desolate herself at missing even such a tiny milestone. She understood that to a six-year-old who had been rehearsing for weeks the starring role in a fairy tale, her absence would not be a minor disappointment. She had even tried to have Gary postpone the court date.

"Are you nuts, Val?" the lawyer had said when she made the request. "We don't want to do anything now that makes it seem as if you're waffling. . . ."

"This is for my daughter, Gary."

"One of them. You've spent five years to get to this point so you could adopt another. Just explain it to Teddie. It's not the end of the world to miss her prancing around for a few minutes; she'll get over it. Five years versus five minutes, Val. I think the choice is pretty clear."

To the adults, yes. But Teddie had cried and screamed

terribly when Val tried to explain. *I hate you . . . you don't love me. . . .* The worst weapon in a child's arsenal of words to wound a mother.

How much worse it would be, Val thought, if her sacrifice proved to be for nothing.

"Oyez, oyez . . ."

The clerk of the court announced the entrance of the judge. Val reached for Gary Felsen's hand and held on as much for dear life as if she was hanging over a precipice. She had paid so much to be here. Not in money alone, nor the energy to fight the long battle. There were times she thought that she might not have lost Andrew if her friendship with Josie hadn't made its claim when it did, times she feared the commitment to Josie's orphaned daughter had damaged the bond with Teddie.

The judge, a portly, gray-haired man with a nasal voice, began to announce his finding. "In the matter of Miss Valentina Cummings's suit for custody of Amanda J. MacMoran, this has been a most difficult case for the court to decide. On the one hand . . ."

Yes or no, yes or no? she screamed within, hardly able to concentrate as he went through a thoughtful but lengthy presentation of the pros and cons on both sides, a recitation of relevant case precedents.

Please God . . .

She was still lost in the prayer when she felt Felsen's strong hand on her shoulder, shaking her. She opened her eyes to see him smiling broadly. "You've won, Val," he said. "Mandy's yours!"

The same afternoon, while Teddie was still in school, Val went to the Brodie home to collect Mandy.

She was waiting downstairs when Val arrived, freshly scrubbed and wearing a new pink dress made for her by Mrs. Brodie, her golden hair tied back with a black velvet ribbon. Mandy ran into a long close embrace with Val, who began crying tears of joy.

"Don't do that, Aunt Val," Mandy pleaded. "There's nothing

to cry about anymore. Things are the way they're supposed to be."

It seemed to be what had sustained the child through the years of waiting for justice, her conviction that there was a plan the grown-ups must eventually have the sense to follow. In keeping with her amazing sweetness and balance, Mandy went from embracing Val to give both Mr. and Mrs. Brodie a hug, and thank them for being so good to her. "If I'd had to stay here," she told the kindly Irish couple, "it wouldn't have been so bad."

"Come on, Mandy," Val said finally. "Let's go home." She took the child's hand and they went out to where Gary Felsen waited with his car. Halfway to the sidewalk, Mandy pulled Val up short.

"You know, Aunt Val, there's a lot of stuff I'd really like to forget. Can you understand?"

How could she not? "Sure," Val said.

"I know it won't be easy," the little girl said. "But there's one thing that would help me a lot, if you wouldn't mind."

"Whatever it is, Mandy . . ."

"Well, that's it—my name. 'Mandy' belongs to another time, and a lot of what I remember about that time was bad, really bad. So I thought, to start fresh, it might be good if I'm not Mandy anymore."

Wanting a different name wasn't an uncommon symptom of a child's desire to step into a new skin. Val had changed her own name for similar reasons, and in the child's case the whim was even more justified. "Have you thought of the name you'd like?" Val asked.

"Oh, sure. It's mine anyway—but my middle name."

Val had never heard it, but she remembered now that in court the name had been read aloud with a middle initial.

"What is it?" Val asked . . . and was told.

So from that moment on, the child Val Cummings would legally adopt as her second daughter was called Jessica.

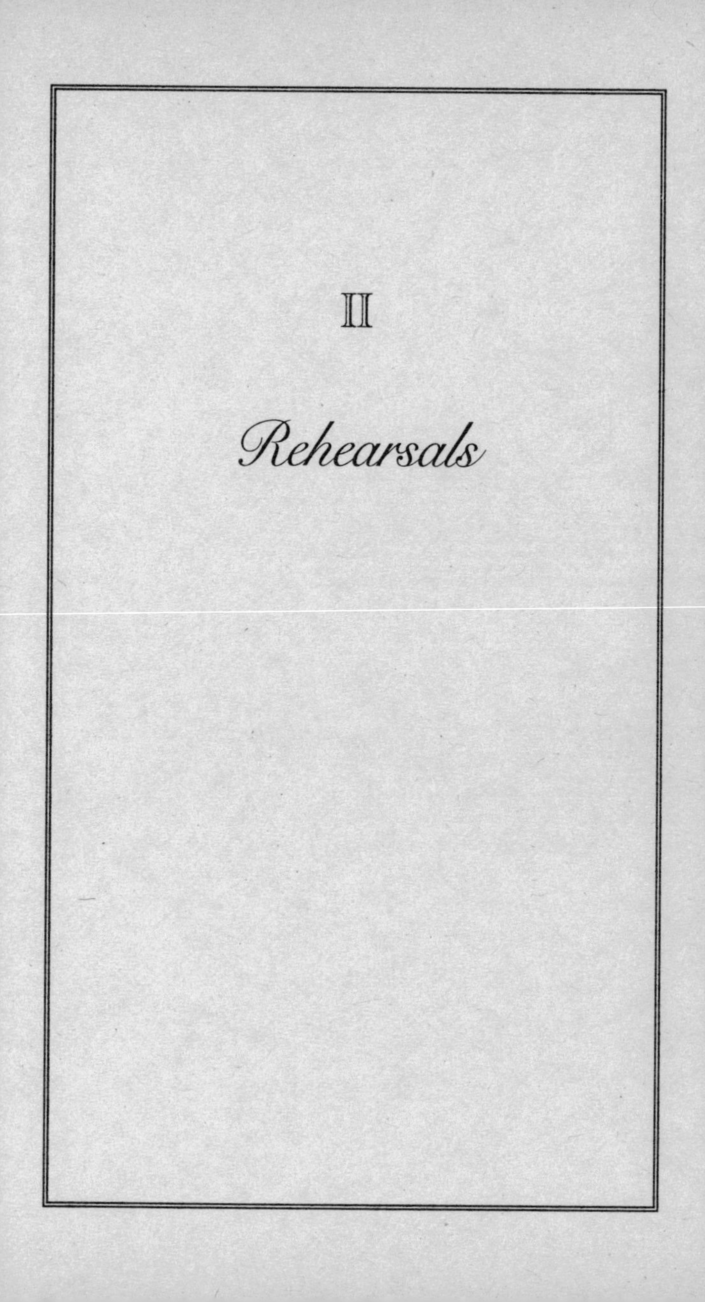

II

Rehearsals

Sixteen

Washington, D.C.
4 P.M.

"Calder . . ." Jess answered the phone on her desk at the newspaper. The call came while she was editing copy for the next day's column, so she was mildly distracted.

"What do you know about this shit?" said a voice, a woman's.

That got her attention. Jess tried to place the voice, but couldn't, though it sounded very familiar and had certainly taken an informal tack. Some senator's press secretary?

Rather than insult a contact she ought to know, Jess replied blithely, "Exactly which shit are we referring to?" This being Washington, the possibilities were infinite.

"This goddamn wedding shit," came the answer.

Now it fell into place. "Teddie . . . ?" Jess asked in hushed disbelief.

"Yeah, who else?"

Jess shook her head. Not surprising that the ice was being broken with a sledgehammer rather than gently melted, nor that the voice had been hard to recognize, well as they knew each other. When was the last time they'd talked? God, how the years slipped by. Could it be ten years ago? No, longer.

"Well, Teds," Jess said, "it's nice to hear from you."

"Listen," Teddie snapped, "suppose we skip all the lovey-dovey sister crap and you just answer the question. You're a hotshot journalist, so tell me: What's the scoop on the invitation I just got . . . ?"

Obviously she meant the same invitation Jess had received before lunch. "If you really want an answer," Jess said calmly, "you might work to get it by at least *pretending* to be nice."

Teddie sighed. "It's been so long, I forgot how. Coach me a little—nice was always one of your strong suits."

Jess couldn't help laughing. "You could start by filling me in a little. How are you? What are you doing? Round it off by telling me if there's a chance you'll come—"

"Okay," Teddie agreed grudgingly. "I'm fine. Still in the same business. I divorced number four two years ago, and I'm on the prowl for number five. And since I'm invited, I wouldn't miss it—if I can learn where and when it is, not to mention if it's for real. So, now, do I get to hear your news?"

"Fine too. Still with Ben. Job good. Kids are in college, Josie at Yale and Matt at—"

"I meant the wedding news," Teddie cut in. "I don't have to hear how fucking perfect your life is."

It was too much. "As it happens," Jess said acidly, "it's not quite perfect. Two years ago I was diagnosed with breast cancer, had a lumpectomy and radiation and I'm okay . . . but you never know."

There was a short silence before Teddie said quietly, "Sorry. I had no idea."

The tone was chastened, with even a hint of sympathy. Jess had never heard Teddie sound that way before. The passing time had brought a change or two apparently. "Of course you didn't," Jess said flatly, and rushed on. "About the wedding, I can't tell you any more than what you already know."

"Why not?"

"Because I don't know either," Jess said. "I don't know one thing more than what's on that invitation."

"Oh, cut the crap, princess. You were always her lady-in-waiting. There's nothing she didn't share with—"

"Not this time," Jess said firmly. "That's the truth."

There was a pause. "And you never lie, do you?" Teddie said, accepting it. "Then just tell me what all the cloak-and-dagger bullshit has to do with getting married?"

"I'm not sure about that either," Jess said. "But I'd have to guess it's superstition—she doesn't want anything to get in the way this time. And maybe the best insurance is not to let people—or even the gods—know too much until it's absolutely necessary. But you'll certainly be told, along with the rest of us, when the time is right. Evidently she wants you there, Teddie." After a moment Jess added, "She always did."

Jess waited for Teddie's response, but this time the silence lasted. "Teddie . . . ?"

But no answer came. Only the click of the line disconnecting.

Seventeen

Pocono Mountains
August 1963

Even sick with worry as she was, Val couldn't fail to notice the many changes since she'd last driven through these mountains more than ten years earlier. Then it had been a rural backwater with a few small family-run inns like the one she and Andrew Winston had visited, tucked in here and there along with farms and a few children's summer camps. Now the roadside was lined with billboards advertising large resorts, many recently built. On all the signs—always printed in a red heart—was a mention of special rates for honeymooners.

The explosion of honeymoon business accounted for much of what had happened in the Poconos. Val had to smile when she recalled her encounter with Rudy Wellstrom—how endearingly eccentric he had seemed, trusting the aphrodisiacal powers of his heart-shaped tub to be the foundation of any successful marriage. The darnedest part of it, though, was that he had been far more right than wrong. It wasn't long after Val had visited The Rainbow Inn that word began to spread about the unique touches it incorporated, and others had hurried to imitate it. The tubs, the enormous heart-shaped beds, mirrored ceilings, fur carpets, fireplaces.

Val had done her part to spur the growth of honeymoon business in the Poconos. The shock of Josie's murder during her visit to The Rainbow Inn had initially distracted her, but a month later she had sent a staff writer to do an article on the inn for *E.B.*'s regular feature on honeymoon ideas. Wellstrom's rooms were soon solidly booked for months. He built more, and they were filled too. Then, rather than build more, he began licensing his patented tub to other hotels in the area. The Poconos had taken over from Niagara Falls as the Honeymoon Capital of the World.

Musing on the way it had changed gave Val only passing relief, however, from the emergency that had sent her racing here from New York. . . .

Three hours before, she had been running an editorial staff meeting about the November issue. The meetings were a regular weekly occurrence, but Val was truly enjoying this one because it was the first Jess had attended. Before graduating high school last month, Jess had announced she was thinking of pursuing a career in journalism, and had asked to be a summer intern at the magazine. Val was thrilled. Jess would be a bright and enthusiastic worker, a welcome addition in any department. In spite of all she'd been through, Jess continued to demonstrate a remarkably positive outlook in all things. After coming to live with Val, she had done exceptionally well in school—had been a leader of student council and member of several athletic teams, as well as editor of her school newspaper. She was going on to Harvard's sister school, Radcliffe. Still, there was one factor in obliging Jess's request for a summer job that had made Val think twice.

From the time Jess had come into her home, Val had made every effort to assure Teddie that it wouldn't mean anything less for her—certainly not less love. "Love's not an object," she'd told Teddie, "not like an apple, or a coin, so that when you take away a piece of it or spend it, what's left gets smaller. That's the magic about love. When you learn to share it, give some to another person, what's left only gets bigger. . . ."

But Teddie didn't easily accept such romantic notions. Her way of tolerating life without a father had been to adopt an absolutely practical view. Never mind what she didn't have, could never have, she relied wholely on what she could grasp as real and tangible. That made the prospect of sharing her mother all the more threatening. Sweet homilies on the inexhaustibility of love, all Val's attempts to explain the importance of honoring a vow to give Jess a home, made no difference. Teddie could see Val's taking in another child only as a rejection of herself.

Recently, Teddie had turned fourteen. She looked physically mature for her age, tall, her body filling out; but in attitude she remained childishly petulant and selfish. Over the past few years, the jealousy and bitterness she felt at what she seemed to regard as a betrayal of maternal love had been more and more openly expressed—in rebellions at home, and at the good private school that Val's growing affluence made it possible for Teddie to attend. Val's initial uncertainty about giving Jess a summer job at the magazine was due to her fear that it might add to Teddie's resentment. Ever watchful and jealous of the limited time Val was able to spend with her, Teddie's feelings were likely to be especially bruised if she realized that Jess would now have exclusive access to their mother all day, every day at the office. So Val suggested that Jess might get her first journalistic experience at another publication. With her contacts in the publishing business, Val said, there would be no problem arranging an internship at another magazine or newspaper.

Jess's reaction had been typically even-tempered. "I'll go wherever you think I can get the most useful experience. But I thought the nicest thing would be to work where you do, Mom, see exactly how you've been spending your time all these years. . . ." Val had been "Mom" to her since the day the custody issue was decided.

"I'd like that too, sweetie," Val said. "But frankly . . . I'm worried about how it'll affect Teddie if you and I work together every day."

"I understand," Jess said. "I don't want to do anything that hurts Teddie. But, Mom . . . does this mean I might never get a chance to work with you?"

That question had made Val decide in the end that the problem might as well be confronted head-on rather than avoided. Val mustn't allow herself to be tyrannized by Teddie's jealousy.

It turned out that all the worrying was needless. The revelation that Jess would work for the summer at *E.B.*—made casually one evening at the dinner table—had elicited no comment from Teddie except "Good luck—I can't think of anything more boring." For herself, Teddie announced she wanted to spend the summer at the same camp where Deb Swaine, her best friend at school, was going.

The camp happened to be in the Poconos. In the first weeks after Teddie went off, Val got a couple of calls from the head counselor reporting disciplinary problems: Teddie and Deb had been caught smoking cigarettes in the shower cabin, or had sneaked out of their bunk one night to skinny-dip alone in the lake. Teenage mischief. But then came an episode where the two girls had ganged up on a third to take candy and magazines her mother had sent from home. The camp had placed Teddie and Deb in different bunks.

Now *this*. On an overnight camping trip, Teddie's sleeping bag had been found empty at sunrise. The campers had searched the surrounding woods without success. Finally the local police had been notified, and Val had been called.

Six times during the two-hour drive from the city, she had stopped to telephone the camp for news. Each time, she was told Teddie hadn't been found.

Val arrived at the camp shortly before noon. The owner, a lean, muscular man named Dan Cartwright, was waiting for her at the large log-sided dining hall, the center of the camp's activities. With a weathered face under a gray crew cut, dressed in jeans and a T-shirt, he gave the impression of being half woodsman, half marine drill sergeant. Val had met him before in New York at a gathering where pictures of the camp were shown to prospective campers and their parents. He had convinced her that he ran a first-class facility, and she still believed that if Teddie had run away, it wasn't because there was a problem with his operation.

"Mrs. Cummings," he greeted her solicitously, "believe me, I'm sick over this. Everything possible is being done to find your child."

Val let the mistake in her marital status go by. For Teddie's sake—to save her being categorized as illegitimate—Val often used "Mrs." before her name. "I suppose you've talked to her best friend," Val said, "asked if Teddie said anything to her."

"Of course. And she did give us a lead."

Deb Swaine's revelation was that for the past two weeks, Teddie had been keeping secret late-night trysts with a twenty-year-old boy who worked as a dishwasher in the camp kitchen. Upon checking, the camp director discovered the boy also was missing.

"You're telling me they've run off together?" Val erupted.

"So it seems. But if they're traveling together, they'll be easier to trace. I think you should be relieved that she didn't run off to roam on her own. It means she's less likely to . . . do harm to herself."

"There are ways a young girl can harm herself," Val observed, "that work a lot better when you're *not* alone."

Over the next few hours spent at the camp, Val was given all the tea or coffee she could drink—she had no appetite—while awaiting word from the police. She sat on the porch of Dan Cartwright's cabin, or walked through the surrounding pine forests, meanwhile going over and over all that happened in raising Teddie. What could she have done differently—other than abandon Jess? She would have liked to give more time to parenting, but she'd had to earn a living. She'd provided a loving surrogate in Leila Falconi, but the Italian widow had died four years earlier—just at a time, perhaps, when Teddie needed her special wisdom and homey authority to smooth the entry into adolescence.

The one "fatal" error, perhaps, had been trying to do it without a man, not marrying.

Suitors had never been in short supply. The more successful Val became, the more she traveled in circles where there were interesting men—executives, others in the publishing business, editors and writers who worked for her. Her beauty as well as her position made it natural for them to court her. She had tried to fall in love, had wanted to . . . had even been attracted to one or two men. But the sparks never ignited a lasting fire.

If only she'd let Andrew finish his proposal, been more clever or patient, let love take root. Had she expected it all to be perfect from the beginning, become a sucker for the dream she sold in the pages of her magazine? A father for Teddie—and Jess—could have made the difference. . . .

What good was second-guessing now? Anyway, thinking about her two daughters, Val concluded that the difference couldn't be solely in upbringing, but in the innate mysteries of personality. Jess's life up to the age of eleven had been a constant ordeal, ten times harder than Teddie's. Yet Jess had somehow remained basically unselfish, trusting, cheerful, industrious—

"Mrs. Cummings!"

She had walked deep into the woods as her mind teemed. The golden sun of late afternoon slanted down through the pines. When Cartwright called, she ran all the way back, sure she'd detected a positive ring in his voice.

He was standing by the door of his cabin.

"They've found her?" Val said expectantly.

"No, sorry. But the police talked to a gas station owner who saw a boy and girl matching the descriptions hitchhiking west along a secondary road. Knowing their direction narrows down the search. I thought you'd want to hear."

"Yes, thank you."

"It's just a matter of time now until they're found."

If they were located before spending a night together, Val thought, that could make a significant difference.

"It's getting late," Cartwright said. "You're welcome to stay the night at the camp."

She hadn't thought of spending the night anywhere. But if it was necessary, she preferred to stay where she wouldn't be whispered about by all the young girls whose grapevine must be buzzing with talk of Teddie's flight. "I think I'd rather go to a hotel," she said.

"There are a number of nice places nearby. I can make a reservation for you."

"I'll manage on my own, thanks."

"Just let me know where you'll be," he said, "so we can give you a call as soon as there's any news."

On impulse, she asked about the one hotel in the area that came readily to mind. She wasn't completely sure of the local geography, but she thought it couldn't be too far away.

"Are you sure you want to stay *there*?" Cartwright said. "That place is mainly—"

"For honeymooners," Val said. "I know." Perhaps the memories could provide a little distraction from her worry, the tiniest bit of comfort.

She found it only nine miles away. But it wasn't The Rainbow Inn anymore; now it was called The Rainbow Resort. The original colonial house and its tacked-on wing had been torn down long before, replaced by a modern nine-story structure with several hundred rooms and dozens of charming outlying bungalows—all featuring bathrooms with the famous heart-shaped bathtub. Rudy Wellstrom's original holding of twenty-four undeveloped acres had been augmented with the purchase of large tracts of surrounding land on which were a man-made lake with a sand beach, a golf course, miles of bridle path, and lavishly landscaped enclosures called the Moonlight Garden, the Jungle Hideaway, the Valley of Roses.

As soon as Val entered the lobby of the main building, she saw newlywed couples everywhere, holding hands or nuzzling as they checked in, sitting on red heart-shaped lobby divans. Their happy togetherness clashed with her mood of solitary anxiety, but she was too drained after a day of worry to move on. She needed a place to wait for news; any place would do once she was behind closed doors.

"I was hoping you'd have a room for tonight," she said when her turn came at the reception desk.

"I'm sorry," the clerk said, "we're full—unless you have a reservation." He eyed her curiously, realizing she was alone. "But this wouldn't be the best place for you anyway."

She smiled ruefully. "I know—it's for honeymooners." She wondered then if she ought to identify herself. Her name would certainly open doors; the magazine was vitally important to places that did a big honeymoon business, not only domestically but in romantic spots around the world. After many years of offering suggestions for exciting honeymoons in its pages and regularly answering bushels of letters on the subject, it had occurred to Val to start a subsidiary travel agency specializing in honeymoon trips. The first announcement of the new service, two years ago, had drawn three thousand inquiries. Since then, *E.B.*'s travel service had booked nearly eight thousand honeymoon trips, earning commissions that added significantly to its climbing profits.

"Is Mr. Wellstrom here?" Val suddenly asked the desk clerk. She knew the innkeeper had become wealthy, but that he still took an active interest in the hotel.

"Yes. He's not in his office, but he's on the grounds. I'll try to find him for you—if you'll give me your name."

Under the circumstances, Val didn't want to draw attention. But she thought it would be nice to say hello, and Wellstrom could surely arrange a room for her. "We're old friends," she said. "I'll look for him on my own."

It wasn't long, however, before Val realized that searching the acres of grounds was a monumental task. After ten minutes she headed back to her car, resigned to finding somewhere else to stay the night.

She was crossing the parking lot when she noticed the desk clerk outside the main building, pointing her out to a tall man in a suit who stood at his side—not Rudy Wellstrom. The house detective, perhaps. A single woman showing up at a honeymoon hotel, asking for the wealthy owner but reluctant to give her name, could be deemed worthy of investigation. Val continued toward her car. They ought to be satisfied if she simply left.

"Hello . . . you there!"

Val turned to see the man she'd assumed was the house detective loping after her with a graceful athletic gait. A lock of his neatly cut sandy blond hair dropped across his forehead, jarred loose by the run. He caught up. "I'm told you were looking for Mr. Wellstrom . . . ?"

"That's right."

"And you were going to leave without talking to him?"

"It was nothing important," Val said. "Just a personal call."

"Oh?" The long look his brown eyes gave her hinted at frank appreciation for what he saw, along with curiosity as to her mission. She didn't object to it. He was quite attractive, a few years older than herself. "Have we met somewhere?" he said.

The oldest chestnut in the world for a pickup, it made her smile. "No," she said. "Not that I can remember."

"But you have 'personal' business with me?"

"Not with *you*. I was looking for Mr. Wellstrom."

"But I'm—" He broke off. "Oh, I see. I'm *Alan* Wellstrom. You must want my father."

"If Rudy's your father, yes. Where is he?"

"If he's behaving himself, he's in Europe with my mother—on the first real vacation they've had since they opened this place."

"I'm glad to hear it, though I'm sorry to have missed him."

"Give me your name, I'll tell him you were here. He calls in a few times a week—can't imagine the place survives without him."

"Val Cummings," she said.

It registered instantly. "*Valentina* Cummings?"

She nodded.

"But I can't let you just drive away! You're practically the patron saint of this place. I've heard the stories, what you did for him in the early days. This calls for popping a champagne cork, rolling out the red—"

"Mr. Wellstrom . . . right now I'm not in a situation where I feel I should be celebrating with you. I would be very grateful, though, now that I'm here, if you could find a room for me."

"You're not on your—"

She smiled faintly. "No, not on a honeymoon. But I need a hotel for overnight, and I thought of this place first."

"I'm glad you did," he said, though his expression darkened; he seemed to realize now that she was in trouble. "The regular rooms are full, but my father has a bungalow on the property. You'd be welcome to stay there." When she hesitated, he added, "You'll have it to yourself. I have a room in the main building."

"I'll take you up on that," she said. "I've had one of the worst days, and I was dreading getting back on the road."

He got in the car with her and directed her to the bungalow, situated away from the main compound. On the short drive, he asked Val what had brought her to the area. When she told him about Teddie, he was very sympathetic.

"I understand now why celebrations aren't in order. Nothing can burn you out as much as worrying about your kids, can it? If there's any way I can help . . ."

"I think everything possible is being done. I've been told she'll probably be located soon."

The four-room bungalow was located in a quiet corner of the property with a nice view from a rear patio over a pond and the manicured golf course beyond. Inside, a living room and two bedrooms were furnished with Early American furniture probably saved from the original Rainbow Inn.

After letting her in, Alan Wellstrom showed her quickly around in the same practiced manner as a bellboy. "By the way," he said, "the bathroom is the only one for miles around that *doesn't* have a heart-shaped tub."

"Why not?"

"My mother can't swim, and she thinks the darn things are too big and she might drown." He winked. "The marriage survived anyway."

It gave Val her only laugh of the day.

He retreated to the entrance. "Help yourself to anything." He pointed to a drinks caddy in the living room with bottles of fine single-malt scotch, brandy, and other liquor. "A little shot of something might do your nerves some good after the kind of day you've had."

"Not a bad idea. Will you join me?" she asked before he could retreat farther. She found Alan Wellstrom's company as therapeutic for her frayed nerves as a drink might be.

While he got ice from the kitchen to oblige her request for a scotch on the rocks, she called the camp and the hotel switchboard. Then she and Alan took their drinks out to the patio.

It was a lovely evening, summer sun sinking low, making long shadows across the vivid green of the golf course. For a minute they sat in garden chairs, quietly sipping their drinks. Considerate of the strain she was under, Alan let the silence last. Val felt a little of the terrible tension soothed away. "It's very nice here," she said.

"Has to be. Honeymoons are supposed to be an ideal time."

She turned to him. "Do you enjoy playing cupid?"

"Me? That's not really my game."

"But aren't you running the hotel now?"

He shook his head. "I'm just here for a couple of days. I know something about how the place runs, so Dad asked me to look in while he's traveling. But he's got a good manager in charge."

"And when you're not here, what are you doing?"

"I'm also in the hotel business, but a different kind of operation. Any newlyweds we get are probably eloping and staying for just one night."

"Oh? Where's your hotel?"

"It isn't just one. I run Festival Inns."

She knew of it, a chain of the sort of no-frills moderately priced establishments that cater to touring families and business travelers. In the last ten years they had gone up across the country, and new ones were being built all the time. "I'm impressed," she said. "I've heard it's one of the best stocks on Wall Street."

"We're doing well," he said modestly. "Though lots of times I think maybe I should have joined Dad. Sitting in the sun and playing cupid probably is more fun and better for your soul than just piling up money and real estate."

"Why didn't you go in with your father?"

"When I went to hotel management school, that was the plan. But a recruiter from Hilton showed up as I was about to graduate, and Dad encouraged me to get the experience. I started climbing the ladder there, and then I met an investor who had this idea about serving the great American public with a cheap, efficient lodging, and he asked if I'd be a partner, handle the nuts and bolts."

From what he was saying, Val realized he had helped to start the Festival chain. Its success had undoubtedly made him very wealthy, but she interpreted a flicker of discontent she'd picked up—his talk of what was best for the soul—as indicating he was still searching for more meaningful challenges.

"Your business is growing rapidly," she observed. "Doesn't that please you?"

He gave her a shrewd glance, as if aware she was fishing. "Maybe too much. I get swept up in the excitement, and there's a price to pay." He sipped his drink, lost in some private thought. Then he looked back at her. "But you must know that. You've also had a tremendous success."

He didn't have to add that she, too, had paid a price. After all, she was there alone waiting for word about her runaway daughter.

The sun was down, the sky shading toward lavender. In the silence between them now, she wondered exactly what was missing in his life that had made him hint at being unfulfilled, what price he had paid. But before she could probe further, he quickly drained the last swallow from his glass and stood up.

"Well, you've had a very hard day. No doubt you could use a chance to rest."

Part of her wanted to cry out *No! stay with me . . . hold me, that's what I need more than anything*. Somehow this man aroused a longing for what was missing in her life more than any she'd met in the past ten years. She felt an instant connection, a desire to know more about him, give more of herself—

But of course she couldn't possibly reveal these feelings to a stranger. She rose too. "Thank you. For everything."

"My pleasure."

He gazed intently at her. Did he also feel a current flowing between them? Or was it even real? She was in a fragile state, prone to imagine wishes as facts, to mistake a small touch of kindness for something more.

He took his glass into the kitchen, rinsed it out. When he came to the door, she was there. She summoned her courage. "Will I see you again?"

"I'll be at the hotel tonight. After you've relaxed, if you'd like, we could meet for dinner."

"I doubt I'll have any appetite, but I'd like the company."

"So would I."

When their eyes locked this time, she knew the silent messages were real. They set a time, half past eight; he'd call for her at the bungalow. There was a charming place, he said, in a village not far away. "Not a honeymooner in sight," he added.

"Sounds perfect."

As soon as he'd gone, though, she regretted making the date. It seemed wrong, even callous, to be involved in a flirtation while Teddie was in trouble.

Yet wasn't that the way life worked, playing tricks, setting traps, taking with one hand while giving with the other? Raise an emergency, then drop a new hope into your path—making you desire a man who might already belong to somebody else.

She phoned the camp and was told the police had reported nothing new.

Then she called the magazine. Jess was still there, worrying because she had heard that Val had rushed away. "Madge told me it was some problem with Teds," she said anxiously. "Is she okay?"

"Physically, yes," Val replied, and explained the situation.

"The poor kid."

"I guess I've really let her down."

"Don't think like that, Mom. You've done the best you could. Let me know as soon as you hear anything."

Thank God for Jess, Val thought as she hung up. For all she'd been through, she remained a source of comfort, pride, and inspiration. Though Val knew that the very strength of her adopted daughter's character set a standard Teddie found hard to match—and, so, easier to resent.

She managed a short nap after the phone call, then took a hot bath to leach away the tension. While the water steamed, she hung the pale amber suit she'd been wearing in the bathroom to take out some of the wrinkles. Having raced off straight from the office, it was all she had to wear—though she trusted Alan would make allowances. Fortunately, she'd learned for the sort of hectic business schedule she maintained to carry a travel toothbrush along with her makeup in her purse.

It was a quarter past eight, and she had just finished dressing when the phone rang.

It was Dan Cartwright. "They've found her—and the boy—in a motel just fifteen miles from the camp."

The need to have every other question answered sent her running from the room as soon as she hung up the phone.

Eighteen

Before being reunited with Teddie at the local police station, Val was briefed by one of the officers. She was told that her daughter and the young man had been found in the motel after spending a few hours there, and in Teddie's statement to the police she had admitted being sexually active with him since meeting him at the camp; she also stated she was not a virgin at the time they met.

Val was incredulous. "It can't be true. She's only—"

The policeman cut her off. "Your daughter's fourteen, Mrs. Cummings, the young man is twenty. So he'll be prosecuted for statutory rape. Your daughter may have thought the charge would be dropped if he wasn't her first."

Either way, Val was devastated by what she heard. She thought back, trying to comprehend her own failure. How had she been so blind to what was happening to Teddie? She had seen that her child was developing into a beautiful young girl—taller than average, which made her seem more like sixteen or seventeen than her true age. She knew Teddie got respectable grades in school and had friends, boys who asked her out for a movie and an ice cream soda, girls like Deb Swaine, who invited her for pajama-party sleepovers. Or so Val had thought. But all the time Teddie was evidently making a different choice—to leave the innocence of childhood behind forever. Now it was gone, and Val had been able to enjoy so little of it with her.

Teddie was sullen and uncommunicative when released into Val's custody. They drove straight back to New York. Dan Cartwright had told Val he would not accept Teddie back at the camp. In the car, Val tried several times to initiate conversation. The theme wasn't to blame Teddie or punish her, but let her know that Val felt she was herself responsible, that she understood her daughter was acting out of a need for love she must have felt lacking at home.

"I'm sorry if you haven't felt it," Val said, "but there's nothing more important to me than doing whatever I can to make the best life for you, giving you whatever you need. That's what it's all been about, Teddie, from the time you were born—even before, from the time I knew I was going to have you. . . ."

However conciliatory Val tried to be, Teddie remained hunched against the passenger door on the opposite side of the car, refusing to speak. It tried Val's patience, but she bit her tongue rather than explode and widen the gulf between them. Even if it took time, nothing was more important than reopening the lines of communication. Val was haunted by the prospect of history repeating itself, Teddie throwing her life off track by becoming pregnant. But Val didn't press for answers now, hoping it would be easier to talk after a night of sleep.

Jess had already gone to bed by the time they returned to the apartment, but hearing them arrive, she rose to greet them. "Hi, Teds . . . I'm glad you're all right."

"Why shouldn't I be all right, Jess? All I've been doing is fucking. Do you know what that is, Miss Goody-Goody? It's not something that'll kill you. Feels pretty great, in fact."

"Stop it at once!" Val couldn't hold back the fury that had been building in the car.

But Teddie would not be stopped. "Of course, Mother dear, you tell the world no one should fuck until they're married, because then they won't be allowed to wear white at their wedding. Nothing means as much to you as all that stupid bridal bullshit! Even if you're raising a bastard yourself."

Val was livid. "That's enough!"

"Sure, more than enough for Jess to hear," Teddie parroted sassily. "Must protect your precious angel's delicate little ears, not to mention her delicate little—"

"Stop it," Val ordered, stepping up to Teddie. Trembling

with rage, she forced herself nevertheless not to shout this time, but to find words that could lead somewhere other than the dead end of mutual bitterness. "Whatever you think of Jess's behavior, do you think your own is really something to be proud of? You're still a child, Teddie. Just getting into bed with a man doesn't make you a woman, and it certainly doesn't make you better than your sister."

"Sister? She's nothing to me, just some poor little orphan you took in. I never wanted that candy-cunt bitch for my sister."

Val made one more herculean effort to fight down the rage. "I'm not going to tolerate any more of that filth. Apologize to Jess. Now."

"Or else what?" Teddie challenged.

Jess spoke to head off a collision. "Never mind, Mom. Teddie's upset. I don't take it personally."

Teddie stepped around Val. "Why not? I sure as hell meant it personally. I hate your guts, Jess! Hate every bit of that goddamn pure-as-snow sweet-ass act of yours. . . ."

Val was so stunned by the venom spewing from Teddie's mouth, she couldn't find her voice. For a second she thought it might be just as well to let it go on a little—let the poison out like lancing an infection.

"Saint Jessica," Teddie went on, snarling at Jess, "the most wonderful, perfect girl in the whole wide fucking world. Takes nothing personally, loves everybody . . . even me. What a crock of shit! If you're really so terrific, Saint Jess, how come your own parents didn't want to live with you? Did you take *that* personally?"

"Teddie!" Val gasped in disbelief at such viciousness.

Staring rigidly back at Teddie with wounded eyes, Jess looked as though she had gone into shock. Val had an impulse to go to her, hold her, yet she stifled it, knowing it would only incite more of Teddie's viciousness.

"That's the cruelest thing you could have said, Teddie," Val observed quietly, more in sadness than anger. "You know it has nothing to do with the facts, nothing at all. For God's sake, tell Jess you didn't mean it."

Teddie's mouth was set in a tight, grim line, a silent declaration that she would not recant.

"Tell her you're sorry!" Val commanded, her fury coming through.

"Hell I will," Teddie screamed. "Who says it's not the truth? From what I've heard, neither her mother or her father cared enough about her to keep themselves alive—*she* let herself be killed, and *he* took the coward's way out—in a car, sucking up exhaust. Why do you think? Maybe 'cause that sweet little Miss Perfect act of hers made them both think they were worth shit and might as well be dead. So then *we* had to get stuck with—"

Val didn't know where the impulse came from—if she did, maybe she could have stopped it. But suddenly her hand was coming around in a swift arc, the crack of the slap as it met Teddie's cheek sounding as loud and final as a gunshot. Val was instantly ashamed; whatever the provocation, there was nothing worse than hitting one's own child.

But Teddie barely flinched.

"Teddie . . . baby . . ." Val stammered, "That was wrong. . . . I'm so sorry."

Teddie smiled thinly, pleased because she had proven that she was the one unloved, sacrificed to Val's adoration of Jess. For another moment they all stared at one another, none able to find words to cut through all the hate and confusion in the air.

At last Teddie broke the silence. "Well, I'm going to bed," she said coolly. "I've had a bitch of a day."

Val's hand almost shot out again to grab her—

For what? Punish her insolence with another blow? Val wrapped her arms quickly around herself, binding her hands from doing further harm. She squeezed her eyes shut and tears seeped between her lashes. How could it all go so wrong? She had worked so hard to make Teddie's life sweeter than her own. That ambition more than any other had molded all her initial choices.

Once Teddie had disappeared, Jess spoke. "It'll be all right, Mom. I'm sorry about this."

Val looked up at her. "You? Why on earth should you be sorry?"

"It's because of me, isn't it? She hates me for . . . all that my being here took away from her."

"You didn't take anything away, Jess. You brought something more to both of us. It's too bad Teddie couldn't be glad about it, but I am, I always will be. If she can't be, that's not your fault. It goes back to who she is . . . the way she's made. I don't love her less for it—she needs more sympathy, I know—but I'm not blind to it either."

Jess solemnly nodded and moved over to Val. "Will you be all right?"

That was Jess all over, Val thought, worrying first about the other person. "I think so. Can I do anything for you—make some cocoa, or—"

"No, thanks." They embraced. "Really," Jess added before going off to bed, "I'm okay."

Through the rest of that night, a phrase that had emerged from Val as she tried to account for Teddie's viciousness kept echoing in her mind. *It goes back to . . . the way she's made.*

Was that the root? Because Teddie was created out of violence rather than love, did that somehow scar the soul, make her less capable of love herself? Or did it come from the part formed out of Willy?

Val stayed home for almost a week after bringing Teddie back, afraid to leave her alone for fear she would run away again. She also came to the decision that her daughter needed to be someplace where she could receive special attention. Communication between them was hopeless. Every one of Val's attempts to express love and concern was quickly derailed by her daughter's inner demons. When Val raised the delicate issue of whether Teddie had known enough to take contraceptive precautions, it was only seized as an opportunity to taunt her.

"You worried I'm gonna get pregnant? And why should that worry you? I'll just have a bastard like you did."

At the end of the week, Val located a camp in Vermont that would take Teddie for the balance of the summer, a place offering closer supervision and a staff of psychiatric professionals devoted to dealing with "problem youngsters." The cost was ten times what the camp in the Poconos had charged, but Val was ready to pay any amount if only the pain and hatred that possessed her daughter could be soothed away. Still, Teddie's lost childhood, her innocence, could never be bought at any price.

In her first days back at the office, Val found it hard to concentrate on work. If not for her child, she would never have fled from a life of limited opportunity, would not have had the impulse to succeed as she had . . . and yet these same achievements had driven them apart.

There were other women who managed to raise children alone without losing their children's love. So what had made the difference with Teddie? The possibility that most tormented Val was that her daughter's unhappiness was not just the result of never feeling truly wanted and accepted, but of never actually receiving absolute maternal devotion. Val hated to think that she might have cheated Teddie out of her unconditional love.

But she asked herself now: Against her own will, had she loved Teddie less because Willy was her father—because of . . . the way she was conceived?

The phone call came in the midst of a meeting about a special promotion the magazine was running: The winning essay in a contest to describe "My Dream Wedding" in two pages or less ("preferably typewritten, double-spaced, though neatly handwritten entries will be accepted") would be rewarded by having that wedding carried out, fully paid for by *Every Bride's*—up to a cost of $20,000, more than three times the current national average spent on a formal wedding.

"Pat, I thought I told you to hold my calls during the meeting," Val said when she answered the buzz of the intercom and heard there was a caller.

"I know, Val, I'm sorry. I told this guy you were in a meeting, but he says he's the head of a very big hotel chain and he'll talk only to you right now about making a huge ad commitment. I though it was worth checking—"

"What's his name?" Val asked quickly, though the mention of the hotel chain made her think she already knew the answer.

"Alan Wellstrom."

Two weeks had gone by since they'd met, and, of course, she had broken their dinner date by running off to collect Teddie. She had never called to explain or apologize—for reasons she assumed he understood, since she hadn't heard from him either. Yet she couldn't help feeling a rush of excitement that after all, he was getting in touch with her.

Telling the others to go on with the meeting, Val went to the cozy dressing room that adjoined her office, a place where she could take a nap, or change clothes if she had to rush straight from the office to a formal event. She sat in one of the chairs upholstered in flowered chintz and picked up the phone beside it. "This is Val Cummings. To which Mr. Wellstrom," she asked playfully, "do I have the pleasure of speaking?"

"The one you stood up for dinner," he said.

"Alan . . . I'm terribly sorry about that, but just as I was going to meet you—"

"I knew what had happened, Val. When I came to the bungalow and you weren't there, I called the local police and they told me your daughter had been found."

She was silent a moment. Perhaps she did owe him an account of why she had never contacted him to apologize, but getting into that would arouse the very feelings she had tried to repress. Indeed, she had picked up a phone that very next day and several times since to talk to him, but had never let the call go through. His sympathetic remark about the particular stress of worrying about children, his mention of paying a price for his own success, had hinted strongly there was a family in the background—not a difficult assumption to make: He was much too attractive not to have married by now. If she had sought him out, she'd want to see him too—and the last thing she wanted to be was a home-wrecker.

Letting so much time go by before calling her indicated he had doubts of his own.

Yet now he was on the line. And she was glad.

The silence had lasted too long. "You told my secretary you wanted to advertise . . . ?"

"Not exactly. What I said—when I needed to get past your first line of defense—was that I run a big chain of hotels . . . and that I wanted to talk to the boss about making a long-term commitment."

"You really think your no-frills Festival Inns are going to appeal to our honeymooners?"

"Hold on, Val—you're jumping to the same wrong conclusion as your secretary. I never said the commitment was for advertising."

She got it now. And as much as she'd liked him, remembered every moment of their first meeting with a thrill, hearing him speak in these terms scared her a little. "Alan, I . . . I truly loved meeting you—"

"I felt the same," he put in quickly.

"But I think it might be a mistake to—"

He knew where she was going, and stopped her. "Val, when you didn't call, it was obvious you were backing away from . . . from whatever happened during that little piece of time we spent together. I didn't call you then because whatever your reasons, I wanted to respect your decision. I still want to." He took a breath. "The trouble is, miracles don't happen every day, so it's not easy to ignore them. There was a certain feeling in the air when we were together. And when I looked at you, I felt I'd never seen anyone so lovely, never would again."

She wanted to hear this, longed to hear it. Yet the fear was still there, the old reflex she couldn't control, a belief that it could go so far and no farther. Once it had been because she was alone with a fatherless child. In recent years the social code had become more forgiving, part of a sexual revolution that encouraged freer love, young, unmarried people living together on communes, even a young president of the country who was called "sexy." But now other factors said it wasn't the time to begin a new love affair. Teddie was clearly in need of being reassured that she came first.

"Maybe I misread the signs," he said, "but I didn't think I was alone in feeling we connected in a special way. So whatever else we have in our lives, I thought we might both be fools not to—"

She stopped him cold. "Alan, you have a child of your own, don't you?"

"Two," he said flatly, "a boy and a girl."

"Well, then—"

"I thought that might be it. Val, I'm separated from my wife. Have been for three years."

"You haven't divorced though."

"I'll explain that to you, but not now. Let me see you again. Let's find out if we only imagined there was magic in the air when we met. You do believe in magic, don't you? I took a good look at your magazine after meeting you—and I know you want all your readers to believe in it. . . ."

"Yes," she said plainly. "I believe in magic."

He would have wanted to see her at once, he said, but in fact he was calling from Los Angeles, where he was planning the construction of two new hotels in the chain, and would have to be there a few more days. "I'll be back next Friday. Can we have dinner?"

She said she would be ready at eight o'clock, and gave him her home telephone number. Then just before saying good-bye she added, "Alan . . . I'm glad you believe in miracles."

When she returned to the meeting, a number of people around the table gave her second looks. She realized then that her eyes must be shining; there was nothing she could do to hide the excitement she felt. More than once someone at the table addressed her, and she was daydreaming like a schoolgirl unable to concentrate in class because she was thinking about a crush. She was glad Jess wasn't sitting in at this meeting.

". . . what would you say it is, Val?" Connie Marcantonio, who had come back to the magazine after marrying and was in charge of the special promotion, was looking at her expectantly.

"About what?"

"I was wondering," Connie said, "if there's any one key to picking the winner in this contest, what you think it might be?"

"Magic," Val answered at once. "The way the dream wedding is described should make us feel it's a time of absolute magic."

On Friday evening he called her at home an hour before he was to pick her up.

"Would you mind if I don't come for you myself?" Alan asked. "I can send a car to bring you where I am."

She understood he must have a busy schedule. "That'll be fine. I can even take a taxi—"

"My carriage will be at your disposal," he said.

"Sounds like I should wear my glass slippers."

"Nothing quite so fancy."

"Where will I be meeting you?" she asked.

"Ah . . . that's part of the surprise."

At eight o'clock sharp the doorman of her apartment building rang on the house phone to say a car was waiting.

"Wow! You look fabulous," Jess said when Val went into the den to say good night. Jess was already settled for the evening on a couch in front of the television. "Who'd you say this guy was?"

"Just someone in the hotel business. . . ."

"He ain't 'just someone,' " Jess said wryly, aware that the casually elegant red silk shift by Cassini—the designer doing Jackie Kennedy's White House wardrobe—was new, and that the loose cut of Val's long hair looked as though it had been touched up that afternoon.

Val smiled. "We'll see. . . ." She bent down to kiss Jess.

"Don't do anything I wouldn't do," Jess called out as Val went out the door.

The teasing remark had an extra edge to it in the light of Teddie's terrible outburst against Jess. Val had talked since with Jess about her reaction, making sure she wasn't concealing problems of her own. There was, after all, some truth at the core of Teddie's remarks, even if they had been framed so brutally. Jess was almost *too* good—and it wasn't hard to understand why she might apply such a high standard to her own behavior. Just six when orphaned by her parents' murder-suicide, at that age a child's view of the world was naturally egocentric; deep within, a part of Jess took the blame for what had happened—*if only I'd been better*—with the result that she could not allow herself any further misstep, fearing it might result in life inflicting another terrible punishment. Val had wondered if Jess reined herself in to an abnormal degree. While not so statuesque as Teddie was on her way to being, Jess was no less lovely, yet she spent many evenings at home curled up with a book, though Val knew she was often asked out on dates. When Val talked about it with Jess, however, she never got the feeling Jess was struggling with any secrets or neurotic repression.

"I'd rather not go out," Jess would say, "unless I know I'm going to be spending an evening with someone whose company I really enjoy. And interesting boys don't grow on trees, Mom. Well, you know that as well as I do. . . ." Over the years, Jess had seen Val spending time alone rather than involving herself with any man merely for the purpose of staying on the social circuit.

Just as tonight, Jess had detected the signs that Val was going to be spending an evening with a man she must feel was special.

A limousine was waiting in front of Val's apartment building, a chauffeur holding the door for her. She didn't ask where they were going, knowing already Alan wanted to surprise her. The car traveled downtown and across to the East River at Thirtieth Street where there was a marina, crowded in the late summer weeks with yachts of varying sizes. The car stopped at the gate, and the chauffeur came around to open the door. "Mr. Wellstrom will meet you on the dock," he told Val.

Alan stood at the head of the dock, dressed in white flannel pants and a loose midnight-blue shirt. With his hair slightly windblown, his skin tanned as though he had already spent the afternoon on the water, he looked even more appealing to Val than she'd remembered.

He held out both his hands to her, and she took them. If he

had pulled her into a kiss at that moment, she would not have resisted. But he just looked at her.

"It's wonderful to see you again, Val."

"I'm happy to be here." Happy—the ordinary word felt as if it had new meaning.

He started to lead her along the dock, still lightly grasping one of her hands. "Thanks again for coming to meet me. I was tied up until a little while ago with some of my engineers. Some run-down waterfront across the river might be reclaimed for one of our hotels, so I felt they had to see the site from the water." They had walked past a number of yachts tied up in their slips. He stopped by a gangplank that led up to the after-deck of a white cruiser with *Wave Dancer* written across the transom. "Here we are," he said.

The sleek boat was fifty or sixty feet long, Val estimated, yet modest compared to other yachts on either side. As she looked up at it, memories flashed through her mind of being brought down to the water's edge long ago by a man she had deeply cared about. And then, again, by Willy . . .

Something must have showed in her face. "Do you mind boats?" he said. "I thought it'd be nice to have dinner aboard, but if you have a problem, seasickness or—"

"No, I'll be fine," she said. "It's a wonderful idea."

An accomplished sailor, he took the helm himself to pilot the boat out into the harbor, though he was helped in casting off by a couple of men who lived aboard, maintaining the boat and acting as crew and stewards. She stood beside him in the open cockpit as they cruised south, gliding out into the wider reaches of New York Harbor. The heat of the city in August gave way to balmy summer breezes. Ahead of them, the illuminated form of the Statue of Liberty glowed in the evening, off to one side canyons of glittering skyscrapers rolled by, occasionally a bridge went past overhead.

Val had never seen the city from this perspective, and she thought it more beautiful than any other view of it. Silently expressing her gratitude for the gift, she slipped her arm through his. Strangely, for a long time there was no need or desire to speak; she was certain he knew exactly what she was feeling.

At last he summoned one of the men to take over the helm and brought Val aft to a salon, where a small table had been set for dinner. Glass doors at the rear opened wide to the vision of the sparkling city retreating behind them.

Dinner, brought up from the galley by a steward, was simple, but as delicious as she could imagine having at the finest restaurant—a cold curried carrot soup, fresh poached salmon, green salad, and a raspberry tart—all accompanied by crisp, fruity white wine. All through it they talked, delivering whatever pieces of their history were needed to advance the process of belonging to each other. For her, it was the story of coming to New York, starting the magazine, how she had come to have two daughters without ever marrying.

He told her about growing up in the small inn his parents ran, his service in the Korean War—the navy, the origin of his love of boating. Finally, over coffee, after the steward had touched some light switches to dim the salon to more intimate lighting and then discreetly vanished, Alan fulfilled his pledge to tell her about his marriage.

He had met his wife, Stefanie, a while after he and a partner had started the hotel chain nine years before. She was an assistant to an architect who had been commissioned to design a number of the earliest Festival Inns, and so they had found themselves together often.

"The chain grew so fast, I didn't have much time for women—or maybe they didn't have much time for a guy who was too busy traveling all over the map, looking for new places to build. But Stef kept showing up at the same places I was, with her boss, and eventually we drifted into being a couple, and—" He paused, took a sip of wine. "What seemed like love was only having someone who knew about my work and didn't mind that I had to be away so much. After we married, she wanted children right away—maybe to keep her company. A marriage can be wrong from the beginning, yet you want to keep trying, believing. Finally, though, we both had to admit it didn't work, never really had. We're friends; she has custody of the children, and she's wonderful with them, thank God, and I spend a lot of time with them. Neither of us wanted to go through the extra wrenching of a divorce—or put the kids through it—unless there was a reason." He paused to gaze at Val, and his hand reached across the table to cover hers. "I think I've found a reason."

With his declaration, her heart started to pound. She was thrilled by it, yet also gripped by the same curious terror. Facing a fresh chance at love, it was as if she were transported back to the times she had lost it.

She had an impulse to pull away, to save herself from whatever tricks fate might have in store this time, but she fought against it, stayed with him. "We hardly know each other, Alan . . . but I won't pretend that I don't also feel . . . well, if I were going to throw caution to the winds—"

"Go ahead," he coaxed.

"Then I'd say I feel . . . we have a future."

"Caution didn't get blown very far."

"For me it's a big leap to say that. Even now there are priorities that come way ahead of taking care of myself."

"Your daughter . . ."

"She needs to know she comes first."

"I won't get in the way of that. I'll be happy with whatever part of yourself you can spare."

She leaned closer across the table to look at him a moment, then brought her other hand up to caress his face. "You're a lovely man, Alan."

"You bring out the very best in me."

Neither of them could wait any longer. He rose, pulling her up with him, and they kissed long and deeply. Then, both breathless, they held each other close.

"Alan," she whispered after a minute.

"What?"

"I don't want to wait a minute longer . . . to begin the future."

She pulled him eagerly into a kiss. With Andrew she had needed to wait, to go slowly, as an antidote to being taken by storm the first time, against her will. But she trusted herself now to know that sooner or later, it would make no difference.

He answered her passion with his own, and so great was the longing for what had been missing in both their lives, they undressed each other right there. Moving to one of the soft sofas at the side of the salon, they made love, lost in passion. The gentle rolling motion of the boat as it circled the harbor subtly accentuated the movements of their bodies, adding to their own voyage into pleasure. He was a glorious lover, taking his time, touching each part of her exquisitely. She rose slowly to the climax, and when she came along with him, she had the feeling that not just these touches, not just tonight, but all that had gone before had been destined to bring them together.

"Yes," he said, holding her after the first waves of pleasure receded and new ones began to rise, "we have a wonderful future."

Nineteen

New York
May 1967

"Elvis got married," Alan said. "It was on the news."

"I know. This morning in Las Vegas." Val lay entwined with him in her bed after making love. She'd known about it before it was on the news. Only a few days earlier, Presley's press people had asked if the magazine would like to send a reporter to the wedding on May 1st . When Val heard about the arrangements being made, she declined. Famous as Elvis was, the popularity of the sort of romantic ceremony *E.B.* encouraged wouldn't be helped by publicizing his wedding—in a Las Vegas hotel suite, Priscilla's dress the least expensive model bought off the rack at a local wedding shop, more of Presley's "Memphis Mafia" present than family, and no reception to follow. Val preferred to cover weddings like last year's nuptials for President Lyndon Johnson's daughter Luci. Johnson was the first president to give his daughter a White House wedding since Teddy Roosevelt's Alice had been married there six decades before. Covering that kind of pomp always gave a lift to the wedding business in general. Val had been delighted to attend personally.

"He'd been courting his bride, Priscilla, for quite a few years," Alan said.

Val knew now why he'd brought it up. "She was just fourteen when they met. He *had* to wait."

Alan propped himself up on his elbow and looked down into her eyes. "What about us? I passed my eighteenth birthday a while ago, in case you missed it."

She smiled, and brought her hand up around his neck, slipping her fingers into his hair, tousled from their lovemaking. "Then what we're doing isn't against the law," she said. "So let's do it again."

"You're changing the subject," he said.

She pulled him closer, fitting her body to his. "Do you mind?" She touched him below, feeling the signs of arousal.

He gave a low moan of pleasure. "Yes and no."

"I'll proceed on the basis of no." After five years with Alan, there had yet to be any decrease in the desire aroused in Val when they were in bed. Yet, it was true, whenever he raised the subject of marriage, Val retreated from it—and he had begun to bring it up regularly since the divorce from his wife had been amicably settled two years earlier. She loved Alan—thought she did—but she was happy enough with the way things were, and had a vague premonition that if she were to make plans to marry, it might all go wrong. Was it that she didn't love him enough? Or was it a fear instilled by the memory that she had lost the only other man she had been committed to marry?

For now, however, he allowed her to escape the subject again. Responding to her physically, his hands glided up and down along her arms as they kissed. Then his caresses moved across her shoulders, down to her breasts, his fingers taking on the curve and then pinching her nipples so delicately, it gave her only the most delicious jolt of sensation. She arched back, and he slid down, his mouth laying a trail of kisses across her throat, the valley of her bosom, the soft swell of her torso, around her hips, to her thighs, until she thrilled to his lips speaking silently to the very core of her sensations. His touches sent her climbing steadily upward in a flight of growing thrills until she could bear no longer not to have him joined completely with her. She summoned him in an urgent whisper and he was there, completely a part of her, and she went flying still higher and higher until she felt they were plunging together into the sun.

They came back to earth in the soft lamplight of her bedroom.

"So," he said at last, "as I was saying . . ."

She was half amused, half exasperated. "Alan, it's too soon

for me to change the subject again. But can't we just put this off until—"

"Until what—Elvis and Priscilla's children get married? Darling, you've asked me to be patient, and I have been: It's four months since the last time I brought this up."

"Not even three," she said. She remembered exactly: The last time he'd mentioned marriage was on a February weekend in Vermont, skiing, a sport she loved since he'd taught her.

"All right, that was winter, now it's spring. I'm going to bring it up once every season until you set a date." He grinned devilishly. "Unless you want to elope."

"If that's what you want," she said lightly, "when the day comes, just put the ladder under my window."

"Even a fire truck hasn't got a ladder that long—and you know it." With Teddie away most of the time, and Jess now enjoying life on her own with a studio apartment downtown, Val had moved last year to a new apartment. The flow of added money from her book on weddings—considered the authoritative source, it had been an instant best-seller—had allowed her to buy an eight-room penthouse with a huge terrace in a building on Fifth Avenue. Nineteen floors up.

"So I guess the elopement is out," Alan went on, sounding genuinely deflated. "Which wouldn't be so bad, Val . . . if I didn't feel sometimes that you may never want to set a date." He rolled onto his back and stared balefully at the ceiling. "You know, darling, for a woman who owes her success to the brides of the world, your aversion to marriage is positively subversive."

She laughed good-naturedly, hoping to keep the mood light. "Alan, marriage doesn't have to be an issue for us. We'll do it when we both feel the time is right."

He pulled himself up again to look at her. "But why isn't *now* that time, Val? You know I'd like to have children with you, and the doctors all agree: At our age, the sooner we start, the better."

"Unfortunately," she said pointedly, "there's one doctor who doesn't agree. And right now he's the most important one."

She was referring to the skilled psychiatrist who had started treating Teddie intensively during the year after she'd run away from camp. Other misadventures had followed—shoplifting, experiments with marijuana. But in the past two years, as a student at boarding school, Teddie's record was excellent. Not that there weren't occasional arguments with Val when she was home during school recesses; Teddie remained sexually active—she had confessed to sleeping with boys who dated her over holidays, and that she knew about practicing birth control. But she was adjusted to going away to school, obeyed the rules, got good grades, and her relationship with Val was much improved—even if still strained with Jess. The psychiatrist, who continued seeing Teddie on school vacations, had said that to save the gains with Teddie—particularly if Val wanted to have a baby with Alan—marriage should wait until Teddie started Wellesley the following year.

Alan knew all this, but he also knew the toll it had taken on Val to have conceived a child as the result of rape, and felt that having a child with him born of love would repair a damaged piece of her heart and soul. "Well, if you can stand waiting," he said at last, "I suppose I can."

Val put her arms around him. "You've been so good for me, Alan. I just need to be completely sure that when we take our vows . . . I'll be as good for you."

He clasped her tightly. "Why on earth would you doubt that?"

"I haven't made everyone happy, have I?"

"Oh, darling," he said sympathetically, knowing it was the rift with Teddie that haunted her. "You've done the best you could. That's all anyone can ask." He kissed her lightly before adding, "All that I ask."

She clung to him and returned his kiss gratefully. But while she found both solace and pleasure in his embrace, she was also aware of the curious relief she felt that for the moment at least, he seemed willing to put aside the question of marriage.

They couldn't have asked for a more beautiful day. Under a bright blue cloudless sky, the manicured green lawns and redbrick dormitory and classroom buildings of the school campus made a picture-perfect setting for the daughters of the privileged to receive their high school diplomas.

The Madeira School was among the most prestigious of the all-female preparatory schools in the nation. Set on a few hundred acres beside the Potomac River in the Virginia countryside not far from Washington, D.C., it had educated generations of children from the families of senators, diplomats, and the corporate elite.

Even so, it had not been Val's first choice for Teddie. When Teddie's doctor had suggested her education might proceed best in the more structured environment of a boarding school, Val had still wanted to keep her daughter as close to New York as possible, and enrolled her at Miss Porter's in Connecticut.

Teddie lasted there only two months. Still rebellious, she had continued to break the rules and had fought so much with other students that at last the school informed Val it would be "best for all concerned if Theodora did not return after the Thanksgiving holiday." Teddie had spent the remainder of that year back in New York, continuing therapy while being tutored.

By summer, when Val was advised that Teddie's therapy had prepared her to behave more responsibly, fresh applications had been made. Some schools simply rejected her outright. Even Madeira had been slow to act, obviously on the fence about admitting a possible troublemaker. Then Val had visited the school to make a personal appeal to the headmistress, a trim and proper fortyish blond divorcée named Jean Frost. Over tea in her house on the grounds, Mrs. Frost had listened sympathetically to Val's appeal to give her daughter a chance to prove herself.

"I don't like to think of a girl not being given a second chance," Mrs. Frost said. "Even someone who knows the difference between right and wrong might have some bad luck and get into trouble. . . ."

Val had left the meeting with hope that her daughter would get her second chance.

A week later, a letter had come from Mrs. Frost to say that Teddie would be admitted to Madeira on the condition that she repeat the year that had been broken by her expulsion from her previous school. As a result, Teddie was a year older than the girls in her class. But that slight edge of maturity had probably been a boon. Along with a good academic record, Teddie had been a high-scoring forward on the volleyball team, chairman of the Social Committee, and a co-editor of the yearbook.

Now, after three years, Teddie was graduating. Last night Val had come down to Washington—on the eve of graduation, Mrs. Frost always gave a cocktail party for the parents of the seniors—and this morning the ceremony was being held in a hillside amphitheater that looked across the Potomac to the Maryland shore.

Arriving twenty minutes before the ceremony was to begin, Val easily found herself a single seat not far from the front. She had come alone only after considerable discussion with both Alan and Jess, neither of whom wanted to do anything that might detract from Teddie's being the proud center of Val's attention.

The ceremony began, music playing through amplifiers, and the graduating class started filing down from the top of the hillside toward their seats at the front of the amphitheater. The parents all turned to watch them. Val easily spotted Teddie, one of the tallest of the girls, also one of the most striking, her long blond hair fanned across her shoulders. Considering the personal battles she'd had to overcome, the social stigma of her early years as a fatherless child, the inner anger that had caused her self-destructive behavior, to see her marching steadily toward this positive milestone brought Val not only a swell of pride, but an inner calm. As Teddie came down the aisle with her classmates, she caught Val's eye, and a smile flickered through the solemn expression the occasion demanded. Yes, the smile communicated to her mother, I made it, I'm going to be okay.

The line of graduates passed down the center aisle, and as they did, Val was able to see across to the section of seats beyond. In the moment before she turned forward again, Val caught sight of something that sent her plunging from the height of pride and elation to the depths of despair.

There, seated in a far corner of the section, near the rear, his eyes firmly fixed on Teddie—*their* daughter—was Wilhelm Gruening.

It was not quite a year before that she'd heard from him again, a call to the office that came on a mild June afternoon, a few days before Teddie's eighteenth birthday. Unpleasant as it was to hear from him, the contact did not come as a total surprise. Val had never forgotten that at the time she'd bought his agreement to renounce a claim to Teddie, he had imposed a single condition: *Once—once at least I want to see her. Sometime . . . somewhere.*

Willy hadn't been unreasonable at first. When Val described the problems Teddie had gone through, he agreed to put off exercising his right—as he thought of it—to see Teddie. He had not called again for several months. Then Val asked him again to be patient. "She's been doing so well. If you care at all for your daughter, Willy, you won't want to do anything now that might upset her. . . ." He had consented again not to intrude, though he didn't hide his irritation. "You can't keep me away from her forever though. You promised me this, Val."

His latest call had come to the office only two weeks earlier. "From what you've told me before," he said, "Theodora should be graduating soon. That's quite an achievement for a young lady . . . obviously the sort of thing a father takes pride in. . . ."

The hint that he might choose this occasion to make himself known to Teddie terrified Val. All the progress Teddie had made in overcoming her doubts of being wanted and cherished could be undone in an instant by learning the truth that Val had not yet been capable of revealing to her—that she wasn't the daughter of a man she'd loved who had died before they could marry, but that she was the accidental result of an act of violence by a crass brute who was still alive.

"Listen, Willy," Val had pleaded. "You've got to give me

time to prepare your daughter to meet you. You've got to understand how this might affect her if she's not prepared."

"All right, do what you have to," he had told her. "But you'd better do it soon."

She had believed then that she'd bought enough time so that Teddie's graduation wouldn't be spoiled. When Val consulted the psychiatrist about the situation, he had confirmed her judgment that she, no one else, must be the one to reveal to Teddie that the truth about her birth had been kept from her, and that it would be best done after she finished with school.

"It's going to be a shock to her no matter when or how you do it," he'd warned Val.

"I should have told her a long time ago," Val said guiltily.

"The recommended procedure is always to tell children such truths as soon as they're old enough to understand. But in Teddie's case there were extenuating circumstances," he added, hoping to relieve Val's guilt. "If you'd acknowledged this man as the true father, it would have meant giving up your adopted daughter. You did a noble thing to rescue the other girl."

"I didn't know the cost would be so high for Teddie. How do I help her now? You said it'll be a terrible shock—"

"There's no way around that, but having her accomplishments to stand on will be . . . like a shock absorber. Let Teddie get that diploma up on the wall, know she's on the path to a fine college—and she should be able to come to grips with this new reality without any serious damage to her self-esteem. Especially as you're the one who'll be revealing the truth, she'll be able to see that it comes from the same source as the lies you once told—your love for her."

Now Val was terrified she wouldn't have that chance.

Throughout the rest of the ceremony, she could barely concentrate on what was unfolding on the stage. A storm of troubled questions raged through her mind. What could she do to head Willy off, how would Teddie react if they met? Her preoccupation was such that during a part of the program when special class prizes were awarded, she became aware that Teddie was one of the recipients only when she heard her daughter's name being read aloud, then saw her crossing the stage. For what was Teddie being honored? Val was so consumed by worry, she'd missed it. Teddie, who'd obviously wanted to keep this achievement as a surprise, grinned happily in Val's direction as she walked back to her seat with an award scroll.

As the program continued through the valedictory and the presentation of diplomas, Val's anxiety grew to a fever pitch. What must she do to stop Willy from committing this devastating act against Teddie, this *crime*? For it seemed no less than that—another kind of rape, a forced assault against her child's personality.

Gripped by a black rage as she sat on the sunny green hillside, Val had to force herself not to leap up and run to obstruct Willy. Several times, though, she looked over in his direction, hoping somehow she could silently convey an appeal that would win one more delay. But his gaze was always fixed as wholly on the stage as any of the other proud parents'.

The presentation of diplomas began, graduates being summoned forward in alphabetical order, parents and friends applauding. As Teddie walked across the stage after the presentation, she looked toward Val again, smiling. Val smiled back as broadly as possible, and raised her hands aloft as she applauded. Was *he* applauding, too, indicating his personal interest in this graduate? Val avoided looking until Teddie was seating herself, no longer turned toward the audience. Then Val swung around to check—

His seat was empty.

Val's eyes searched the perimeters of the audience. Nowhere to be seen. Gone. Relief flooded through her. Thank God, he had come only to share as a witness, but had made a decent retreat, not the assault she had feared.

Still, it was also a warning that he could come this close again whenever he wished. Val knew she couldn't wait much longer to tell Teddie about him.

The ceremonies came to a close with the graduates marching in solemn recessional up the hillside. At last, they gave out a unified whoop of joy, and broke ranks, each girl running to find her loved ones. Val climbed up the aisle and found her daughter.

"I made it, didn't I?" Teddie said, beaming.

Choked with emotion, eyes filling, Val said, "I'm so proud of you. . . ."

"To tell the truth, Mom, I'm pretty damn proud of myself. And you too. I've never said it before, but I know how hard it must have been for you—right from the beginning. Thanks for . . ." Teddie faltered, holding back her own emotions. "Well, you know." She looked around. "Jess didn't come, huh . . . or Alan."

"They would have, but—"

"I know. I scared 'em off. I'm sorry about that now. I realize it's my loss. From now on I'm going to be—"

"Hello, Val." Involved in their emotional reunion, neither noticed him approach. The voice, instantly recognized, was enough to send a cold shaft knifing through Val's soul, destroying the warmth of the moment. She turned to him, speechless.

"Well, aren't you going to introduce me?" he asked calmly.

She managed somehow to form a few words. "Teddie . . . this is . . . an acquaintance from when I lived in Buffalo, Wilhelm Gruening."

"No," he said sharply. "It's William. Remember, I call myself William now." He put his hand out to Teddie.

Before taking it, she glanced between him and Val, sensing the disturbance in the atmosphere, like that electricity in the air before a lightning bolt strikes. "How do you do, Mr. Gruening," she said.

His eyes lingered on her after she retracted her hand. Then he turned to Val. "You said she was lovely. But I had no idea just . . . how much. . . ."

There was a silence.

Teddie was staring at Val, obviously in need of an explanation for the presence of this man when others had been kept away.

Willy turned back to Teddie. "You have no idea, do you?"

Val could stand it no longer. "Willy . . . I beg you. . . ."

At that moment, Teddie realized where she had heard the name before. "Gruening!" She clutched at Val. "That was my father's name, wasn't it? Theodore Gruening." She glanced to Willy. Her shrewd eyes scanned his features, picked out the resemblance to the face she saw in the mirror, calculated ages. "Brother! You're his brother. That's it, isn't it? My father's brother!"

That was too much for Willy. To give credit to Ted for this beauty when his own life had been empty of achievement. "No," he said. "It wasn't him—"

"For God's sake, Willy," Val cried out, "what's the point?"

He ignored her. "*I'm* the one. *I am* your father."

Teddie stared back at him. It was all too clear by the expression that came over her face that she was taking an instant inventory of things that hadn't seemed to quite add up in the past . . . and that suddenly did. She whirled to Val. "All these years," she murmured, shaking her head as if to clear it. "Why?"

Val reached out to her. "For you, Teddie, for you. I wanted you to believe the best—"

"Lies!" Teddie said, backing away. "I believed lies."

"But you need to hear it *all.*"

"Yes, tell her," Willy crowed.

Teddie screamed at Val: "No, I don't want to hear any more. Certainly not from you! *Liar!*" Pressing her hands over her ears, she backed away farther, flicking a glance at Willy that was filled with disdain for what she saw, hating him as much for bringing the truth as she hated Val for concealing it. "Him! Jesus, how could you?" Abruptly, she spun away and broke into a furious run, dodging through the happy groups of graduates and their guests, bumping aside anyone in her way.

"Damn you, Willy," Val shrieked at him, a cry that made all the other happy groups around them go silent and stare at her. "Damn you to hell!"

Then she went racing off to search for her daughter.

Twenty

Val didn't find Teddie that day . . . or the next.

When Teddie ran back to her dorm, she had grabbed only the cash squirreled away from allowances, her Nikon camera, and a double strand of pearls Val had given her on her sixteenth birthday] and left before Val could catch up. From there she had hitchhiked into limbo.

Val engaged the services of a private investigator named Frank Stecchino, who had a good reputation for locating long-lost relatives. As the weeks went by, everything other than finding her became secondary. Constantly checking in with the investigator, worrying when no leads were produced, Val had difficulty concentrating on work. Fortunately, helpers who'd been with her from the beginning knew how to take up the slack. Madge and Connie were still there, high-salaried, each given a bloc of shares as bonuses; Kath Storrow had come back and taken over the honeymoon bureau after her marriage to an investment banker—starting with a hundred-thousand-dollar wedding—ended in a painfully hostile divorce.

Val was further distracted from work by her vendetta against Willy. In her fury, she yearned to extract some form of justice, and began to have papers drawn for a civil suit charging Willy with alienation of affection of her daughter. Then she realized fighting him would only forge more of a connection than she wanted to maintain. Willy's punishment, Val decided, was simply to be the man he was, destructive and cruel, alone and unloved.

The summer passed without any success in the search. Alan urged Val to concentrate on moving her life forward, and over the Labor Day weekend, he finally persuaded her to spend four days relaxing aboard his boat, cruising the waters around Cape Cod.

They had dropped anchor off Martha's Vineyard on Saturday night, and were sitting on the afterdeck, when he thought Val offered an opening for him to express the feelings he'd been holding back since Teddie's disappearance.

Rising from the table where they'd had dinner, Val carried her wineglass to the stern railing and gazed across the dark harbor at the lights of Edgartown. "I can never look into the darkness," she said, "without thinking about her—wondering where she is out there, what she's doing. . . ." She sighed. "How long, Alan . . . when will I be able to go on with my life again?"

Joining her at the railing, he put his arm around her. "In the time we've been together, Val, I got to know Teddie pretty well. She could be a terribly willful kid at times, tough and stubborn. But there's a good, positive side to the same character: She's strong, determined, fearless, resourceful. . . ."

Val looked at him, knowing he was leading up to something.

"So if she wants to survive on her own," he continued, "she can and she will. You've got to be ready for that, Val—ready, too, not to expect too much even if she's found. Whatever healing has to be done between you two will take time." He made his point: "Use that time instead of throwing it away. Use it with me."

She understood, but she could not yield. "Alan, don't ask me to marry you now."

He took her in his arms. "I want a life with you, darling—a whole, good life."

"With children," she said. "No need to marry otherwise."

He looked hurt by that. "There *is* a point to marriage anyway—always has been. It's a bond of love unmatched by any other kind of commitment. And yes, I do want us to have children too. More than ever, I think we should have a family."

"Why is that so important to you?"

"Not just to *me*. Val, with all you've accomplished in your life, the one thing that's torn you up for years is your guilt—the idea you failed as a mother. I want to see you—"

She didn't let him finish. "You can't change the truth. I did fail—badly. It would be wrong for me to have another child."

"That's crazy! You did everything you could for Teddie, and under the most difficult circumstances right from the start. And look at Jess! You've been a fabulous mother to that girl. Don't you take any credit for who she is, the success she's made?"

After working at the magazine for a couple of years, Jess had decided to get more journalistic experience. She had sent out her résumé and had received a positive response from *The Washington Post.* When Jess traveled to Washington for an interview with the editor, Ben Bradlee, it went so well that an offer had been made on the spot for her to report on women's issues, with an occasional column on Washington's social scene. Jess had accepted—subject to Val's approval. Of course Val had endorsed the change, knowing it was best for Jess to carve out her own identity in the media rather than stay at the magazine. Now, Jess had been at the *Post* for a couple of months and was doing very well.

But Val could take no credit for it, nor for the unusual person Jess seemed to be. "Jess hardly needed a mother," she said now. "She was just created that way—and not by me."

"That's equally wrong-headed," Alan said impatiently. "You were there for that kid at the worst moment any child could face—fighting for her from the time she needed you. And she knew it. You think none of that made a difference? Don't you think it's time you forgave yourself and—"

Val broke down. "I can't. Not unless Teddie can."

"She may never be able to, Val, that's what I'm saying. But it won't be your fault."

She wiped her tears and looked at him bleakly. It was so awful to contemplate that her child might be lost to her forever.

He took her back into his arms. "I can give you all the love in my heart, but I think what you need most now is to believe that part of you isn't a failure. Have *our* child—children!—with a father who'll be with you, love them as you do. Then you can stop blaming yourself for Teddie, you'll see that what you give as a mother is as good as any—"

"Can you guarantee they'll be happy and healthy and lovely and sweet-tempered? And are you so sure that I really will do what's right for them?"

"I know you'll try to do what's best. You always have. As for the rest, life's always a bit of a crap shoot. But you win nothing unless you roll the dice."

She looked away. "I don't like to think of the most important things in life being a gamble at best."

"And that's the real trouble," he said. "You won't take a chance on the most important things, because you're so damn afraid it won't go your way."

She said nothing while his words echoed in her mind. Was he right? She thought of Andrew, with whom she might have found love, marriage. . . . Other chances she'd ignored—like that sweet doctor who'd brought Teddie into the world. Yes, she'd always found some excuse not to take the risk. Even with Alan. Was this why she had kept him waiting? Or because the love she felt wasn't whole, wasn't enough?

Or was it because losing Ted had left her terrified to approach that moment again. Even if she could see objectively, that would be foolish, that didn't make the terror go away. There ought to be a word for it, she thought, as there was for those people who were terrified of stepping out of their own homes—agoraphobics. A woman who was phobically terrified of being a bride, what would that condition be called—groomaphobia?

She laughed to herself at the irony. Of all people to be a—well, one of . . . whatever they were called.

He was still beside her, hoping his plea had changed her mind. "What's so funny?"

She told him her thoughts. "God, imagine . . . if my readers were to find this out," she said then, "that maybe I'm more afraid of being a bride than of being burned at the stake."

He took her in his arms again. "Maybe we should do something about it before the secret gets out?"

She imagined it, her wedding, all the people she cared about gathered together. But as the mental picture formed, she saw the blank space, too, the place that would *not* be filled by her child. In some ways, it was worse than an absence caused by death—to know that someone you loved *chose* to keep away; it would poison what ought to be the happiest occasion of her life.

If she were even to answer the question of whether she truly wanted to marry Alan, Val realized, she must have the antidote for that poison.

"I've got to find Teddie," Val said abruptly, looking into the darkness. "That has to come first."

There was no use arguing, he realized then. No use discussing it again.

It was February of the New Year before Teddie was finally located by Frank Stecchino, living in the Haight-Ashbury section of San Francisco. The center of the city's hippie community, the neighborhood was a natural magnet for rootless young people from all across the country. The report presented by Stecchino contained a major shock for Val. Teddie was married.

Her husband's name was Mark Handler. Now twenty-two, he had been a student at the University of California at Berkeley, where he had been one of the leaders of a student revolution centered around opposition to the Vietnam War escalating under President Johnson. Handler's ability to give articulate and fiery public speeches had made him a spokesman for war resisters, a leader in large campus protests such as flag burnings—which had resulted in his expulsion from the university. He continued to agitate, though, often appearing to preach "peace and love" wherever crowds of young people were drawn together, like rock festivals. He and Teddie had been together since meeting at the largest of one of these—in Monterey, California, last July.

They had married in October. The investigator's report included a brief description of the wedding—perhaps because he understood that Val in particular would expect such details. It had been an ad hoc affair, with several hundred of Handler's adherents and friends walking through the streets of Haight-Ashbury to MacArthur Park, and taking vows written by the bride and groom themselves. The music was played by a variety of rock and folk musicians from the San Francisco music scene, and the legal pronouncement of wedlock made by a municipal judge who had become a supporter of the antiwar movement after his son was killed in Vietnam. The guests had gotten stoned in the park—and several, including Teddie and Mark Handler, had been arrested. The first night of Teddie's "honeymoon" with her new husband had been spent in a jail cell.

The wedding was the antithesis of the traditional ceremony and the values it represented that meant so much to Val, and were glorified by her magazine. Realizing this, Val's initial reaction was to feel it as a deliberate slap in the face.

Jess helped restore perspective after Val had sent a copy of the report to her in Washington, and they spoke on the phone.

"Mom, this is the way more and more young people are being married these days."

"With marijuana instead of champagne," Val observed, "and a honeymoon in jail?"

"Not that part," Jess said. "But for the ceremony, they just don't see the point in spending thousands of dollars on a lot of unnecessary things." As part of reporting social issues that affected women, Jess had lately been to a number of non-traditional weddings.

"Beautiful romantic traditions are *not* unnecessary," Val declared.

"But the ones really worth preserving are marriage itself . . . and vowing love and loyalty. All the rest, and especially the cost of it, doesn't make any sense to the kids. Maybe it's part of their rejecting other traditional ideas—like spending tens of billions of dollars on a stupid war."

"Celebrating love is a very good way of preventing war. I can't help feeling something wonderful will be lost if all it takes to make a wedding is to stand on a plot of grass at sunset, slip a strand of love beads around your neck, and promise to love the person standing beside you—for a few weeks, at least."

"I hate to say it, Mom, but you're beginning to talk like a real old-fashioned fuddy-duddy. I've always thought you were more of a trendsetter."

"Well, if caring about beauty makes me a fuddy-duddy . . ."

"The beauty isn't being lost," Jess persisted. "The beauty is just in the feeling. That's all that really matters."

On reflection, the conversation with Jess persuaded Val it was wrong to regard the style in which Teddie chose to be married as deliberately hurtful. Still, it hurt badly enough that she had been excluded from sharing this significant moment in her daughter's life.

The private investigator's report on Teddie included her current address and phone number. Val tried communicating first with a letter, an explanation for all that had gone into the decision to hold back the truth about her father, an avowal of love, a plea for reconciliation. By the time it was finished, the letter ran to nineteen handwritten pages.

But not one page came back from Teddie. Not a word.

Late one Sunday evening, after a few weeks had gone by, Val telephoned the number Stecchino had provided. A man answered. Val asked if she was speaking with Mark Handler, and when he said yes, she identified herself and asked to talk to Teddie.

"I'm sorry, Miss Cummings," the young man replied, "Teddie's here, but she doesn't want to speak to you."

"I didn't hear you ask her," Val objected.

"I don't have to. She's told me—more than once—what I should say if you ever called."

"But how can she be this . . . this unfair?" she pleaded to the son-in-law she had never met. "Didn't she read my letter? Doesn't she understand that I—"

He cut in. "I can't say what's fair. I just have to respect my wife's feelings on this. I am sorry," he added gently before hanging up.

A couple of days later Val dialed the number again, hoping

Teddie herself might pick up the phone. An operator intercepted and said the line had been disconnected. Within a week Val's private investigator was able to provide Teddie's new, unlisted number, but Val decided it would be futile to call.

"Go to her" was Alan's advice. "Get on a plane, go where she lives, put your foot in the door, and talk."

It was Jess to whom Val listened, however. What Teddie needed now, she said on one of their regular phone calls, was "space," as the kids put it—a chance to build a foundation for restoring a shaky identity. If Val intruded too soon on Teddie's territory, she would be rebuffed, positions would harden, and a rapprochement might become more difficult, even impossible.

"Give her more time on her own to think things through," Jess advised. "She'll come around."

Maybe. But how long would it take? How long would Alan wait?

The months passed, and then one day Val realized it had been a year since she'd last seen this daughter, this child whose conception and birth had so shaped her life. At last she could shrink no longer from taking the first step to some answers. She picked a date just after the release of the September issue, when editorial duties would slacken off for a few days, cleared her business schedule, and made the flight and hotel reservations.

On the afternoon before she was to leave, she was in her office when she was told by her secretary that a lawyer named Gary Felsen was calling. Val grabbed up the phone.

"Gary! It's wonderful to hear from you!"

"Nice to hear your voice too, Val. . . ."

They hadn't spoken in many years. After he'd won her the right to adopt Jess, they had tried for a while to keep in touch; as a virtual godfather to Jess, he'd sent birthday and Christmas presents into her teen years, and Val would respond with notes about Jess's progress in school and other developments. Then he'd married a younger woman, also a lawyer, and they left the city when a firm in California offered her a position. The contact faded.

"Are you in town?" Val asked. "I'd love to see you."

"No, I'm at work. I've been a partner in a firm here in Los Angeles for a few years."

"Doing the same kind of work?"

"We run the gamut—corporate, matrimonial, liability. The only time I get into a custody case is when a movie star's divorcing and there's a battle for the kids. Now, before anything else, tell me what's happening with 'my little girl'?"

The way he'd always referred to Jess. Val crowed proudly for a couple of minutes about Jess's journalistic success, and reported on a recent visit to Washington, when she'd met the man Jess was dating seriously. A tall, attractive orthopedic surgeon named Ben Calder—already successful though only in his mid-thirties—Val had liked him enormously.

"You hear the sound of wedding bells?" Felsen asked.

"I'm keeping my fingers crossed, but it could be a while. The trend these days seems to be to try out married life long before taking the vows. Jess told me she may move in with him."

"Well, she's a big girl now," Felsen said, "she must know what she's doing. If and when there's a wedding, I hope I'll be on the guest list."

"On the bride's side, you go right at the top."

She asked about his own life; he told her his marriage was solid, there were two kids now, one already in high school. Then Felsen shifted gears. "Val, this call isn't just for old time's sake—it's also work. I'm calling on behalf of one of my biggest clients, a man named Glen Majer." He said the name as though confident Val would know it.

"I've heard of him. Didn't he just open a big new resort in the Bahamas?" Through the magazine's travel business, she was familiar with owners and operators of the larger resort hotels in places popular with newlyweds.

"That's the guy," Felsen said. "He also has a couple of hotels in Las Vegas, and one in Lake Tahoe."

Val's association with the name came into sharper focus. Majer's establishments were all located where gambling was legal; he wasn't so much a hotelier as a casino operator. She understood now why a lawyer had been brought in to approach her. On several occasions, agents for Majer's hotels, as well as for others in Las Vegas and other gambling havens, had wanted to advertise in *E.B.* and sell honeymoon packages through the travel agency. Val had vetoed accepting such business. She didn't want to steer newlyweds to places they would gamble. A honeymoon was a time when couples were naturally feeling expansive, so they might easily bet to excess and find themselves in way over their heads. Val not only declined business from gambling resorts, but made a point of specifically advising newlyweds that whatever fun and adventure they sought on a honeymoon, gambling was best left out of it. "Marriage is enough of a gamble," she'd written in one of her monthly advice columns. "You don't need to start out by playing at games where the odds are always stacked against you."

Now she heard Gary saying, "He'd like to do business with you, Val."

"I know, Gary, he's been trying for years. But it's my policy not to take any advertising or travel business from casino—"

"Wait, this isn't about that kind of business. Majer has a much better proposition for you. He wants to buy the magazine."

"To buy—" She didn't even have to think about it; *E.B.* was her life. "Now I'm *really* not interested."

She heard Gary laugh. "I told him that would be your first response. But just for the hell of it, would you like to hear what he's offering?"

"It's no use, Gary, I wouldn't—"

"Forty million dollars."

The number stunned her. "You did say . . . ?"

"Forty." Pause for emphasis. "Million."

Waves of astonishment kept washing over her. Val was aware that the value of the magazine had appreciated sharply in the twenty years since she'd started it. She had seen her own earnings go from nothing more than living expenses to the $250,000 annual salary she now took home, seen advertising revenues climb, profits accumulate—all reflected in the growth of its staff, their increased wages and benefits, larger and grander offices.

Yet she had never stepped back to assess exactly what she had built, how much it would bring if sold. Why should she have? She couldn't imagine handing it over to anyone else, and there was never any pressure to do so. It was essentially her own, except for small blocs of shares given as rewards to her earliest employees, and the shares that remained with Andrew Winston, his own and those he controlled for the estate of Nate Palmer. He had never interfered with her running of the business, however, and in fact Val had no contact with him, only his representatives. Andrew had married a couple of years after Val had broken with him, had come into his share of his family's wealth as well as making his own success with Atlas Air, now a huge international air carrier. By now, Val assumed, his share of her company was a relatively small part of his holdings. Though she regularly sent business letters to inquire whether Andrew might sell his bloc, the answer always came back—via his lawyers—that Mr. Winston was keeping his piece of the magazine "for sentimental reasons." Now she realized it was also shrewd business.

"Hey," Gary said as her thoughtful pause continued, "you didn't faint, I hope. . . ."

Val was jogged out of her thoughts. "To be honest, Gary . . . I don't know what to say."

"Why not say maybe instead of no. Majer would like to meet with you. He'll come right away, if you're available."

"I'm not. I'm going to San Francisco tomorrow. Teddie's out there," she added without further explanation.

"But that's even better. Majer's been here in L.A. He'd fly up to Frisco to—"

"Gary, no, I need to spend all my time with my daughter."

"Forty million dollars, Val. For that kind of money, can't you spare my client just thirty minutes? You owe it to yourself—owe it to your kids, in fact. This'd put you all in clover for the rest of your lives."

That made her think. Maybe it wasn't just the money she owed her kids, Val mused, but the time. If she gave up the magazine, she might feel better about having children with Alan . . . children for whom she could be completely available. In her desperation to reunite with Teddie, Val even considered that being able to give her some of this new wealth might bring her closer. As Alan had said, Teddie was practical.

"All right," she said. "I'll meet Mr. Majer if he comes to San Francisco."

She spent another minute with Gary to tell him she would be staying at the downtown Festival Inn, and gave him a choice of times when she would make herself available.

"I'm glad you're keeping an open mind about this, Val," Gary said before hanging up.

The first thing that occurred to her afterward was that it would be wise to contact Andrew Winston and let him know about the offer. A sale would be less complicated if he didn't withhold his own shares. She reached for the phone—

Then drew back. She didn't have to talk to him yet; she could wait until the proposal was confirmed . . . or perhaps until she decided to act on it. She still felt uncertain about how he might respond to her. Did he still blame her for Nate's death? Damn, if there was one decision in life she wished she could have back, it was the way she had kept Teddie a secret from him. Perhaps if she had let him know right at the start . . . then had done what he asked—given him time . . .

Val pulled herself out of the daydream. Those had been such different times. What seemed possible now simply hadn't been possible then. Having Teddie had ruled out any chance of pursuing that romance.

As now it was Teddie who figured in her reluctance to marry. The realization gave Val fresh resolve. She would make every effort to heal the breach with her daughter. But whatever happened—even if Teddie made the decision to reject her—this time she would feel free to seize her own chances for happiness.

Twenty-one

Val gazed across San Francisco Bay, watching as the cables of the Golden Gate splintered golden beams of the early morning sun, turning them to fingers of light that seemed to be strumming a mammoth harp. Stecchino had advised her to come in the early morning if she wanted to be sure to catch Teddie at home.

At last she could delay it no more. She turned and looked along the quay at the colorful variety of houseboats lining the Sausalito waterfront, some so large and lavish they looked hardly different from suburban homes—except that the "lots" they sat on were water—others no more than jerry-built shacks that floated on gangs of empty oil drums.

From the canvas shoulder bag slung over the rain jacket she wore to ward off the mist of northern California, Val pulled out the color photograph snapped with a telephoto lens—Teddie and a handsome, dark-haired young man as they crossed a small gangplank, leaving their houseboat. She matched the picture to the view in front of her, and headed along the quay toward one of the small cabinlike houseboats with sides of weathered gray shingling.

Crossing a gangplank to a narrow deck of the rectangular floating shack, she went to a door painted with a free-form design of psychedelic colors. She knocked, waited, and knocked again. The door cracked open and a young man peered out drowsily. A stranger—her son-in-law. He was naked but for the towel wrapped around his waist, his dark hair disheveled.

"Yeah . . . ?"

"Hello, Mark. I'm . . . Teddie's mother."

His narrow, handsome face took on a troubled expression, the sleepy brown eyes focusing more sharply.

"I've come a long way to see my daughter," she went on before he could make a decision. "If she wants me to go away and stay out of her life, I've got to hear it from her."

He hesitated another moment, then stepped back and opened the door. "However you want it," he said.

Inside, the houseboat looked hardly different from any college apartment. There was a living room furnished with various pieces of unmatched furniture—a large cable spool standing in for a coffee table, huge burlap-covered pillows lined up as a sofa. The space was separated by a counter from a galley kitchen, and continued into an "L" alcove, a dining room that ended at a glass slider. Through the glass Val saw a broad sundeck facing across the bay to the city skyline. Beyond the kitchen and alongside the dining room was a walled-off area that Val assumed must be a bedroom with its own access to the sundeck. A pleasant place to live. Val was glad to know her vision of Teddie leading a dark, impoverished existence had been wrong.

"She's still sleeping," Handler said. "I'd wake her, but I recommend you do it—if you want to be sure of talking to her." He pointed her to a door beyond the galley, then set about making coffee.

The door opened into a short hallway with a bathroom at one side, an opening to the bedroom beyond. Val stepped into the bedroom. Slatted bamboo shades were rolled down over the glass sliders, but in the dim light she could see Teddie lying on her back in a futon bed, her nude body only half covered by a sheet. Moving to the bed, she looked down at her sleeping daughter, appreciating her in repose. An adult now—fully formed, quite beautiful. A married woman. Val was stricken with the pangs of having missed her daughter's wedding—and much of her childhood as well, occupied so often with scrambling to succeed.

"Teddie?" she said softly, lowering herself to sit on the edge of the futon.

Teddie stirred and rolled over, still asleep, her back to Val.

After a moment Val simply began to speak, possessed by an urge to pour out her feelings, like those mothers who stood at the side of children put into a coma by an accident. What she was impelled to say might better reach Teddie while she was in her unconscious state, with no defense at work.

"I wish I could go back and change the things that made you so angry with me. I don't blame you . . . I understand how hard it must have been for you all along, not having a father . . . not having enough of me. It wasn't much comfort, I know, to be told that I had no choice. Too much to understand when you were young. But I've never wanted anything but the best for you, even for you to think you *came* from the best. Please—can't you forgive me for not wanting you to know your father was . . . a man who . . ." She faltered as the horror of that moment when Teddie had been conceived was suddenly real again, and she was overcome by the sense of being powerless. It struck her suddenly that her surroundings were similar to the place where it happened—a little cabin on the water. She put out a hand and caressed her daughter's back. "Oh, baby . . . please. Give me a chance to—"

Abruptly, Teddie turned over, her eyes open, staring up at Val. "I thought for a second I was dreaming . . . hearing you. . . ."

Val stared back, trying to determine if the look in her daughter's eyes was hostile or forgiving. "I had to come, Teddie. I can't bear what's happened between us."

Teddie stared up at her for another moment. Then, in a whirl of movement, she leapt up from the futon. "Mark!" she called out shrilly as she wrapped a sheet around her nakedness. Handler appeared at once. "Didn't I tell you a hundred times what to do if she ever showed up?"

Stunned, Val rose and waited to hear the young man's defense.

"Teddie, for Pete's sake, it's your mother. She came all this way. You owe—"

Teddie didn't wait to hear more. She spun toward Val. "What do you want me to tell you? That we can kiss and make up and all be one happy family? Well, it's not that easy. Not when you've never been happy—or a family. I just want to be on my own now. So go home, Mother, home to where you've still got a child—the one who's so good and easy to love, the one you fought so hard to get, not the one you must've fought to avoid getting pregnant with. You don't want me. You never did."

The words of rejection knifed into Val's heart. "Of course I want you, Teddie. You've got to get over this idea that because I took in Jess it meant I felt any less—"

"No!" Teddie broke in. "You don't get it, do you? I don't believe you! *Can't!* If I ever wondered how much I meant to you—why I always felt somehow that I wasn't as good as Jess—I finally got an answer when I saw *him*. My father!" She spat out the word with contempt. "A useless fucking jerk, somebody you couldn't have possibly loved—"

"That's right, Teddie, I didn't. I didn't choose him to be your father. He . . . he forced me."

"Yes, *that* I believe. And it explains why you can't really love me—why you resent me, the kid you never really wanted!"

"Oh, baby, that's not so." Val was weeping now, wounded not only by her child's unjust rejection, but from an empathetic feeling of Teddie's pain. "So many things happen in life by accident, without our planning them or wanting them. But that doesn't always mean we're sorry about them. Everything good in my life happened *because* of you . . . because it made me leave one life to find a better one—for us."

"Well, then," Teddie said coolly, "you should be able to understand if I want to do the same thing. I've got my own life here. I don't want to be a part of anything that came before. So get the hell out and leave me alone."

Val was dumbstruck. Nothing she could say held any hope of touching Teddie. Automatically, she started toward the door. Teddie said nothing, though her husband tossed up one hand in a small gesture of apology.

Before going out of the room, Val turned. "There's a man who's asked me to marry him," she said. "More than anything in the world, I'd like you to be part of my wedding. Any other way, it wouldn't seem right."

Teddie shook her head. "Weddings," she said scornfully. "Perfect fucking weddings, that's all you ever think about. Do me a big favor, will you? Don't even bother sending me an invitation."

Returning to her hotel by midmorning, Val went straight to reception and asked the clerk to prepare her bill. She had booked four days originally, thinking she and Teddie would need time together. But Teddie was a lost cause, she knew that now. All she wanted to do was get on a plane as quickly as possible and go back to the things in her life that promised happiness.

"Are you sure you want to check out?" the desk clerk asked in surprise. "I took a phone message for you just a few minutes ago from Glen Majer." There was a trace of awe in the way the clerk said the name. "He said he'd pick you up here this evening at seven o'clock. . . ."

She'd forgotten about Majer. Seven o'clock—was that what she'd agreed? Drained of energy and purpose from her demoralizing encounter with Teddie, Val couldn't remember clearly what plans she'd made. She might have booked a business dinner . . . though she certainly couldn't go through with it now. "Did he leave a number to call back?"

"I'm afraid not."

She had the number at Gary's office; he could cancel the dinner with his client.

Then, as Val imagined the lawyer's irritation—his impassioned urging to think about the huge amount of money at stake—she decided to keep the appointment after all. It wasn't the millions that lured her, just the idea of cutting loose from the magazine. All these years she had been avidly selling the most perfect vision of love fulfilled . . . and it had kept her from achieving the same fulfillment in her own life. Her heart couldn't be in it anymore.

From the edge of the sprawling cliffside terrace, Val looked down at the path of moonlight striping the rolling surface of the ocean, the silvery clouds of spray that fountained up from waves crashing on the rocks a hundred feet below. Along the coast the lights of other dwellings could be seen, but only as distant pinpoints.

"It's spectacular," she said as Glen Majer returned to her side and handed her the refilled glass of champagne.

"I hoped you'd think it was worth going a mite out of the way. . . ."

She smiled at the understatement. "A mite out of the way" had meant taking her from the hotel by a Rolls limousine to a heliport by the bay, from there being piloted in Majer's private helicopter an hour down the coast to his huge ranch, several thousand acres of land on a high plateau looking out to the Pacific.

Along the way they had both avoided discussing the subject that had brought them together, laying a different kind of groundwork for negotiation by exchanging information about themselves. Val had told him most of the story behind her creation of the magazine, and later, while they were served a steak dinner on the terrace behind his seaside house, she had gotten Majer to fill in a few of the gaps in what she knew about him—though there weren't many. Before leaving New York she'd had someone in her research department cull other magazines and newspapers for the pieces that had been written about him over the years. It added up to a lot, and they told a colorful story.

Born in Arizona only a few years after it became the forty-eighth state, when the Great Depression rolled across the land Majer was still in his teens and working as a cowboy earning three dollars a week. The nomadic cowboy life had taken him down across an empty corner of Texas, where he'd noticed his horse's legs getting coated with some sticky black ooze while riding across a nearly dry streambed. He'd taken his whole meager grubstake and spent several weeks playing in every poker game he could find to raise the money for forty acres of that land. No good for grazing, it had sold cheap. He sank one good well on the first try, then sold his holding to an established oil company for a million dollars. Not a bad price back then, though the local wildcatters said he'd been stupid, there had to be more wells in that property, dozens more millions to be made. Majer's reply was that he didn't know shit about the oil game; he'd ridden into a piece of dumb luck—his horse had actually—and the smart thing was to know what he didn't know and quit while he was ahead.

The dumb luck kept happening, though, until people realized it wasn't all luck, and none of it was dumb. With a piece of his million he'd bought stock in a company providing a service that was bound to do well in the wide open spaces—the phone company. And while sweating down there in the tropical heat of the Texas Panhandle, he figured that a bottling franchise for some stuff called Coca-Cola might be worth another flyer. Cattle he knew, so he also bought ranchland. With one thing and another, by the time another world war broke out, he was worth thirty million. During the war he'd more than doubled it—some said by selling black-market beef during rationing. Then when peace came again, he'd gotten in on the ground floor of the casino business in Nevada. As poker games had provided the cowboy's first stake, he still believed gambling might yield the biggest payoff. And it had—between casino hotels, and raw desert real-estate in places that began to grow by leaps and bounds. With a couple of hundred million in hand by the time he was in his fifties, he'd slowed down—gambled in the stock market, built the occasional hotel in other gambling havens like the Bahamas. His "dumb luck"—as he still insisted on calling it—had by then taken him from being a dirt-poor cowpoke sleeping in a bedroll to a man who could lay his head down in any one of seven homes around the world, all fully staffed. Both his history and Val's made good telling, and they had found each other's company so enjoyable, there was little hurry to start fencing over matters that were merely practical.

"I'm glad I didn't break our date," she said now, turning from the view to face him.

"You were thinkin' of it?"

"A few hours ago I was going to return to New York."

"Does that mean you had doubts about doing business with me?"

"Nothing to do with that." She paused. He seemed sympathetic, and she was tempted to unburden herself of the doubts swirling through her mind since Teddie's absolute rejection. But she held back, realizing that if it did come to negotiating with him, revealing her emotional vulnerability would put her at a disadvantage. "The truth is," she said, "I'm probably more disposed to consider your offer today than I was before I made this trip."

He held up his champagne glass, inviting her to a toast. "Well, then, let's drink to doing business together."

Val clinked her glass against his, and they sipped their champagne. Looking at him over the rim of her glass, she became even more strongly aware of the force field that surrounded him, a physical magnetism she had felt the minute she had met him in the hotel lobby. She had simply never been exposed to a man like this before. The men who'd attracted her, with whom she'd let herself become involved, had all been gentlemen. Majer didn't fall into that category. He was obviously shrewd enough to play the part when necessary, but Val didn't doubt that his own basic nature, formed early by his vagabond life, was more primitive.

Retreating from this allure, she said, "Perhaps it's time we got down to brass tacks." She went back to sit at the table where they had eaten dinner.

"Gold tacks would be more like it, Valentina. You know the amount of money I've put on the table. . . ."

"Yes. It almost seems too much," she remarked impulsively.

He smiled. "You tryin' to tell me I should pay less?"

"That was the champagne talking, I guess."

He joined her at the table. "Don't worry, I'm not backin' down. Forty million is a fair price, I've been over the numbers. You're selling three hundred thousand issues of *E.B.* every month at a price of a buck and a half per—that alone is an annual gross of more than three million. Unlike most magazines, you sell more off the newsstand than subscriptions because it's an impulse buy for the girls thinkin' of marriage, not something they need long-range. Then there's your advertising revenue, and the honeymoon travel business. It's a neat little money machine, and that makes it a sound investment. Payin' ten times annual profit is a fair price."

"But why invest in this?" she asked. "There are a dozen things that seem like a better match for your interests."

"You know one reason: I've been building a hotel business—"

"Casinos," she corrected him.

"Okay, that's part of it—and I know that's why you've locked me out of your advertising. Which has made other bridal magazines think twice about taking my ads, or recommending my resorts to newlyweds. So the policy hurts. You know as well as I do that the most lucrative single segment of the travel market is honeymooners."

"So one way for you to change our policy is to buy the magazine."

Majer opened his large hands and smiled, a confession that made his plan seem the most innocent maneuver.

But if he succeeded in luring another three or four thousand couples a year to his resorts, how much more did that represent in money left at his gaming tables and slot machines? Val wondered.

"You have other reasons for buying *E.B.*," she asked, "aside from helping your casinos?"

"None but the obvious," he admitted. "You've got a good product, something that will never go out of style as long as women want to be brides. And it's part of an industry that I'm betting will only get more important and more valuable as time goes on—publishing and communications. Yours isn't the only magazine I'm bidding for. I'm planning to put together a conglomerate."

Val drank some more champagne. "You're starting to convince me that your offer may even be too low."

"You haven't heard it all. I'm firm on the purchase price, but I'll also want you to stay on to run things. I'll give you a five-year contract, at six hundred thousand a year."

Another three million dollars in all! Was it the lofty numbers she was hearing that made her feel light-headed, or the alcohol she'd consumed? As owner of the business, Val had always been careful about costs—even keeping her own salary relatively moderate. But if another owner wanted to pay her more . . .

Yet this new element only confused the situation. "Are you still interested in buying if I don't stay on?"

He frowned. "Never occurred to me you wouldn't. *E.B.* is your baby."

The very expression underlined the yearning she had for a different path. "It may be time for me to do other things with my life," she said.

"Like what? You've got a good track record so far, Valentina. I might even give you the backing."

She laughed. "These things, Glen, are the kind that don't need an investor."

"Personal stuff," he probed, though only in the mildest way.

She thought again of speaking openly with him. He was a man who'd come up from simple beginnings—as she had—but had seen a lot more of the world. "At times," she said, "I think I haven't really lived my life yet, at least not the one I planned on and dreamed about when I was growing up."

"Creating a multimillion-dollar business isn't a good enough dream?"

"Funny, that's what ought to be the ideal—and I'm not saying it hasn't been satisfying. But I wanted . . . the simple things."

"Home, family, Mom's apple pie."

"Well, it would've been *my* apple pie," she said.

"You wanted to be a mom, but business got in the way. . . ."

She smiled ruefully. "Not quite. I had children. I just . . . never had time to bake them the pie."

He heard the nuances of regret and guilt, and while he said nothing, he looked at her in a way that clearly told her he was ready to hear as much as she wanted to share.

It just flowed out of her then—the reason she'd come to San Francisco, the history with Teddie, her adoption of Jess, and her thoughts about having more children. Though she found herself holding back when it came to mentioning the man who might figure in her plans.

Majer sat silently for the most part, speaking only those occasional phrases that let her know he was paying attention, and was moved. He had a talent for listening, she thought. Looking into the handsome, weathered face, she imagined it was a talent formed around cowboys' prairie campfires, exchanging long stories of wanderlust and hard times.

At last, talked out, she fell silent. Only then did he offer an opinion. "You're bein' much too hard on yourself, Val, if you think anythin' you did accounts for how this girl of yours is actin'. Almost every herd has a rogue heifer that'll wander far off by itself. You try to keep 'em in the pack 'cause that's where they're safest, but sometimes you got to let 'em go so you can follow the main trail to your destination. Have more kids if you want, but don't expect 'em to turn out better or worse just 'cause you're in the kitchen bakin' pies rather than out in the world bein' a boss lady. Doin' what makes *you* happy is better for your kids than if you're miserable."

"Is that what worked with your children?" She knew he'd already been married once or twice.

"Me? I got no kids. I've just got a big mouth, and opinions on everything."

She laughed. No way to tell whether his advice was good or bad, but she knew it had made her feel better to talk to him.

As they talked, he'd opened yet another bottle of champagne, and kept pouring for them both. Now he reached for the bottle again.

"No thank you, Glen. I should be getting back to my hotel."

He glanced at the gold Rolex on his wrist. "Val . . . it's half past three in the morning."

"It can't be!" It seemed they'd been together two or three hours, not eight.

"I'd guess around midnight my whirlybird pilot figured you were stayin' over, and hit the hay. I'd wake him, but there's extra room here and I think you'd be comfortable. . . ."

Val glanced at the sprawling house. Extra room and

comfortable were understatements. "All right," she said, "let him sleep."

As he led her into the house, it occurred to Val that the evening might have all been prelude to a planned seduction. It seemed even more likely when he led her upstairs to a luxurious guest suite already prepared, welcoming by soft lamplight, a bed with the covers turned down. She steeled herself to fend him off.

But at the threshold of the room he stopped. "Sorry if you were inconvenienced, Valentina," he said, "but I was having such a fine evenin', the hours just slipped away."

"It's not an inconvenience, Glen. There's nowhere else I really have to be."

He nodded. "Good." He paused, and Val realized she wouldn't mind at all if he kissed her—just that, a gentle ending to the kind interest he'd shown earlier.

But he just gave her a soft smile and said, " 'Night now, lady. Sleep well."

He turned away, and she retreated into the room and closed the door. She stayed right inside, though, half tempted to call him back. Not mind a kiss? It went beyond that. She wanted him, all of him. But she reined in her desire. It couldn't be anything more than a passing whim—a result of the wine, the Pacific night, the self-doubt raised by Teddie.

Couldn't be. Good Lord, wasn't she virtually engaged? Resigned at last to leaving things with Teddie as they were, wasn't she ready again after all these years to become a bride? But maybe this evening showed her that she wasn't as ready as she thought, that Teddie was not the real obstacle to her marriage to Alan.

Twenty-two

Waking, Val saw brilliant sunlight pouring into the room. She glanced over at a bed table. The hands of a gold Cartier clock stood at a few minutes before noon.

She had a weird moment of disorientation when she rose. Lying over a bedside chair she saw her own peignoir—the one packed for the trip. But she'd left it at the hotel! Was her evening with Majer all a dream? She moved to the bathroom within the guest suite and found her toiletries and perfume arrayed neatly on shelves. She went to the huge walk-in closet: Her clothes were on hangers, and carefully arranged in the built-in drawers; her luggage was stacked in a corner.

Evidently Majer's private pilot had been sent on an early morning mission. She marveled at the thoughtfulness, though there was a disconcerting side to this casual display of Glen's wealth.

Casually dressed in slacks and a cashmere pullover, she went looking for him and found him at a table beside the enormous swimming pool at one side of the house. His clothes were pure cowboy—jeans, filigreed leather boots, a black shirt with slit pockets and pearl buttons. A young, pretty woman sat in a chair facing him, a steno pad in her lap, jotting down dictation. Dishes of fresh fruit, a coffeepot, and cups were on the table. As soon as he saw Val coming, he said a few quiet words to the stenographer; she vanished into the house, and he stood.

" 'Mornin', Val. Hope it's okay I let you be. You said there was nothing pressing on your calendar."

"Fine. I must've needed a good rest." She took the chair the young woman had vacated, and he sat down again. "That was quite a little trick—fetching all my things."

"I thought you'd rather not get up and have to put on yesterday's stuff."

"Very thoughtful."

He picked up the hint of wariness. "You've still got your room at the hotel," he assured her. "Though I'll level with ya, Val. I was thinkin' you might spend a little more time here."

"We still have business to discuss?"

"Some. I'd like to talk you into remaining as editor even if you agree to sell the magazine."

"Anything else?"

He smiled. "I'd like to get to know you better, and there's no time like the present."

She gazed back into his ruggedly handsome face. He was a charmer, all right, with all that just-plain-folks stuff to go with the intelligence and tremendous sophistication he'd acquired through the years of being enormously rich. She ran a risk, if she stayed, of having her business judgment clouded.

"I can stay for the day," she said.

After breakfast he asked if she had ever been on a horse. When she admitted she never had, that didn't stop him. He took her to the ranch stables and picked out a sleek gold and white palomino as her mount.

"His name's Sultan," he said. "And he's so gentle, a baby could ride him straight out of the womb."

That succeeded in coaxing her into the saddle. Once they were riding at a walk across the broad open reaches of his land, Val felt completely at ease.

They climbed up into rolling hills from which they could look down and see the ocean. Cattle were grazing everywhere in valleys and on green plateaus. It was like riding back into the past, a simpler time when this was all there was, no highways beyond the far horizon.

Eventually, he encouraged her to try a trot, and told her how to hold the saddle, and then she went to a canter.

"You're a natural," he called, riding alongside. "Get used to this pace, then we'll try a gallop."

"That might be too much. . . ."

They rode to a broad shallow stream that rushed across the land. While the horses watered, Val and Majer strolled by the stream. She felt wonderful, exhilarated by the ride, and thrilled by the scenery, the endless expanse of pasture rolling gently away to more hills.

"All this space," she said. "It's like medicine to be in the middle of it, not to feel hemmed in, to have no boundaries."

"That's what I love about it. Same thing I loved about the life I lived when I didn't have a dime. The difference now is I can afford to keep the wide open spaces from gettin' cluttered. The places I used to love to ride are gettin' all covered up with cities and shoppin' malls."

"This is all yours?" She swept her hand in an arc.

"In a manner of speakin'. I talked to a Sioux man once, and he told me his people believe a man can never own land, it's just on a loan from the spirits. So you might say I got a lease on this for as long as I live. I've already planned on giving it over to a nature group, with some money so it'll always stay this way."

She regarded him with fresh appreciation. His reputation in business was for being a ruthless brigand; certainly, his desire to have the magazine become a means to lure more newlyweds into his hotel-casinos seemed purely venal. But she got a different perspective from knowing he put his wealth to good use. "You're an unusual man, Glen," she said.

He gave her a slow smile. "Now, that kinda talk could give a man the idea he just might be good enough for you."

It was the opening to continue the exploration, and she took it. "I hope I'm not just—what do the cowboys say?—being sweet-talked to keep me on the job."

He moved up in front of her and gripped her arms in his large hands. "Tell you what, lady: No matter what happens, I won't expect any promises from you."

What he was saying, too, was that she shouldn't expect any promises from him either. But at least he was honest about it. Accepting the terms, she lifted her mouth for his kiss.

It was everything she was craving. Mature as she was, this felt like having an adolescent fantasy come true—a kiss from a movie star. Overtaken by desire, she wanted him right there, and it was obvious to him as she pulled the pearl snap-buttons of his shirt and breathed warm kisses onto his chest. Matching her move for move, he undressed her, pressing his lips to each inch of her skin as it was bared, breasts, stomach, going down onto his knees to kiss her thighs as he lowered her panties. The clothes that dropped at their feet he kicked into a pile to make a place to rest on the grassy ground. With the blue open sky above them, the warm sun on her shoulders, Val felt a release of natural passion as never before. They were the first lovers, unwatched in Eden. . . . No, they were animals, without any reason for restraint. In the midst of a place without boundaries, she was herself unbound, and she gave him every part of herself, and took everything from him. He came into her, and brought her to a shattering climax that made her cry with joy and pleasure.

And still she wanted him again, riding atop him, her eyes filled with the blue of the sky so when she came she could almost believe she was flying up into the heavens.

"Do you have this effect on every woman?" she asked frankly when they were lying quietly at last. For hours they had made love. She hadn't believed she could be so insatiable; she hadn't believed a man could be so potent. The sun was just settling low enough so she was aware of the faintest cooling breeze wafting across the hills.

He chuckled softly. "Lord, if I did, I'd be dead long ago," he said. "This was chemistry, darlin'—the kind that don't come along more'n once in a purple moon."

She almost wondered aloud if that rarity made it something they should both want to hang on to, but she wasn't sure what her own answer would be, so it was better not to raise the question.

They dressed and remounted their horses for the ride back. After they'd gone a short way, he said, "How about tryin' a gallop now? It's like a canter, only faster and much more exciting."

"God help me," she said, "right now I feel I can do anything."

He told her a few more things about how to balance in the saddle, and hold her feet in the stirrups, and keep her knees in, and when she said she was ready, off they went. The exhilaration she felt ran a close second to the sex. One instruction he gave her she found particularly helpful: As long as you settled back unafraid of the speed, going at a gallop gave you an even smoother ride than going slow.

It was a lesson, she thought, that she could take away and apply to other parts of her life.

She stayed another two days. They made love at night, and went down to the ocean the next morning to swim and make love on the beach, and took the horses on another long ride, bringing food and wine this time, and again making love under the blue sky. They went in his helicopter to a vineyard in the Napa Valley, where they had dinner before flying back to make love by his swimming pool before going to sleep entwined in the same bed.

They never spoke about the future. Val simply understood that whatever existed at the moment was too rare to be sustained. Probably, it couldn't even have happened except for the circumstances leading up to it—Teddie's rejection sparking the need for a boost to her self-esteem, the sense of freedom that came with being alone and far from home, the attraction of a last fling before settling down.

On the morning of their fourth day, after breakfast by the pool, she said it was time for her to go.

"So soon?" He sounded genuinely disappointed.

"I thought you wanted me at the magazine, making sure it's shipshape and worth buying."

"I thought I did too. Now I'm not so sure."

"About buying it—or me running it?"

"About not keeping you close to me."

She gave him a long look. "Glen . . . I don't think there's been another four days in my life as perfect as these. But we're not starry-eyed kids, Romeo and Juliet who think this is all there ever is. We should know that something this perfect can't last."

"Wouldn't think I'd hear that from you, Valentina. Perfect

love and happily-ever-after . . . isn't that what you're sellin' month after month?"

"Yes, that's what every bride wants to believe she's getting when she marries. And the purpose of a wedding has always been to make that dream seem real. That's why so much effort goes into making the moment flawless, ideal." She smiled wistfully. "The irony is that in ninety-nine cases out of a hundred, it will never be that perfect again."

"Sounds like maybe you've lost a little belief in your product. And if that's the case," he added after a second, "I might want to put in a new editor."

"I think I'm still the best person for the job," she said. "But that'll be your decision to make. If I sell."

He smiled. "Before we reach that point, it could help if you tested the proposition that maybe something perfect *can* last. Do a little consumer research for your readers . . ."

"How would you suggest I do that?"

"Try it with me."

She stared at him in amazement. "Glen . . . are you . . . proposing?"

"Well, darlin' . . . that would be a little presumptuous on such short acquaintance. But I am askin'—even if you leave today—not to close the book on us."

Her astonishment ebbed, but she remained uncertain of how to reply. She flirted with telling him that there was a man waiting back east who wanted to marry her. At last she said, "I'm not sure how I'll feel once I've left this behind."

"Okay. So let's leave it right there for now. In a couple of weeks I'll come to your neck of the woods and you can see if I look different to you stacked up against all those city slickers. Meantime, suppose we don't even talk. By the time you see me again, you'll have some perspective on your feelin's."

Would she? Val imagined him being in New York, the temptations and complications that were bound to result.

He must have seen the doubt in her eyes. "I should come anyway, Val . . . if we're goin' to make a deal."

She wasn't sure whether it was the lure of wealth or the desire of her heart that persuaded her she would have to see him again.

Twenty-three

When she returned to New York, she found that Alan was away for a week in London, launching an international extension of Festival Inns. Though they retained separate apartments, he had been staying with her most of the time, and Val was glad to have this time alone in familiar surroundings to prepare for their reunion. She was troubled by her infidelity, uncertain of how to deal with it. When she had departed for California hoping to heal the breach with Teddie, it had been understood that however it went, when she returned home it would be time to plan their future. Alan had more or less said that it was "now or never" to set a date for their wedding.

To take her mind off the dilemma, Val was grateful for the distractions of business. If a sale were to be consummated, many things needed special attention. She engaged a Wall Street accounting firm to take a good look at the financials and make sure the price was fair. She needed to consult a lawyer—someone other than Gary, who worked for "the other side"—about how to structure the deal. And there was still the day-to-day running of the magazine. Partly as a result of suggestions from Jess—whose coverage of women's issues made her sensitive to the need for updating—Val had been working with graphic designers on new typography and layout, commissioning articles with more substance . . . even considering a cover with something other than a white wedding gown.

While engaged in these efforts, she wondered frequently if she could ever adjust to being a woman who didn't preside over a business domain. Perhaps this was all she'd ever really been cut out for—not homemaking, or even marriage.

As she continued to waver on the idea of selling the magazine, she didn't forget that Andrew Winston would have to be a party to any decision. His holdings represented a minority share, yet all dealings would be easier if he endorsed her decision. Even before Majer came to New York to finalize the sale, Val realized, it would be diplomatic at the least to inform Andrew of what was in the works.

On Friday, at the end of the week after her return from California, she made a call to the offices of Andrew Winston at Atlas International Airways. She was told by his secretary that he was "unavailable."

In the special language spoken by secretaries, Val knew that particular word meant one of two things—either Andrew was really somewhere else about which no further information would be given, or he was avoiding her call.

"It's quite important that I speak to him on a business matter," she persisted. "Is there any way of reaching him?"

"He'll be calling into the office, Miss Cummings," the secretary said. "I'll see that he gets your message."

Val left it at that. But after putting down the phone, she sat there for a long time, wondering about Andrew. . . .

Later in the day, she got a call from a man named Dwight Jeffries. From her past inquiries about buying the outstanding shares of *E.B.*, Val knew Jeffries as a somewhat crusty Wall Street lawyer who handled Andrew's investments other than his airline holdings.

After greeting her cordially, the lawyer said, "I imagine, Miss Cummings, that your message about a business matter means you're making one of your periodic inquiries about whether Mr. Winston wants to dispose of his interest in your magazine. His instructions to me haven't changed. He has no desire to sell to you, or change anything about this investment. He approves of the way the magazine is being run, and he continues to express a strong attachment to the business—one that he always describes to me as 'sentimental.' "

"That's nice to hear, Mr. Jeffries. But I'm calling about

something different than in the past." She told him about Majer's offer.

"Ah, yes, I see. Forty million, you say. Well, that is quite another thing. I'll have to discuss this with Mr. Winston and get back to you. Good-bye, Miss Cummings."

"Mr. Jeffries—wait! Would it be possible for me to talk directly with Mr. Winston? I'd like his advice about how to proceed—if he's willing to talk to me."

There was a short pause from the lawyer, as though considering whether to comment. But all he said was "I'll pass along your request."

It was near the very end of the day when Val's secretary buzzed on the intercom to say that Andrew Winston's office was on the line.

Taking the call was a simple matter of pushing a button. Yet Val found herself overcome by a rush of nervous excitement, distracted by an avalanche of memories. Barging out into the rain and colliding with him . . . their rendezvous at Pennsylvania Station . . . the weekend at his family's estate in Oyster Bay . . . their lovemaking at The Rainbow Inn, ended so cruelly by the news of Josie's death. . . .

And she remembered, too, how much she had wished there could have been hope for their love to last—

Val shook her head, reproving herself for the foolishness of being swept even for a few moments into wishful dreams. They had nothing but business to discuss. She took a deep breath, picked up the phone, and said hello.

"Hello, Valentina. It's Andrew Winston."

Nothing but business, she told herself again. But it didn't help. His voice stirred up her feelings, transported her back to the past, back to the hopes and heartbreak, the dream and the disappointment. It took an effort to speak, and hide the emotional turmoil. "Andrew . . . thank you for returning my call."

"I was told you're considering a sale of the magazine."

"Considering it, yes. I'm not sure it's the right thing to do. I thought you might advise me."

"You don't need any advice from me. You've been managing brilliantly on your own for a long time."

He sounded a bit cold, she thought. Or was she just hoping for more involvement and concern than it was reasonable to expect? "I never could have gotten *E.B.* off the ground without your help, Andrew. You were there when I started. If I'm going to step down, it seemed to me you ought to be involved in the decision."

There was a pause. "The magazine is yours, Val. The idea was yours, the accomplishment is yours . . . the decision should be yours. I'll just say this: If the business isn't going to be in your hands, I have no wish to be involved. I'll sell my stake at whatever terms you accept. Is that good enough?"

"Yes. Thank you."

Now their business was done. But she couldn't bear to break the connection. Suddenly she wanted so much to see him, to say a hundred things it seemed had been left unsaid the last time they were together.

"Andrew . . . could we meet?" The words flew from her lips of themselves. "I mean, just to confirm our agreement. . . ." No, she didn't mean that only, but how could she explain the longing she felt to revive what had been left behind so long ago?

There was another brief silence before he answered. "I don't think there's any need for that, Valentina. You have my word that you can count on my cooperation."

She found the will to say good-bye, though it emerged as barely more than a whisper.

Long after she had hung up the phone, she was still sitting in her chair, looking out at the view of the city rooftops as the sun set. Why was she feeling such a loss? she wondered. She had more than enough emotional entanglements in her life right now. What on earth had she hoped? That there was some possibility of exploring what might have been?

Some chances, once lost, could never be recovered.

The picture on the front pages of all the New York tabloids this October evening was the same news-service photo to be found on the front pages of newspapers from Tangier to Tokyo and every other major city on the globe.

In all her demure beauty, draped in a black mantilla, the thirty-nine-year-old widow of President John F. Kennedy was shown leaving the Greek church on the private Aegean island belonging to the groom at her side—shorter, gray-haired, considerably older—the Greek billionaire, Aristotle Onassis.

As Val took a cab across town to meet Alan for dinner at Patsy's, the folksy Italian restaurant that was one of his favorites—as well as Frank Sinatra's—she saw the image in multiple on every newsstand, gripped in the hands of bus riders and pedestrians.

She'd already had a full day of being besieged by calls from various news organizations wanting the comments of a wedding expert to accompany stories on this unlikely match that would glut the media for days to come. Val's reaction was sought on everything from Jackie's choice of dress to her choice of groom. And whether Val thought prenuptial agreements, like the one Jackie was said to have made—twenty-five million payable simply for saying I do, an agreed budget of a million dollars a year for clothes, a pledge that she need not spend more than a set number of nights per year in the same bed with her new husband—were going to become a more popular part of wedding customs?

Whatever view she might have, Val kept it to herself. She understood why there were people who found the pairing unbelievable—a woman who had become the quintessential symbol of restrained elegance and aristocratic style marrying a man who had piled up one of the world's largest fortunes by a life of rough-and-tumble opportunism that verged on piracy. But who was she to judge? Lately she had crossed paths herself with a wealthy man whose scruples were not so unlike those of Onassis, and Val knew how easy it was to give in to fascination with such a man.

In the weeks since she had been with Glen, Val hadn't managed to take any steps to resolve the uncertainties created by their passionate fling. Alan had returned from Europe, and they had fallen back into a routine: evenings spent together—usually over quiet dinners in her apartment, sometimes dressing up for opera or theater. As for making love, at first she had held him off with excuses, unable to go quickly from the arms of one man to another. Eventually, though, she wanted him—wanted, at least, the comfort of hoping they might go on as before.

Now, though, she measured their predictable enjoyment of each other against the new thrills and passionate sensations she had found with Majer. The quest for more of such excitement might not be reason enough to abandon what was steady and stable and reassuring on a daily basis; there were thrills in riding a raft over white-water rapids, but you couldn't possibly tolerate more than a limited journey—and the thrills alone were the usual reason for taking the ride, not a desire to get from one place to another. Still, she wasn't yet able to resign herself fully to the steadier course. She had to see Majer again—once more, at least—before she could commit herself wholeheartedly to going on with Alan.

Meanwhile, she agonized over the question of whether or not to confess the slip of her heart that was clouding her vision. She owed Alan no less than the truth—though what would be gained by that confession if she saw Glen again and she realized that the enchantment of those brief few days was over?

So when, inevitably, Alan raised the subject of marriage again, she replied that she wanted to wait to make any other plans until the sale of the magazine was consummated.

He obviously wasn't happy with her answer, but he didn't force the issue. He knew Glen Majer was expected to come to New York soon; without knowing any more than Majer's role as the potential buyer, he understood that the trip would result in clarifying Val's thinking.

This evening, however, as Val entered Patsy's she was feeling especially guilty about her recent evasions. All the attention given the Kennedy-Onassis marriage had the effect of making her think about Glen—making it seem not so unlikely she could choose to be with him. It would be selfish and unfair not to let Alan know exactly where he stood.

He was already waiting at a table, and rose to give her a quick kiss of greeting. "You look great—especially for a working girl who's had a hard day."

His sweetness and gallantry touched her. Why couldn't she make the easy choice?

A waiter brought menus and inquired about drinks. When Val ordered a martini, Alan shot her a glance as he requested the same; he knew that she almost never had strong cocktails.

"I didn't realize it was *that* hard a day," he said.

Too soon for cards on the table. "The phones never stopped ringing," Val said.

"And what sort of quotable quotes did you hand out?"

"Nothing much. I said Jackie looked beautiful, and she's entitled to marry whomever she likes, and left it at that. Frankly, I think it's just awful the way she's being hounded by the press."

"It isn't just about her, of course," Alan observed. "It's what this wedding represents."

"What do you think that is?"

"The end of innocence, the death of romance. America's one and only fairy-tale princess marrying not for love, for all the world to see, but for money. When she kisses this frog in the morning, he won't turn into a prince. He'll stay a frog . . . but at least he'll be all green."

"That's very cynical, Alan. I've heard people say Onassis is a fascinating man. You don't think she could truly love him?" The question was double-edged, of course.

The drinks arrived, and Alan took a swig of his. "Val, there are all kinds of weddings beside the lovely fantasies you sell—plenty where love isn't involved at all. In a big part of the world people get hitched only because their families have made a marriage contract. Right here people marry for companionship, for tax reasons, or just because it isn't quite as fashionable to be single. And sure as hell, some marry for money. When enough is involved, the fairest princess will marry a man she doesn't love."

But Val knew that the fantasy she sold was the fantasy she wanted to believe in—no matter how hard it might be to fulfill. "When I marry," she said, "it has to be for love—first, last, and always."

"For us it will be." He smiled at her. But then the smile

faded. He had seen the clouds in her eyes, could feel the vibrations of doubt bouncing back at him.

"What is it, Val?"

She fortified herself with another sip of her martini. "Alan . . . this is the hardest thing I've ever—"

"You're calling it off," he broke in. "That's what all this is really about, isn't it?"

"Calling it off isn't the way I would have put it—since we never exactly called it *on*."

"It's always been on as far as I was concerned. Just a question of when."

"Maybe that's still the question. I don't want you to give up on me, Alan. But right now . . . I'm afraid I can't . . . go ahead."

He studied her, then the smile faintly came through again. "You of all people, the great bridal problem-solver, you're having a good old-fashioned case of—"

"No. I wish that's all it were."

Her anguished tone caught his attention. He waited for more.

"When I went out west, I . . . I met someone and—" She forced it out. "I was unfaithful." She searched his face for a reaction, but he was like stone. "It wasn't planned," she continued. "The last thing I was looking for was anything that would stand in our way. But . . . then I met this man. . . ." She gave up on words and lowered her eyes, ashamed and sorry for having hurt him.

The waiter chose this moment to saunter over to take their dinner orders, but from his quick reading of the way Val was sitting, her companion staring at her, he realized it was the wrong time and left.

"Who is he?" Alan asked at last.

She raised her eyes for the confession. "Glen Majer."

This time he couldn't hold back a reaction. Almost as though he had absorbed a physical blow, he flinched. "Oh, Val," he murmured. It had a pitying edge to it, as though he were grieving more for her than himself.

"I know," she said. "He's practically a professional heartbreaker. Probably has to make a conquest of every woman he meets. I had my guard up . . . and all the same I did get swept off my feet. I wasn't sure how much it meant. Not then, and not now. I just know . . . I'm at sea right now, and it's been killing me to lie to you."

He eyed her solemnly for another second. "I'm glad you were honest with me," he said finally. "If it had to happen, it's certainly better now than after we walked down the aisle." He leaned closer to her across the table. "But for me, Val, it doesn't change what I'd like for the future. I still want to marry you."

He was making it as easy for her as possible, she thought. Hadn't even asked if she loved Majer. Though maybe he just assumed love wasn't part of it, or her confession would have started off by saying she was in love with another man instead of only confessing to infidelity. Or maybe he preferred not to know—as long as she could put it behind her, rededicate herself to him.

Forgiveness did not come more simply or graciously; it made her appreciate him all the more—made her wish it could be as easy as swearing right then that she would never see Majer again. But she was too afraid she couldn't keep that oath. A part of her had come alive in those few days that couldn't be boarded up with no more than a promise. And as Alan had remarked, whatever must happen was best faced before the vows were taken.

"He's coming here soon," Val said, "to finish the magazine deal. I'm going to see him, Alan—I'd have to, if just for business. Until I do, until he's standing right in front of me, I can't be a hundred percent sure of what I'll feel, what words I'll want to say. . . ."

Alan gave a slow nod of resignation. "You're too special and too important for me to simply toss in the towel. So for the moment I'm going to look on the bright side and hope the decision could go my way. Until then, until you know what you want, it's probably best we don't even talk." He stood abruptly. "So I guess there's nothing else to say except . . . give me a call if we're getting married." He tossed a fifty-dollar bill on the table to cover their drinks and her dinner if she wanted, then started away.

Her vision blurred by tears, Val saw only an indistinct form retreating. She wanted to call him back, but it wouldn't be fair unless she could tell him to stay forever.

Then, as if hearing her, he stopped suddenly, took the few steps back to the table, and reached into his pocket. "Just remembered. I've had this for a while, but tonight . . . I thought the time had arrived to bring it along." He set something down quickly in front of her and hurried off.

Wiping her eyes, Val saw the ring box. She flipped open the lid—to punish herself.

He hadn't stinted on this symbol of how devoted he was. The diamond was large and flawless. She felt each sparkling ray of light that struck her eye as a splinter in her heart.

Twenty-four

Returning from lunch the following Friday, Val found her office overflowing with several hundred long-stemmed white roses, each bunch of two or three dozen in its own Baccarat crystal vase.

Her secretary was apologetic, knowing Val liked her office uncluttered. "I tried to keep the delivery men out, but they said they'd been paid to put the flowers where you work and marched right past me. There wasn't any card."

"It's all right, Pat. I know who sent them." The gesture had all the excessive extravagance of a frontier miner who had struck gold.

Val told the secretary to help herself to one of the vases of flowers, and spread the word in the steno pool that each woman could take a dozen roses home.

Alone in her office, Val looked around at the floral blizzard and surrendered to a delighted laugh. "You crazy cowboy," she said out loud.

Suddenly she had the oddest sensation—almost as though, wherever he was, he'd heard her, and would answer any second. She turned to stare at the phone on her desk, certain it would ring. "Go ahead," she dared. A sign she belonged with him.

She stared at it another few seconds, then laughed again—at herself, though she was actually surprised she'd been wrong. Forget ESP, she had a sense of Majer's style. She'd been sure he'd want to hear her reaction before it got stale.

The intercom buzzed. She grabbed it up.

"Mr. Majer is on the line," her secretary said.

She understood the man! "Put him through."

"How are ya, darlin'?" he greeted her breezily.

"Up to my ass in roses at the moment."

"I guess I should've asked if you have hay fever."

"I don't. It's a lovely gesture, Glen. A little over the top, but very lovely."

"Just my way of sayin' I'm ready to make all your dreams come true."

"My one request is a simple one. I'd like to see you—soon as possible."

"Just what I had in mind myself. Car'll be in front of your office in five minutes—"

"Glen, these are business hours—"

"Soon as possible, you said. Anyway, business is just what we've got to talk about."

No point arguing further. He'd hung up.

She emerged onto the sidewalk in front of her office building five minutes later. A plainly dressed, burly man with graying red hair stepped right up to her. "Miss Cummings?" When she nodded, he led her to a car—not the limousine she expected, but a dusty gray sedan. He started to open the rear door, and she hesitated, surprised to see the backseat empty.

"Where's Mr. Majer?"

"He had business. I'm taking you to meet him."

It felt a bit like being abducted, but she went along—though she opened the passenger door herself to ride in front. As they rode together, Val made conversation—all with the goal of drawing out whatever she could about Majer. She learned that the driver was a New York police detective named Brady who had moonlighted for the past few years as a chauffeur and bodyguard to Majer whenever he was in town.

"Why does Mr. Majer need a bodyguard?" Val asked.

"Doesn't everybody?" Brady said wryly. "This is New York."

"Seriously, Mr. Brady," Val said. "If *I'm* in some particular danger by being with your boss, I think I've got a right to know."

He glanced at her apologetically. "I wouldn't say it's really dangerous, ma'am. But it's a wise precaution for Mr. Majer. Being a top guy in the gambling business, he's got to hold his own against some very tough people, the kind who'll take things away from you if you show any signs of getting soft."

"But Mr. Majer isn't soft. . . ."

Brady smiled. "No, ma'am. He can hang with the best of 'em."

The "best" seemed to mean the worst. If she had any sense, Val thought, she'd ask him to stop the car, get out, and run straight to Alan. But she was held by the memory of the excitement she'd felt with Glen.

The car brought her to a strip by the Hudson River, where a chartered helicopter was waiting. "You said you were taking me to him," she reminded Brady.

"First leg of the journey."

"Journey to where?" she asked suspiciously. With Majer, she was learning, anything was possible.

"He's at the beach, ma'am."

With him, it could be any of a dozen beaches—could even be somewhere in the Caribbean—but she didn't ask. The mystery was beginning to amuse her.

The helicopter settled down less than thirty minutes later on a wide stretch of white sand on the south shore of Long Island. From the topography she'd seen below, Val thought they had landed in Southampton. Facing the beach was a sprawling gable-roofed, brown-shingled mansion with a colonnaded porch that ran across the front. Except that it was so large, it was exactly the kind of old-fashioned beach house Val would have chosen for herself—if she could afford such an extravagance.

A path from the beach cut through fifty yards of lush green lawn and ended at steps to the porch. Majer was watching from the top step, and he strode forward as soon as the helicopter rotor stopped turning. As though there were an electrical field surrounding him, she felt a charge of energy as he came nearer, a prickle on the skin—even a tangible sexual itch. It felt dangerous to be so easily aroused by just the sight of him, as though she had lost all her willpower.

When he was right in front of her, he seemed to know exactly how she was reacting. He said nothing, but looked down into her eyes for a couple of seconds, gave her the ghost of a smile, then seized her arms in his hands and pulled her up into a kiss.

It left her breathless, almost ready to plead for him to take her straight to bed. But she blocked the urge, resolved to behave like a mature woman, not some fluttery adolescent. "Is that how you say hello to all the girls?" she said.

"Not by a long shot, Val. Forgive me if I took too much for granted, but . . . I'd forgotten just how lovely you are."

Winning words. It was getting harder to maintain control. "You have the most amazing effect on me, Glen," she admitted as she ambled toward the house. "I feel things . . . I've never felt before."

He strolled alongside. "Well, I hope they're things you don't mind feelin'."

"That's part of what's amazing—and confusing. I'm not sure if I mind or not."

"How can that be? Feelings are the easiest things to decide about. Either they feel good, or they feel bad."

"Put it this way: These feel very good—but I'm not sure they're good *for* me. Especially now. We've got business to discuss, and personal feelings could get in the way."

They had reached the porch steps. "Point taken," he said. "So let's get all the dull palaver out of the way, then we'll see what's left when the talkin's done."

They entered through French doors into a large living room. If Val had approved of the house from a look at the exterior, she was utterly enchanted as soon as she stepped inside. The furnishings of the living room combined an artful blend of wicker chairs with pillows upholstered in silk florals, antiques, a couple of exquisite Tiffany lamps, and an Aubusson carpet of flowers and vines faded to perfect pastel. She imagined Glen favoring a more masculine decor for a beach getaway, but this was so much to her taste, it was as if he'd consulted people who knew her.

"Your house is exquisite," she said.

"I'm glad you like it," he said. "Though it's not mine. I'm renting it."

"Oh." So much for this idea that he was devoted to satisfying her whims. She was trying too hard to talk herself into believing he could be the right man.

However, he went on to say he'd taken the house because it came with an option to buy—furnished as is—and he thought it one of the nicest beach properties he'd seen. "I don't really go for modern places. Got one out west because the old ones are hard to find. But the ocean is old as time, ain't it, so maybe the best way to enjoy it is to look at it from an old house. Helps me to believe that things can last." He dropped into a chair, stuck his long legs out, and watched Val as she circled the room, appreciating the decor. "I'm not sure, though, this place is worth the investment. The lady who owns it wants a lot for it, and it remains to be seen how much I'd end up usin' it. Seein' it suits you, though, could help me make up my mind."

The references to how much time he might spend here, and figuring her into his decisions, brought her guard back up. She sat down facing him. "Let's talk business, Glen. I think you said that's the reason you brought me here."

"Not quite, darlin'. The reason I brought you here, frankly, is to make love to you. But I did say business was what we had to *talk* about. . . ."

Without a stop he launched into describing a situation they had to resolve before he would finalize his offer to buy. From public records relating to the ownership of the magazine, his lawyers had found that the largest minority shareholder was an eastern socialite named Andrew Winston. The lawyers had then approached Winston's representatives about selling his holding.

"You see, Val, I have a rule about investing. I'll go into the stock market and buy shares in a corporation where I've got a million partners. But if I go into a business I intend to own, then I don't want partners—not a one, big or little. It has to be mine, lock, stock, and barrel."

"That won't be a problem," she said. "I've talked to Andrew

and sent a memo to employees of mine who got stock bonuses over the years. They're all willing to sell if I do."

"That's not exactly the feedback I got from this fella Winston. He passed a message back through my people that he'd happily sell out if the magazine was no longer in your hands."

"Yes, that's just what I was told. So where's the problem? Has he gone back on what he said?"

"Not at all." Majer stood up and paced around, his hands stuck down into the pockets of his jeans. "But I think you took it to mean something other than what he intended. He's saying that as long as you're there runnin' things, he wants a piece of the action. I guess he believes you'll keep on makin' it more valuable. You see the problem now, darlin'?"

"You mean . . . even if I sell, but I'm still editor—"

Majer nodded. "Then he won't let go. Sorry, sweetheart. It's not my play. I was thinkin' I'd keep you on. But this adds a little twist to what you've gotta decide."

Val shook her head in dismay. Andrew's conditions didn't sound like they derived so much from the sentimentality Mr. Jeffries claimed for his client as from a maneuver designed to accomplish one of two things: to force Val out of remaining as editor, or else throw a monkey wrench into the sale. Either way, it struck Val as troublemaking. She thought back to their conversation. Andrew Winston must have undergone quite a change from the unpretentious, pleasant young man he'd been when they met.

"Well, then," she said to Majer, "I guess it's all or nothing for both of us."

"What's your decision?"

"Give me the weekend to decide."

"Sure, take a few days. You might also want to get on a phone and talk to Winston, see if he'd sell without conditions."

She didn't need to go back to him to know it would be pointless. "I'll give you my answer Monday morning."

"Fine." He moved close to her chair and got down on his haunches right in front of her, like a cowboy warming himself at a campfire. "Meantime, I was hoping you'd spend the weekend here with me."

He had already said he'd brought her there to make love to her. "Glen—I don't know. I . . . I'm not prepared. I was at the office, nothing packed . . ."

He laughed lightly and laid his large hands on her knees; their touch filtered through the sheer silk of her skirt. "Now, honey, you know that's not gonna be a problem."

Did he mean she'd spend the weekend wearing nothing . . . or that he'd have her clothes fetched as he had the last time she stayed with him? The answer didn't matter. His touch built on the excitement still lingering from his kiss.

He stood, and bent to pull her up out of the chair. "Let's go see if you approve of the way the bedroom's decorated."

Only one thing surprised her: that as good as it had been with him before, this time it was even better. Somehow he tapped into a well of passion and vigor that she had never known waited within her. It seemed almost perverse to feel herself stripped of every other desire and ambition but to want him with her, inside her, to give herself to him in every way she could, endlessly. Before they lay back, their hunger for each other sated, night had fallen, the bedroom dark except for the silvery glow of moonlight.

Glen proposed taking her out for dinner, urging her to look in the closet and see if she could find something suitable.

"Your landlady might not like strangers wearing her clothes," Val said.

"They're not hers," he said. "They're yours."

The clothes she found filling the hangers of not one but two closets in different bedrooms were all new, expensive designer originals along with stylish production-line beach clothes. He'd noted her size when she was with him in California, he explained.

He must have supreme confidence in predicting her moves, Val thought, if he could buy twenty thousand dollars' worth of new clothes to hang in these closets on the assumption she would surely come. Once more she wondered if she was truly in control of herself, or could be so easily manipulated.

Looking through the array of dresses that might be suitable

for the evening, she couldn't help noting again that he was well attuned to her taste. She liked every single one.

Where there degrees of perfection? At the outset, the weekend seemed more perfect than the last. Glen had chartered a sixty-five-foot sailboat for a cruise on Saturday morning. The October day was sunny but brisk, perfect for an invigorating cruise during which she took the helm. Later, while the charter captain took over, they went below. A champagne and lobster lunch was laid out in a teak-paneled dining salon. Afterward they made love and napped in the forward cabin.

In the evening he gave her a choice. There were other movers and shakers with houses up and down the beach, and invitations to several parties had been extended. Or they could stay in; the house had a screening room, and he'd arranged to have several first-run movies on hand, as well as some Buster Keaton and Charlie Chaplin silents.

Val opted for seeing the silents. "I like what happens with you," she said, "when there's not so much talk."

A light supper of various salads was prepared by one of the several servants who came and went so unobtrusively and efficiently that Val never knew if there were two or twenty. They took plates into the screening room, and sat side by side nibbling while they watched Chaplin's benighted tramp hilariously trying to impress a pretty young girl and stumbling all over himself. Val laughed at first, but the image of love gone awry started to weigh on her. When Majer saw she wasn't laughing, he punched a button and instructed the projectionist to stop the film.

"What's wrong?" he asked when the lights came on.

"Watching that little man in a derby make a fool of himself for love has me wondering if I'm doing the same thing."

"Honey, why is it so goshdarn hard for you to simply relax and enjoy what we've got?"

"Maybe 'cause I'm not sure exactly what that is." She gave him a direct look. "Glen, at the time I met you . . . I'd been with someone else for a long time. We were going to be married. Since then, of course . . . the plans have changed." A self-amused smile touched her lips. "I can't deny it, I've always dreamed of being a bride—but one thing or another always keeps getting in the way—and now that thing is you. . . ."

"I don't want to be an obstacle to your happiness, darlin'. Quite the opposite."

"You do make me happy," she said, then paused, fearful that even the slightest pressure could be as destructive as a fingertip touching a soap bubble. "But you see why I keep wondering if it's enough?"

"I understand why the first time I mentioned stayin' together, you wondered if it was a proposal. You're afraid of tradin' in a good old reliable mule who's always ready to carry your freight for a sleek racehorse who might bolt on ya at any moment."

She smiled. "I wouldn't have put it that way," she said—she certainly wouldn't choose to compare Alan to a mule—"but I guess it captures the essence of how I feel."

"Well, let me spell it out for ya, then, Val. What's happenin' between us isn't an everyday thing for me anymore'n for you. I wanted to know if you liked this house, 'cause I want you to feel right at home with me." He shook his head. "But marriage? I can't truly say yet—and that's partly 'cause I think I love ya. I'm a ramblin' type, honey. To date, I've had two wives, and I married 'em knowing I'd probably cheat on 'em sooner or later, but soon as I gave 'em a sweet enough payoff, they wouldn't mind all that much. I know it's got to be different with you. If I take those vows, I've gotta be sure I'm never gonna hurt you. If you can't wait till the verdict is in, then I'd have to advise ya to go back to your other fella and get that knot tied."

She was as grateful to him for his honesty as she had been to Alan for his graciousness. "That's laying it on the line, I guess. Thank you, Glen."

"And . . . ? How's it shake out?"

She slid her hand across his thigh. "Can I take till Monday on that one too?"

She took his prescription, relaxed, and enjoyed what existed. On Sunday evening, after rising late and spending a good part of the day in bed, she knew already what her decision must be.

She told Glen she wanted to get back to the city that evening, and he summoned the helicopter to fly them in.

As he was gathering papers he wanted to take with him, he reminded Val she could pack any of the clothes in the closets she wanted to take with her.

"Leave them in the closets," she said. He looked disappointed until she added, "I'll want a choice next weekend."

He gathered her close, and his kiss assured her there had never really been a choice.

Twenty-five

The brilliant colors of her autumn were not just in the leaves of the trees, but matched by all the shades and intensities of emotion in this new season of life. Saddened as Val was by the end of one love affair, she was rejuvenated by the other. Anxious as she was about relinquishing the work of the two decades, she was excited by the prospect of exploring new possibilities. Once she was committed to being with Glen, the final decision about the magazine fell into place. To kill the sale would leave a divisive loose end, so she could not stay on as editor. As long as she was with him, however, she could still exercise a degree of influence over the magazine, even if it was unofficial.

Through Glen, the pleasures of being very rich—as she would soon be in her own right—were becoming a regular part of her existence. During October and the first half of November, Glen attended to his casino business during the weekdays, arranging to have all his weekends for Val. He flew her to Bermuda for a few days away from the New York chill, to Sun Valley for skiing, to the Caribbean for cruising on a chartered yacht. Could it go on being so idyllic?

They targeted the end of the year as a convenient date for ownership of the magazine to change hands. It allowed time for Glen to comb the publishing ranks to find a replacement editor, Val to prepare the transition.

In the course of reviewing contracts and other papers sent by her lawyers dealing with the sale, she saw Andrew Winston's name regularly cropping up. He was cooperating as promised, prepared to sign for the same terms of sale as she—though unwilling to sell if she remained as editor. Puzzled by the strict line he had drawn, and his avoidance of meeting with her, Val took the opportunity when talking with her own firm of lawyers to ask what they knew about Winston.

"I doubt it has anything at all to do with you, Miss Cummings," she was told by one of the more venerable members of the firm. "Mr. Winston seems to be less of a social animal these days than he was in the past—some say as the result of some personal unhappiness. . . ." The story told to Val was that Winston's only child, a beautiful girl of sixteen, had been killed two years earlier in the crash of an automobile driven by a drunken Dartmouth freshman who had invited her for her first college weekend. A year later Winston's wife had left him. He lived alone now, and was rarely seen on the party circuit or elsewhere in public.

Recalling the gregarious young man she had once known, Val was moved by hearing of the losses that had apparently turned him into a somewhat reclusive man. She gave some thought to reaching out to him; perhaps she could invite him to spend time with her and Glen—

No, that would be too awkward. What had happened in his life was sad and unfortunate, but for the present she doubted she could help. With the sale still pending, he might even be suspicious of her motives.

A week before Thanksgiving Jess called and asked Val to come to Washington for a family get-together. "Ben's folks and his sister are coming from Minneapolis. How about bringing this new man of yours too? About time I looked him over."

They spoke regularly once or twice a week, so Val had known for a while that Jess was living with Ben Calder, and had told Jess in turn that her long relationship with Alan was over. Jess was shocked. She had liked Alan and urged Val to marry him. Val had also mentioned that another man was involved—and had kept Jess abreast of developments at the magazine—yet she had never linked the two events, or provided any details about her new lover. She deflected Jess's natural curiosity by saying, "You'll find out everything when you meet him."

"Mother, why won't you even tell me his name?" Jess had asked recently. "Is this someone notorious—Frank Sinatra, Cary Grant? Or is it some Mafioso?"

"Don't be silly, Jess. I'm sure you'll approve of him . . . but more if you meet first than if I just tell you his name and vital statistics."

Now Jess was pressing for that meeting. As Val considered putting Glen under her daughter's scrutiny, she realized she was no less nervous than if *she* were the child bringing home a suitor to meet her parents. Jess was so level-headed, the fact that Majer was enormously wealthy would mean nothing to her. She would care only if he was the man to make Val happy. And was he? Being with Glen was intoxicating. But the high could wear off very quickly. With her own doubts stirring, Val feared having them reinforced by Jess's second opinion.

"I'm not sure about Thanksgiving, dear," Val said now. "So much is going on here with this magazine sale."

"Mother, it's one day. Why are you making excuses?"

Sharp old Jess. "I . . . I'm not sure a big family get-together won't make me blue. That kind of thing always gets me down now that Teddie's never there."

"Must that come between you and me? I want you here Thursday, Mom, with or without Mr. X. Listen, I was going to wait and tell you when you were here . . . but Ben and I have decided: We'd like to be married in June. That's why his folks are flying in too. We thought you should all meet, even start to do a little planning. It's not too early, is it?"

Val was instantly energized. "Oh, no, sweetheart, not if you want a formal wedding. Is that what you'd like?"

"With all the trimmings," Jess said. "Valentina Cummings's best."

Val sighed with relief. She would see at least one of her daughters married! "Well, then it's certainly not too early to start making arrangements." She went on for another few minutes nonstop about the preliminaries before she caught herself. "But we can talk all about that Thursday," she said.

"Will you be coming alone?"

"I'll let you know."

When she was with Glen on the weekend, she brought up Jess's invitation.

"I was thinkin' of flyin' us over to Paree for one of them five-star turkey dinners," he said.

"They don't celebrate Thanksgiving in Paris, so I doubt we'd get turkey."

"They'd still do a hell of a job with the trimmin's. Never mind though. You want to be with your daughter, that's fine by me."

"The invitation is for both of us," Val said.

He grinned. "Guess it is about time I let the family look me over."

When Glen entered the Georgetown condo where Jess lived with her boyfriend of the past year, outfitted in his Stetson and western-style suit with the three-thousand-dollar alligator and gold cowboy boots, Ben Calder did a small double take. And Jess's eyes went wide when Val introduced her to Majer: Working on a newspaper, she had seen the name enough to know exactly who he was. But before long Glen had disarmed her and the rest of the family. It started when they sat down to the perfect feast Jess had prepared and he volunteered to say a blessing, then recited the moving appreciation of small things that had been a common grace said by cowboys on the range: "Thank you, Lord, for a place to sleep out of the wind and rain, and bringing me to where my horse can water after a hard day's ride." Later he engaged Ben Calder's father, a physics professor at Marquette University, in a lively discussion of the higher mathematics involved in figuring casino gambling odds. In between he was an attentive listener who displayed obvious affection for Val.

"So what do you think?" Val asked when she found a moment alone with Jess in the kitchen during cleanup.

"He's a catch," Jess said as she put some leftovers into the refrigerator.

Val waited until Jess was facing her again. Avoiding eye

contact while giving an all-purpose compliment signaled less than full enthusiasm. "Yes, he's already been 'caught' a couple of times before," Val said. "But the question is, do you think I'm the one who ought to catch him again?"

Jess busied herself covering the remains of a pumpkin pie. "Mom . . . I'm your kid. Who am I to give you advice?"

"You're the person I asked, that's who—the one person I trust to tell me what you really think."

Jess turned around and leaned back against the counter. "I suppose it may just take some getting used to—you know, I had you married off already to someone else. Or maybe what throws me a little is seeing how much of what happens between you and this guy is . . . is, well, so involved with . . ." She tossed up her hands. "I mean, Mom, I've never seen you like this."

"Like how?"

"It shows every time you two look at each other: This guy really pops your cork, doesn't he?"

It took Val a second to understand exactly what Jess meant—and adjust to speaking with her on this basis. Then she gave an embarrassed laugh. "I suppose that's one way of putting it."

"Fine. I'm glad you have that in your life. But . . . Glen Majer doesn't strike me as someone who's going to be good for the long run. Not for you."

"Maybe he doesn't have to be permanent," Val said defensively.

"Maybe not. But I guess . . . I wanted more for you." Jess shook her head and smiled. "Hey, that's the mother's line, isn't it? But I don't like to think of you ending up alone. What Alan was offering—"

"I think that's over, Jess," Val said.

There was a brief silence, then Jess came over and embraced her. "Just be happy, Mom. However you do it, that's all I wish. Now . . . since we can't start planning your wedding this weekend, suppose we go to work on mine. C'mon, Ben's mother is waiting to tell us how many of her side we've got to put on the list. . . ."

* * *

Without the small but potent dose of perspective provided by Jess, Val would have drifted along thinking that eventually the quicksilver excitement of her time with Glen Majer would solidify into something lasting. Now she admitted a truth to herself she had been previously unwilling to face. She was infatuated, intrigued, intoxicated with Glen . . . but not in love. He touched her and excited her in a way that was new and thrilling; she was charmed by his style, his legend. Yet she wasn't sufficiently attached to the man himself, his values and ambitions, his interests. In bed there was a wildfire between them, but its sparks didn't ignite a blaze that extended to the mind and soul.

On a weekend visit in mid-December, Glen proposed flying abroad in his jet to spend the holidays. "We'll celebrate Christmas in London with all Dickens's Christmas ghosts, spend a few days skiing in the Alps, then drop down for New Year's in Paris at Maxim's. Make it a party. You can invite Jess and Ben, even some of the girls from the magazine to come along, if you want. Then we'll fly back and finish up the magazine deal."

It sounded wonderful, though she wasn't sure about making it a traveling circus. The idea of bringing family along appealed to her, but it also projected her into anticipating—yet again—the sadness of Teddie's absence.

Rather than stew over it, she decided to use the opportunity to make a fresh approach to Teddie—ask if she and her husband would like the free trip to Europe. But Teddie's phone had been disconnected. Val had been paying for only occasional reports from Frank Stecchino. She knew that Teddie had gone to work for a catering firm while her husband started law school, knew the couple fought occasionally but were still together, knew they continued to live on the houseboat. That at least had been the situation when Val decided that even if it was done out of love, it was wrong to keep spying on Teddie.

She called Stecchino and asked him to use his people in San Francisco to locate her daughter again.

He told her not to worry, he would get back to her as soon as he had the information.

For the rest of the morning Val was on edge, nervously drinking three times as many cups of coffee as usual, pacing the office, unable to concentrate on work. Teddie's disappearance, the mere thought that she might not be found again, threw Val into a fresh sense of loss. She was gripped by a presentiment that something more serious had happened to Teddie than simply moving to a new address. Worrying over it actually began to make her feel ill, the kind of faint nausea that struck when you lost your inner equilibrium, as on a rocking boat. Or was it just too much coffee?

When her secretary told her only two hours later that Stecchino was calling back, Val leapt at the phone, so worked up by her own imaginings that she was steeled to hear the worst.

"No trouble at all finding your daughter," the investigator told her. "She and her husband vacated the boat two months ago when they split."

"They're not together?"

"Unh-unh. She's moved in with a new guy named Dirk Brandon, somebody she met when that caterer she works for did a wedding for his business partner."

"What kind of business?" Val asked.

"A record company. I'm told he's pretty successful, but I'm getting more details for you, Miss Cummings. For now I thought you'd just like to know your daughter's okay, and she hasn't dropped out of sight. Oh, I've got phone numbers for Brandon's home and business if you'd like. . . ."

Val wrote down the numbers, though she realized she wouldn't use them—not soon anyway. She foresaw that Teddie would resent having her whereabouts traced, and feel defensive about Val's knowledge of her brief failed marriage.

Relieved as she was to know Teddie was well, Val's nausea didn't go away. She felt sapped of energy to a degree that wasn't characteristic. That afternoon, after dictating a long memo to the staff about the coming change of management, Val stopped her secretary as she was leaving her office. "Pat, can you get me a doctor's appointment? Later today or early tomorrow, if possible."

"Will do. You okay?"

"Fine. But I may be taking a long trip for the holidays; I want to be sure I'm not coming down with something before I go."

Three mornings later, at a quarter to nine, Val entered the spacious professional office suite of one of New York's most successful Park Avenue specialists. She had been told to come fifteen minutes before the office's standard opening time so she could get in ahead of the crowd of regular patients.

After receiving the result of tests administered earlier in the week, it had taken her two days just to absorb the news she'd been given and decide how to deal with it. Once her decision was made, she called the one man she believed she could talk to about such a personal matter.

"Miss Cummings," the nurse said, "the doctor will see you now. He's in his office, straight ahead." She pointed the way along a corridor. "Oh, Miss Cummings," the nurse added as Val passed her desk, "I'd like to thank you. I got married in September; we did everything according to the way you suggested in your book, and it turned out perfectly."

"I'm glad," Val said. "But I can't take all the credit. The mood—the emotion—is always the main ingredient when it turns out right. And that came entirely from you."

"And my Dave," the nurse said, nodding. Val started to move on. "Oh, good luck," she called after her.

The doctor rose and came around his desk the moment Val walked into his large office. "Valentina," he said effusively, "this is the nicest surprise I've had in years." He stretched out his hands to her, and she took them in both of hers.

"Hello, Walter."

In his early fifties, Walter Kendall still had not lost his teddy-bear appeal, though his curly brown hair had gone gray, and his round face, masked by black-framed spectacles, had given up some of its cuteness to accommodate the confident dignity of a man who had become a leader in his field. "My goodness, Val, how good it is to see you—one of my most famous patients. . . ."

"What flattery, Dr. Kendall! From what I know about your practice, I'm small potatoes." Walter Kendall had become the chosen obstetrician of many celebrities and socialites. The plain no-nonsense rules he had once insisted on when he was just a green resident—for example, absolutely no smoking or alcohol during pregnancy—had since become commonplace, but he was still pioneering new ideas for healthful prenatal care and birthing. Lately he had been part of a group of specialists exploring prenatal surgery to correct birth defects.

He moved behind his desk as Val took the facing wing chair. "I'm sorry I didn't return your call personally yesterday—I was in delivery—but I told my nurse to fit you in first thing this morning."

"I appreciate it, Walter. This isn't exactly an emergency."

"What is it, Val?"

She let out a breath it seemed she had been holding for days. "I'm pregnant again."

From the subdued way in which she made the announcement, Kendall understood that she was less than happy. "Would I be correct that it wasn't planned?"

"That would be putting it mildly. I don't know how it could have happened."

He smiled. "I didn't think you'd need to be educated about that."

His gibe eased the tension a little. "You know what I mean—I took precautions." Well, *most* of the time, she admitted to herself; there had been a few times with Glen when she was carried away, unmindful of consequences she thought so unlikely.

"There's nothing foolproof," Kendall said. "But why dwell on the down side? Having a baby is always a miraculous event."

"At my time of life, it's less a miracle than a disaster."

He gave an avuncular shake of his head. "Let's see—if I've got my arithmetic correct, you're . . . just forty. Everything must be in good working order, or you wouldn't have conceived in the first place. From my perspective, Val, your age is no problem at all. With the right regimen, only a small amount of extra care—"

"The problem isn't my age, Walter. I'm not married. And I'm not in love with the father."

He nodded slowly. "I guess lightning can strike twice."

"It's not exactly the same this time. Nothing was done against my will. But you see . . ." She was fighting a wave of emotion that was all the stronger for being a replica of twenty years ago—being with the man who had helped her then. "Since I found out, I've been struggling with the question of what to do."

"Well, you couldn't have done anything better than come to me. Nothing will please me more than to see you through. I'd rank you as my all-time favorite patient." He looked down, suddenly boyishly shy. "I don't know if you realized it when I took care of you last time, Val, but I had quite a crush on you. If I'd been more sure of myself . . ." He shrugged. "Well, so it goes."

She smiled. "I did sense something. And I was fond of you too, Walter. But at the time I wasn't in a position to be with anyone." She glanced over at a photograph on the wall she'd spotted when she entered, Walter and a slim, pretty woman on a sunny beach with three children of various ages lined up in front of them. "Looks like it worked out fine for you."

"Yes, it did." An awkward silence took the place of his openly wishing her family life could have worked out equally well. "But to business: We'll start with a basic exam. Then I'd recommend an ultrasound, routine these days, just to make sure the fetus is—"

She stopped him. "Walter, you said you'd see me through, and I'm counting on that. But I don't think you understand why I'm here. I came to you as a friend hoping you'd help me . . . do what I'd like in the safest way."

He gave her a long, probing stare. "Are you talking about an abortion?"

She nodded.

"You're sure that's what you want?"

"I've spent two sleepless nights thinking about it."

He rose and came around his desk to perch on a corner right in front of Val. "Tell me why you'd make that choice."

"Some of it I've mentioned already. I'm not married, and I don't think I want to bring this child up with the man who's the father. But more than anything . . . I've proven to be a lousy mother. That child you brought into this world, Walter, she doesn't talk to me anymore. She's mad about having to grow up the way she did, stigmatized, given too little love and attention because I had obligations to work, to friends." Val couldn't hold back the tears. As they spilled down her cheeks, Walter Kendall pulled a tissue from a box on his desk and handed it to Val. "Dammit," she said as she blotted her face. "Do I have to explain any more? I just couldn't bear to make another child so angry and miserable. I couldn't have made this choice the last time, Walter, it was against the law then. But it isn't now. You can do this for me, can't you?" She gazed at him imploringly.

"Legally, I can," he said. "But . . . I'm sorry, Val, I can't square it with my own views. I don't believe it would be right."

"This is my *choice*, Walter. Don't you think I have a right to my choice?" There were no tears now. His reaction plunged her into an icy reality that banished all emotion.

"I do. And there are circumstances in which I'd help carry it out. But in your case I can't."

She was shattered. It had been hard enough to bare her desire—a weak and ignoble one, she felt—to this gentle man she trusted. She didn't think she could do it again to a stranger. "Walter, I came here because I needed a friend. . . ."

"That's why I'm saying no to you, Val—because I *am* your friend." He stood, and paced in the space between his desk and a window that looked out to Park Avenue. "I'm giving you an opinion—a medical opinion based on dealing with thousands of other women, and being asked more and more to help in this same way. I think a time would come when you would regret this terribly. Especially because at your age it's apt to be your last chance." He paused, letting that sink in. "Up to a couple of years ago, it was my custom to agree when asked to end a pregnancy. I understood the motives—the baby wasn't planned, it got in the way of a career, the woman didn't *like* children, the father didn't want it. There are only a few basic reasons, they don't change. But what I've seen, as time passes, is that the patients *do* change. Far more often than not, they wish they had the decision to make again." He stopped in front of the window and looked out. "I suppose I'd also have a different perspective, if I were tending to underprivileged women who can't afford to feed another mouth, or are too young to take on the responsibility. But here, seeing women who are bright and successful, with every reason to be optimistic about the sort of life they can make for a child . . ." He turned back to Val. "You're the chosen ones, you see. Your children can grow up to be fine, caring, responsible people. And we need them. I won't be the one to cheat humanity out of a person who can do it some good any more than I want to cheat that child-to-be out of the pleasure of . . . playing in the sand or the snow, smelling a flower, all the wonders of life."

Val was silent, absorbing it. At last, quietly, she asked, "You don't believe it's possible that you're condemning this child to a life of unhappiness? I've already ruined one young life."

"Have you? Let me ask you a few questions—just answer yes or no. Is your daughter healthy?"

"Yes. . . ."

"Is she making her own way in the world?"

"I told you she wants nothing to do with me."

"Is she reasonably intelligent, mentally stable?"

"I suppose . . . yes."

He came back to sit on the corner of the desk by her chair. "I don't know what the issues are between you and this girl. I don't know if they'll ever be solved. But it doesn't sound to me like you've ruined her life. You've produced a strong, independent individual. It's not certain she's unhappy. Oh, I understand *you're* unhappy about the situation between you, but it doesn't persuade me you can't be a good mother. If there were mistakes made, Val, you might even be glad to have a second chance—to work out the kinks."

She sat with her head bowed, not looking at him. His

kindness and common sense made her even more ashamed of what she had come to ask than she had felt walking in, though she had no real change of heart. The decision she had reached earlier might be hard to live with, but it had the virtue of forcing no one but herself to live with it.

He coaxed her out of her silence. "It's not the easiest way to go, I know. But I'll help you all along the way."

She looked up at him and smiled. "Thank you, Walter. You *are* a friend, and I take everything you've said in that spirit." She stood. "I'll have to think this through some more." She gave him a quick kiss on the cheek and turned to the door.

He followed her. "You'll let me know what you decide."

"I'll be in touch—soon—if I need a full examination."

She was stepping out of the office when he said, "Let me know either way, Val. If you need the sort of help I can't give, I'll send you to the best."

Twenty-six

There was a week of wrestling with the choice—a week of also avoiding Glen while she tried to reach a clear decision on her own. Once he knew she was pregnant with his child, he would certainly try to make her act according to his wish, and he was a forceful man. What his preference would be, she didn't know. He'd had no children yet, he might want one to carry on his dynasty.

For a week she made excuses to him—deadlines, a minor flu, an emergency with Jess's plans that required being in Washington, whatever kept him at bay. By the second week the excuses were wearing thin, and Val felt so exhausted by the nights of sleepless indecision, she feared it could affect the health of the baby. At last she decided it was his right to know.

It was the weekend before Christmas, and they had agreed to meet at the beach house he was still renting. Friday evening she drove out from the city alone and was waiting in the living room when he was shuttled there by helicopter after his jet landed at JFK. He had read too many faces across too many poker tables not to know the minute he walked into the room that she was holding a bad hand. He wasted no time.

"What's the problem? The magazine deal? Got a better offer and you're afraid to tell me? Or is it just a personal adios?"

His concerns seemed so relatively insignificant, she almost laughed. "Nothing so simple, Glen." Nothing to do but say it. "I'm pregnant."

He stared at her for a second, then pushed back his large black Stetson so a lock of his silver hair fell across his eyes. "Well, shiver my timbers—aren't we somethin'?" He came to her chair, reached down to take her hands in his, and pulled her up into his arms. "Guess there was more to our fireworks than sizzle and sparks, eh, lady?"

She couldn't quite read the reaction. Searching his face, she said, "You sound almost . . . glad?"

He shrugged. "Glad? No, hon' . . . I wouldn't say that. I just don't see it as any kind of problem." Yet he said it so breezily, he almost made her believe it—that his wealth and generosity would somehow make it easy no matter what the decision was. Then he went on. "Easiest thing in the world to take care of these days. Couple hours in some fancy clinic, and you're rid of it quicker'n a heifer gettin' hog-tied."

Maybe it was just his words—his no-frills cowboy expression—that cast his choice in such a harsh light, but she was instantly furious, and protective of this still-unborn part of herself. Thrusting him back, she spun out of his arms and walked across the room. " 'Rid of it'?" she repeated. "You make it sound like some . . . some unwanted, useless thing that can be just thrown away like a . . . a dead battery."

He tried to smooth it over. "Okay, darlin', I put it badly. But you can't think it makes any sense for us to have this kid?"

She regarded him defiantly. "Why not?"

"You really need me to spell it out?"

She challenged him with her silence.

"Okay," he went on, "start with this: The way I feel about havin' a child is the way I feel about anything else I'd own. It's got to be mine outright—which means givin' it my name, investin' my money in it. So there we are, darlin', I couldn't let you have this baby unless we were married, and together all the time. . . ."

Hearing Majer talk about the child as something to be "owned" and "invested in" depressed her, and made her aware that she didn't want to rear a child with him even if they could agree to do it outside the bounds of marriage. As he continued, though, it was clear that during the weeks she had been defining their relationship for herself, he had come to similar conclusions.

"When it comes to tyin' the knot," he said, "I got a hunch

you feel as I do—it would be a mistake. I love ya, Val. More'n that, I admire ya. But I've been a tumbleweed too long to think I'd ever tie myself down permanent. What we have might've lasted as long as it was fun and games, you and me. But as a mammy and pappy bringin' up a papoose?" He shook his head. "Honey, I'd just head for the hills the first time I heard the little critter bawlin'. So there it is. While there's just you and me, we might keep goin' . . . even have a good long run. But with a kid in the picture, there's not a mite o' hope."

So he was asking her to choose. Between him and the baby—though not even promising he'd be around for any longer than the day when the fun and games lost their appeal. She couldn't be angry about it. She'd gone into the affair with her eyes wide open, and she had wanted him as he was.

She took a long, deep breath. "I still can't . . . give it up."

He looked down, kicked the expensive carpet with his foot as though turning over a clod of prairie dust. "Too bad," he said. When he raised his eyes to meet hers again, there was no softness left in them; she saw the same hard, impenetrable look that he had taken into every business deal where he had beaten down his competitors. "But it's your decision, not mine. And so that's how it'll be all the way. Have this baby, Val, and I'm tellin' ya straight, here and now: I won't be any part of it. Don't ever expect any cooperation from me, any bein' a daddy, any kinda support. You understand? That's the choice you're makin'. Your choice. Not mine."

She knew there were ways she might yet force him to accept responsibility, but she couldn't bear to think of having another child of hers become the source of anger and bitterness. Nor did Majer's position seem altogether unfair. It was her choice, and in rejecting marriage, they were of the same mind.

"I understand," she said.

He stood gazing at her another moment. "Looks like it was adios after all," he said. Touching the brim of his large Stetson in a cowboy's gesture of good-bye, he turned, and without another word walked back out the door.

A minute later she heard the engine of the helicopter come to life.

It should have been easy for him to give her at least some money. He certainly had plenty, and he had always been generous in the past. But money wasn't the issue with him—it was purely a matter of power. He couldn't tolerate that she would act against his "orders," that this was a circumstance in which the final decision wasn't his to make.

He had a surprise for her though. On New Year's Eve, when she was alone in her city apartment, a package was delivered by a bonded messenger along with a bottle of champagne. Inside, Val found a deed to the Southampton beach property in her name. There had been no contact with Majer since they'd parted, and no note of any kind accompanied the document. But it was clear that the house and all its contents was being given to her as full and final settlement. A generous one at that; she knew the asking price for the house had been well over three million dollars. She couldn't drink the champagne—against Walter's rules—but she understood the symbolic toast to the end of an affair.

But his gesture did not signal a surrender on all fronts. Following their personal break, Val had reappraised her decision to sell him the magazine. On the one hand, she saw the advantages of being free of work and financially set for life when the baby came; on the other, she no longer felt sanguine about putting the business into the hands of a man who had behaved so coldly. Her heart was too much in the institution she had created—one that depended on a belief in romance. She met with her lawyers and announced she had reversed her decision to sell the magazine.

To let her control *every* decision was too much for Majer. In response to the letter from Val's lawyers informing him that the magazine was no longer for sale, Majer had his own lawyers serve papers declaring that an "implied" contract already existed, backed up with considerable documentation showing that she had already agreed to sell, and the terms were set.

At that point it turned into the kind of bitter contest that often moves in to fill the vacuum of emotion after good feelings die. Charge and countercharge issued from battling legal firms like artillery shells flying across a battle zone.

Initially Val expected that Majer would soon give up; surely, the magazine itself couldn't mean as much to him as it did to her. He had so many other ways of making money. The gift of the house seemed to indicate that more than a remnant of good feeling remained.

But demonstrating how much she cared about the magazine only made him want to wrest it away all the more. The wrangling of lawyers continued for week after week, going on into months. It became so stressful for Val that Walter Kendall expressed concern that it could interfere with her pregnancy.

"Maybe you should toss in the towel, Val," he said in April, when she was entering her fifth month.

"Are you *telling* me to surrender, Walter? Are those doctor's orders?" He had given her wonderful care, and she had no doubt that whatever he advised would be carefully considered and important for her health and the baby's.

"It hasn't reached that point yet," he said. "But think about it. This is a time when you should be free of worry, getting more rest than usual—not less. You're wearing yourself down, Val." Though he had encouraged her to believe her age would not be a factor, he explained that there could be higher risks if she let her health deteriorate.

It did seem foolish to risk the baby when surrender would do no worse than make her rich.

A few days later she was on the verge of instructing her own legal team to yield and settle according to Majer's terms, when she received a phone call one afternoon from Dwight Jeffries, the Wall Street lawyer who had contacted her previously on behalf of Andrew Winston. He explained that his client had been staying on the sidelines for the past several months, prepared to honor his pledge to act in concert with Val's wishes, whatever they were.

"But I should tell you, Miss Cummings," Jeffries said, "since you withdrew from negotiations to sell, I have been contacted repeatedly by representatives of Mr. Majer with offers to purchase my client's percentage of ownership independent of yours."

The revelation alarmed Val. Andrew Winston held a minority share—but except for her own holding, it was the largest single bloc; if Majer took possession, it would be easier for him to meddle in the running of the magazine and wear down Val's resistance to a takeover.

"The offers have been steadily getting larger," Jeffries added, "far exceeding what Mr. Winston would have been paid originally as a party to your transaction."

Val thought she knew what Jeffries was leading up to. "Mr. Winston has been very good to stand by me as long as he has. Tell him that if he feels he ought to sell, I'll understand."

"He hasn't made any decision. Though frankly, Miss Cummings," Jeffries admitted, "I've been urging him to divest. But that's why I'm calling. To make a sensible assessment, the time has come when we need a clearer picture—questions that need to be answered. Why did you flip-flop on this sale? Is this just a maneuver to push up the price? Or do you intend now to continue with the magazine for the long run?"

Andrew deserved no less than her cooperation in helping him make an informed judgment about his investment. But up to that point Val had told no one the actual reason for breaking with Majer—even if people close to her must have figured it out—and Majer had evidently been equally discreet, or Jeffries could have gotten his answers from the grapevine and wouldn't need to ask her.

"Mr. Jeffries," she said, "let me assure you that I'm not flip-flopping to—"

"I didn't mean you have to tell me," he interrupted. "It's Mr. Winston who wants to hear the answers."

"Andrew?" she said, surprised. "I'd be glad to meet with him." More than glad.

"A meeting isn't possible," the lawyer said. "Mr. Winston is away for an extended period." But he gave her a number and said Winston was waiting by the phone to take her call.

* * *

When he answered the phone and she identified herself, his greeting was cordial. Yet there was an edge of remoteness in his voice too. She thought of what she'd learned about him since they'd last spoken, the losses he'd suffered. She longed to say that she knew he'd had a difficult time, and would do anything in her power to restore his spirit to that exuberance she'd once known. But there was a chasm of time and experience that was hard to bridge.

"How are you, Andrew?" she asked simply.

"I'm managing." The quick, dry answer seemed to plant a Keep Off sign in the personal area. He emphasized the wish by moving straight on to business. "Dwight told you I'm being courted by Glen Majer?"

"Yes."

"You know I've always believed in you, Valentina. You had a clear vision, and that inspired my faith. Whatever happened between us personally, I never lost that belief."

She thought she heard a softening in his tone. "Certainly I know that, Andrew. And I'm still grateful to you for—"

He cut in. "I wasn't fishing for gratitude. I mentioned my past feelings as a prelude to saying that lately I've been less clear on what your vision is. If you thought it was the right time to sell the magazine, that made it right for me too. But suddenly you've done an about-face. I can't support you unless I know what's behind the way you're behaving."

"You don't need to support me, Andrew, if it's not good for you."

"I know I don't *need* to." He sounded edgy and impatient. "But I'm still entitled to know exactly what's going on. You're spending bushels of company money for lawyers so that actions you approved only a few months ago can be declared void. Why, Val?"

She could have fudged it, let him make his decision on the existing facts. But after twenty years of his loyalty, she owed Andrew nothing less than what he'd asked for—the truth.

Summoning all her courage, she gave it to him in one piece. "I used some very bad judgment, Andrew. I met Glen Majer through his interest in buying the magazine, but . . . we became involved. It's been fairly brief—and it's over now. But I . . . I am carrying his child." She paused, expecting there might be a reaction, but there was only silence. She hurried on. "However, the problems caused by that aren't the only reason I reversed the sale. I love *E.B.*—no less something I conceived than a baby—and I can't hand it over to someone who no longer seems trustworthy."

The silence lasted another couple of seconds. "Majer's a very smart businessman," Winston said then. "That hasn't changed, has it?"

"No," Val admitted. "I'm sure he'll do well with any business, but I woke up to the fact that this one in particular runs best with someone who . . . who really understands a woman's heart."

"Perhaps your feelings about this man are clouding your judgment."

"They could be," Val answered honestly. "You'll have to decide. I've told you everything I can."

"Thank you, Val," he said. "It's helped me understand. Good-bye."

"Andrew—" she said quickly before he could hang up.

"Yes?"

She wanted to say that she'd like to see him again sometime. But then she decided it was pointless. He'd sounded so distant, he wasn't likely to be won over by having heard about her affair with Majer. "It was . . . nice to talk with you again."

He hung up without even a reply. She realized then how blandly insincere she must have sounded. Nice to talk? It might have been if she could have broken through his shell—and if she hadn't had to make such a shameful confession.

Three days later she was called down to the offices of the legal firm handling her defense against Majer, and informed by them that the complexion of the case had undergone a sudden change in her favor—thanks to Andrew Winston. He had not only fired off a letter to Majer strongly expressing his solidarity with "the current management of *Every Bride's* magazine," but had engaged counsel of his own to launch a suit against

Majer, accusing him of illegally breaching various technicalities and disregarding ethical practice in his attempt to undermine "the management."

"The real legal merit of Winston's claims is dubious," Val's lawyer said, "but Majer's going to have to think twice now about whether to pursue his case against you."

"Why—if it's all bluster?"

"Val, the firm Winston has engaged is a top Wall Street powerhouse. And Majer knows it. Putting them on the front line is a signal that the whole financial establishment is pissed off by his attempt to nail you—a warning that he could find it hard to make richer deals in the future if he doesn't throw in his cards on this one. Why Andy Winston's gone all-out for you over his minority share when selling would be so much easier, I'm damned if I know. But you sure got yourself one hell of an ally."

Two weeks later Val was informed that every legal action Majer had instituted against her and the magazine had been dropped without the usual legal feinting, not even a nothing-to-lose offer to settle.

In the wake of her victory, Val's lawyers suggested they might raise the question of recovering her own legal costs from Majer, and she agreed. Subsequently, Majer paid them without protest. Even her own lawyers were astonished. For a man of Majer's power and ruthlessness, his swift unconditional surrender was puzzling.

But Val didn't think the power play was the whole explanation for the outcome. No doubt Andrew's firm support had made Glen think twice about going ahead. But with reflection, Glen had probably recovered that more decent, generous spirit she had known. After all, Val reasoned, she could never have been so beguiled by him if he didn't have some redeeming qualities.

On the second weekend in June, Val watched Jess married in a full formal ceremony at the Washington Cathedral, followed by a dinner and dance for three hundred at the Shoreham Hotel. Jess's work as a journalist had already brought her into contact with some important people in government who liked her and had become friends, and quite a number were present for the occasion.

Whatever the trials and losses Val might have suffered over the years for having kept the vow to Josie, they were far outweighed by the joy of seeing her child—*their* child—reach this milestone. The tide of emotion also erased any lingering doubt that she could do anything else than keep and raise one more child—a child she knew from amniocentesis and ultrasound testing was going to be a daughter.

Visibly pregnant at seven months, Val provoked a full gamut of reactions as she encountered other guests at the reception who asked how she came to know the happy couple, and she answered, "I'm the bride's mother." Probably all the more startling because she was only approaching forty-one, while Jess had just turned twenty-eight.

The world was changing. Val could look ahead and see a time when an unmarried pregnant woman would not be such a rare guest at a wedding—or so rare a bride.

It occurred to Val, indeed, that as soon as she got home she ought to write a chapter on the proper etiquette covering such situations for the next edition of her wedding book.

III

Vows

Twenty-seven

Las Vegas, Nevada
9 P.M.

Teddie walked into the vast lobby of the Shangri-La and stopped to stare. She should be immune to spectacle, having arranged so much of it herself, but she couldn't help being dazzled by the sight of the hotel's indoor atrium. The length and breadth of two football fields, at the center was a lake sizable enough to have its own island in the middle, a tropical paradise with miniature mountains and curved white sand beaches. On the lake's aquamarine water, scaled-down pirate galleons sailed under remote control, their decks loaded with stacked golden ingots, and chests with pearls and jeweled necklaces spilling over. This tribute to greed might seem to some people to be nothing more than excessive decor, but actually it was a shrewd spur to business. Seeing all those exotic riches so near yet out of reach spiked the appetites of the customers to run to the banks of slot machines standing everywhere on the lobby's "dry land" to try winning a fortune.

Teddie wasn't there to gamble though. A desire for greater wealth might be her motive, but she was angling for more of a sure thing.

Across the lobby, past the main elevator bank, she turned a corner and entered an alcove small enough to be ignored by those who weren't looking for it. A single elevator there serviced only one floor. The car was waiting, a burly uniformed man standing in rigid military fashion beside the open doors.

"Mr. Majer is expecting me," she said, "Teddie Darian."

The man pushed a button on a keyboard set into the wall, and a picture of Teddie appeared on a computer screen to confirm the appointment and her identity. He turned to Teddie and held out his hand. "Purse, please. . . ."

"Do I look like I'm carrying a concealed weapon?"

"Please," he repeated in a humorless monotone.

With a sigh, Teddie handed him the evening bag that matched the slinky low-cut black sequined evening dress under her white fox jacket. Glen Majer couldn't be blamed for his caution. Even among those who were supposedly friends, there was probably no shortage of people who'd enjoy killing him.

The elevator man finished checking the purse and handed it back. "Not going to frisk me?" she said, following him into the elevator. "I like being frisked."

He acted as if he hadn't heard. The elevator swooped upward, and the doors opened onto the opulent entrance hall of the penthouse that took up half the hotel's top floor. A maid took Teddie's coat, and conducted her down a long, marble-sheathed gallery opening into an enormous living room edged at one side with a sizable indoor garden complete with grass, rosebushes, and fruit trees. Beyond the garden, a long wall of glass gave onto a view across the city's sparkle to the dark plain of the desert.

Glen Majer stood beside an apricot tree, studying it, a small curved pruning saw in one hand. After a moment he reached up and started to saw away a branch.

Teddie watched, assuming he hadn't realized she was there. Could he truly be approaching eighty? she wondered. His body, clothed at the moment in jeans and a denim work shirt, still looked amazingly youthful, lean and erect. The iron-gray hair was thick—almost too much of it in that swept-back mane. What was his secret? There had been at least a few face-lifts, but that didn't explain his vigor, the whole aspect. Perhaps it was the hardy constitution built up in his early years of rugged outdoor living.

"They're a bit like women," Majer said while he concentrated on pruning the tree. He was aware of her, after all, though he had yet to look at her. "You want 'em to flower fully and give you the juiciest fruit, you have to cut 'em down to size a little now and then."

"You know, Glen," Teddie said, "these days that kind of talk to a woman can get you killed."

The branch dropped to the ground, and at last he turned to her. "That's why I have the bodyguards. So I can go right on saying any damn thing I want."

Of course, coming from his background, Teddie thought, he had to be forgiven if he hadn't gotten rid of his macho swagger. No doubt there was a certain amount of public relations hyperbole in the colorful legend surrounding Glen Majer, but there was also a surprising amount of truth. Since the time he'd nearly bought *Every Bride's*, his fortune had grown by a billion or two—which he still referred to whimsically as his "grubstake"—and he had erected the Shangri-La, four thousand rooms all filled year-round with people who couldn't help getting beaten by the odds. He lived atop the hotel when he wasn't traveling, using his money to play at any deal that took his fancy, buying big slices of movie studios or car companies as easily as if he were ordering a piece of pie.

"Well, Teddie-girl, you're lookin' mighty fine for all the time gone by since I saw you last." His eyes rested on her as he wiped his hands on his faded jeans. "Just how long's it been . . . ?"

"Let's just say I wasn't much more than a kid then."

"Some kid. You knew how to negotiate, all right. Made me pay pretty well to do me the favor that helped me solve that little problem I had with your mama."

Teddie was silent. Ready as she was for yet another betrayal of her own blood, she didn't like to dwell on a past sin.

Majer walked out of his indoor garden onto the polished black granite floor of his living room. "S'pose we sit down over a little rotgut, and you tell me what brings you 'round all of a sudden?"

His kind of rotgut ran the gamut from fifty-year-old whisky to hundred-year-old brandy, but she said a martini would be nice, and he pressed a button somewhere—they were all over, in the walls, floors, even hidden in the trees—and a maid appeared to take the order. He requested a scotch, and they went to one of the sitting areas scattered around his enormous living room.

Teddie had called only that morning from Beverly Hills seeking an appointment right away. To the assistant who asked for an explanation she would give none. The message had come back that Majer would be happy to talk to her whenever she liked; but not on the phone, he wanted it face-to-face.

Now Teddie opened her purse and pulled out the invitation she had received yesterday. She thrust it at him. He took it and glanced at it. Not a trace of reaction in his face. Teddie had to remind herself he was one of the world's great poker players. "Well?" she said.

"Well what?"

"Is it you? I've heard you two are kind of friendly again."

He stared at her a moment, then laughed, a cowboy's hearty bunkhouse guffaw. "Me? You thought—? Oh, Teddie-girl, that's a good one . . . that really is."

She wasn't convinced yet. "Why wouldn't it be?"

He hesitated as though deciding whether he cared to convince her. "For one thing, you know your mama's gotten too old for me."

"She wasn't always," Teddie observed.

"Well, back when I was young and foolish, I liked 'em closer to my own age."

A maid brought their drinks and left. They each took a swig.

"There are other factors besides age that might attract you," Teddie said. Reaching out, she pulled the invitation from his hand and scanned it. "The way I read this, it could be a kind of puzzle. Maybe what she means here by 'the man of her dreams' isn't about the old lovey-dovey kind, but about someone who helps her achieve all her dreams in business. And where she says the wedding will be 'in paradise' . . . isn't that kind of a synonym for Shangri-La . . . ?"

"That devil's mind o' yours is working overtime, Teddie. Sure, your mama and I can be in the same room these days without one takin' a swing at the other, and true, we had a thing once—"

"More than a thing," Teddie observed tartly.

"Whatever. But if the knot didn't get tied then, there's a whole lot less reason for it to happen now."

Teddie hadn't bought it quite yet. "Making money's always a good enough reason for you to do anything, Glen."

"Not where your mama's concerned. Remember, back when I went for her, it wasn't all about dollars and cents. She was quite a pistol. . . ." He frowned and shook his head slowly, a bit tiredly, letting his age show for a second as he contemplated the changes that time inevitably brought.

That finally persuaded Teddie. "Well, I'm relieved," she said.

He chuckled. "Don't think I'd make you a good stepdaddy?"

She laughed. "Oh, I think you'd be the best—tell me the best fairy tales every time I climbed into your lap." He laughed too, and raised his glass as if toasting her before draining it. "But then," she went on, "what I have in mind would be . . . almost a kind of incest."

His eyes brightened. "Oh? Would it?"

"In a *financial* sense, you could call it that. I mean, if you and I were to get into bed together . . . in the business sense, that is, you giving me the benefit of your very sizable . . . wherewithal, that would strike some people as a fairly unholy combination."

He cocked his head inquisitively. "Let me understand this: You're here to make me a proposition?"

"I think it's time for me to be at the top of my business," she said.

"The wedding business, you mean. I thought you were already doing pretty well at it."

"I want to do better. I'm tired of simply planning the absurd spectacles that people like you—people with too damn much money—call a wedding. For some reason, you all think that the more you spend, the better chance it gives the marriage to last. When, actually, it works the other way around."

"Does it? I'll remember that the next time I get hitched." Up to then, Majer had been married six times—though not in the past ten years—always with lavish celebration, and not one of the unions had lasted more than two years. He had paid out upward of a hundred million dollars in settlements and alimony. "So let me understand this, Teddie, you want to take over your mama's business—usin' my bankroll?"

Teddie nodded.

"You really think you can run it better than she does herself?"

"Better? Hard to say," Teddie answered honestly. "But at least as well."

"In business terms, what's the point of making a change if you can't improve things?"

"You'll make money out of it, that's the point."

"But for you," he said, "money's not the point, is it? You still can't forgive her. . . ."

Teddie was silent a moment, letting the bitter words that rose to her lips die away unspoken. "We don't have to get into that, Glen. All that matters, if you really don't figure in my mother's plans . . . is that you could figure in mine. If she's really getting married, it's time for me to take over." After a pause, she added,"You owe this to me, you know. I helped you out once."

He smiled at her. "As I recall, you got paid very well for your help."

"True. You also told me you'd always appreciate it, and if I ever needed anything . . ."

He leaned back in his easy chair, his long legs spread like a cowboy relaxing after a long ride. "I suppose this deal of yours could make sense," he said. "Tell me: How much you figure the honeymoon business alone adds up to these days?"

As if he didn't know, Teddie thought. But she answered. "According to the latest figures, American honeymooners will spend about nine billion dollars this year."

"And she has a fair say in how a good portion of that gets spent." He chewed on it a moment. "You know, this proposal of yours does perk up my interest. Life was just beginning to get a little dull, nothin' to do but clip coupons and prune the trees. Starts to make a man feel old."

"You'll never be old," Teddie said throatily, playing up to his vanity, anything to win him over.

His shrewd slate-blue eyes rested on her thoughtfully. "You're some piece of work, Teddie—ready to stab your own mother in the back."

"Not the back," she said evenly. "She knows where I stand. I've always come at her from right up front."

Still, he hesitated.

He was her best chance. She couldn't let him slip away. "Is there anything else I can say or do to push our deal through?" she said. "Anything . . . ?" She leaned forward and reached across the gap between them to lay a hand on his knee.

He glanced down at her hand. "We seem to be gettin' closer to a kind of incest all the time."

Her hand moved along his thigh. "Just stop me if I get too close."

He hesitated another second, then clapped his hand over hers and pulled it away, holding it in a tight, painful grip. "I don't need that, Teddie, not from you."

She pulled back, yanking her hand free. "What about my . . . *other* proposition?" she asked anxiously.

He smiled slowly. "What the hell. Let's see where it leads."

Twenty-eight

Southampton
Summer 1981

"Dice! Time for the cake! Dicey—where are you?"

Val stood on the wide span of white sand in front of the house, turning to scan the view of ocean and the broad lawn. A couple of picnic tables had been brought down to the beach, and the five girls invited to celebrate her daughter's twelfth birthday with her had stopped building their sand castles and splashing in the surf to sit down for the ritual singing of "Happy Birthday," and eating cake and ice cream. Also present were a few of Val's oldest associates—Connie and Kath, their husbands, escorts, children they'd brought along, and Madge. As the most senior of Val's friends, Madge—still sporting vivid red hair though deep into her seventies—had become de facto grandmother to Val's youngest daughter. This time Val hadn't felt the need for secrecy that had accompanied the birth of her first child; she had been completely open, had welcomed all the help and extra love that came from providing an extended family.

Val looked to the group of young girls, friends of Diana's from other families who summered in the area. "You're all sure she wasn't swimming?" she asked anxiously.

In ragged chorus they confirmed that Diana had come out of the water more than half an hour before.

Reassurance came from a more trusted source. "I had my eye on her the whole time she was in the water, Miss Cummings," said Jimmy Lavelli. "I watched her come out and dry off. I'm sure she didn't go back in."

Jimmy had come to work for her three years earlier, recommended as a man with the skills and the temperament to provide the protection Val believed she needed for herself and her youngest child. In his forties, with prematurely silver hair, he still maintained the kind of muscular body that by itself was a warning. Starting as bodyguard and driver, Jimmy had gradually taken on all the odd little chores that would have been handled by a husband if Val had one—cleaning the pool, teaching Diana to water-ski and play tennis, making the occasional batch of scrambled eggs on the maid's day off—while continuing with his primary duty to provide security.

"Please check the house again, Jimmy," Val said anxiously.

"I came from there when I brought the cake down, and I didn't see her . . . but okay." He sprinted off the beach and across the lawn. Once a Green Beret in Vietnam, he had been forced out of the service by a shrapnel wound that had torn up his lower body. He had rebuilt himself to excellent condition, and no outward sign of his injuries remained. But there were some wounds that could not be repaired. He'd never talked about it, yet his utter platonic loyalty to her and Diana in the absence of any attachment to either a man or a woman during the years he'd worked for them indicated he was probably no longer sexually functional.

A couple of minutes after being dispatched to the house, he emerged on the porch and shouted to Val. "I've found her!" He made a beckoning motion indicating Val was needed to coax her daughter back to her own birthday party.

She hurried to join him. "What's wrong?"

"Nothing's wrong. I heard noise coming from the attic—sounds of cheering. So I went up and there she was, in front of that old television set up there. Squirreled herself away because she didn't want to be dragged off until she'd finished watching."

"Watching what? Has she turned into a baseball fan?"

Jimmy smiled. "You of all people—don't tell me you forgot what's all over the tube today."

Val's jaw fell. No, she hadn't forgotten; she just hadn't imagined her young daughter would consider the event more important than her own birthday party.

Val found Diana sitting on the floor of the little attic room in front of the vintage television console, gazing with total concentration at the image of a beautiful young woman riding in a coach drawn by teams of white horses, accompanied by phalanxes of horsemen in shining plumed helmets with swords strapped at their sides. The young woman waved and smiled at crowds of people that stood twenty deep on each side of a roadway. A captivating sight. Val moved up to watch alongside her daughter.

"Isn't it incredible, Mom?" the girl said. "Like Cinderella—only better, because it's not make-believe. She's in a golden coach . . . on her way to marry a real-life prince."

Incredible indeed, all this regal pomp and splendor surviving in the modern world. But that was what made it so fascinating that billions of people wanted to share in this wedding as witnesses. Every television channel around the globe was broadcasting tapes of the wedding of Prince Charles and his princess that had taken place earlier that day in London.

"It's a little weird though," the girl at Val's feet said.

"What is?"

"You know, 'cause of her name. Every time they mention it—Diana's doing this, Diana's wearing that—it makes me feel it could be happening to *me*. . . ."

"Maybe it will someday," Val said. "There ought to be one or two princes left by the time you're ready."

"I don't think they'd want me. I'm not the princess type—not like her." Diana Majer gazed wistfully at the image of the young blond woman who stood on a balcony of Buckingham Palace with her groom and her new in-laws, waving to the masses below.

Val wondered what she could say to her daughter to ease her adolescent insecurity. Diana was at the age when hormonal tides were playing havoc with her complexion and growth spurts made her body look as if it weren't quite the sum of its parts.

"It looks wonderful at the moment to be a princess," Val said, "but I'd guess she'll have the same problems in the end as anyone else. You know I believe in beautiful weddings. But for a beautiful life it's what happens after the wedding that counts. Now, how about coming outside and cutting your own cake?"

Val's daughter pulled herself to her knees, eyes still fixed on the television screen.

"C'mon," Val coaxed. "They'll show it again later, the wedding, the procession—the whole bloody thing, as the Brits say."

Diana turned off the television and popped to her feet. "Whatever happens to the princess now," she said, "at least she can say she had the best wedding ever." She gazed earnestly at her mother. "You don't mind, do you—about missing it?"

Val smiled, amused by the irony that her daughter had been so interested in seeing the royal wedding that she had deserted her party—when Val herself had been offered a chance to attend as a commentator for one of the American television networks—and had turned it down rather than be away during her Diana's birthday. It was part of keeping a vow taken at the time she decided to have this child that she wouldn't make the mistakes she had made with Teddie. Work would never come first.

"I would have missed being with you a lot more," Val said, drawing the girl into a tight hug.

They stood for a minute in the embrace. The idea of being absent at one thing or the other had put both their minds on the same track: For now, this moment, they were together, where they wanted to be. But tomorrow things would have to be different.

Val broke from the embrace. "Let's go," she said, eager to concentrate on the positive. "Time to make your wish."

"You know what I wish, Mom . . . ?"

"Yes." Val knew exactly. And they both knew it was a wish that couldn't possibly come true.

She had devoted herself in the years since Diana's birth to two things: raising this child—her first priority—and working to keep *Every Bride's* magazine the leading bridal publication.

Both tasks had gone well. Diana was bright and healthy, with a natural artistic talent and an even temperament jarred only by an adventurous streak—the sort of kid who'd plunge into the ocean and uncomplainingly let the waves toss her around before she had even learned to swim. It was that quirky appetite for risk that made Val think of her daughter as a gambler—the father's genetic influence?—and gave rise to the nickname Dice.

The magazine was equally healthy—if not as adventurous. Despite its popularity, *E.B.* was regarded by some as becoming too conservative, changing little over decades that had encompassed vast social evolution. But Val turned a deaf ear to those critics. In a world where everything else was changing, and romantic values were imperiled by hard realities, she was committed to providing reassurance that somewhere in life there was one solid foundation, one hope for the heart, that would endure. That message was embodied in a wedding, and its symbols, from the first promise of marriage represented by a ring set with a diamond; to the ceremony where vows of "forever" were spoken; to the honeymoon, which betokened that together a man and a woman could make their own Eden and enjoy times of absolute bliss. If it was old-fashioned to uphold those beliefs, so be it.

Still, the ceaseless momentum of progress was not ignored altogether. The days were long past when formal weddings were the province of an elite who didn't have to worry about costs; as the country traveled in and out of recession, *E.B.* published blueprints for budget weddings with all the flair of the most elaborate. Codes of etiquette were revised to take into account the changing balances between men and women. The photographic honeymoon sections became more daring, with coverage of safaris, ballooning trips, and even Arctic exploration for newlyweds.

By 1980 between two and three million marriages a year were being registered, and among first marriages of people under thirty years old more than seventy-five percent chose a full formal ceremony. Val's audience had grown accordingly. A publishing division now turned out specialized books; the travel agency expanded to operate air charters to the most popular spots in the Caribbean and Hawaii; a licensing division selected wedding-related items to be marketed under the *Every Bride's* name, or with its endorsement. Val was sure another leap in the revenues of her company would be spurred by the worldwide fascination with the Charles-Diana fairy tale.

Whether Majer would have capitalized on the boom to the extent she had, Val couldn't know. But even if he hadn't succeeded in buying the magazine, his desire for it had been no less shrewd than his moves in other areas of business. The price he had offered was only one tenth of the amount at which the company was presently valued.

Knowing Glen as a man who would never suffer any loss gladly, she kept expecting delayed repercussions in the first years after their break. But year after year not the least ripple came from his direction. Sometimes she saw his name or picture in the business news; he had gone ahead with his plans to assemble a communications conglomerate, and had joined the growing ranks of moguls who were described as billionaires. Once, when she happened to be watching the televised Kentucky Derby, he was shown in the winner's circle after the race, the owner of the winning horse—the stunning, much younger woman at his side identified as his wife. Otherwise he remained as totally cut off from Val—and from his child—as he had sworn he would be.

At the age of five, Diana began asking questions about her father. Val delivered the information over time in small, relatively painless doses. The divorce rate had mushroomed since she had faced the same questions from Teddie, and so it was easier for Diana to adjust to the situation. Half the kids in her school were being raised by a single parent.

As for Teddie, Val had never given up hoping that there would be a détente between them someday. Although any letters she wrote were mailed back unopened, Val continued to write to her—and to receive up-to-date reports from the private investigator. She knew Teddie had left Dirk Brandon for yet another man whom she'd married, then divorced; moved from San Francisco to Los Angeles, where she had lived alone for a couple of years, then married a wealthy businessman and now lived with him in Beverly Hills. Val had also learned—only through Stecchino—that Teddie's move to L.A. had been facilitated by an inheritance of $37,000, left to her by a man named William Gruening, who had died of unknown causes the year before last.

It was when Diana turned nine that Majer had abruptly reentered Val's life. He had turned up one morning at her office, her only preparation the voice of her secretary on the intercom saying he was in the waiting room.

The ten years since she'd last seen him was time enough, she thought, to inoculate her against emotions she couldn't control. "Send him right in," she said without even taking a moment to compose herself.

They took seats in the comfortable sitting area of her office and chatted pleasantly for a while. They told each other how well they looked. She asked about his interest in horse racing, said his wife had looked very beautiful. That wife was gone, he said, though he'd kept the horses.

Then he started talking business. "I have to congratulate you on the way you've managed your company, Val. At the time you decided to hang on instead of sell, I thought it couldn't be purely a business decision. But now it looks like it was, and a right smart one. You've turned this into one of the best blue-chip companies in the publishing game."

It was a gracious concession . . . and Val fooled herself into thinking that this must be why he had come: to touch base in a way that said bygones could be bygones—and launch another attempt to buy *E.B.* But then he hit her with the real reason.

"I want to see her," he said. Not a request but a demand.

She understood at once, and all the ambivalent feelings she had thought she could master boiled to the surface. "Why?" was the only word she could form in the first hot flush of anger and confusion.

"She's mine . . . and I'd like her to know it. Does a father need more reason than that?"

Her fury was all the greater for having lived through a similar circumstance once before. In the past, of course, it had been her own decision to keep a daughter from the father who'd intruded himself so damagingly into her life. But this instance was all the more brutal and unfair—for it had been Glen's willful decision to utterly abandon this child.

"Yes, you sure as hell need a lot more reasons," she shot back. "You told me you wanted nothing to do with her, and for nine years you've been as good—or as bad—as your word. No sign of interest ever. Not when she was born, not on a single birthday. If once you'd shown some feeling, I could understand this. But she's learned to live without a father now. She's fine and happy, the world makes sense to her as it is. You don't have the right to march in here and say the rules have changed." Val's rage only grew as she saw him sitting so calmly in front of her, his wealth and power embodied in the cool way he stared back. She bolted up and stood over him. " 'She's mine,' you say just as confidently as you once said 'get rid of it,' as if you're talking about a piece of property to be written off, or held for your portfolio." She shook her head, her voice rose. "Goddammit, no, Glen! She's not yours. *You* got rid of her, I didn't. That was your choice, and you'll have to live with it."

"Are you so sure she's better off not knowing me?" he asked calmly.

"She's better off not learning to look at things—at people—the way you do."

He nodded philosophically and said nothing. In the silence, Val's words played back to her. Was she being unfair? Was her reaction based on her fear that what happened with Teddie from being exposed to her father would happen to Diana? Glen was such a different man. As she looked at him, she could guess that the moderation in his stance might have come simply from growing older. He was in his sixties now, the far horizon of life's end was at least in sight, and he'd had no other children. She remembered him talking about all his possessions only being "on loan"; he could feel that a child would be the only meaningful thing he left behind.

Maybe the most reasonable thing, Val thought, was to ask Diana her wishes. She was about to back down, say that perhaps she'd talk to Diana, let her decide—

But Majer spoke first. Rising to look down at Val from his full height, he said, "You got to call the tune last time, lady. But I don't think your Wall Street friends are going to stop me from winning this one. I've come around to wanting to take a hand in what happens to my daughter. You can try and stand in the way, but it won't work. For your own sake, Val, you'd best step aside."

Her first reaction to the threat was to take it literally: She stepped out of his way, and without another word he walked out of the office. But she knew he'd meant something more. Glen never put limits on himself. If he started by angling for a chance to spend time with Diana, sooner or later he might want to take Val's place and control his daughter's upbringing.

Val was left frightened. She had never forgotten what she'd learned from that moonlighting policeman, Majer's bodyguard, on visits to New York. Glen was a man whose control of casinos made it necessary for him to deal with and understand the threats that came from a shady element of society. If there was something he wanted enough, perhaps he was capable of applying methods used by that element.

It was then that she had sought protection, hired Jimmy Lavelli to escort Diana to and from school, live in their home as a protective presence. Val felt much better having security in place, though not the least threat of an abduction was ever seen.

Majer did launch a legal assault, however, an onslaught of writs and suits and summonses carrying accusations against Val for everything from mere "alienation of affection" to actual child abuse in the form of keeping Diana a virtual prisoner. Absurd charges, and yet they had to be answered. Playing out such a legal chess game couldn't be done in two or three moves either. It had continued for the past three years.

Then, just a month earlier, a court order had come down. Majer was awarded one month's trial custody of Diana as of the girl's twelfth birthday. There were mothers, Val knew, who reached this point in the legal process and elected to defy the courts by running, taking a child and going abroad, vanishing, giving up their lives for the sake of their child's.

But was Majer so dangerous that such a drastic response

would be justified? Val resented the way he'd conducted himself, and the confusion it had created in her daughter's life, but she couldn't think of Majer as evil. He had been her lover. He was Diana's father, and at least she had been created out of willing passion, not out of force and violence.

Now, on the day of her twelfth birthday, in three more hours, Val had to deliver her daughter to the airport, where Glen Majer's private jet would fly the girl west to spend a month.

On the beach, in the warm sunshine, the party continued. Perhaps it was the adventurous streak in Diana's character that allowed her to face being torn away from the one home she knew and loved without sinking into moping and tears. But Val was pleased to see Diana return to her friends and enthusiastically blow out all the candles, and laugh gleefully when they all got caught up in a messy cake-throwing contest before plunging back into the ocean to clean off the goop.

Later, the party over, Val was getting her ready for the drive to the airport, when Diana said, "It's all right, Mom—about going. I didn't even bother wishing I didn't have to go. Want to know what I wished instead?"

"There's a rule about not telling if you want it to come true."

"Yeah, but the odds are so long on this one anyway, it doesn't matter. I wished someday I'll have a wedding just like that one—the other Diana's. Or even better."

"How would you do it better?" Val asked.

"I'll make my own gown."

Val smiled. Odd, the little links of heritage that could suddenly emerge. She had told Diana some time ago that her grandmother had been a dressmaker, and had been known especially for her beautiful wedding gowns. "Well, if that's what you want," Val said, "all you have to do is find a prince."

"I will. I might even start looking as soon as I get back home."

For the month that Diana was away, Val lived with the fear that Majer might hold on to her.

He abided by the court-ordered custody terms, however—though he stretched his rights to the absolute limit. His visitation was to last through Labor Day, so he timed his private 737 jet to fly into Kennedy Airport late Monday night. By the time the plane taxied to a stop, the ramp rolled up, and Diana came at last through the doors of the corporate gate, Val saw that her wristwatch showed 11:57 P.M.

She took it as an omen that having staked his claim, Majer would always take for himself the full measure of whatever rights he won by law. But at least he seemed willing to play by the rules.

To judge by Diana's first experience with her father, he could afford to play it that way. From the moment she rushed into Val's arms, Diana couldn't stop chattering about the way her days had been filled during her month away.

"We went to this ranch he's got . . . and he gave me my own horse, the most gorgeous golden color with a white mane, called a palomino . . . and you know what, Mom, he was trained already, so all I had to do was whistle and he'd trot right up to me and put his nose up to my cheek. Do you know, Mom, a horse's nose feels just like velvet . . . ?"

The report went on all during the ride back to the city apartment . . . and continued at mealtimes for days afterward. There had been a morning at Disneyland too—Majer paying out a fortune so that the place would be closed for five hours during which Diana had been able to call the place her own. And a few days in Los Angeles, visiting with movie stars—easily arranged, since Majer's communications holdings included a stake in a studio. And a final few days spent in Las Vegas, where Diana saw Frank Sinatra and Paul Anka and every show on the Strip from a ringside table.

Having been treated like a princess herself, Diana could hardly be blamed, Val thought, for returning from the month totally in awe of her father, and ready to revise her worst beliefs. It was encouraging to see that she nevertheless managed to settle back easily into her routine, doing well in school, with no lessening of affection toward her mother.

The following Easter, when Majer petitioned to have Diana for a week of her school holiday instead of waiting for his summer visitation rights, Val started by protesting. But Diana was made aware of what Majer wanted in a letter he wrote to her, and she pleaded. To refuse, Val realized, would only drive a wedge between herself and her daughter in a different way. She gave permission.

That April week was spent in Paris, meals at the best restaurants, a two-day limousine trip through the château country, ringside seats at all the fashion shows. Diana's feelings about her father when she returned were even more effusively positive. Whizzing from continent to continent in his private jet, elevated suddenly to a kind of celebrity status in her own right as "the billionaire's daughter," she was understandably dazzled. Now Diana not only began lobbying for spending more time with her father, she criticized Val for having failed to appreciate him, thus depriving her of another full-time parent.

"Why couldn't you have stayed together?" Diana asked at a Sunday breakfast after returning from Paris. "Jesus, Mom, what's not to like about him? He's great-looking, he can ride a horse as well as Clint Eastwood, and he's lots of fun to be with. Not to mention, he's got more money than God. I don't get it. Seems to me you had to be crazy not to want to be with him."

Val knew she had a fine line to tread when she answered these questions. To knock down Glen in any way might only spur more of Diana's resentment against her. "Is that the way he explained our not being together?" she said. "That I didn't want it?"

"Not exactly. He tells me pretty much what you do—that it just didn't work out. Except he did say that he was ready to give being together more of a chance than you did. I mean, I got the feeling that you were the one who made the choice to split up."

Almost true—as far as it went: It was making the choice to have Diana that had made it impossible for their affair to go on. But Val had to consider it only momentarily before she knew this part of the story shouldn't be shared with her daughter.

"Someday, when you've been in love once or twice yourself," she said, "I hope you'll understand how it's possible for a man to look absolutely perfect . . . and yet not be the right one to share every day with. It doesn't always make sense, not when you think about it. Only when you listen to your heart."

"Well, right now my heart tells me that if I ever meet a man like my father, he'll do just fine for me."

Val smiled. You couldn't be covering the wedding scene without knowing that it was a pretty common statement for brides to make: They had picked a man who was as close to their daddy as they could find.

Val's one subtle effort to help Diana view her father realistically was to ask if he had ever explained why he had been willing to let the first nine years of her life go by without even caring enough to send a birthday card.

"Sure, I asked him."

"And what did he say?"

Diana gave a little laugh. "That *he* had to grow up a little before he was ready to be a father."

Not a bad answer—though Val realized Diana would have forgiven him no matter what he said. What continued to worry Val was whether or not Majer had grown up enough to be able to go on sharing the love of his daughter rather than needing to own it completely as he liked to own everything else.

He applied pressure for more time with Diana by offering her wonderful opportunities. A whole summer of cruising the Mediterranean. Christmas he spoke of taking her skiing in St. Moritz. His plane would come for her whenever she asked, he told her—hers to command. In effect, he was romancing his daughter, putting a rush on that no thirteen-year-old girl could resist.

It was hard for Val to know what choice would be in Diana's best interest, where her own selfishness might supersede good judgment. Did it hurt if Diana saw more of the world?

Val opted for letting Diana have more time with her father, hoping that her values had been established firmly enough that she would not always be so dazzled and would make mature, decent choices for herself.

Over the next year Diana was often with Majer. More trips abroad, expensive gifts, one-of-a-kind experiences like the summer day on Ronald Reagan's ranch in Santa Barbara riding horses with the President and her father, and a spring excursion to Rome, where she and Majer were received privately by the Pope.

Yet it seemed to be working out the way Val hoped: The more familiar Diana became with the glitter and flash, the faster the luster faded. Returning from a July weekend in Las Vegas not long after her fourteenth birthday, she told Val she wanted to spend the rest of the summer with her, and Thanksgiving, and Christmas, and not be shuttling around so much.

"Dad's so rich," Diana said, "used to having so much, I get the feeling sometimes I'm just one more thing he wants to own."

Yes, Val thought, her tactic had been the right one.

Then, as Thanksgiving of 1984 drew near, Majer pressed to have Diana spend it with him for the first time. Diana was on the fence about it, since Jess—soon to give birth to her first child—was having a big get-together in Washington with Ben's folks also flying in, and Diana loved her half sister. But in the end Diana chose to be with her father, and was relieved to know she could leave Val without abandoning her to a solitary holiday.

He flew to New York, watched the Macy's Thanksgiving parade with Diana from the V.I.P. reviewing stand on Thirty-fourth Street; then they flew back west for a turkey dinner on the ranch.

Val timed her return on a shuttle from Washington to be at the airport on Sunday evening when Majer would return Diana. But Majer's plane didn't land at the corporate terminal at the scheduled time. Val waited only five minutes before going to the airport desk that kept track of corporate and private flights.

"Can you tell me the status of the plane belonging to Glen Majer? It was supposed to have landed by now from California."

The controller at the desk knew the plane and its registration; it flew in and out of New York often enough. He looked through the records. "No flight plan was filed for Mr. Majer's plane," he told her.

Val knew the regulations. "But a plane like his, a large jet, is required—"

"To file a plan," the controller said, "that's correct—if it's going to be en route across country . . ."

Val's heart iced over. She knew at that moment that what she'd feared all along had finally happened. There was no flight plan, because the plane had never taken off: It wasn't coming. Majer had taken full possession of his "property."

She tried making contact with Majer or Diana—to lodge a protest, vent her rage, but Majer had erected a wall of silence and locked their daughter behind it. Within days the lawyers' papers were already piling up. According to Majer, his daughter had sought asylum with him from "the cruel, restrictive environment of her mother's home," a demand for total obedience that—as stated in the documents—constituted a form of mental abuse. For a man as rich as Glen, Val quickly learned, the old adage that possession is nine-tenths of the law had to be revised; in his case it was closer to the whole of the law. He didn't have merely teams of lawyers to call upon when needed, he had batteries of them, armies. Fight them and win one piece of high ground, they moved their artillery to another.

Val had no way of knowing beyond doubt whether Diana had made a genuine decision to stay with her father. She knew only that her rule in parenting this child—making every effort to be more careful than she had been with Teddie—had been to respect Diana's feelings, listen to her, try to do what was best by consensus rather than laying down the law. Clearly, Majer had exerted either extraordinary powers of persuasion, or he had used force, to subvert Diana's desires and perceptions.

But while he stayed with their daughter in California, where the judges were his friends, beneficiaries of his political contributions, he managed to gain first rulings in his new bids for custody. And residing on large, well-guarded properties, he had no trouble keeping Val away.

While the legal battle raged, Val knew Majer was winning

the time to change Diana's mind into believing the things he claimed.

Finally Val called her trusted private investigator, Frank Stecchino.

"Nothing new on Mrs. Darian since my last report," he said as soon as he came on the line.

"It's something else, Frank. My youngest daughter has been taken by her father."

"Isn't her father Glen Majer?"

"That's right."

"Taken, you said. You mean illegally."

"I have custody, but he has visiting rights. She went with him to California for Thanksgiving and never came back."

"So she's living with him all the time," Stecchino said, "in one or another of his houses . . . ?"

"That's right."

"What do you need from me, Miss C.?"

"Pictures, information—the same sort of stuff you got when Teddie first ran away. I've been trying just to get a call through to my daughter, and I can't. I have no idea how she is, whether she's happy or not." Val started to break down as she spoke about it. "Frank, this is worse than before. . . ."

There was a pause. "I won't kid you, Miss C. You've got a hell of a problem. I know a little about the way Majer lives, and he's got about as much protection as Fort Knox—goes with being in the gambling business. So I don't know if I can get close enough to give you what you want."

"Just do your best, Frank. Get whatever you can."

Two weeks later Val received a report and a packet of pictures taken with a telephoto lens. From these Val learned that whenever Diana left Majer's property, she was accompanied by a pair of armed bodyguards. She had been privately tutored for the first several weeks after going to live with her father, but since then had attended an excellent private day-school near the ranch. During her hours in the school, the guards remained stationed in a car outside. Even so, Stecchino reported, spending those hours regularly outside the walls of Majer's home, with her peers, was a good indication that she wasn't being held against her will. The bodyguards were a standard precaution the mega-rich took against the kidnapping of their children.

Diana turned sixteen without Val being able to set eyes on her again. Val could only put her faith in the desperate hope that eventually the injustice would have to be rectified by law. At last her lawyers informed her that there had been a definite movement in her favor: It looked like Majer would be ordered in a California court to surrender custody.

But then the most devastating turn of all cut the ground out from under Val. Majer managed to locate Teddie, and procure from her an affidavit that supported his claims that Val was an unfit and unloving mother, undeserving of custody.

"Who knows what he did to get it?" Gary Felsen said to Val. "Made friends, flew her to Paris, or just paid her more money than she'd ever seen before. Anything he paid would be in cash, of course," Felsen added. "We could never prove it." Disgusted by what Majer had done, the lawyer had resigned all work for the billionaire—despite his being Felsen's most valuable client—and offered to assist Val's efforts free of charge.

The betrayal by her first child that robbed her of another was the most crushing blow Val could have suffered.

But it made the fire of Val's determination to recover Diana burn that much hotter. It seemed she had lost one daughter forever; the other she would stop at nothing to get back.

Twenty-nine

Aspen, Colorado
1985

Skiing down the fall line, where the pylons for the Bell Mountain chair lift ran down the snow-covered mountainside like a row of huge concrete trees, Val felt perilously tentative. Since she had started to ski with Alan Wellstrom, it had been a favorite winter pastime. On school holidays with Teddie and Jess, and later Diana, she had passed along her enthusiasm for the sport to the girls, and developed her own natural ability to become a more than competent skier. But the fall line was the place where only the best skiers ought to be testing themselves, the steepest of inclines. It was taking a tremendous risk to be in an area generally reserved to daredevils.

But then, that was the least of the risks she was taking that day.

As Val sped past the pylons, she noted the black numerals boldly painted on their circumference denoting their sequence in the line. She passed the one marked "13," and at the next, swung her skis uphill, came to a stop, then herringboned off the cleared area beneath the lift into a clump of pines.

Pulling back the sleeve of her ski jacket, Val checked her wristwatch and saw she had arrived several minutes early. In the shadow of the pines, invisible to skiers riding the chairs passing above, it was cold. She hoped the others would be there soon.

She heard the scrape of skis along the fall line, and peered through the pine branches to see fantails of snow rise in the air as a couple of speed demons in white ski suits came to instant stops. Val held her breath. Were they *chasing* her? In their knitted head masks and yellow fog goggles she couldn't see their faces to identify them.

They moved into the trees. One reached up and pushed his goggles back on his brow. Val exhaled with relief as she saw it was Jimmy Lavelli.

"How're you doing?" he asked.

"Holding up," she said.

Jimmy nodded to the second man, who kept his goggles down over his eyes, the rest of his face sheathed in a black knit ski mask. "This is my friend," Jimmy said.

"How do you do," Val said. In the circumstances, the normal amenity struck her as absurd the moment she heard herself say it.

The second man only nodded. It had been agreed that it would be best if Val met him only once, never saw his face, and didn't know his name. Apparently, she wasn't even to hear his voice. She knew only that he and Jimmy had been very close when they served in Vietnam together, and that to secure his help today Jimmy had agreed to pay him twenty-five thousand dollars in an untraceable cash transaction. Another friend with the same credentials—and price tag—was also involved, but he must have remained at the top of the mountain.

"We're down to the wire," Jimmy said.

"You've seen them . . . ?" Val asked.

"Yes, they're on top, having lunch as usual at the Sundeck. Around two they'll start a run down. That's the time for us to move. Any doubts?" He stared at Val, needing her final approval. When she hesitated, he said, "We won't get a better chance than this, Val. The guy skiing with her is pretty far off the pace. Dice goes for the black-diamond trails every time, and he can't keep up. She doesn't give a damn, never looks back. . . ."

Val looked down at the clean white snow. No matter how many times Jimmy had assured her he could pull it off, she knew it was dangerous. Knew, too, that whatever her justification, it would be breaking the law, and embarking on a path that could make the rest of her days a constant trial, perhaps even without achieving her goal.

But she was at the end of her rope. "All right," she said.

Jimmy didn't move. He waited until she raised her eyes again to look into his, to see the fire confirming the words.

"Go," she said more emphatically. "I'm not changing my mind."

Only then did he jam his poles into the ground and push off, gliding between the trees, followed by his anonymous silent friend until they were back on the fall line. There they seemed almost to plummet away into space as they raced down the mountain to catch the chair lift back to the top.

The idea had come from Jimmy months before. "Turnabout's fair play," he said. "The sonofabitch took Diana from you, we'll just take her back." He had plenty of friends from his time with the Green Berets who could help put together a professional operation commando-style—go right over the walls of any property Majer owned, knock out guards, do whatever it took.

Val laughed it off the first time he raised it. She valued Jimmy's loyalty, but this was overzealous and plain wrong. Such a step could only work against her—unless she was ready to be a fugitive, surrender every other part of her life to stay on the run. Not that other women hadn't done it; there was said to be a kind of underground railway for women who had to abduct their own children in order to take them from the richer, more powerful fathers. But Val hadn't thought she could be pushed that far.

Until Majer had used Teddie. She knew then that counting on justice was hopeless. Knew Glen would do anything to have his way.

Once decided on the abduction, they had waited for the best opportunity. Over Christmas a year earlier, Majer had taken Diana skiing. Through Frank Stecchino, Val learned that for this year's holiday Majer had rented the Aspen chalet of a movie director who was abroad making a film.

The best thing they'd have going for them, Jimmy said, was

that Majer wouldn't really expect it: He would be counting on Val's basic decency. So far it seemed to be true. Diana was accompanied everywhere by bodyguards, and a man was even detailed to stay with her on the ski slopes. The man was a competent skier, but not nearly up to Diana's level. She regularly sped far ahead, then waited at the base of the mountain so they could ride the chair lift up together.

Having observed that routine for the past few days, Jimmy Lavelli and his cohort had picked out a place on each of several trails where Diana would be out of sight of her surveillance for long enough that she could be hijacked into some thick woods and taken across to a neighboring trail to descend the mountain to a base area, where Val would be waiting. At the wheel of a van waiting with her would be another former Green Beret who was also a licensed pilot; they would then all drive to the local airfield and fly out. That, of course, would be only the beginning of what was required.

Even succeeding that far wasn't a sure thing, of course. The biggest uncertainty was how Diana would respond in the first phase. Jimmy believed that as soon as she recognized him, and he could explain why they had chosen this method, she would go willingly to see Val. But if she didn't—if she panicked before recognizing Jimmy, shouted for help—there was no predicting where and how the escapade would end.

"You mustn't force her," Val had insisted. "Promise me, Jimmy: Bring her to me only if she *wants* to come."

Now, waiting by a van in the flat snowfield where some of the lesser-used trails ended, Val swept her gaze back and forth over the white slopes, searching for a trio of skiers—or would it be one, racing hell-bent to stay ahead of two others.

Suddenly they were up there, skimming over a ridge several hundred yards away, hitting moguls and flying, landing, turning. She was sure it was them, two figures in white, a third in a designer outfit of striped colors, coming on at Olympic speed. Val's heart started pounding with joyful anticipation. For she could see from the way they were moving, traversing the same lines, the figure in colors flanked by the other two, that they were skiing in unison. Diana had come willingly.

Val locked her gaze on the middle figure as it rocketed closer, came on straight, swiveling the skis around at the last second to glide right up to her. Val's arms were already open by then, and she held them open as Diana flipped the goggles off her face and pulled the mask from her eyes so eagerly that she just tossed it away. For a moment, her face wet with snow and tears, Diana could only stare. Then she fell into Val's embrace. "Mom, oh, Mom," she cried, "I'm so *glad*!"

Jimmy allowed them only a couple of seconds of clinging together. "C'mon. If anyone picked up our trail, they could spot that rainbow Di's wearing from a mile away. We've got to get out of here fast."

Val paused only long enough to hold Diana at arm's length and make sure she understood what was happening. "This was the only way I could do it—you know that, don't you? The only way he'd let me be with you again . . . ?"

Diana looked puzzled, as though not quite sure of what Val was telling her.

But she had come willingly. It was acceptance enough. "Let's go," Val said.

They flew in the small two-engine plane only as far as a remote airport in Idaho. Jimmy remained with Val and Diana to watch over them; his two anonymous friends departed at once.

A rented cabin an hour's drive from Sun Valley was waiting, a safe place to stay while Val became reacquainted with her daughter and determined how much Diana was prepared to continue cooperating to ensure she would not have to return to Majer.

Over a week, in talks with her daughter as they strolled along open roads or sat in the evening beside fires that burned long into the night, Val came to understand how Diana had been instantly willing to flee from her father—yet for much of the time she'd been with him had been content to stay.

Majer's manipulation of her will had been deftly managed from the first to avoid stirring up any resistance. That Thanksgiving more than a year before when he'd kept her away,

Diana had been told she was being kept only at her mother's request—that Val had met a man with whom she wanted to take a vacation, and had asked Majer to keep Diana for an extra three weeks. By then, of course, Christmas was approaching, and as much as Diana had wanted to spend it with her mother, she had accepted Majer's story that Val had extended her own romantic holiday. Diana's pain and disappointment were eased by the gifts Majer showered upon her—a puppy, her first "serious" jewelry, more clothes than she could wear. Just fifteen then, Diana was in no position to question her father's authority—or his veracity.

Still, she had wanted to make contact with Val, so Majer had switched his tactics. He'd found Teddie, paid her lavishly to come to his ranch and befriend her younger half sister—to tell Diana her own reasons for no longer speaking with Val. Listening to Teddie's vitriol for several days had eroded Diana's belief in her own judgment.

At New Year's, when Majer told Diana that Val had agreed to let her stay with him for six more months while she pursued her love affair, the child had accepted it as the truth.

The vicious campaign to subvert Diana's love was reinforced by Majer's own constant affection and the endless flow of gifts he lavished upon her. At the same time, he had Diana watched to make sure she didn't stray from his control. At school, on dates with her friends, she had always been under surveillance—and she knew it. She accepted Majer's explanation that it was a normal precaution for a man of his wealth to guard against kidnappers.

But as the year passed, her natural desire for independence developed. Her willingness—indeed, eagerness—to go with Jimmy Lavelli when he had confronted her on the mountain did not spring solely from a desire to be reunited with Val, but also from a sixteen-year-old girl's basic hunger to be free from the controlling presence of all those people who were always keeping her under guard, reporting everything she did to her father.

And the moment Diana had seen her mother waiting with open arms at the bottom of the mountain, the wall of feelings that had been carefully constructed against Val by Majer's manipulations had crumbled.

Diana's fury and hatred of her father only grew as she came to understand how much he had lied to her, the enormity of the crime he had perpetrated against both her and Val.

"I never told your father he could keep you," Val explained the first evening they were together. They were sitting on the floor, facing the fireplace, Diana leaning back against her mother. "There was no new man in my life, none at all—still isn't. There were never any long, lovely travels to far-off places. I've spent every spare minute doing nothing but trying to get you back."

"If only I had known, Mom. I feel so awful for leaving you—for believing him. . . ."

"Never never blame yourself, Dicey. It was beyond your control. We're together now, and that's what matters."

"Don't you think he'll try to get me back? If you can hire men, so can he—even more of them. Mom, we'll never be safe. When Daddy wants something—"

"I know, Dice. But I think I can persuade him to leave things as they are."

"How?"

"We'll talk about that at another time."

Diana stared into the fire silently for a minute. "I wouldn't mind if you had somebody kill him," she said then.

"Oh, Dice." Val sighed. She understood the torrent of feelings that could make her daughter speak so rashly, but she knew it would be important to quell the hatred if she was going to keep Diana from being permanently warped by the experience. "What your father did to us was terribly cruel and selfish," Val went on. "And it would be easy for me to hate him for it. What's hard, much harder—but worth trying—is not to give in to hate. All the time you've been with him, I've tried every day to remember that at least part of his motive was his love for you."

"How could it be love? To lie to me that way, to twist me around so I'd hate you . . ."

"It was wrong, Dicey, dead wrong. But you've got to

forgive him. He's your father. You can't hate him without hating a piece of yourself, and I never want you to feel that."

It was what kept Teddie from fulfilling herself, she knew: The contempt for her own father—and hatred of Val for lying—were what undermined Teddie's faith that she herself was worthwhile. They were what kept her from being able to forgive, from being able to love in a way that allowed her to stay with one man.

"Gosh, Mom," Diana said, "I understand what you're saying. It feels awful to lose the good feelings I had about Dad. I don't want to hate him. But knowing the truth of what he did, I feel almost as if . . . as if I was . . ." She really had to pull the word out of herself. "Raped. I mean, what he called love was just forcing me to be completely his. That's what rape is, isn't it? Forcing someone to love you? I sure don't ever want to see him again."

"Maybe you never should," Val said, "at least not for a very long time. But try, Dice, try with all your heart to keep hate out of it."

It might take Diana a while to absorb the lesson, Val knew, but it was one worth teaching.

Even while preaching forgiveness, however, Val had known as soon as she committed herself to taking Diana that keeping her would probably require the same no-holds-barred tactics that she could expect from Majer. What was needed to block Majer from hounding her again through the courts, or else similarly taking the law into his own hands, was a quick preeemptive strike, something that would force him to let things stand as they were—at least leave Diana to choose for herself where and how she wished to live.

Val's weapon for this strike had been designed and waiting to be launched even before the abduction. It began with a telephone call to Majer from his former lawyer, Gary Felsen, only hours after Diana was in Val's hands. Felsen warned Majer that unless he was "one hundred and ten percent certain" that he could defend his behavior with Diana over the past year, and that his daughter would similarly find no fault and willingly choose to return to him, he would be wise to lodge no charges against Val.

Knowing that his lies would be revealed once Diana had talked to Val, Majer elected to heed the warning.

The second phase of the plan was simplified by Diana's reaction once she understood the extent of Majer's deceit. The force of her own fury came through in one of the first things she'd said to Val—that she felt almost as if she had been raped.

"Well, it was a kind of mental rape," Gary Felsen said to Val when she phoned to report the conversations she was having with Diana. "And it'll work perfectly for what we have to do next."

"Gary . . . I'm having second thoughts about—"

"Do you want to keep your daughter, Val?"

"Of course I do. But I don't want to be guilty of manipulating her."

"Even if it's for her own sake?"

"Glen must have excused himself with the same alibi—that it was for *her* sake. If I can't be honest with her, how can I feel for sure she's better off with me than him?"

"Dammit, Val," Felsen barked, "you don't have to be a saint to deserve your daughter." His patience was frayed by the thought of Val disregarding their careful plans, putting herself at risk again. Regaining his composure, he pleaded quietly, "Just let me play your cards. With any luck, Majer will fold right away, and you won't have to bring Diana into it."

Hearing Felsen put it in poker terms hardly reassured her. Glen, she never forgot, was a great card-player, had raised his first important grubstake at the poker table.

But by then there was no way to play her hand except to go for broke.

The lawyer contacted Majer again—and his second warning was more severe, even if couched in coded language dictated by a need to observe the ethical canons of the law.

After recounting what Diana had told Val, Felsen said the girl was willing to sign an affidavit attesting to those facts.

"You can't win, Glen," Felsen said, "because the girl

doesn't want to live with you again, and she's ready to give the kind of testimony that would guarantee the court wouldn't make her. Val will use the media too—where she has friends of her own—to win support. Diana may be only sixteen, legally still a minor, but that's an age when many judges would already be inclined to give whatever she says the same weight they'd award to the statements of a full-grown woman. For all practical purposes, that is the way they'll see her. And if she speaks of feeling raped—a word she's used—it'll open a can of worms. For your sake as well as Diana's, I'd urge you to do everything possible to avoid that."

Listening to Felsen, Majer could hardly believe that what he'd heard between the lines was correct. "You can't be thinking Diana would ever say—that Val would ever *let* her say—I'd forced her to . . . to do anything . . . unnatural."

"I don't know what she'll say. Just as no one can know for sure what the truth is," he added, careful to speak as if he were not party to fabricating anything in case the conversation was being recorded. "But I know that girl wants to stay with her mother. If it gets ugly, that'll be too bad for everyone. But remember, Glen, it was you who started us down this road."

Majer didn't have to think about it more than a few moments before he made his choice. He knew how it would look if the charge was made: He'd been married already to a few women much younger than himself, had no other children, and Diana had indeed begun to look much more like a woman than a girl.

"You got me, Gary," he said to the lawyer. "That lady client o' yours plays dirtier'n a hog in a shitstorm, but, hell"—he let out one of his good ol' boy guffaws—"can't say as I blame her. Just do me one favor, will ya, Gary, for old time's sake?"

"Within reason . . ."

"Tell Diana my door'll always be open. She's somethin' I can be proud of, all right. Even ready to fight like her old man."

Val's lawyer kept to himself that whatever he'd threatened, probably neither Diana nor her mother would have been willing to fight quite so dirty.

Fortunately, it seemed to be the one time in Glen Majer's life he'd been outbluffed.

* * *

Despite the upheaval in Diana's life, she readjusted well to her life in New York with Val, secure in the belief she wouldn't be torn away again. And Val devoted herself entirely to her daughter.

As Diana reached that time in her senior year of high school when she had to start making college applications, it seemed likely that she would have no trouble being accepted any place she wanted to go. Her private school had an excellent placement record, her grades and SAT scores were well above average, and she was a starter in girls' volleyball and edited the senior yearbook.

It came as a shock, then, when Diana told Val one night at the dinner table that she didn't want to go to college.

"You can't be serious," Val said. "College is a must these days."

"Not for what I want to do."

It struck Val that there had never been any mention of a particular ambition. Diana had always seemed happy-go-lucky, ready to take things as they came, without a plan. "And what *is* it you want?" Val asked now.

"I'd like to"—Diana gave a diffident shrug as though acknowledging it might be a foolish whim—"to design clothes. To be . . . a couturier." She pronounced the French word with exaggerated flair, almost mocking it—another symptom of embarrassment.

Val had noticed, of course, that her daughter had an excellent sense of style, evident in the wardrobe she had compiled at the time Majer was giving her an almost unlimited clothing allowance. Most of what she wore was still drawn from this source. But occasionally she would also stitch together some minor invention—a skirt made out of various scarves, a blouse adapted from an old piece of lingerie—that showed flair and inventiveness. Yet Val had never thought it was anything more than a hobby.

"How long have you had this ambition, Dicey?"

Diana looked down, and half swallowed the answer. "Since Daddy took me to Paris."

Val leaned back and smiled to herself. So that was why Diana had never spoken about it, guarded her ambition like a guilty secret. It was hard to acknowledge that she owed anything to her father.

"It was wonderful, huh?" Val said. The best thing she could do for Diana was to neutralize the guilt, help the ambition flower fully.

"Oh, gosh, Mom, the most wonderful week of my life. I loved every minute of it. We sat ringside at all the fashion shows, and saw all the new designs . . . and I came to understand that it's a kind of art, you know, creating with fabric the way some people sculpt or paint. The city was so beautiful too. Notre Dame, and the Louvre, and . . . gosh, just everything. I loved the whole adventure of being in such a different place, hearing a different language, tasting different foods." Diana took on a reflective look, then giggled endearingly. "Dad was so funny. He really didn't like it all that much. Kept grumbling he'd rather have a good thick steak any day than all those French things with sauces, and he thought blue jeans and a nice western shirt looked better on anyone, man or woman, than all those—as he put it—'frog frills.' And yet . . . he was the one who took me there, wanted me to see it, gave me a look at something I've never stopped dreaming about since. Funny, huh?"

Perhaps, thought Val, it was the combination of being exposed to it by her father, yet knowing it was a world he didn't particularly favor himself, that made it take root in her.

Encouraged by Val, Diana talked more about what she remembered of the fashion shows, and then revealed that she had a realistic understanding of what it would mean to go to Paris and work as an apprentice in a designer's atelier. The job would not be easy to get, would not be well paid, and there could be years of backroom drudgery before she was in a position to try designing for herself.

"It could all be easier, of course," Val pointed out, "if you used your father's name."

"I don't want to do that, Mom. I don't want to owe him the tiniest part of what I achieve. Anyway, starving in a garret is part of the scene. I just think it'll be a real kick to live abroad for a little while until I learn the ropes—and as much of an education as going to college. Of course, if it doesn't work out, I can always come back and go to school." She reached across the dinner table and took Val's hand. "You had an ambition once, Mom," she said, "a desire to make something on your own. It was an adventure, and you succeeded. Now I want to have the same chance."

Val might have told her that she hadn't carved out her path for the sake of adventure; there had simply been no other choice, and it had been goddamn rough for a good part of the way. Yet, looking back, her success achieved, she knew she wouldn't have wanted it any other way. Diana's wish to make the same kind of success for herself was the highest form of admiration; and wanting to do it on her own was the proof she hadn't been spoiled by the interlude with her billionaire father.

"If that's your dream, darling," Val said, "I'll help as much—or as little—as you want." After a pause she added, "I can't pretend, though, that I'm not the tiniest bit scared for you."

"If I fail, I fail," Diana said. "I'm not afraid of failing."

"Nor am I. What scares me is that once you're there, alone . . . he might try to take you again. . . ."

Diana smiled, tolerant of her mother's anxiety, but knowing within herself that she had the strength and wisdom now to keep her freedom. "It doesn't make sense anymore, Mom. I'm grown up now. He's lost me—forever!"

Oddly, as she heard those words come from her daughter, Val was seized by a feeling she had never imagined she could have: sympathy for Glen. She knew how heartbreaking it was to be forever rejected by one's own child.

Someday, she told herself, someday she might even be moved to help Diana love her father again.

Thirty

New York
Spring 1995

To mark the forty-fifth anniversary of the publication of the first issue of *Every Bride's* magazine, a special promotion was planned. Val had decided not to wait until the fiftieth—since that would fall in the year 2000, and there would be so many special parties and promotions and celebrations associated with the millennium that her celebration might be lost in the shuffle.

In the months leading up to the anniversary, the magazine ran two contests: One invited women who had been brides when the first issues of the magazine were published in 1950 to write accounts of their weddings, and the ways in which *E.B.* had influenced their plans. Of course, women celebrating their own forty-fifth wedding anniversaries wouldn't themselves be current readers of the magazine; but no doubt many would have granddaughters who consulted it for their own bridal plans, and would bring the contest to the older women's attention.

The second contest offered a $100,000 gala wedding in June to the woman who wrote the most affecting letter explaining why, though she couldn't possibly afford it, she would like the kind of wedding such a huge amount of money could buy. Ten winners from the contest for early readers would be brought to New York, all expenses paid, to attend the wedding ball that would be combined with the gala ball celebrating the magazine's anniversary.

In choosing a place to hold the special event, Val considered dozens of the special venues offered by New York. The ballrooms of the Waldorf or the Plaza, the greenhouses of the Botanical Gardens, the restaurant atop the World Trade Center with its astounding eagle's-eye view, the outdoor terraces of the Tavern-on-the-Green in Central Park. All were eager to be associated with an event that would generate publicity and bring more bridal business.

But in the end Val decided there could be no place more appropriate to hold the event than in her own home, the beach estate she had finally christened Silversands.

When she presented the idea to her staff, they were astounded.

"It's going to be a huge crowd, Val. Better let a hotel handle it. . . ."

"Why have all those strangers running around your house, treading on your lawn?"

"Goodness, you wrote the book on it, Val. It's all right to have a *family* wedding at home, but a shindig like this . . . ?"

Of course, that was at the heart of her decision: "This *is* a family wedding," she explained. "Not only for the family of the winner . . . but for me. My readers are my family. Haven't I been as involved as any mother in planning their weddings?"

The attachment Val felt to her readers had only grown as her true family life had diminished. She was close to Jess and Diana in emotional terms, but now they had very busy lives in other places; and of course Teddie remained lost to her. There were no other especially close attachments. She was still vigorous and beautiful—those who didn't know Val Cummings's true age took her for ten or fifteen years younger—and over the past decade a number of successful and attractive men had courted her, but she hadn't found one to whom she could devote herself. She didn't think she had simply gotten too old to believe in romance; if anything, she was as much a believer as ever. She just needed to fall hopelessly in love or not at all—as she had been with her first, as she had been on the very brink of being with Andrew. If ever she did, she still thought it was possible she might marry.

But only if she met the right man. Marriage, she still believed, should be forever. Never mind if it was a long forever or a short one.

In the absence of that love, and with her children gone, she was content to have the extended family of women everywhere who put their fondest dreams into her hands. Once Val's staff understood the significance of using her home for the wedding ball, they changed their tune. Yes, no matter how large the crowd, it would have a warmth and intimacy that could never be equaled in a public place.

With the decision made, the invitations went out to the hundreds of people who had been involved in the history of the magazine. To staff and their relatives—even grandchildren of some of the earliest employees like Connie Marcantonio; Madge Truesdale, though now almost ninety and retired to Arizona, who would fly in for a week; advertisers of the past and present; the owners of honeymoon resorts that had long done business with the travel bureau; and other leading lights in the magazine publishing world such as *Cosmo*'s Helen Gurley Brown and the editors of *Vogue* and other fashion monthlies would be there.

In preparing her own list of people to receive engraved invitations to the event, Val confronted a few difficult choices, a couple that were even painful. Alan Wellstrom? He had become an important advertiser, and his family was still in the honeymoon business; Val felt he ought to be invited, and she believed he would come. He had been happily married to his second wife for a long time, she knew; it should be easy, even if bittersweet, for them to meet again.

A harder decision involved Glen Majer—and what his attendance might mean for Diana. By then, her eight-year run as a so-called supermodel kept her busy flying around the world, but she had promised to clear her schedule to be in New York for *E.B.*'s anniversary. More, she had told Val that she wanted to be the one to appear in the bridal gown on the anniversary issue. Inviting Majer to the gala, Val thought, presented an opportunity to show her own readiness to declare the peace between them and also to bring Diana together again with her father. She wouldn't do it, though, without Diana's permission.

"I don't think I'm ready for it, Mom," Diana said when Val reached her in Rome while the event was in the early planning stage. "It sounds like it's going to be a really great party, and I'd rather not take the chance of spoiling it."

So that was that.

A week later, though, Diana called back. "If it's not too late, I've had a change of heart. What you told me once about not hating him if I'm going to like myself . . . that finally sunk in. I'm pretty damn proud of myself these days—and it seems like a good time to bury the hatchet. I want my father to know me and be proud too. That would make my success complete."

"We could do it another way, if you'd prefer," Val offered, "another time . . ."

"That's up to you, Mom. But for me, this way sounds perfect. I'll be at my glamorous best, we can toast with some champagne, have a nice father-daughter dance . . . then everybody goes home."

Val sent the invitation to Majer.

Then there was Teddie. The pain came not in making the decision to invite her—Val never stopped trying to bring her close again—but in sending the invitation to the ball and anticipating that it was almost certainly a pointless gesture. None of Val's efforts to communicate with her first daughter had been answered. Not the long letter many years before in which she told Teddie that she understood and forgave the anger that had prompted her to join Majer in his battle to keep Diana. Not the telegram of congratulation she'd sent after learning—through Jess, whose sources for all kinds of gossip had to be extensive—that Teddie had taken her fourth husband, James Darian, a successful motion picture studio executive. Nor the note expressing her concern and sympathy when Jess had mentioned later that Teddie was getting divorced yet again. More recently, Val's attempts to raise a response had been limited to a card and a gift on Teddie's birthday, or the few affectionate words she might occasionally scribble down on an evening when she was alone and overtaken by nostalgia. Sometimes she would look at these notes the next morning and tear them up, finding it too painful to send them off into a void. Just as often she mailed them anyway, always hoping there might be a breakthrough.

Finally, reviewing the guest list brought her to wondering about Andrew Winston. Of course, he was due to be invited as a matter of form. Though Val's generous employee incentive programs had absorbed a substantial amount of the magazine's equity over the years, Andrew still owned the largest percentage of the privately owned company with the exception of Val herself.

Yet he remained an enigma. She had not talked to him since the time when he had decided to go on supporting her against Majer's attempts at a takeover—and not for want of trying. Yet no direct response from Andrew would come back. She supposed, if the mood ever struck, she could locate him, pick up a phone and talk to him. But he had made it so clear he had no pressing desire to speak to her that to violate his wishes seemed to be a crass invasion of privacy.

Her reticence was tested, however, when it came to planning the anniversary party. A week after mailing an invitation to Andrew's home address in New York, the envelope came back marked by the post office as undeliverable due to the addressee having moved, no forwarding address in their files. Val instructed her secretary to place a call to Andrew's office to get a more recent address. "And get Mr. Winston on the line," she said in a burst of bravado. She would underline her eagerness to have him at the anniversary with a personal appeal.

After fifteen minutes, the usually efficient secretary still hadn't buzzed back to say the connection was made. Val called her on the intercom: "Pat, are you trying to get Mr. Winston?"

"Like crazy," said the secretary. "But I've struck out on everything in the Rolodex and the directories."

"Impossible. You must have a number for Atlas Airways. It's one of the biggest—"

"Not a thing. There is no Atlas Air."

It was unlike her secretary to be so slapdash, but this was obviously a mistake. Perhaps the old number was defunct because they'd moved to new headquarters in another city. Rather than berate a trusted employee, Val dialed information herself and asked for any number under Atlas Airways, even one of the depots at any of the airports serving New York.

Nothing.

She turned to her personal Rolodex and hurriedly found the number for the legal firm of Lane, Compton, & Jeffries.

"I'm sorry," she was told by the switchboard operator when she asked for Andrew's trusted adviser. "Mr. Jeffries is deceased. Mr. Gilkey handles his clients now. I'll put you through. . . ."

When Val explained her history of dealing with Andrew's lawyer to Mr. Gilkey, and expressed her condolences, she was told that Jeffries had been ninety-four years old, had never missed a regular workday up to the time he died two months ago, and in his sixty-eight years with the firm had handled not only Andrew Winston's personal business, but that of Andrew's father and uncle.

"And are you handling his affairs now?" Val asked Gilkey.

"No. Since Mr. Jeffries's death, Mr. Winston hasn't dealt with the firm."

"Then could you tell me how to contact Mr. Winston? I haven't even been able to get a number for Atlas Airways."

There was a curiously heavy pause before the lawyer asked, "How long have you and Mr. Winston been out of touch?"

There was no one answer to the question, Val reflected. On some levels they had been out of touch much longer than others. "We haven't spoken in many years."

"Are you free anytime in the next day or two, Miss Cummings? If you're going to be in contact with Mr. Winston, I feel an obligation to fill you in first on . . . certain developments."

Evidently, the lawyer assumed Val's desire to reach Andrew was based on business, but so much the better if it meant he would clarify the mysteries. "Can we meet in half an hour?" Val said.

She didn't want the trail to Andrew Winston to cool by a single degree.

* * *

Lionel Gilkey was a trim, compact man with close-cropped black hair and a shrewd, narrow face, one of many young associates in the firm that occupied five floors in an office tower on Wall Street. As Val entered his office and saw the young man in a vested suit standing behind his desk, she thought at first glance that he was probably typical of what law schools were sending out to Wall Street these days—determined, ambitious, a bit chilly. As she went nearer, however, his face broke into a broad, warm, sunny smile that utterly revised Val's first impression.

"It's such a pleasure to meet you, Miss Cummings," he said, shaking her hand.

"It is?" Val answered ingenuously.

"Wait'll I tell my wife . . ."

Val understood now. "How long have you been married?"

"Eight months. And Deborah planned the wedding straight out of your book, soup to nuts—no, come to think of it, nuts was about the only thing we *didn't* have at the wedding—if you don't count some of my relatives."

Val laughed, and took the seat across from him.

He sat down and put on his lawyer face again. "Strictly speaking, Miss Cummings, I'm going just a little outside the guidelines to talk to you about an ex-client. But I'm familiar with Mr. Jeffries's files, so I'm aware of your business relationship with Mr. Winston . . . and when you mentioned Atlas Airways, it was clear to me you ought to be briefed."

"Is Mr. Winston all right?" Val asked in a sudden panic; recalling Nate Palmer's death in a plane crash, it occurred to her that perhaps Gilkey had some disastrous news he'd thought it best to deliver in person.

"As far as I know, he's quite well personally. But not the airline. Atlas Airways went bankrupt . . . six years ago."

Val was speechless. How long had it been since she'd last seen something in the business news about the air-freight company—or had been in a plane taxiing across an airport, flying off to a convention of honeymoon resorts or returning from a vacation with Diana, and had seen Atlas Air's yellow and blue jumbo jets lined up by a hangar in fours and fives. All she'd known then was that the company Andrew had started with Nate Palmer had grown into an international giant.

Seeing her disbelief, Gilkey went on. "It's a very competitive business. When fuel prices ran up in the early eighties, they got loaded down with debt for their new planes and never dug their way out." He shrugged. "Happened to a few of the biggest, you know—Pan Am, Eastern, Qantas, several others. Disappeared. The bigger they were, the harder they fell."

If it hadn't been solely a freight carrier, Val guessed she might have heard. But learning now that one source of Andrew Winston's fortune had vanished only made it more puzzling to Val that he'd never sought to realize any gain from his holdings in the magazine. "What has Mr. Winston done since his company failed?" she asked. "I haven't been able to find him at any of his old addresses."

"He may have had to sell some assets—such as his homes—to clear liabilities in connection with the business."

"But surely he would have sold the stock in my company first? It's become extremely valuable."

"I don't know how or why he made the decisions he did."

"I guess he's the one to ask, then. Are you able to tell me where he is, how to contact him?"

The lawyer nodded and picked up a slip of paper on his desk. "Documents still come to us occasionally in connection with old business. Mr. Winston deals with these matters himself now, and this is the address we've been given for forwarding." He handed the paper across to Val.

She glanced quickly at the typed address—Andrew's name on the first line . . . and then simply "Trireme Project, Doğanbey, Turkey."

"Turkey?" Val burst out. "What's he doing there?"

"I have no idea. Running from his creditors for all I know."

That couldn't be. He could have had tens of millions of dollars for his share of E.B., Inc.

But Lionel Gilkey had given her as much information as he could. Val thanked him and left.

When she emerged from the Wall Street office tower,

Jimmy was waiting with her limousine to drive her back to the office. He came around to open the door, but Val paused in the sunshine, lost in thought. Why Turkey? What was the Trireme Project? It smacked of foreign intrigue. . . .

Jimmy called her out of the reverie. "Miss Cummings, everything okay?"

She moved toward the car. "Not everything, Jimmy," she said wistfully. "But maybe it's not too late to do something about it."

She ate alone at home that night, a plain salad and some steamed asparagus she prepared for herself, accompanied by a glass of white wine.

After dinner she moved to the large outdoor terrace of her penthouse apartment, bringing with her a sheaf of her personal stationery. Looking out over Central Park and the glittering city beyond, thinking of how far she had risen above that rain-swept street where she had encountered Andrew Winston a lifetime earlier, she tried to compose the letter she wanted to write and drank a few more glasses of wine to fuel her courage. She remembered those past occasions when she had thought of reconnecting with him, letting him know he occupied a unique place in her life. Finally enough time had passed that whatever had driven them apart at a crucial moment no longer seemed to matter. Was it his disillusion with the secret she had kept, her disappointment at his inability to commit to her in spite of it, guilt or anger in the wake of Nate's death? She hoped it would have faded for him too. And that he would be glad to hear from her.

Though she doubted that her excuse for writing now—to invite him to be with her at the anniversary—could be meaningful enough to him that he would make the trip from overseas.

Sometime after midnight, having finally penned half a dozen pages—so pleasantly high on the wine that beyond saying it would mean a lot to her to see him again, she had only the most general idea of the words she'd set down—she sealed the envelope. Tomorrow she would send it express from the office.

Doğanbey, Turkey . . . the Trireme Project. As she wrote the address on the envelope, she wondered: What on earth could he be doing?

Two weeks went by without an answer. She checked the mail daily at home and at the office with an anxiety that continued to surprise her. Having finally leapt a hurdle to reach out, it was all but unbearable to think he might not answer.

When she saw the letter with the Turkish airmail stamp in her office mail early in the third week, she grabbed it as though she were the one isolated in a distant place where mail was a rarity. As soon as she opened the envelope and pulled out the folded pages, a photograph fluttered free onto the surface of her desk. Val picked it up—a man standing on the deck of a boat, fitted in scuba gear, a diving mask hanging from one hand. Even with the thick hair that fell across his brow changed from brown to white, his face creased by myriad wrinkles—deepened all the more by a wide smile, white teeth vividly contrasting against a deep tan—she recognized him at once. Though he was in his late sixties, his body was athletically slim and flat-bellied, and didn't appear at all out of place in a wet-look bikini bathing suit. What impressed her even more than his condition, however, was how happy and relaxed he looked.

The letter was two pages, typewritten. He began by saying how glad he was to hear from her, and described where he was and what he was doing. Doğanbey was a town on the Turkish coast of the Aegean Sea that was being used as the base for a marine archaeological project funded by a midwest university and some private contributions to recover a pair of ancient Greek vessels—triremes—that had sunk at the time of the Peloponnesian Wars. He went on to explain that after the bankruptcy of the airline had freed him to pursue interests other than business, he had taken some extension courses in archaeology, which had led to his current interest.

"This work is exciting, and interesting . . . and fun," he wrote. "So I have no regrets about the way things worked out.

My only wish is that I'd learned sooner that I could have followed my own stars instead of living so much by the usual rules. That would have made a difference to us too, Valentina. Remember? I lost you because I didn't think my family could accept you as you were—just as I became a businessman to make a lot of money because that was what they understood as a sensible life. I married someone from a similar family because that also seemed the right thing to do. But neither the business nor the marriage lasted, which allowed me to discover that I would have been happier all along if I'd never been involved with either one."

Val paused in her reading. She remembered being told that Andrew had a daughter who'd died in a car accident, and his wife had left him afterward. She'd always assumed that the pressures of the tragedy had dissolved the marriage, but evidently there had been an initial weakness in the bonds, so they tore easily.

She looked back to the letter: "I'd like very much to see you again, Val. Over the years I've often wished we could renew our friendship, but then some new obstacle would pop up. . . ." She stopped again, moved by the thought that he had shared the same wish as she. But what obstacles was he talking about? She didn't think she'd raised any, had always been accessible. . . . It didn't matter now. They had made the connection at long last.

"So I'd like very much to accept your invitation . . . but I'm not sure I'll be able to get away from this work in time. I'm a member of a team here, and they depend on me. Even if I can't be with you on your anniversary, my thoughts and my best wishes are with you. I hope the invitation will be open for sometime in the future. Or you might even come to visit me." In his own hand he had written, "Yours as ever, Andrew."

Visit him? The very thought made her pulse race, sparked a fantasy of making arrangements right now. All that he'd said—his own desire to renew their friendship, his memory of losing her, as he'd put it, because of following the narrow restrictions of his social order—coincided with the feelings she had whenever she thought about him. The notion that if only they could have a second chance . . .

She caught herself before the fantasy could go too far. Shared memories, shared desires for friendship . . . they were to be expected; but at this late point in life, *both* their lives, it would be foolish to think they were the omens of a new romance. Especially since he didn't seize the chance she had offered, wasn't accepting her invitation to the ball.

On this third Sunday in June, the sky was a cloudless blue, the flowered borders everywhere around the estate and along the path that the wedding procession would follow were in full bloom, and the breeze was just strong enough to faintly rustle a bridal veil.

Of all the wedding scenes Val had seen or described, she believed this to be one of the most beautiful. Once she had thought that ceremonies performed in the outdoors were a hippie invention that bordered on being irreligious, but over the years she had revised her thinking. All nature could make a perfectly suitable cathedral, a cliff above the sea a lovely altar. Even the sacredness of the vows came less from their linkage to any religious liturgy than from the pureness of the intentions with which they were spoken. These days marriages didn't last a lifetime simply because they were decreed to do so by ministers or lawmakers; they lasted only if and when they united two people whose hearts and minds fully embraced, without reservation or limit, the vows they were taking.

As she walked to her seat near the front, just behind the relatives of the bride and groom, Val reflected on the myriad details that had involved weeks of planning. The woman who had written the letter to win the dream wedding was named Sheila Donaldson. A twenty-six-year-old computer operator from Columbus, Ohio, she had been engaged at the age of twenty-three to a fireman named Dennis Lane from the same city, a wedding planned for later in the same year as their engagement. Then, while trying to control a ten-alarm blaze at a shopping center, her fiancé had fallen through a flaming roof and had suffered burns over most of his body. Weeks of intensive care were followed by months of rehabilitation, then there had been several operations for plastic surgery. Even with health coverage, the young couple's savings had been entirely eaten up. Sheila Donaldson had written that it wasn't to fulfill her own dream she wanted the formal wedding; she would have happily married the man she loved in a bedside ceremony "as long as he was conscious to say the vows." But her "Denny" wanted her to have the kind of wedding they would have had before his misfortune, and had been stalling until they could afford it.

No more deserving entry had been received. Val was gratified to be able to provide the fulfillment of a dream for this couple and their families.

Among the hundreds of guests Val passed as she walked to her seat set up on the lawn to face the ocean, she saw the faces of almost all the people who had led her to this day, participants in her accomplishments, her triumphs, as well as her occasional failures and sorrows. The staff of the magazine, Madge, Connie, Kath, with many of their nearest and dearest, Dr. and Mrs. Walter Kendall, Alan Wellstrom and his family, even Glen.

And in the front, her daughters—but just two of them. Teddie's absence was one of two disappointments that marred the occasion; the other was that Andrew couldn't be there.

The seats had filled, and Val glanced back over her shoulder. She saw the bridal party forming on the porch of the house to begin the procession down to the edge of the sea.

The organist sounded a few introductory notes on his portable instrument, a hush came over the people as they all turned their heads, and the procession began. Bridesmaids, gathered from Sheila's friends from college, work, and the hospital where her groom had been cared for, started out, followed by a full complement of firemen in uniform, marching for the groom. A little niece of the bride's was flower girl. Then, with his best man, the groom, recovered and rehabilitated, just a small area of his neck above his white collar showing the scar tissue that had covered his body.

At last on her father's arm, the bride—a lovely young

woman with long auburn hair and green eyes. In her white silk and lace gown, her arms filled with a bridal bouquet of white roses, she was exquisite. Coming along the aisle, she caught Val's eye and the solemn ceremonial expression she had worked to keep gave way to a warm smile of thanks.

Val couldn't hold back the tears—she never could at weddings. In some small part, she always felt, they were the remnant of tears she had shed for her own lost groom of long ago. Though mostly they were tears of joy for the bride, for all brides—all the lucky ones who had their dream come true.

The procession reached the altar, and the minister began the ceremony. As always, it was magical, and Val became lost in the quintessential romantic moment.

". . . do you, Sheila Carol Donaldson, take this man . . ."

Oddly, as they came to the point of taking their vows, Val felt her attention to the ceremony come curiously unstuck. She wasn't sure what did it—a cloud passing across the sun, a cough from one of the guests, a missed heartbeat—but suddenly she lost her concentration on the scene in front of her. Then, as if a voice only she could hear had called to her, she turned to look behind her.

He was there, standing just inside the portal to the garden. Not watching them take the vows, but with his eyes fully on her, as if he had meant to call her with the silent force of his gaze.

Her breath caught as she looked at him, and a hand flew up to her chest as if to keep her heart from flying out of her body. How handsome he was still! The hair silver, but still full enough so that a lock fell boyishly over his brow, eyes still clear and bright. Somewhere along the way between the far ocean and this one, he'd found a tuxedo.

Her lips moved, forming his name without thought, and he smiled back. And at that moment she thought she knew how her whole life might have been different—both their lives—if only they could have been braver when they were young. If only the world had been ready to let them be so brave.

At last she tore her gaze away to look forward again and

listen to the bride and groom finish taking their mutual pledge. But already in her thoughts she was beginning the conversation with him.

When the ceremony ended, Val was surrounded by a crowd of well-wishers before she could make her way to where she had seen him. For a while then she let the tasks of her position keep her apart—pictures with the bridal party, talking to guests, and checking with the caterer to make sure the waiters started passing champagne.

It was really nerves, she knew, this circling around him, an inner clash of impatience to fly across the long span of years, with a terror that once she did she might yet be disappointed.

At last she could wait no more, and she looked for him in the mass of people who filled the open lawn where champagne was being passed, and a band was already playing next to a polished dance floor that had been laid over a portion of grass. In the milling hundreds, she couldn't find him.

Had he been an apparition? Conjured by a heart yearning so much to see that it created what wasn't really there . . . ?

She ran into the house. Perhaps he'd gone to freshen up. He would've had to make a long journey, after all, to be there.

Inside, the formal rooms were all quiet, deserted, the guests outside. Val looked up the stairway, then stopped herself. This was foolish, of course, *unladylike*. Fine for a girl of fifteen to go hunting down someone because of his smile, not for a woman of her years. They would find each other when the time was right. She turned back to the front door to leave again.

"Valentina!"

She was at the threshold when his voice reached out to her. Her heart, already racing since she'd entered the house, began to pound. She spun around.

He was at the top of the wide stairs, and neither said another word as he descended and walked up close to her. Though she wished something would come—something to make her sound at least slightly in possession of herself—she simply couldn't speak. In her mind she was as shy and stunned as she had been the day she had collided with him in the rain. In her eyes he was unchanged.

And she, too, in his. His next words told her. "You're as beautiful as I remembered," he said quietly, standing before her. "Even without the rain."

"It's very nice to hear that you did remember," she said.

He took a breath as though to speak, then hesitated, obviously overwhelmed.

She was groping for words too.

Outside, the band had begun to play, and the music floated in through windows left open to the breeze. As it filled the silence, she became aware that it was playing one of the songs from that time, "These Foolish Things."

At last he said, "Would it be too late, do you think . . . ?"

"Too late for what?"

"That dance with you I never got to have."

"No," she said. "Never too late."

He took her hand in his and encircled her waist with his arm, and right there, together alone in the hallway of the house, they began to dance smoothly, in perfect step, as if they had been dancing together all their lives.

Thirty-one

New York
April 1997

Inspiring awe and envy from many of the secretaries she passed who knew that she was one of the world's supermodels, Diana Majer strode briskly along the halls of *Every Bride's* magazine. The flowing white caftan she'd been allowed to take away from one of the recent shows billowed around her. She turned into the door of Val's office suite. She had come straight from the airport, to be sure she was there at ten A.M., a time her mother was always in her office. She kept going past the secretary, not concerned with being announced or barging in on any meeting in progress.

Val was at her desk, working over an article on the resources available through the Internet for wedding planning. The magazine had brought itself into the computer age years before, issuing products on disc and CD-ROM, but more recently it had started its own bridal planning services on the World Wide Web. Val looked up as the door flew open.

"Darling!" she greeted Diana, coming out from behind her desk to embrace her. "What a wonderful surprise."

Diana accepted her mother's embrace before pushing her back to arm's length and saying tartly, "I thought one good surprise deserved another."

Val understood at once. "So you got the invitation. Nothing nicer than accepting it in person."

Diana took a couple of steps back and folded her arms. "Do you know where and when that invitation arrived?"

"I knew you were supposed to do Angeloni's big show at the Coliseum, so I arranged for a messenger to—"

"And you already knew it was going to be my last show, didn't you?"

"You told me weeks ago."

"I thought so!" Diana said sharply. "It was deliberate."

Val was taken aback by her daughter's accusing tone. "Well . . . yes. I thought it would be an especially meaningful time—"

Diana stamped around in a circle. "I just never thought you'd be so . . . so inconsiderate of my feelings. There I was, getting all rigged up in a wedding gown of all things, and I get *this* news." She stopped and stared at Val. "Do you know I walked the runway spilling buckets of tears. Of course, they all loved it, thought it was part of the show! But I was really miserable."

Val reached out to her. "Darling . . . why? I never imagined you wouldn't be happy for me."

"I am! Of course I am . . . for *you.* But not for me. I mean, the way you wrapped the whole thing in mystery . . . I could only assume it was because you were ashamed to tell me everything. And there's only one reason I could think you'd be ashamed." She paused, as if to give Val time to confess.

Val didn't cooperate. "And what reason is that?" she asked.

"Because you're marrying *him*!" Diana cried.

"Your father?" Val said incredulously. "Dicey, how can you think that? He and I have patched up some of our differences—we can be in the same room these days without going for each other's throats. But marry him? This is my first time, remember. I still have the dream it should be forever."

Diana's mood was softened by Val's humor. Still, her hurt wasn't soothed. Quietly she said, "There's something else."

From the way she said it, Val detected the second matter was no less serious than the first. "What, dear?"

"I'd always thought—" Diana stopped, choked up again by the sadness of even having to spell this out, feeling cheated by her mother's failure to perceive without being told.

"What, Dice? Please . . ."

Diana looked down, hiding her face. "You know what I've always dreamed of doing. I think the dream was planted by hearing you talk about your own mother . . . the beauty of those dresses she used to make—like the wedding dress you wanted to wear that got lost in the war." She looked up at Val. "I always thought when you got married that you'd give me the chance to dress you. And here I am, giving up everything else to start designing, but—"

"But, darling!" Val broke in. "Of course I want you to design and make my dress. I can't imagine having anyone else do it."

Diana stared back with wide eyes. "But . . . it sounded so much like everything was already planned, complete, the arrangements made."

Val smiled. "Oh? I didn't give an actual date, did I? What day did I say—'the first day of the rest of my life'? Well, that won't come until everything's in place. And everyone. So I'm ready to wait until you've done the last stitch on the dress you want to make for me."

Diana appraised Val for another moment. "There is a man though? You *are* definitely planning to be married?"

"Oh, yes, my love. I'm going to have what I've waited for all my life."

Diana's eyes narrowed shrewdly. "So just what's going on? Why all the mystery?"

Val smiled cunningly. "Because like every bride, I want my wedding day to be completely and absolutely perfect, the answer to all my prayers. In my case, getting it that way takes a little extra work. And it seemed that keeping a couple of secrets would also make it easier. But you'll find out everything in good time, my love. Now . . . would you like to take my measurements? I have a tape measure in my desk."

As Val walked to her desk, Diana regarded her with a mix of bewilderment, admiration, and love. "You old fox, I'd love to know what you've got up your sleeve."

"Make me the sleeve," Val said, holding the hand with the tape measure toward her daughter, "and you'll find out."

Once the measurements were done, they sat over tea discussing the gown, with Val calling on memories of the beautiful dress her own mother had once shown her, and Diana offering her variations on the theme. At last Diana left, eager to get to a drawing board and to start looking at fabrics—in effect to begin her new life. Val had promised that if the dress turned out well, it would go on the cover of the magazine. No designer could ask for a more surefire launch for a career.

As soon as the office door had closed behind Diana, Val hurried to her desk, picked up the phone on her desk reserved for personal calls, and punched in a number.

Good, he was there, answered for himself.

"It's me," Val said. "Diana was just here. Guess what she wanted?"

She heard no words from the other end, just a low chuckle.

"Now," Val asked, "what's the news at your end?"

"Looks like we're right on schedule, lady," answered Glen Majer. "For that matter, maybe even a little ahead . . ."

Thirty-two

New York
June 1997

Teddie just didn't get it. Why were they meeting here, of all places, in this dingy office building on a side street off lower Fifth Avenue? Not the kind of place where takeovers involving hundreds of millions of dollars were usually discussed. A suite at the Waldorf, a table at "21," or a Wall Street executive suite would have been more appropriate—and certainly more to her liking. Nevertheless, the money backing her was Glen's, so there wasn't a choice but to go along with whatever arrangements he'd made.

After getting out of her taxi, Teddie stood in front of the building for a couple of minutes. She knew Glen couldn't be here yet or there would have been a chauffeured stretch limousine idling in front of the address. Where was he? She'd flown to New York with him on his jet, but at the airport he'd pleaded that he had private business first that would take him farther out of the city, so he had sent her back to New York alone, pledging to be there at the appointed time.

Teddie glanced at her wristwatch. Only a couple of minutes before three. Was she in the right place? She checked the slip of paper on which Majer had jotted the address, and the room number where the meeting would take place. She looked at the numerals over the street door. Yes, this was it.

Perhaps she'd better go ahead. Not a good idea to keep the man they had come to see waiting, not when they were there specifically to negotiate an agreement. Best to demonstrate that they could be relied upon to perform as promised.

She entered the building. The lobby was dimly lit, the walls bearing smudges of graffiti that had been only partially washed away. Teddie was aware that the man waiting for them had been in some economic difficulty in the past, yet he was still a man of means, or they wouldn't be dealing with him. So why operate out of such a dump? She understood now why he had a reputation for being eccentric.

Teddie rode the elevator to the twelfth floor, walked along the corridor to the designated room number. She paused before the door, reading the black stenciling on the frosted glass pane: BYTE-RITE, COMPUTER REPAIR. The whole deal was beginning to seem beyond weird, even a little scary. She looked again at Glen's note, still in her hand.

This was the right number.

Teddie opened the door gingerly, half expecting to see some Peter Lorre look-alike leering back at her. Just inside was a small anteroom furnished with a desk and file cabinets. The desk was unoccupied. Two closed doors apparently led to two inner offices. With her first sight of the empty space, Teddie's uneasiness grew. She had the strangest sensation of déjà vu, an absolute certainty deep within her consciousness that she knew this place, had seen it before, though she couldn't remember ever being here.

"Hello . . . ?" Teddie called out, announcing herself.

At once one of the doors opened. A man emerged. From what she knew of the person she and Glen had been scheduled to meet, this must be him.

"I'm Teddie Darian," she said. "Are you—"

"Yes, Teddie," he said. "I'm Andrew Winston." He shook her hand and held on to it, as though trying to sense something in her grasp that would tell him if there was any reason not to do business with her.

"What is this place?" Teddie asked nervously, retracting her hand.

"Well, it's been a lot of things over the years. But once upon a time it was where it all began."

"Where what began?"

"The magazine—the thing we're here to talk about."

Teddie looked at him curiously. "Why did you want to meet here?"

"For luck," he said cryptically. "Shall we get started?"

"We can't until Mr. Majer arrives. It's his money, after all."

"But he won't be coming, Teddie. He wanted us to settle this without him."

She regarded him now with alarm. That wasn't the way Glen operated, not at all. He didn't do a business deal unless he had his hands on the controls. Something very odd was definitely behind this. From everything she knew about him, Andrew Winston wasn't the sort of person she ought to fear, but this was too odd. "He has to come," Teddie said, trying to keep her panic from showing, "if we're going to reach an agreement. It's his money," she repeated more vehemently.

"But you won't need his money."

They still hadn't sat down. Teddie took a couple of nervous backward steps away from Andrew Winston. "Mr. Winston, Glen told me you'd agreed to sell your shares. He brought me here to New York on that expectation. You understand that we want your percentage of the ownership to give us a base to challenge . . . the present management. Without his money, I can't—"

Andrew broke in. "I think what Mr. Majer must have told you—because it's what I told him—is that I am indeed willing to let you *have* my shares. But I never actually spoke of selling them."

Teddie stopped to stare at him. "But that is what you meant, isn't it?" She let out a nervous laugh. "I don't imagine you'd give them to me."

He gazed back earnestly. "But I would, Teddie. That's exactly what I'm prepared to do—*give* you my shares. Providing you'll meet certain conditions."

It was beyond odd, she knew now; it was sheer out-and-out nuts. Hand over an investment worth tens of millions? And yet she'd heard he was eccentric—that money meant nothing to him anymore, and he happily spent most of his time on dry, stony islands far away, diving around rotten old boats. Maybe he was just crazy enough to be serious.

"Okay," she said, bemused. "Let's hear your conditions."

Before he could answer, the door leading to the second office swung open. "They're not actually *his*, Teddie. They're mine."

Paralyzed with amazement, Teddie stood and stared silently as her mother came toward her.

Two years had gone by since Val and Andrew had found each other again. It was a time in which they had confirmed that they were truly in love—that in a sense had always remained in love, though fate had conspired for decades to keep them from exploring that truth together.

At their first reunion—in that wedding dance—they had both confessed that they had never stopped thinking of the other, never ceased to consider reaching out again. . . .

Andrew had been held back by problems of his own. The death of his daughter, the collapse of his marriage—coupled with a career that gave him little satisfaction at the time—had led to problems with alcohol. In fact, on that occasion when he and Val had spoken on the phone while he was "away for an extended period," he had actually been at an alcohol treatment center in Minnesota, finally getting himself back under control. A guiding aspiration at the time had been to restore himself as a man who could present himself to her and hope to deserve her respect and interest. Then, when they'd spoken, he'd learned she was pregnant with Majer's child.

With that history far behind them, however, they were able now to make plans for a life together. At the same time, they also tried to proceed sensibly and cautiously, doing nothing to jeopardize their new bond. Each had obligations from which they couldn't easily tear loose, activities that were a basis for their own pleasure in living, indeed for the joie de vivre each admired in the other. Neither could, or would, ask or expect the other to give up the work that engaged them.

Having taken a lifetime to find something that engaged his intellect and adventurous spirit, Andrew meant to continue with it. He had returned to Turkey and the Trireme Project, while Val, having used a lifetime to create a huge, successful enterprise, refused to simply abandon it. She wasn't quite ready to retire from the position of power and authority she'd held for almost fifty years—wasn't sure she could survive without that excitement. Though even if the time came when she was ready to leave, an orderly transition still had to be arranged to preserve the value and integrity of what she had built.

For twenty-three months, therefore, they had seen each other only at intervals. Val would fly to Turkey to spend a week or two; Andrew would rendezvous with her for a week's holiday somewhere else—Paris or Rome or a Caribbean island—or return to the States to visit her in New York. And throughout that whole time, Val had not boasted to a single soul, even to Jess or Diana, of once more being—in the golden afternoon of her life—engaged in a love affair.

In some part, her secrecy arose from trepidation that the girls might chide her for not "acting her age." But the larger reason was that conducting her affair with Andrew in secret—almost as if they were adulterous lovers—gave it an edge that made it all the more delicious and exciting.

Of course, her trips abroad and the general sparkle she exuded from the rejuvenation of love did arouse some suspicion. Jess, for one, had questioned Val more than once about it.

"Flying off to Europe again? Mother, I can't remember you ever traveling so much in the past. . . ."

"I miss Diana," Val might alibi—since she usually did stop off in Rome if her daughter was there. Or she would say, "When am I going to see the world if not now, darling? I'm not getting any younger."

Which was the very point Andrew had also made to her when he had said not long before that perhaps it was time to make it official, publicize to the world how they felt about each other. "We should be living together, Val, enjoying each other twenty-four hours a day. This catch-as-catch-can stuff isn't enough anymore, dammit."

When he said this, they were sunning themselves on a

Turkish beach. Looking out at the blue ocean, lying beside him in the sunshine, Val also felt the longing to make her life completely with him. But she confessed one reservation. "I'm ready to set a date, Andrew. But . . ."

"But what?"

"I want it to be the most perfect, happiest day. And every time I think of it—" Her voice broke, and she looked away.

He knew what was bothering her. "Suppose you just try again," he said.

"She won't ever come. She won't even speak to me. I'm dead to her, have been for such a long time." Val always grew especially emotional when talking of Teddie to Andrew; after all, he was the man she would have been with long ago but for the existence of her firstborn.

"You're not saying that you won't marry me unless she's there?"

"No, no . . . I don't think I am anyway. But . . . I guess I've dreamed that everything could all be made right at the same time."

"Perhaps it can't be, Val. Maybe you'll have to settle for just having me."

She smiled at him. "I can live with that," she said.

From that time, they had talked marriage and setting a date. But their plans were also snagged on the matter of where and how they would make their life. Which occupation, his or hers, would be sacrificed to togetherness?

"You know better than anyone that my whole life has been tied up with the magazine," she had told him in one of their transatlantic phone conversations. "I just wonder if I'll stagnate as soon as I'm not part of it—become boring, someone who doesn't interest you." She was feeling it especially because it had been an exciting day at the office, circulation figures reaching a new record high.

"If that worries you, then don't sell *E.B.* Turn it over to someone to run for you—someone who'll let you keep a hand in when you want. Jess would be perfect. She's an experienced journalist."

"No, that wouldn't work for half a dozen reasons. She's too

good at what she does, and too happy and successful to give it up. What's more, she's not really the type. She doesn't have the ambition that keeps priming the pump, doesn't want to be saddled with all the dry organizational stuff. That's why she works alone. Anyway, she's settled in Washington, where her husband has his practice, and she's got friends in government from top to bottom."

"Diana wouldn't be up to it either," he acknowledged. "Too bad. It would have been nice if you could have passed it on to one of the kids. . . ."

It was at that moment that it struck Val that if she could pass the magazine on to anyone, her choice would have been Teddie without a doubt. Teddie had everything the job required, the drive, the ambition, the knowledge of running a business—the wedding business in particular. The hitch, of course, was that the way things stood, Teddie wouldn't take anything from Val, certainly nothing that shaped the future of her life.

"If only Teddie would accept it," Val said sadly, "let me just . . . hand it over to her. But if I ever wanted to make such a proposition, I couldn't even get that child to sit down with me and listen. The only way I think she'd want the magazine is if she could feel she was snatching it away from me. Getting even," she added sadly.

After a moment Andrew said, "Then let her."

"What?"

"Give her the feeling she wants. Let her take it away. Let her *win* something from you—or think she's going to, at least until she's on the playing field, where you have a chance to talk with her. . . ."

That was how it had come about.

As she watched Val come toward her, Teddie was a mass of warring emotions. She knew she had been tricked into going there, into lowering the barrier that she had worked so hard to keep up for so long; even Majer had been in on it apparently. That annoyed her, sparked an urge to foil all their clever planning by turning and marching straight out the door.

But she didn't move. There were selfish practical reasons to stand her ground, for one thing. Andrew Winston had spoken of turning over his share of the magazine to her, and he had the look of a man who never said anything unless he meant it.

And beyond that, try as she might to dig down into her reserves of resentment and anger, she simply couldn't find the will to make the feud with her mother last another day. Whatever annoyance Teddie felt, it was not the fury that had once driven her away. What she realized only now—couldn't have realized until actually confronting her mother—was that somewhere along the line that fierce rage of her youth had burnt itself out. All the years of lost closeness suddenly seemed such a terrible waste.

God, if she let herself think about it, she might crumble. Teddie forced herself to concentrate instead on the matter at hand: conditions, they had mentioned conditions.

"I'm listening," Teddie said.

Three weeks later Val and Andrew were married at the house in Southampton, Val in a gown designed and sewn for her by Diana—peach-colored, not white. Unlike the last wedding at Silversands, this was not a blowout gala. Just a family affair, though once grandchildren and old friends and even a past lover or two were counted in, it amounted to a congenial crowd of more than sixty.

As it happened, the reconciliation between Val and Teddie had progressed more rapidly and happily over the past few weeks than either would ever have predicted. All the doubts that had once afflicted Teddie about the truth of her mother's love were erased at a stroke by finding herself the welcome recipient of all that Val had built. She understood, moreover, that healing the breach between them had been the purpose of Val's strategy in sending out those first three wedding invitations, and the reason they were written to reveal nothing. For if Teddie had known Andrew Winston was to be the groom, she would never have agreed to fly east with Majer in the belief that he would cooperate with them to undermine Val. Nor could Val actually pinpoint a day and time for her marriage until she knew how long it might be before Teddie took the bait, and decided that the marriage provided an opportunity to "steal away" the magazine. As for concealing the location of the ceremony? Paradise would be wherever she and Andrew finally took their vows.

Yet there was one mystery about the wedding invitation that continued to plague Teddie. She had wanted the answer as soon as she understood Val's game, yet she had resisted asking—the last remnant of pettiness, this unwillingness to acknowledge how well her mother must know and understand her.

Today at last, though, she could resist no longer.

The chance to ask came after the ceremony, when photographs were being taken for an album.

"I want one with my girls," Val said, "just my girls."

When they lined up, Val held an arm out to Teddie, making sure she was close at one side.

Arm in arm with her mother, Andrew beaming at them from behind the photographer, Teddie finally had to ask, no matter how much satisfaction it gave Val to crow about it. As soon as the shutter snapped, Teddie turned to her.

"Just tell me one more thing," she said. "How the hell could you know that inviting me to the wedding would make me jump in just the direction you wanted? What made you so sure I'd start thinking of a takeover?"

"Oh, I didn't plan it that way at all, sweetheart," Val replied. "I'd worked it out quite differently. I'd already asked Glen to help—well, I told him, he'd taken one of my daughters away from me for a while, he owed it to me to help get you back. So he agreed that a couple of days after the invitation was delivered, he'd call you and say he'd heard I was getting married, comment that it was bound to make me loosen my hold on the reins at *E.B.*, and then he'd ask if you'd like to run it for him if he took it over. Then he'd bring you to New York to meet Andrew. But as it happened, Glen never had to ask. You called him first."

Teddie smiled. "Now I know what makes *me* so clever," Teddie said, and they embraced.

There were a dozen more family poses taken, and then the jazz trio started to play for dancing on the portable floor set up in the open air. Andrew reached out to Val, and they linked hands and walked out to have the first dance by themselves. Two songs were played while they danced, one requested by each. Andrew's was Kern's "All the Things You Are"; Val's was Gershwin's "Our Love Is Here to Stay."

As Andrew spun Val, she saw her beautiful daughters watching from the sidelines, the three of them together, side by side. How lovely they were. It struck her suddenly that she'd never seen them all together before. Even with all the missteps to get to this moment, Val thought, how lucky she'd been.

But then a flicker of concern touched her expression, and Andrew caught it. "What are you worrying about now?" he asked.

"Diana . . ."

"Of all things! Diana? That girl has the world by the tail." From being a supermodel, she'd gone straight to being a hot designer: Valentina Cummings's own wedding dress on the cover of this month's *E.B.* had brought Diana Majer orders from department and bridal stores all across the country, and they wanted the rest of her collection as soon as it was ready.

"Yes," Val said, "she has her work. But she's so beautiful, and yet . . ."

"Mmmm?"

"She still isn't married."

Andrew threw back his head and laughed. "Darling," he said then, sweeping his bride into an agile spin that made the crowd around the floor applaud and remark to each other how very young they both looked, "you ought to know by now that finding the right man takes a little time."

From Elaine Coffman, the New York Times *bestselling author who has captured the hearts of countless devoted readers, comes another dazzling tale of the crimes of the heart.*

ESCAPE NOT MY LOVE

U.S. Deputy Marshall Jay Culhane had tracked down outlaw gangs and renegade Indians, but he'd never encountered a prisoner as infuriating as the beautiful schoolteacher Jennifer Baxter. From the shimmering desert to a magnificent Texas ranch to the genteel drawing rooms of Savannah, he would pursue her relentlessly, ruled by a fierce passion for the woman who dared him to believe in the redeeming power of love.